DELIVER US

RICHARD JOHN THORNTON

DELIVER US FROM EVIL

THIS STORY IS DEDICATED TO EVERY CHILD THAT HAS EVER SUFFERED AT THE HANDS OF AN ADULT.

PROPHECY

That the defenceless shall rise against their persecutors and curse them as they were once cursed.
Without warning; without motive; without reason.
Simply for the sake of the act itself.
For if the sin deemed itself just, then so doth the penance.
And in due turn, those same defenceless will be armed only with the stealth and will of mind that so coldly accompanied the administration of their own, torrid plight.

REFLECTION

Fear is something only felt when aware of imminent circumstance. Fear is a defensive emotion that evolves through experiencing aspects of life that are displeasing or alarming. If the scent of danger is familiar from some other previous encounter, the mind and body will respond accordingly and automatically place a person on their guard.

Yet how can the mind react protectively if it doesn't behold a learned understanding of a situation? How is human instinct supposed to signify trepidation if nothing seems particularly wrong? Indeed, why would one be wary of circumstances that have never occurred before? Tragically, in most instances, only in retrospect does immense risk become truly evident.

Only on tasting real horror for the first time can the psyche truly appreciate subsequent solace. Only the renewed sensation of liberty brings to bear the fraught anxiety of imprisonment. But those boys…they were just eleven years of age. They were supposedly raised to be wary of the unknown. Their parents warned of the perils that lurked around every corner of every street of every town within this increasingly degraded world.

But of course, when confronted with such demons for the first time, there was little chance of those boys acknowledging such menace. By natural default youth incurs such vulnerability. Innocence is the logical human precursor to susceptibility. Hence, the young are never compelled to protect themselves.

Because the young can never sense the fear.

And so, rendered completely defenceless, they are easy prey for the vultures that circle the reddened skies above…

PROLOGUE

He watched in silence from behind the glass.
Contemplative of the next move, his gaze wandered among the vibrant activity beyond the window.
Yet that pleasant scene was no place for him.
Not before.
Not now.
Not ever.
His role had been ordained.
He was to be the unseen observer.
Not for him to tread the path of normal men.
For he had been robbed of such luxury long ago.
The female voice resonated in his ear as a necessary irritant.
He could be nothing without her; yet he so resented her constant presence by his side.

'Are you ready? Have you chosen yet?'

The question halted his patient moment of selection.
He did not gesture with his hands.
A merest nod of the head indicated the designated targets.

'Those two?' she confirmed.

Tilting his head once more, his lungs slowly inflated with anticipation.
No further exchange was deemed necessary as she set her mind to the task ahead.
Sating his every whim.
Tending to his every desire.
She would always be there for him…

HEAVEN

CHAPTER 1

Summer; 2008. Hazel Leavesdon was losing patience. She switched position in the front passenger seat and faced the two boys sitting behind her.

'Peter…I know you're excited but stop showing off in front of Michael. Your dad's trying to concentrate on the road.'

Her husband David briefly glanced at the pair of impish young faces in his rear-view mirror before diverting his concentration back to the steady stream of traffic ahead.

'He's alright, Hazel. He's entitled to act the clown a bit in front of his best mate.'

'Well…I'm just thinking of you being distracted, dear. That's all.'

An unsteady compliance with the order for peace prevailed in the back seats, but the feigned act of obedience did not endure for long as the boys covertly recommenced their game of punch and kick.

Less than thirty seconds had elapsed before Peter's mother swivelled in her seat once more with a stern glint of maternal authority casting itself over the smiling opponents. A pointed forefinger accentuated the warning.

'Right…Peter. If I have to tell you once more, then you can forget all about going to watch the film and there will be no McDonald's afterwards…okay? One more wrong move and this car will be heading for home. Do you understand? You've been a good boy up to now. Don't spoil it. Now you've got to do as you're told for five minutes. Is that clear?'

Another subdued silence resumed as the car employed the slip road to depart from the dual carriageway and eventually navigate the roundabout that would guide them to the multiplex cinema. The attention of the two eleven-year-olds soon became fully engaged by the impressive sight of the large billboard displaying the current batch of movie screenings.

David glanced in amusement at his wife as he weaved through the car park toward a vacant space and stationed the car.

Straining his neck to observe the growing expressions of excitement on the faces behind him, he wilfully opted to increase their youthful vigour as he released his seat belt.

'Okay boys...which film are we watching, then?'

Not satisfied with the partially obstructed view from behind his father's head, Peter kicked open his door and jumped out, still transfixed by the large white board daubed in red plastic lettering.

'Can I choose any film I want, Dad? Honest?'

Quickly joining his son at the rear of the silver Ford Focus, they studied the films and show-times together.

'Yes...it's you and Michael's evening. So, it's your choice. But no horror movies! I know what you're like when you get scared. You'll have nightmares for weeks. What about the latest Disney one? What's it called...Wally...or something daft...isn't it?'

Peter grimaced in childish disgust and shook his head.

'Dad...it's called Wall-E. And Disney films are for girls! What do you reckon, Michael?'

Michael Tompkins closed the car door and assisted with the analysis. Browsing the selection of movies, he swiftly offered a suggestion.

'I know. What about...The Dark Knight? We both look old enough even though it's a twelve certificate. Don't we Mister Leavesdon?'

David didn't get chance to respond as his son showed immediate vocal and physical support of the recommendation.

'YEAH, DAD! BATMAN! PLEASE! PLEASE, DAD! CAN WE? PLEASE?'

Peter tugged excitedly at the hem of his father's t-shirt, resulting in a further automatic reprimand from Hazel.

'Don't jump about like that, Peter. You're not a baby anymore. Stand still for Christ's sake. Anyway, we can't choose yet until Michael's parents get here and check it's okay with them. I'm sure they aren't too far behind.'

Fuelled by the prospect, the boys began to enact an imaginary fight between hero and villain in the middle of the car park, much to the enjoyment of the watching parents. However, Hazel could not help but eventually voice her usual sense of concern.

'What do you think, Dave? Will Batman be a bit too violent?'

He turned and faced his wife with a self-explanatory smile.

'Are you kidding? I've waited all summer to see this! A brilliant choice by Michael if I say so myself! And I'm sure Jim will agree with me when he gets here! Oh good – he's just pulling in now, look!'

The metallic green Vauxhall Astra containing James and Sharon Tompkins floated through the entrance to the central car park and slowed to a stop in the vacant space beside the waiting group. Michael's parents alighted and joined the throng, with James' gaze immediately following that of David's, who was now pointing avidly toward the billboard.

'Hope you don't mind, Jim, but Michael's chosen the new Batman film.'

'Great stuff. We'd better get a move on, then. It's twenty past four, now. Only ten minutes until it starts.'

The two sets of parents followed the buoyant pair of youngsters across the car park to the pedestrian footpath and made their way toward the tinted glass double doors of the cinema entrance.

'Peter, slow down!' cried Hazel to her oblivious offspring as he scampered off in front.

In contrast, Michael walked at a more sedate pace with the adults before courteously holding the door open for everybody, whilst his best friend had already bounded inside and across the maroon-carpeted foyer toward the refreshment counter.

'Erm, Peter…don't you think you'll need some money if you're queuing over there?'

As usual, her son pretended not to hear his mother's persistently restrictive tones. Transfixed by the large transparent cabinet brimming with his favourite sweet popcorn, he pressed the palms of his hands against the warm glass and stared at the golden bounty inside.

Sharon quickly opted to intercede on the next inevitable maternal imposition.

'Come on Hazel. We'll sort the boys out with some sweets. I wouldn't mind some chocolate myself. The men can do something useful for once and fetch the tickets. Small coke is it, Jim?'

'Yes. Please. And…erm…a packet of wine gums.'

'Greedy.'

'Yeah! Of course, I am!'

David scanned the array of confectionary before declaring his choice and joining James in the line-up for tickets.

The mothers moved to supervise at the kiosk and duly ordered an armful of food and drink to silence the impish baying of her son and his comparatively calm best friend. The boys' enthusiasm was rapidly beginning to infect Sharon, who dearly appreciated the sight of her son having an enjoyable time.

'It seems ages since we came to the flicks together, Hazel. It feels like being a teenager all over again. Can you remember when we went to see E.T. all those years ago? You started crying halfway through and never stopped...even after we left the cinema!'

Hazel reluctantly smirked with affection at the distant memory as she retrieved the first batch of popcorn from the assistant.

'Here you are, Peter. And don't eat it all before the film starts, either.'

Her son's instinctive response was to grab a ridiculously large portion of yellow puffs and cram them forcefully between his lips, which greatly amused Michael. Unfortunately, Hazel failed to see the funny side and pulled her son closer to offer a cautionary whisper.

'Peter...I said don't be silly. What did I say to you in the car about showing off? Now hold it steady so you don't spill any.'

Sharon declined to comment as she handed Michael his portion.

'There you are, my love. A drink is coming.'

She had secretly always felt that Hazel henpecked her only son far more often than was necessary and that she had seemingly still not grasped the fact that boys were boys and took many years to grow up.

That's if they managed to grow up at all.

It was true that Peter was an exuberant child and easily excited, but so were many of his age. Sometimes she wished that Michael was a little more outgoing, but she also deemed his natural shyness to be an inherent attribute which rarely encouraged even the slightest need for parental authority to be enforced.

Michael's temperament was indeed something of a blessing. He was a considerate, abiding child and one who always knew his own mind for such tender years. Peter on the other hand was immature and overly dependent for his age, but the families had become very intimate over time and the mix of personalities worked very well.

The boys had always played happily together since infancy. Hazel and Sharon had been the best of friends at school and the bond they had nurtured for over thirty years looked set to be justly repeated by the next generation.

James and David returned from the ticket desk and helped ease the burden of goodies that their wives were struggling to carry.

Peter began to jump up and down at the sight of his father clutching the admission slips.

'Can I hold my ticket, Dad? Please? Can I?'

'No. Just you concentrate on not throwing that food everywhere!'

A husky-voiced public announcer revealed that the film was about to start, and the admitted groups shuffled their way along the semi-lit corridor toward the theatre. Needless to say, there was no holding the boys back. Again, Hazel bowed to her authoritative compulsions.

'Peter, don't run with your popcorn! You'll lose it all over the floor just like last time. I know you will.'

Sharon looked at the anxious expression on her friend's face and then in turn glimpsed at James, who acknowledged his wife's reaction by rolling his eyes and giggling quietly to himself.

'Now, boys…wait for us…' requested David just as his son almost sent Michael flying by yanking open the door to the screening room.

Both boys laughed loudly as Michael steadied himself and just about saved his own carton of popcorn from being up ended.

Standing against the open door, Peter then centred his gaze on the four silhouetted adults that were following behind and bellowed his instructions.

'Come on, hurry up you lot! We'll miss the movie at this rate!'

Right on cue, Hazel issued her response.

'Peter! Stop shouting! You have to be quiet now we're going in here!'

*****

A chortling Michael and a hysterical Peter raced out of the cinema exit door and into the amber-hued car park. Swinging karate chops and shooting imaginary guns, the boys were quick to enliven the sanctity of their surroundings.

'That was totally amazing!' Peter yelped. 'Come on. I'll be The Joker. You can be Batman!'

The four parents gradually followed their sons into the arena of super-hero battle, with Hazel naturally issuing the obligatory caution.

'Watch where you're going, Peter. That car's reversing over there. He might not see you.'

James put his arm around Sharon's shoulder and admired the deep crimson sky of the late summer dusk, which separated distant blackening rooftops from the dark blue of encroaching night.

'Christ Shaz, it's got chilly quick. How long were we sat in there?'

Sharon glanced at her watch as James kissed her softly on the cheek and then held her hand as they strolled.

'Well…it's nearly half-seven. And I don't know about you but I'm starving.'

'You're kidding! The film didn't feel that long. Now you mention it, my belly's rumbling as well.'

Out in front, Hazel led the group back to their cars whilst David declared his support of the call for food.

'Big Macs all round, then. We'll go to the Mcdonald's nearer home, though. This one's always packed, and you can never sit down!'

The Tompkins travelled separately behind the Leavesdon's Focus, with James and Sharon occasionally laughing at the antics of the two urchins in front as they performed varying poses and faces though the rear windshield of David's car. A compelling novelty that was soon to be cut short again as Peter's mother gave the customary order to behave.

'Come on, boys, face front! Seatbelts please. You know the rules. You don't want a policeman to tell Daddy off, do you Peter?'

The youngsters begrudgingly swivelled round and smirked at one another as they clicked themselves into place. Then Peter's attention centred on the next leg of his treat.

'I want a quarter-pounder with cheese meal. Is that okay, Mum?'

'Yes…if you're good. Now sit back! Michael…you want to go for a burger, don't you? Your mum and dad are coming too.'

Michael instantly smiled as the thought of food entered his head.

'Yes, please Mrs. Leavesdon!'

Peter interrupted with an urgent query.

'Michael's still sleeping round my house tonight, isn't he?'

'Yes…as far as I know. Better ask his mum and dad if it's still alright first, though!'

Peter's shout of joy was accompanied by a flick of a loosely clenched fist toward his friend's shoulder, whose contemplative gaze had settled on the mystic view beyond the passenger window. Michael momentarily studied the ebony skirt of the early evening sky and wondered at the rapidly retreating hem of red that trailed away beyond the horizon.

The colours seemed to belong to another world far removed from the car and the road they were travelling on. It seemed like a safe place; a place to have pleasant dreams.

A place far away, where fantasy became reality.

Michael suddenly flinched in pain as his cheek received an unexpected slap from Peter's hand. The playful antagonist sat chuckling in anticipation of a similar response, but Michael simply looked at the beaming expression of his friend and uttered the first word that entered his head.

'Idiot!'

Peter's chuckles now erupted into booming laughter as he attempted to repeat the mischievous act, much to his mother's relayed disapproval.

'Come on, leave Michael alone or he's not staying over tonight. We're not far away from Mcdonalds now!'

Both cars pulled into parking spaces beside the brightly illuminated frontage of the burger bar. Within seconds, Peter had unbuckled and sprung from his seat. Pushing open the door with his feet he squealed with delight and jumped across to the partially lit pavement that flanked the restaurant. Michael adopted a rather more civilised approach and waited patiently for the four adults, supplying a ready quip regarding his friend's ever reliable appetite.

'I can't believe he's still hungry. He ate most of my popcorn, too.'

Furtively loitering at the entrance, Peter let the door clang into Michael's face as he went to grasp the handle. On witnessing the act, Hazel quickly followed her son inside and grabbed him by the hand to try and stem the overly energetic enthusiasm. Her son nodded avidly before scampering off toward some window seats and proceeding to daub greasy patterns on the glass. Hazel shook her head and turned to the others to take their orders.

'We'll buy these tonight, Shaz. You're our guests after all. Michael, what did you want to eat, darling?'

Michael's gaze alternated between Hazel and her mother as he considered the plethora of options.

'Erm…I'll have a chicken sandwich meal, please.'

Finally seated together at a table across from the boys, the group endured ten pleasurable minutes of virtual silence whilst they ate, until not even a solitary limp French-fry remained.

'Thanks for that, you two. That…was…fab!' exclaimed James as he leaned back in his chair and patted his stomach, much to Sharon's amusement.

'Looks like you need to attack a few salads judging by that paunch, Jim.' remarked David, as he sucked Sprite through a straw.

James offered a wry smile in response and opted to change the subject. He observed the tormenting expression on his son's face as the boys began to mildly aggravate one another.

'When are these two scallywags back at school, anyway? It seems like they've been on holiday for six months…not six weeks.'

Ever one to be organised and on hand with the relevant information, Hazel intervened with the required answers.

'Not until next Wednesday, I'm afraid. Monday and Tuesday are inset days for the teachers, apparently. Then its big school for these young men.'

Alarmed by his mother's revelation, Peter glanced across to her for confirmation of the statement.

'You mean…we aren't going back to junior school?'

'No, Peter. You know very well that you're not! You've moved to Riverlands across town. You're both in Mrs. Gray's class according to the paperwork you brought home last June. You spent a whole day there…remember?'

Hazel's son frowned as he sampled his strawberry milkshake.

'I think Mrs. Gray's horrible. I wanted to stay in Mrs. Jackson's class. She let us mess about all day!'

David laughed at the blunt innocence of youth.

‘Well…no more messing about from now on. It’s time to grow up for you two. Though…that won’t be as difficult for Michael as it will be for some…not too far away…not mentioning any names…’

The adults laughed as Peter scowled once again and flicked his drinking straw at Michael, adorning his friend’s shirt with droplets of thick, pink liquid.

‘Oi. Pack it up. Fool!’ requested Michael, sharply.

Grinning from ear to ear, Peter could not help but emit his familiar impish chuckle.

‘But I’m The Joker, remember? So, I can do what I like! So there!’

The act was reciprocated, and milkshake soon began to fly in all directions across the table. Of course, Hazel did not hesitate to bring the childish hostility to a close.

‘Right, if you’re going to throw your drink around it’s time to go, I think.’

Both boys immediately stopped launching their liquid missiles and burst into fits of giggles.

James also laughed as he observed the game come to an end.

‘Well…I’ll say this. Taking you two lads out for the night has been nothing if not entertaining! I can’t wait for the next date. I don’t know about you lot but I’m ready for bed. I’ve got to be up early.’

‘How is work at your place, Jim? Still busy?’ enquired David.

‘Oh…yeah, alright I suppose…although the upholstery trade is bursting with competition at the moment. We’ve got a few orders to keep us going until Christmas but after that I’m not sure. If things go pear-shaped I might have to train myself on a computer and apply for a job at your firm!’

Sharon laughed heartily at the mere suggestion of the idea.

‘You? Working with computers? You’d be swearing in seconds with your temper!’

James observed his wife as she enjoyed her moment of affectionate mockery.

‘Well…I’d just have to get our Michael to teach me the ropes, wouldn’t I? He’s pretty good with technology.’

Still Sharon continued with the teasing.

‘Stick with the day job…making beds and chair frames! Stick to what you’re good at, love!’

James looked across to his male counterpart, who was grinning broadly at the jousting spouses.

'Doesn't your missus have any faith in you either then, Dave?'

'None at all, Jim! But for totally different reasons. You see, I'm crap at D.I.Y. Whereas you're great at mending stuff, Hazel won't even let me pick up a hammer!'

'That's because you wouldn't know which end to use!' declared his wife with practised timing.

Laughter abounded around the table as the milkshake war recommenced across the aisle, giving motive for the party to make their departure.

'Are you sure it's alright for Michael to sleep over with you tonight, Hazel?'

'Yeah, of course. By the way, if you want, I'll take them both to school on Wednesday in the car.'

'Well…I reckon my boss will let me go into work a little later, so I'll hopefully be able to come with you the first day.'

'Great! We've can see our little boys finally become men together!'

The two families exited from the restaurant and headed for their cars. The evening air had become considerably colder during the past half hour, with the navy sky of earlier now portraying itself as ominously black. Peter looked up at the shimmering moon and pointed the spectacle out to the group.

'I'm going to live up there one day.' he declared.

'You're a saddo! And no saddos are allowed on the moon!' came the chuckling reply from his best friend.

'Give us a kiss then!' whispered Sharon as she leaned into Michael's face, accompanying the peck on the cheek with a hug. He then made a request of his parents as they got into the car.

'Mum…Dad…can I have a mobile phone when I'm a teenager?'

Peter supported his friend's claims by instantly barking the same request to his mother and father.

'Maybe…yes…perhaps when you're a teenager, Michael. You're still a bit young, yet! You'll only lose it, drop it or get it stolen! And I'm not paying your monthly bills, either.'

'Maybe…when you're thirteen.' James agreed.

Sharon's reply was enough to encourage an expression of earnest contentment to broaden her son's face.

'Have you got everything you need for tonight, love?'

'Yeah...I packed my bag this morning. It's on Mister Leavesdon's back seat'

'Okay. Good lad. We'll pick you up tomorrow. Thanks for having him, Hazel.'

Peter's mother laughed as she pulled open her passenger door.

'Don't thank me, Shaz. I ought to be thanking you! At least if Michael's around it means Peter will be giving *him* the headache instead of me!'

With waves of farewell, the pleasant engagement was brought to an end. Both cars followed one another out of the restaurant car park and filtered with the sparse main road traffic en route home. Driving in front, James watched in his rear-view mirror as the Leavesdon's Focus flashed its headlamps and veered off toward their house in Cromford Road.

Issuing a deep sigh of fatigue, he glanced across to Sharon.

'Is it me or is Peter bloody hyper-active? Jesus Christ. Hazel wasn't joking when she mentioned headaches!'

His wife simply smiled and nodded in agreement.

'You get used to him. He's good company for Michael, anyway. He's still a bit of a baby at the moment. Good night though, wasn't it? I enjoyed it. In fact, those boys have had a good summer holiday, really. They've been to some places. I tell you what...it's going to be a real shock to the system is secondary school.'

James navigated the Astra into Basford Lane and pulled onto the driveway of number twelve.

'Home, James! By the way...Wallace will need taking for a walk before you settle down on the sofa.'

'Yeah...funny how it's always my turn to take him for a walk.'

Sharon unlocked the front door as the family's German Shepherd hurtled toward them along the hallway and offered his customary greeting on hind legs. Evidently pleased to see his masters arrive home, his tail whipped itself into a furred blur and his long pink tongue commenced a very moist exploration of his master's face. Sharon giggled at the display of canine affection.

'Well, as you can plainly see, he's your dog. So as his owner...*you've* got to walk him.'

Reaching for the leather lead hanging behind the front door, James yawned as he attached it to Wallace's collar.

'Yes…he's my dog, alright. But as I recall…you laid a pretty firm claim to be the owner when he was a puppy.'

'Well…he was small and cute then…and he used to do his poos in a tray! There's no way I'm walking the streets carrying a bag of that stuff twice a day! I don't mind once a day, but not twice.'

Wallace began to jerk with impatience as he poked his nose through the open door and eagerly sniffed the night air.

'Yes...amazing isn't it how now he's all grown up and needs four miles a day you hand him over to me!'

'Yes…and when you've finally grown up, I'll be handing you over, as well!'

'Very funny, darling! Tell you what…now we've got the rare chance of a night alone together, why don't you run us both a bubbly bath? You know…just like we used to do in the good old days.'

Sharon noticed the familiarly enticing glint in her husband's eye as he battled to keep Wallace from pulling him into the front garden. She nodded without any obvious expression yet indicated her approval.

'Good idea! Hurry up, then!'

With Wallace now tugging relentlessly on his leash, James kissed his wife full on the lips and reluctantly obliged the dog's enthusiastic trail.

'I'll be fifteen minutes.'

Sharon watched her husband depart into the shadows of the amber-lit street as his escort panted and tugged them away into the murk.

'What…a quarter of an hour? Is that including the poo-stop or is the poo-stop extra?' she giggled. 'Okay, lover! Your time starts…now! And Watch out for bogeymen!'

'It's alright madam. I've always got my pet dog to protect me!'

'That big soft thing won't protect you. He'll probably roll over and want the bogeyman to rub his belly.'

Sharon again chuckled under her breath as she lovingly observed her husband and his faithful companion stride away into the enveloping darkness, before shutting the front door and trotting upstairs to the bathroom.

CHAPTER 2

'Michael! Hurry up! It's gone seven o'clock! Big day today! Come on, please! You haven't time to waste this morning!'

With her head eagerly poking through the bedroom doorway for the third time in fifteen minutes, Sharon watched her son stir under the duvet and listened as he supplied another accompanying grunt of displeasure.

Still adorned in her nightwear, she was still only mildly convinced that Michael was trying to rise from his nest and duly skipped across the landing to the bathroom.

Once dressed and bounding down the stairs, she grabbed the mail as it poked through the letterbox. Her mission continued onward to the kitchen where she let the dog out of the conservatory, laid out breakfast cereal and tripped over Wallace's tail as he curiously observed the morning rush.

With the radio blasting out the latest tunes and tiredness still a relevant issue, Sharon's senses remained ever so slightly numbed to the fact that today was Wednesday - the first day of the new school term.

Michael's inaugural day in Year Seven at Riverlands Secondary.

And despite having the best intentions of making an organised and early start since James left for work at just after five-thirty am, Sharon had instead opted to turn over in bed and grab herself an extra forty winks. Subsequently, yet completely as per normal, everything was now running drastically behind schedule.

Not that her schedules were ever set in stone. But Hazel Leavesdon had always been a stickler for punctuality, and would no doubt be knocking on the door at eight o'clock exactly to collect them just as she had pledged.

The pressure of decreasing time was mounting as Michael forced himself from underneath the bedclothes and begrudgingly sauntered downstairs.

Ever eager to see his adoptive human brother, Wallace sniffed the air in recognition and immediately jumped to attention before setting his sights on Michael and bounding into his midriff as he entered the kitchen, nearly knocking him flying back out into the hallway.

Having quickly hung a clean load of washing on the line in the back garden, Sharon returned to the kitchen only mildly pleased to confirm that her son had finally opted to declare his presence.

'Come on, Michael! Don't dawdle today! There's Cheerios or Shreddies on the table. We haven't time to mess about. Did you get your school bag ready last night as I asked you to?'

Having sufficiently sated the dog's appetite for a good morning lick and wrestle, Michael yawned and perched himself wearily at the kitchen table as Sharon ran a sink full of hot bubbles for the breakfast pots.

'Michael? I said is your school bag ready?' she repeated, now becoming concerned as she briefly eyed the clock ticking ominously towards seven-thirty.

'Yes, Mum.' he yawned. 'It's all done. But I can't find my new uniform'

'It's on the sofa, my love…all ironed and ready for you.'

Michael's voice barely carried above the sound of cereal falling into his empty bowl.

'Has Dad gone to work?'

'Yes, love. Ages ago! He's on twelve-hour shifts at the moment. But he said that I've got to give you a good luck kiss from him, though. He's thinking of you on your special day.'

Sharon stared lovingly at her son as he placed the box of Cheerios back on the table. The urge was too much to bear. Creeping up behind him as he added milk to the mix, she gave him a warm hug from behind and kissed the top of his head as he searched for a dessert spoon.

'Ohh…I'm so proud of you today! I've got to have a photo of you when you're ready in your new gear! I'm going to use it as my computer wallpaper. Right, come on! Eat up please time's running against us!'

Michael gradually crunched his breakfast as any remnants of slumber quickly gave way to gradual excitement at the prospect of the day ahead.

With vital minutes elapsing, his breakfast bowl was emptied, his face was washed, teeth were brushed and hair carefully gelled before he wandered into the lounge, yawned again and dressed himself. Once in full academic regalia of black trousers, white polo shirt and red pullover, he stood posing reluctantly for his mother who held her digital camera aloft at various angles and proceeded to click to her heart's content.

'You've put too much gel on your hair! It's shining! And you shouldn't put it on until you've got your clothes on! Look! It's all over your shirt collar!'

'Leave it, Mum! It's how I like to do it!'

Wallace scampered in and out of the lounge in a supportive display of enthusiasm for Michael's imminent venture to secondary school.

'Right! It's just gone a quarter to. The dog needs a quick walk around the block and then we'll be ready!'

Michael duly grabbed the leash from behind the front door. Now in expectation of his morning exercise, Wallace obediently followed and sat wagging his tail manically whilst Michael clipped the leather strap to the collar around his thick furry neck.

'Mum…won't we be late if we take Wallace out?'

'It's okay. We'll make it a quickie. I've got a watch on. We must be back here by five to. Off we go, then!'

The trio left the house and were immediately bathed in the warm sunshine of the late summer morning. There was definitely something invigorating in the air that brought good omens for Michael's initial foray into young adulthood.

Sharon smiled as Wallace yanked energetically in front, giving her son little choice but to increase his stride into an intermittent gallop. She observed Michael and his canine friend as they weaved their way through the estate to be greeted by the distant outline of the local parkland.

The opportunity for a final little heart to heart presented itself as mother and son passed through the park gates.

'Are you excited about going to your new school, Michael?'

'A little bit, I suppose. I'm a bit nervous too, though. They'll be a lot of kids there we don't know, won't there?'

Sharon nodded in reserved agreement.

'I bet Peter's excited, isn't he?'

'Oh God, Mum! He'll be unbearable, today! He can't help showing off, can he. I bet the teacher tells him off for something. He's always been naughty in class.'

'Yes…well, so long as he doesn't distract you and get you into mischief as well.'

Michael looked at his mother to vigorously defend his own corner.

'I'm the one who normally tells him to be quiet! I get him out of scrapes all the time. He'd be in no end of trouble if it wasn't for me.'

'Glad to hear it. I'll tell you what, son. You do look smart in your new outfit! You handsome thing, you!'

'MUM!'

Sharon's responsive chuckles were interrupted as Wallace attempted to bolt for freedom along the tree lined pathway, forcing Michael along with him at quite a pace. Eventually catching the pair up, Sharon unhooked the dog from his lead.

'Let him roam for a couple of minutes. He won't go far. Oh God! I hope he doesn't do a poo, though. I forgot to bring a carrier bag.'

Michael observed his canine brother as his mother's humorous concerns registered. Then, in that very instance, Wallace ceased his inspection of the undergrowth and duly positioned himself over a tuft of flattened weeds before making his deposits in full view of the watching audience.

During the act of bowel evacuation, the pointy-eared gaze of the German Shepherd never averted from that of his owners. It was almost as if the dog was aware of the ensuing predicament as he bared his teeth in gleeful relief.

'Bloody hell fire, Wallace! I do not bloody believe it!' shrieked Sharon.

Michael's instant laughter resounded around the wooded avenues of the park as his faithful friend eventually completed his business and trotted contentedly back towards them. Quickly sympathising with her son's mirth, Sharon too began to laugh hysterically and put a hand to her mouth.

'Quick, Michael! Let's get out of here before the park's poo squad turn up and arrest us!'

Now both consumed by uncontrolled fits of amusement, Michael re-attached the lead and the trio made for the iron-railing exit and back for home.

Completely unaware of the very necessary crime he had just committed, Wallace gave intermittent glances of curiosity to his companions as they skipped alongside him continuing to laugh out loud.

Finally, back in Basford Lane and safely outside the front door of number twelve, Sharon had managed to calm down somewhat and delivered urgent instruction as she checked her watch.

'Right…I'll lock dirty drawers in the conservatory with his morning feed and you fetch your school bag…and make sure you give it one last check!'

Having been imprisoned once again behind the glass double doors of the rear garden extension, Wallace looked suitably perplexed as Michael re-appeared in the lounge and gave him a wave goodbye.

Barking once in fraternal response, the dog then wolfed down a dish of biscuits before curling up on its rug for a barely earned doze.

With the front door now wide open, Sharon kept an eye on the road for the Leavesdons' silver Focus whilst commencing a final inventory of Michael's school equipment.

'Okay…PE kit?'

'Check.'

'Pencil case?'

'Yep!'

'Writing pad?'

'Yep.'

'Anything else you need? Dinner money?'

'I don't know what things cost. They said they'd give us a menu today. I think today is free but I'm not sure.'

'Okay. Well…take this tenner for now. But make sure you keep some change for tomorrow as well.'

Handing Michael the note, Sharon held her breath in trepidation as she ushered her son outside and locked the front door. The familiar form of Hazel's motor car pulled to a timely stop in the road beyond. With three eager pips of the horn, the driver declared she was ready and waiting.

Pressing his portly features through the back seat window, Peter frantically waved to his best friend before pushing the door open with the toe ends of his new shoes.

'Come on! Are you ready?'

Michael observed his friend's thick mop of blond hair and crimson cheeks that book-ended the sincerest of smiles.

Nodding without word, he walked tentatively with his mother along the path.

'All set?' a grinning Hazel called from behind the wheel.

Michael joined his friend in the rear whilst Sharon slipped into the front passenger seat.

'I think so. Well…it's too late now if we're not. What do you say boys? No turning back now! Shall we go for this, then?'

There was no reply from the pair of eleven-year-olds. From beyond the glass, Michael gazed back up his driveway to the welcoming frontage of home and thought of the happy times he had enjoyed during the six-week summer holiday. Lazy lie-ins. Long sunny days. Walks with Wallace. A fortnight break in Greece. Picnics and barbeques. Calling round for Peter most mornings.

Suddenly the thought entered his head that the time for fun may well be truly over. Life had suddenly taken on a very serious twist and in all truth, Michael wasn't overly in favour of the fact.

'Had a right rush on this morning, Hazel! Didn't think we'd be ready in time! Had to take the bloody dog to the park and all. And I had no bag to pick his bloody mess up with!'

Hazel giggled as she checked the wing mirror and lifted the clutch.

'What time you due at the shop, Shaz?'

'Oh…the boss said I could have the morning off. I start at one today…until closing time. Anyway…how come you've got the car? I thought this was Dave's pride and joy? Taking a risk isn't he?'

'Very funny! No…he said I can use it for the school run so long as we need it. He's on his mountain bike for the time being.'

The silver Ford navigated its passage out of the estate and onwards through to the town of Shireheath, with the intrigued young passengers in the back seats providing an uncharacteristically peaceful backdrop to the journey.

As the car gradually neared the hallowed territory of Riverlands Secondary School, increasing numbers of similarly uniformed children ambled along in the same direction.

Judging by most of the expressions on the faces, very few appeared to be relishing the prospect of another three full terms before the next summer holiday came around.

As was normal, Peter peered through the passenger window with his nose against the glass and proceeded to mutter a series of rhetorical queries under his breath.

Then he made an observation which demanded an immediate resolution from the two mothers in the front of the car.

‘How come no one else’s mum or dad is taking them to school?’

Michael was suddenly alerted to the situation and sat up in his seat to gaze at the scores of youngsters trooping dejectedly along the pavement. Hazel kept her eyes firmly on the road ahead as she answered.

‘I’ve driven you because we live quite a way away. About two and a half miles. It’s a long walk for your little legs just yet. Plus, Michael’s mum and I wanted to see you both walk in together on your first day. Anyway, we won’t be the only parents here. Why do you ask? Are you ashamed of us all of a sudden?’

Peter was not overly convinced by his mother’s explanation.

‘Not really…but…we’re old enough to walk on our own now, aren’t we?’

‘Yes…probably. But you’d be late every single day, wouldn’t you! At least this way I can make sure you don’t mess about and get you there on time.’

Peter looked across to his friend who volunteered no contribution to the debate, leaving Peter to continue defending their case alone.

‘Well…we could get the bus in the morning…and then we could walk home after school finishes?’

Hazel dropped through the gears before pulling into Friar Road, at the end of which, the Riverlands complex was situated.

‘Yes…maybe, you could catch the bus…but for now…I’d rather take you by car. Perhaps, in a week or two…if you can show me you can be trusted to get yourself to and from school on time, then I might think again. Okay?’

Peter mumbled in begrudging agreement as his mother crunched the car into second gear and crawled along the road looking for a space to park.

‘Christ…its busier than I thought it would be, Sharon. Looks like there are quite a few parents here after all.’

In her rear-view mirror, Hazel spotted a white transit van facing the other way and supposedly indicating to pull out. She watched as it remained stationary yet still displayed the intention to depart.

Applying the brakes, she clanked unceremoniously into reverse, eventually pulling to a stop adjacent to the driver’s side of the van.

Winding her window down to speak, Hazel noticed Peter had forced his plump features to appear over her shoulder.

'Peter…sit yourself back, please. There's nothing to see. And put your belt back on!'

The harsh-featured woman behind the wheel of the van did not look at Hazel, who quickly enquired about the parking spot.

'Excuse me, love? Are you leaving this space or not? There's nowhere to park down there and we're running a little late for school.'

Still the female driver did not acknowledge Hazel's curious glance; nor did she offer any attempt at a vocal response. Hazel turned to Sharon and both shrugged their shoulders in bemused frustration. Intending to repeat her question with a little more persuasion, Hazel was cut short by the noise of the van's engine as it began to rev wildly.

'I think she's decided to leave after all!' murmured Sharon beside her.

Sharon's forecast proved correct as the van quickly manoeuvred from its location and sped away along Friar Road toward the T-junction.

'Well, I don't know why she couldn't just answer me?' snapped Hazel. 'People are so ignorant these days, aren't they?'

Within seconds the car had been stationed with the two boys and their mothers standing on the pavement among a myriad of flocking students.

'You two have gone a bit quiet, haven't you?' quipped Sharon.

Peter and Michael smiled without word as they nervously clutched their new school bags.

'You'll be alright once you're in the classroom. All first-year kids are scared on their first day. I know I was! But there's nothing to be afraid of. Not when you're at school.'

Hazel's supportive commentary did little to appease the trepidation now evident on the faces of the two eleven-year-olds. The boys glanced at one another and tried in vain to appear youthfully stoic before the inevitable call to order was announced by Sharon.

'Okay. Come on! Be brave! You know where you're going once you're inside, don't you?'

Peter was momentarily tempted to climb out of his shell.

'Yes. Room six. Mrs. Gray's room. We're going to sit at the back in the middle, aren't we Michael? Where we sat before!'

His friend simply nodded before delicately declaring his wishes.

'Mum…will you watch us when we walk into school? Will you stay at the gate…just until we're inside?'

Sharon placed both hands on her son's shoulders and whispered in his ear.

'Of course I will, my love. And we'll still be here if you decide you don't want to stay and want to be taken home again!'

The eyes of pure innocence illuminated with genuine excitement before Sharon rained on the youngsters' temporary parade.

'Oh...did I say that? Sorry! Only joking! Off we go, then!'

Michael stood rooted to the spot as the other three marched onward.

'MUM! THAT'S NOT FAIR!'

Hazel and Sharon sniggered as they led the boys amid the noisy throng of pupils. The large, white-painted metal school gates became ever more imposing. The door to an unknown world. Michael was intrigued by the fact that many of those around him seemed calm and quite assured of their imminent day at Riverlands. He was also quite curious about one or two other noticeable aspects of his fellow pupils.

'Mum...most of the kids have got mobile phones...look! And there are a lot of older kids that are smoking too!'

Sharon eyed her son with a knowing glint.

'Yes, love. But they are naughty. So don't go getting any big ideas, will you?'

His heart began to beat rapidly as the foursome reached the large iron gates. Peter held up his arms compelling his mother to give him a tight hug. Michael saw the moist signs of uncertainty in his friend's eyes and opted to try and stay strong for the pair of them. He kissed his mother on the cheek and faced the entrance as she conveyed a final supportive message.

'Be a good lad, Michael. And don't look back. Keep going forward until you're inside those doors. You'll be fine after that. I promise.'

Reluctantly disengaging himself from his mother's grasp, Peter secured his bag over his shoulders and the pair slowly marched into the school grounds.

Sharon and Hazel watched as the diminutive figures adorned in brand-new uniforms shuffled toward their mutual fate. The only obvious physical difference between the pair as they approached the looming frontage of the building was the colour of their hair.

Peter's blond head entered school first, followed by the dark brown gelled spiky crown of Michael. The glass doors swung shut behind them, enclosing them in for the day.

And then, they were gone.

They did not revert their gazes back to their mothers even once, who had now both succumbed to the emotional swell of the moment and commenced drying their tears of pride with the tissues that Hazel had conveniently provided. Sharon linked an arm of comfort into her companion's.

'They'll be fine now, Shaz. That's the hard bit done.'

'Yes…they'll look after each other, Hazel. We needn't worry, anymore.'

Peter's mother engaged with the now smiling expression of her best friend.

'It's almost like we've lost them to somebody else, now, isn't it?

It's like they're not our little babies anymore. Like someone has taken them from us! You know, Shaz…I'm not sure I want my little boy to grow up so quick after all!'

Sharon began to giggle as she recalled her husband's comment from the other evening.

'Well, like Jim said, hopefully it's going to be a good while before either of those two manages that!'

The friends laughed together as they began to walk back to the car.

'I tell you what, Hazel. Being as I've got the morning off, do you fancy a bit of retail therapy in town, just to cheer ourselves up?'

'Brilliant idea! Just what the doctor ordered. We'll go into Shireheath and browse around some shops. I'll treat you to a cafe lunch and then take you to work afterwards. Should be fun!'

'Great! We can go now if you want. I don't need to go home. Wallace has had his morning walk.'

Now injected with a renewed sense of happiness, the pair ambled arm in arm back to the silver Focus. Hazel shut her door and placed the key in the ignition as Sharon slid in beside her friend and buckled up. Shifting the car noisily into first gear, she checked the road ahead and behind before employing the clutch.

'Okay, then! Town here we come!'

As the car began to move, Sharon's thoughts once again turned briefly to her son.

In the next instance, Hazel slammed her foot down on the brake pedal, narrowly avoiding a blurred flash of white that sped past the front of them, averting a collision by a split second.

Hazel's verbal reaction was almost as instantaneous as her physical one as she gripped the steering wheel and shouted in anger.

'FUCKING IDIOT! WHERE DID YOU GET YOUR FUCKING LICENCE FROM? KELLOGGS?'

'Jesus!' exclaimed Sharon in relief. 'It's double-parked all the way down here! He must have been doing at least fifty! What if a little kiddie had stepped out? They'd be dead! He'd have never stopped in time!'

Hazel observed the red taillights of the culprit vehicle as it came to a stop at the junction ahead before quickly merging with the other main road traffic and disappearing from view.

'Bloody idiot! I'm not sure, Sharon...but I reckon that he was actually a *she*. I'd swear it was that same miserable cow that ignored us from earlier on!'

Sharon shook her head in disbelief.

'Never mind. Lucky escape. No harm done. Forget about it. We've got some serious shopping to do and only four hours to do it in!'

The mothers chuckled as they glided away from the school grounds, now content with the idea of leaving their two sons to deal with today's destiny on their own.

CHAPTER 3

Mrs. Gray stood before the bustling throng of pupils in the outer corridor and waited patiently for quiet to prevail. Eventually, the group awarded her its full attention as she commenced the first instruction of the day with clasped hands and an earnest smile.

'Okay, boys and girls. If you have coats with you, would you please hang them up on the pegs out here and then file sensibly into the room? I don't mind if you wish to sit with friends. I'm quite laid-back regarding seating arrangements…for now.'

Lugging his overstuffed rucksack, Peter avidly pushed his way to the front of the jostling congregation in ensuring he would be in pole position to enter room six.

He peered through the open doorway, immediately focusing his attention on the very same table he had occupied with Michael during the previous June's influx taster day. Holding a firm stance at the head of the scrum, he waited impatiently for the word to pounce.

Only when fully assured that the word had been given, he bounded clumsily through the classroom's open door and along the right-hand aisle, quickly staking a claim for his chosen destination by launching his rucksack onto the desktop from a good five yards away. The bag proceeded to slide off the table and clattered into the chairs behind.

Peter then confirmed his victory with a glorious yelp back toward the rest of the incoming group.

'Hurry up, Michael! I've got our places!'

Being particularly careful not to collide with anybody who might well take exception to the fact, Michael politely awaited his turn to enter the room as the bottle-necked group shuffled forward. However, his efforts in offering some gentlemanly consideration quickly backfired as he inadvertently stepped onto the toe of somebody's protruding shoe.

Responding to the female wince of pain, he immediately turned to the victim fully armed with a ready apology. A blue-eyed girl with a blond hairstyle that sported black streaks looked him sternly in the eye as they stood shoulder to shoulder.

'I'm sorry…I didn't mean it!' quivered Michael.

Then the girl's initially harsh expression softened and rapidly evolved into a captivating smile.

'It's okay. I know you didn't. It's all those other idiots shoving from behind. I'm Chantelle, by the way. I take it your name's Michael. I heard your big-mouthed mate shouting it.'

Michael sniggered as he watched the girl sidle into the room in front of him and veer off toward her own table of choice, before his concentration was broken once again by the familiarly buoyant shrieks of his best friend.

'Michael! Come on! Hurry up! Before somebody else decides to sit next to me!'

Slightly enamoured by the accidental brief encounter with his new female classmate, Michael reluctantly obeyed the instruction from Peter who continued to wave his arms frantically from the rear of the room.

'Don't stress, you fool! I'm here, aren't I?'

The two friends were finally reunited on the back table of the middle row which they both considered to be the ultimate vantage point in their newfound arena.

Peter's anticipation was almost unbearable for him to contain.

'I was a bit worried that somebody else would want to take your seat before you got here'

Michael smirked at the rosy-cheeked expression of genuine relief that his companion displayed and offered some reassurance on the matter.

'Believe me, Peter…there's not much chance of *that.*'

The pair sat and observed the rest of the pupils that were still considering their options regarding where to locate themselves.

'It's great that we can sit together, isn't it?' beamed Peter.

Michael sighed as he studied the teacher who positioned herself in the doorway whilst watching the class gradually settle. She then closed the door behind her and moved towards the large desk situated underneath the blackboard.

'Yes, Peter. It's brilliant. Now calm down a bit, will you?'

Finally, with all pupils positioned, Mrs. Gray appeared ready to begin the day's schedule as Peter began to punch Michael's arm. Michael had insisted that Peter tried to at least listen to what was said and behave himself for just a few hours.

Unfortunately, a very familiar giggling sound began to emanate from the seat next to him just as Mrs. Gray began the opening monologue to her new form class. Michael was forced to whisper a request to his friend.

'Oh God! Don't start laughing Peter! There's not even anything funny happening!? Stop hitting me and control yourself, you idiot!'

In attempting to divert his attention from the persistent chuckles, Michael's eyes wandered around the room and inadvertently rested on the girl with black and blond streaked hair.

As if by telepathic response, her eyes darted back across the void and met with his. Her instant smile was accompanied by a gentle wave and a swish of her short ponytail. Appreciative of the gesture, Michael blushed unashamedly and quickly faced the front of the room once more.

After a few minutes of barely concealed mirth, Peter's nervous tension gradually eased, and his mind settled on the business at hand – namely the tedious tasks of filling in school forms and checking through timetables.

For the moment at least, both boys were convincing in performing their new role as new Year Seven pupils, with the carefree days of junior school quickly being eclipsed as a relic of the recent past.

*****

'I hope they're alright, Hazel. I keep having this recurring image of them both bursting through the main doors in tears and wanting to come home.'

Hazel giggled as the pair entered the designer clothes shop.

'Thick as thieves, them two, Shaz! It'll take a lot to upset their applecart! God! I bet our Peter's running riot as we speak. That poor teacher!'

Sharon laughed out loud as another thought flashed through her head.

'You know what! When we do decide to let them come home on their own it'll be real fun for the other kids on the bus. Peter will be up and down the aisle like a jumping bean!'

Hazel concurred with jovial affection.

'What about the unlucky sod driving them home? If me and Dave can't keep him quiet and sat still for five minutes what chance has anyone else got?'

The pair meandered around the shop, browsing among the overly expensive blouses, dresses and skirts to sate their partial curiosity.

'What do you really think about them coming home on the bus, Hazel? I'm willing to give it a try if you are. It'd save you traipsing there and back twice a day. My parents won't mind looking after them a couple of nights a week, you know. God knows they've done it enough times before.'

'No honestly, I'm glad to do it, Sharon. I haven't got to go to work like you have. I've got the car and I've got the time. Plus, I want to make sure they both get into a steady routine. But they need to prove to us they can be relied upon to actually get on the damned bus, first of all! You're lucky...Michael's very sensible, but I wouldn't trust our Peter to get his shoes on the right feet. I think we'll have to take things one step at a time.'

Back out into the growing bustle of the High Street, Sharon glanced at her watch.

'I wouldn't mind a look in Past Times, Hazel. Always some good stuff in there. Where did you want to eat, later?'

Hazel observed the milling troops of shoppers as she gazed up toward the market square.'

'What about slowly working our way up to O'Reilly's? They do a brilliant brekkie and drink for a fiver! My shout!'

'No, Hazel...you bought the Mcdonalds the other night!'

'Look, I'm not offering again!'

'Go on then! You've twisted my arm!'

*****

Giving his full concentration to the teacher's conveyance of general school rules, Michael was distracted by Peter's right foot connecting under the table with his left ankle. Whilst causing him a jolt of discomfort, it also compelled him to glance across to the hand-written note being covertly displayed under his nose.

It contained four words that broached a simple question:

WHEN IS DINNER TIME?

Fully aware of his friend's consistently hefty appetite, Michael could not conceal the instinctive smirk that instantly spread broadly across his own face. He opted to whisper a selective response to his dumbfounded and obviously hungry pal.

'I don't know when dinner time is, you fool!'

Peter unsubtly reinforced his urgent need for food in an unsuitably loud tone.

'But I'm starving! I only had four slices of toast and jam with peanut butter for breakfast! Oh...and two bowls of Sugar Puffs!'

Now Michael was the one becoming consumed with mirth and his stomach started to twitch as laughter threatened to erupt. He placed a hand over his mouth to try and hide the encroaching episode from the teacher.

'But it's only ten o'clock you greedy git! There's a clock on the wall, look!' he muttered in fitful response.

Despairing at the hunger pangs that were now rumbling uncontrollably, Peter quietly heaved his bag up from the floor and on to his knee before proceeding to rummage inside.

'What are you looking for?' enquired a cautious Michael.

'I'm sure I've got a Mars Bar in here somewhere!'

'But you can't sit and eat it in the classroom, you dummy!'

Unbeknown to the conferring duo, Mrs. Gray had now detected the very audible source of disruption emanating from the back table of the middle row.

She observed their barely private conversation for a few seconds before declaring her undying interest.

'Now then, you two...Peter and Michael, is it? I don't mind you sitting together but you must pay attention whilst I'm speaking. If you can't listen then I might have to split the pair of you up.'

Peter looked up from the open maw of his rucksack, temporarily interrupting the desperate search for chocolate. Michael offered his best friend a warning nudge as the attentions of the whole class centred toward the rear of room six, including the girl named Chantelle, whose reason for her slightly deeper interest in proceedings remained firmly secret.

Michael hissed a curt warning to his friend.

'Peter...stop messing about! You've got to sit still and concentrate...or you'll be in trouble! We've only been here an hour! Put the bag down.'

To Michael's eventual relief, the advice seemed to register in Peter's brain for the remainder of the first morning session as Mrs. Gray introduced the new form group to the ritual process of legislative paperwork that all new pupils had to endure.

Homework diaries were promptly issued, giving cause for a token of protest from Peter and resulting laughter from the rest of the class.

'Homework? You mean…work…that we have to do at *home*? I haven't got time for homework! What about time for playing on my X-Box?'

The teacher grinned and presented him with his solitary option.

'Homework comes first…X-Box definitely comes second.'

A map of the school layout was given to each pupil and raised several natural queries, with Peter predictably displaying an avid interest in the precise location of the canteen.

It soon became evident to all that Mrs. Gray was not the domineering kind. Short in stature and with a mop of greying hair that framed kindly features, she was an experienced hand in dealing with the excitable new entrants that invariably needed careful guidance on the first few days of term.

Aside from her unspoken authority, she had discovered over time that a liberal amount of leniency was also vitally important when welcoming the annual influx.

It was just as well, because Peter Leavesdon had unknowingly tested her patience for much of the first half of the morning. But nevertheless, the necessary tasks had been achieved and the first two hours had passed relatively quickly.

The piercing resonance of the school bell indicated a timely opportunity to liberate the children into the lingering sunshine. Break time would offer a chance to burn off some pent-up energy.

Complying with the teacher's polite request to stand quietly and place chairs under tables, Peter bounded to his feet, forcibly scraping his chair along the polished tiled floor which served to produce a shrill screech. The echo ricocheted toward the front of the room, again giving cause for Mrs. Gray to stare discomfortingly toward the persistent source of mischief.

Failing to hide his giggling, scarlet-hued features, the perpetrator was duly beckoned to the teacher's desk with a curled forefinger.

'Peter. Would you come here and remain standing beside my desk until all other pupils have vacated the room, please? Okay class…the rest of you may go. Out of the door…turn left along the corridor and left again through the main hall doors.'

Michael shuffled along with his best friend, rankling with an undue sense of guilt at the potential punishment that Peter was about to endure.

Obviously loitering, he tried in vain to offer some support.

'He didn't mean to be naughty, Miss. He's always like this. He just acts a bit silly at times.'

However, Mrs Gray had no wish to hear the testimony of a character witness. She had deduced all she needed to know about Peter Leavesdon for the moment.

'Run along, Michael…off to the playground. Don't worry about this one. I just want a quick word. He'll be with you shortly.'

Now verging on partial upset, Peter watched as the room slowly became vacant with a sense of juvenile fear beginning to envelop him. The sudden vulnerability caused the youngster to sway on the spot, leaving him only to wonder what the teacher was about to say and do.

However, fully expectant of shouting and remonstration, he was gladly disappointed. Mrs Gray remained in her seat with her arms folded and asked Peter to take the seat beside her.

The voice was soft yet carried a definitive tone of commandment as he now finally found himself compelled to listen to her every word whilst wiping both eyes with his thumbs.

'Now look, Peter. I fully understand that you are a little daunted to be here and I'm also fully aware that junior school was probably far more fun for you. But as you have seen, the rest of the class is adjusting pretty well. They are attentive and willing to sit still. This is what you must do for me. Okay?'

Peter did not initially wish to engage with the gaze of his teacher, but courteous necessity dragged his attention from the floor at his feet and up to rest on her friendly smile as she continued with the gentle sermon.

'Now…after break time we will be doing some handwriting assessments. Do you think you can concentrate for this? Because I need to see how you're writing has progressed these past few months. I bet you haven't done any writing over the summer holidays, have you? I bet it's been one video game after the next!'

Peter stared vacantly as his teacher continued.

'Well? Are you going to be a good lad and do as you're told, for me? Or do I need to involve Mister Ford the Headmaster? And I should warn you now…he is a lot scarier than I am!'

The begrudging smile on Peter's face was accompanied by a very relieved nodding of the head.

'I'm sorry, Miss. I'll listen to you after break. I promise! Don't fetch Mister Ford!'

'Good boy! I thought you'd see sense. So…its eyes down, listening carefully and working hard. Okay? No more throwing pieces of rubber. No more thumping the boy sitting next to you. And no more making silly trumping noises with your armpit. Okay?'

Peter's chuckles were welcomed and unrestrained, encouraging a similar response from Mrs. Gray as she laid a hand on his shoulder.

'Now…you've got ten minutes left of break time. I suggest you go and make the most of it before coming back in here. Please feel free to burn your excess energy off! And guess what? I'll be giving out the dinner menus after break, as well! That should capture your interest, shouldn't it?'

'Thanks Mrs. Gray! Do they have pizza?'

'I don't think so…no. Now go on…hop it!'

Without further word, Peter jumped to his feet and scuttled from room six to navigate his way toward the playground. Mrs. Gray followed him out and along the corridor on the way to the staff room for a much-needed coffee.

Her endearing smile never threatened to diminish as she observed the blond-haired youngster clatter into the glass double doors with both hands and gallop across the tarmac toward his waiting friend.

*****

'I'll pick the boys up at three-thirty and I'll feed them both. Peter won't want to wait long for his tea! That's a dead cert! I can drop you at the shop now if you want me to?'

Sharon unbuckled her seatbelt outside the driveway of number twelve, Basford Lane.

'Thanks, Hazel. It's fine. Wallace will need a walk, anyway. I should be round from work about half-five. And thanks for this morning, as well. It made a really nice change. Once the boys get used to ferrying themselves about it won't be such an issue. I've decided I'm going to get a key cut for Michael so he can let himself in.'

Hazel watched her friend depart from the car and shut the passenger door behind her. Winding down the window, she shouted through the opening.

'Good idea. Somehow, though, I get the nagging feeling that could be an issue with Peter. Still…we'll have to wait and see. I'll see you at ours at about five-thirty-ish, then!'

Searching through her handbag for her own key, Sharon confirmed the arrangement as she wandered up the drive.

'Great! See you later!'

'Don't forget your poo bag this time!'

Sharon chuckled as she watched the silver Focus trundle away along the road. Entering the hallway, she retrieved junk mail from the doormat, proceeding to drop it at the foot of the stairs. Then it was onward through to the conservatory, to be greeted by the bright-eyed perky-eared vision of Wallace who pressed his nose against the glass in anticipation of welcome release.

Once freed from his dormitory, he immediately sniffed the air and wandered in and around the ground floor rooms of the house as though searching for something. Sharon noticed the display of canine curiosity and quickly ascertained the cause.

'Is it Michael you're looking for? Ahh…are you missing your brother? Are you? Well…I'm sorry…you'll have to wait until tonight, Wally. Come on! Walkies now! Then din-dins! Then work for Mummy!'

Now with his attention firmly fixed on the impending scamper, he fetched his own lead from the hook in the hallway and presented it between his jaws to Sharon as she followed from the kitchen.

'Good boy! Daddy has taught you well, hasn't he? It's got to be a quick one, though. Mummy's due at work in half an hour!'

Backtracking into the kitchen drawer for an emergency poo bag, Sharon's thoughts reverted to her son and the indescribable maternal euphoria she suddenly felt at the prospect of seeing him later that day. She ruffled the thick brown fur around Wallace's neck as she spoke to him.

'Mikey's at big school now! Yes! He's growing up! Yes, he is!'

Now with his mind occupied by only one thought, Wallace pulled Sharon through the front door, affording her just enough time to lock it behind her before being chaperoned toward the local park.

*****

After obliging the wishes of his new form teacher, dinner time duly arrived and was by far the most positive aspect to Peter's first day at Riverlands, although the menu on offer left him a little bemused to say the least.

Having whetted his appetite with thoughts of some real sustenance, he and Michael had lined up with the rest of the school faced with a rather frustrating buffet selection.

After two or three minutes of deliberation at the counter, both resorted to ordering a chicken pasta salad apiece accompanied by a cereal bar for afters.

'Don't you do apple crumble and custard?' exclaimed a dejected Peter as he passed through the cash-tiller. The rotund woman grimaced at the inquisitive boy standing before her as he conveyed his disillusionment.

'Sorry, love! Only healthy options, these days! No more fatty food for school kids! It's because of that Jamie Oliver off the telly! He's stopped sausage and chips and all that stuff! Anyway, today's meal is free for Year Sevens. Lucky you, eh?'

Less than satisfied with her reply, he offered a parting shot as he retrieved his tray from the counter.

'Well…I'll just have to have chips at home tonight, then'

Peter turned to follow Michael in the search for a vacant spot to sit and eat. Hovering among the other diners, they finally settled on a table in the corner which by sheer coincidence also happened to be where the girl called Chantelle was seated with her friend. The boys tentatively took their places as Chantelle's companion stared coldly in response to the intrusion.

'Hello.' smiled Michael to the chewing duo.

'Er…did we say you could join us?'

Mildly startled by the comment, Michael glanced at the source of disapproval perched next to Chantelle. She looked to be the nasty type. Narrow eyes and lank brown hair did little to accentuate the bluntness of her features. Just as a verbal retort was forming, Chantelle stepped in to defend the unexpected guests.

'It's alright, Kim. I don't mind.'

'Well, I do, Chaz! Especially him! The fat one with the gob! Never shut up all morning in class! Gave me right ear-ache!'

Partially distracted from the plastic tray of chicken pasta, Peter drew his attention to the willing antagonist and conveyed his reply.

'Don't worry about me, spotty! I can get thinner but you'll always be ugly!'

Kim screwed up her spiteful features and extended a bony forefinger across the table.

'What did you say, lard-arse? Repeat that if you want a slap!'

Michael and Chantelle exchanged brief glances of amusement as the argument began to gather momentum. To his friend's amazement, Peter typical shyness in front of strangers immediately evaporated as he boldly stood his ground.

'I said…can I have your leftovers if you're finished? These portions are way too tiny for me! I've got to keep my weight up, you know!'

Impressed with the diplomatic repost of his friend, Michael focused on Chantelle's face which looked even more attractive whilst seeming rather concerned about the ensuing battle of wits.

'Leave it, Kim! Let's get out of here! You'll only start something you can't finish.'

'I want to know what fat-boy said. And he's going to tell me. Aren't you, fat-boy?'

Peter's face began to redden as though he had suddenly lost his brief grasp on confidence. He looked at Michael who was now becoming annoyed at the girl's constant references to Peter's weight.

'Oi! Lumpy! Are you deaf or something? Did you call me ugly? Do you want your friggin' teeth knocking out?'

Michael could not control his temper any longer as he sensed Peter's encroaching upset.

'Chantelle…why don't you take your mate out onto the playing field to eat some grass or something?'

Chantelle nodded in agreement and took her now incensed friend by the arm. The girls stood to their feet and began to depart, but not before Peter had uttered the last word to accompany their departure.

'See ya, Kim! Can I have your other sandwich then, or what?'

Michael giggled as he gently patted his pal on the back.

'You are a bleedin' nuisance! But a funny one at times!'

'Silly cow!' replied Peter, through a morsel of chicken. 'I tell you what, though. That Chantelle kept looking at you! I reckon she's interested!'

Now Michael was stumped for words as he registered his friend's un-typically insightful comment. Failing to summon an adequate reaction, he felt contented to say nothing about the girl with blond hair and black streaks.

'Peter…'

'Yeah?'

'Just eat your dinner.'

*****

The afternoon session with Mrs. Gray comprised a series of aptitude tests and an informal class discussion to allow some familiarity to develop between pupils.

In truth, Michael and Peter had watched the clock tick slowly by, with Peter in particular finding the whole experience something of a chore. One or two scornful glances were offered from the occupants of the third desk by the second window, at which Chantelle and Kim were sat, but nothing more was said between the four.

Three-thirty seemed to take forever to form itself on the clock face, and there was an atmospheric sigh of relief to accompany the teacher's request for the class to stand and place chairs neatly onto the tables in readiness for the cleaners.

With hands clasped in front and smile at the ready, Mrs. Gray observed her form group as they waited impatiently for the final home-time bell.

'Well…I hope you all enjoyed your first and easiest day at Riverlands, boys and girls. And please bear in mind that it only gets harder from here on in!'

The class chuckled in response, also realising that the next few weeks were indeed likely to be a stern test of discipline and organisation.

'If you brought coats with you this morning, don't forget to take them with you on the way out. Also…look at your timetables and maps tonight to confirm your lessons tomorrow and the rooms in which they are located.'

The welcome resonance of the droning bell clattered around the building, immediately igniting a crescendo of voices.

Subsequently, Mrs. Gray struggled to be heard above the din.

'And by the way…it's Year Seven assembly in the hall tomorrow morning. So don't come in here for registration. Go straight to the hall from the playground. Good afternoon, class. And please be careful on your way home.'

The young congregation vacated their desks and amassed in the doorway in the united attempt to claim liberation. A convergence with the scores of hustling, swaying bodies and booming voices from other classrooms slowly squeezed its way through the cloakroom and beyond the main glass doors of the school.

Kim eyed Peter through the crowd with a view to maybe continuing with their exchanges of earlier, but she was quickly ushered in the opposite direction by Chantelle.

For Michael's part, he was just happy that they had made it through the first day in one piece and without more hassle than was necessary. He noticed that his friend had continued to stare after his chosen enemy long after she merged with the rapidly increasing mass of vibrant pupils.

'What's up with you?'

Peter adorned a mischievous smirk and revealed his thoughts as the pair embraced the freedom offered by the main doors.

'I just noticed something.'

'Yeah? Noticed what?' asked Michael.

'That Chantelle girl…looking at you again…she's definitely interested.'

A thoughtful pause from Michael was ended with a positive suggestion.

'Peter…'

'Yeah?'

'Let's just go home.'

CHAPTER 4

Peter pressed himself forcibly through the exit amid dozens of other crushed bodies a good twenty seconds before Michael eventually emerged. From the main doors, he ambled along with the swelling crowd toward the large, white-painted gates.

The sun felt good on their faces and a sense of genuine achievement encroached on having completed their first day at Riverlands.

Michael's slow meander toward the gate brought to mind endearing images that flashed vividly across his conscience. The prospect of seeing his mother and father later that evening suddenly seemed something to long for. He had also missed Wallace and decided at that moment that he would accompany his father on the traditional evening dog-walk through the park.

It would also be something of an adventure to sit and eat with Peter and his mother in a short while, although an entire school day in the company of his best friend had already proved ample.

Michael gazed wearily at the heaving mass of teenagers in front of him, noticing Peter gamely trying to push past the crowds in order to meet with the small group of parents gathered on the other side of the school boundary wall.

The sun-bleached golden crown of his most favoured pal suddenly turned, with the scarlet face beneath it displaying an expression of growing concern. Peter's tone was laced with childish alarm as he pointed frantically to the line-up of adults.

'Michael…can you see my mum, yet? I can't see her! There are quite a few grown-ups here, aren't there? But I can't see her! I can't see my mum!'

In unwelcome consideration of the surrounding pupils that had just witnessed Peter's momentary panic, Michael felt mildly embarrassed by his friend's naive outburst. He caught up with Peter who had by now stopped his impatient stride, causing those behind to alter their course and veer around him. Subsequently, Michael was first through the open gate, avidly scanning the smiling faces of the adults as the search for Hazel commenced.

Still transfixed by his mother's apparent absence, Peter accidentally bumped into Michael from the rear. His attentions were now re-focused on activity elsewhere that readily eclipsed the importance of his mother's seemingly belated appearance.

'Hey…Michael…look! Over there! Somebody's waving to you!'

Peter's hand wrenched heavily on his friend's right shoulder forcing him to turn toward the mysterious source of intrigue.

'Ouch! That hurt! What are you on about, you fool?'

'Look! Over there! By the corner. Look!'

Michael switched his head roughly in the direction depicted to see the blond-haired girl with black streaks eating a bag of crisps. He stood and observed her as she intermittently crunched whilst glancing in the boys' direction.

Then, without further word, Chantelle blew Michael a kiss from across the road and continued laughing as she turned on her heel. Her friend Kim simply sneered at the minimal male audience and both girls disappeared along the alley linking to the adjoining street.

Contemplating the cringe-worthy moment, Michael's juvenile discomfort was disturbed by the tones of a familiar voice emanating from the flowing congregation around the school gate.

'Hey, boys! Peter! Michael! Over here!'

Hazel shrieked with excitement as her son finally responded with an enormous grin of relief. Man-handling his way through the home-time rabble, he tugged Michael's arm to once again point him in the right direction.

'There's Mum! Come on!'

Finally back together, the reunion was tender and maternal with Hazel feeling far more inflated at seeing the boys than she presumed she might have been. Squeezing her son tightly in a loving embrace, she kissed him on the cheek as he squirmed away in childish disgust.

'Mum! I'm eleven now, you know! People are watching us!'

Hazel laughed out loud as she observed Michael shaking his head and smirking at the comical scene.

'I can't believe he just said that, Mrs Leavesdon. He was nearly crying for you a minute ago.'

Peter glared at his friend for the minor betrayal as Hazel feigned her offence.

'You're never too old to be kissed by your mother, Peter! In fact, I'm quite offended! Well? Did you have a good day, then? And furthermore…did you behave yourself?'

The youngsters exchanged knowing glances before Hazel opted to continue her questioning by engaging with the more reliable one of the pair.

'Well, Michael? Did he behave himself?'

Ever supportive of his friend's cause, Michael obliged with the answer that was begging to be heard by a mother and son.

'Of course, he did! Never took his pen off the page. Did you, mate?'

'Excellent!' beamed Hazel.

'Except…'

Michael's additional commentary caused Hazel's mouth to fall open and her eyes to widen in expectation of some disastrous revelation.

Luckily, Michael squashed her trepidation in an instant.

'Only kidding, Mrs Leavesdon. He was cool. Really.'

She offered her son a concerned stare as he adjusted the straps of the rucksack hanging awkwardly on his back.

'What about Mrs. Gray? Was she as nice as you thought?'

Peter nodded, yet his dubious expression conveyed mild disappointment which of course Hazel could not ignore.

'Are you sure? Okay, Peter…what happened?'

Her son glanced to Michael before disclosing his quandary.

'Yeah…she was alright, I suppose. But she said I can't play on my X-Box until I've done my homework, though.'

Hazel chuckled at her son's earnest displeasure.

'That's a good rule to start with. You spend far too much time on that console as it is. I'm afraid school has to come first now, my lad. Anyway, let's not stand outside here all evening or it won't be worth us going home at all, will it?'

The trio navigated their way from the school premises and slowly joined with the unpredictable ebb and flow of youngsters trekking steadily along Friar Road.

'I had to park on the next street. It's ever so busy here, today. When do your lessons start then, boys?'

'Tomorrow…after assembly.' replied Michael. 'We mostly just did some handwriting and talking today.'

'Yes…I bet he did most of the talking! Was your dinner nice, Peter?'

Hazel stopped her stride as the boys loitered slowly behind.

'Yeah…alright I suppose. For saying it cost nothing.'

'What did you have?'

'The same as Michael…some cold gooey chicken stuff. Didn't really like it but I ate it anyway cos I was hungry.'

Hazel looked puzzlingly at Michael for some clarity on her son's vague description.

'It was chicken pasta with tomato salad. We sometimes have it at home. The woman at school said you can't get fatty food at school now. Kids have to eat healthy.'

In an effort to encourage a sense of urgency into the departure, Hazel adjusted her position and continued to march slowly behind the boys where she could attain better view of the two new starters.

'Well hopefully we'll soon wean Peter off his burger and chips diet, then!'

The surrounding presence of his many school counterparts prompted Peter into an inevitable yet familiar query as the three shuffled along the pavement.

'Mum?'

'Yes, love?'

'Can Michael and me go to school on our own tomorrow?'

'No, Peter. I told you this morning. You need to show that you can be trusted. For the first week or so I'll be bringing you and fetching you home. Then maybe when you've made friends with other boys who live near to us you and Michael can walk or get the bus with them. Okay?'

Peter mumbled something indecipherable as a gesture of his disgruntlement before looking across to Michael for some backing on the issue. However, his friend was not forthcoming with an opinion.

Changing the subject seemed to be an appropriate plan.

'Guess what, Mum?'

'What, Peter?'

'Michael's got a girlfriend already.'

Hazel stopped before trotting in front of the boys and turning to face them with a broad grin. She glanced down at the scarlet hue gaining youthful density on Michael's face.

'No! You're joking! Wait until I tell your mother! You don't hang about, do you, Michael? Come on, then! What's her name?'

Michael's initial effort to try and dampen down his friend's wildly exaggerated claim was immediately quashed by Peter's increasingly loud enthusiasm to reveal more.

'It's Chantelle! Isn't it, Michael? It's Chantelle! She's got weird hair, though! There's all black bits in it! And she's got an ugly friend called Kim who wanted to punch me at dinner time cos I asked if I could have her sandwich.'

Hazel raised a hand to intercede on her son's accidental confession, which caused more than a little inner satisfaction for Michael.

'Erm...do I really want to know about this? What did you just say? Surely you haven't been fighting on your first day? And surely not with a girl?'

Peter shook his head and adopted an air of male nonchalance.

'Nah! I didn't hit her. But I called her spotty. She got scared off!'

Michael now simply grimaced at the highly likely prospect of Peter unveiling another creative theory about Chantelle to his mother. Thankfully the subject matter changed swiftly once again due to the reliably regular cycle of Peter realising he was hungry.

'Mum...what's for tea?'

'I don't know, love. I haven't been shopping so there's nothing fancy in at home. What did you have in mind?'

The two boys confirmed a mutual preference and announced their plan in perfect vocal harmony.

'Pizza!'

'With chips.' Peter confirmed.

Hazel shook her head and chuckled.

'What an amazing surprise! You'll end up looking like pizzas, you two will. Okay, pizza it is. But we'll have to go to the supermarket on the way home.'

The lethargic manner that had accompanied both boys since they burst forth from the school doors suddenly evaporated.

Peter declared the specifics.

'Great, Mum! Can we have meat feast?'

'Yes.'

'With cheese crust?'

'Yes...okay.'

'Twelve inch?'

'You'll never finish a twelve-inch.'

'Deep-pan, though?'

'Yes…yes, if you want. By the way, more importantly…did you get given any homework today?'

Peter looked blankly at his friend as they walked.

'No! I don't think we did, anyway. Did we get any homework, Michael?'

His friend sighed in disbelief as he gazed at the crowd of bobbing heads in front.

'Peter…did you actually listen to anything that was said in the lesson today?'

Hazel and her son exchanged sheepish glances.

'A little bit. Why? I did Mum! Honest!'

Michael readily put the debate to bed.

'No, Mrs Leavesdon. We didn't get homework today.'

Peter's overwhelming joy at the news incurred another upward shift in volume.

'Great! That means we can go on the X-Box! I'm going to play you at Weapons of War! And you're going to die!'

Hazel was a little concerned about Peter's willingness to commit simulated murder.

'Don't say that, Peter. That's a horrible thing to say to your friend.'

Michael smirked as Peter grumbled a humble apology.

Hazel and the two boys had reached nearly halfway down the street. Although they had walked along in total shadow, the sunshine was still high and very warm for early September centred amid a pure azure sky.

'Mum…hold on a minute…I'm boiling! I need to take my jumper off!'

'Okay love. We'll keep walking slowly. It's not far now.'

Peter stopped to wrestle his rucksack from his back and dropped it from waist height onto the pavement behind him. Tugging the brand-new school jersey from over his head, he promptly tied it around his waist via the arms, retrieved the bag from the floor and continued to follow his mother and Michael who were now a few paces in front.

As he snaked among the gradually dispersing throng of schoolchildren, the path of all was partially obstructed by a vehicle door as it suddenly swung open across the pavement.

Altering his step with the others to manoeuvre around the obstacle, it was quickly pulled shut again just as he approached to pass.

Ever curious, Peter instinctively glanced across to identify the driver of the white van, which was parked tightly against the curb facing back toward the school. As he briefly studied the occupant, Peter visualised the gnarled and gaunt features of a man in his mid to late thirties with a cigarette hanging limply from between his lips.

Beside him in the passenger seat was a woman of similar age and profile carrying a very similar expression of distaste. The gaze of both adults followed Peter's approach as he stared back in unwitting bemusement. Just as Peter passed the open driver's window, the man's head tilted slightly in his direction. Peter instinctively engaged with the man's wild glare for a split second.

His slight alarm at the gesture quickly faded as the man's indeterminable grimace then flickered into a half-smirk which slightly raised the tip of his cigarette, obliging Peter to respond in kind.

And then, in the next instance, Peter had passed by the van and increased his stride to catch up with his mother and Michael.

The van driver's attention rested on the vision in his wing mirror as he observed the flow of children making their way home. He watched certain individuals that caught his eye as they came adjacent and then cast his gaze on their reflection as they passed.

Not a single person that fell under his covert scrutiny was alerted to the fact. Indeed, no one had even noticed the driver of the white van as he speculated upon the marching children. No one that is, except Peter.

'Come on slowcoach! This way! I told you I've parked in the next street!'

Hazel directed the boys down a side alley that separated two blocks of terraced housing and with a swift right-angled turn, the trio departed from Friar Road and through the alleyway toward St John Street.

Once out of the twitchell, the silver Focus honed into their view and Hazel released its central locking with a click of the key fob leaving the boys fighting to gain first entry to the back seats.

'Don't push, Peter. It's rude.' barked Hazel.

Checking the boys were in the car she shut their door and slipped behind the wheel before observing the evidently weary two-some in the rear-view mirror.

'Are you sure you still want pizza?'

'YEAH!' was the fatigued dual response.

'Okay then. It'll save your mother cooking for you later won't it, Michael. Seatbelts on then, please. Don't want a policeman to have to stop me because of you two, do I? There's good lads.'

With the boys buckled in, Hazel started the engine and checked her mirrors once again before slowly guiding the car away from its space and along St John Street toward the main T- junction.

Pulling to a stop at the give way lines, she waited patiently for a gap in the main road stream of traffic to appear before lifting the clutch and merging with the germ of the afternoon rush-hour.

Looking directly ahead as she straightened up the wheel and simultaneously flicked on the radio, Hazel did not notice a white van enter the junction they had just vacated.

Nor did she have cause to acknowledge the curious expressions of the driver and his companion, who stared intently at the departing silver Ford before it quickly vanished from view.

CHAPTER 5

Hazel opened the front door, folded her arms and smiled at Michael's mother as she marched quickly up the driveway. Sharon's inner excitement was barely concealed as her own smirk broadened rapidly.

'Well? How are the little men, then?'

Hazel gestured with a thumb back inside towards the staircase.

'Do you mean the latest posse to hit Riverlands? They are up there... playing army. They are fed, watered and fighting each other on the X-Box. Happy as pigs in muck.'

Sharon entered the Leavesdon's hallway and removed her summer jacket.

'Work alright, Shaz?'

'Yeah...sorry I'm a bit late. Things got a bit behind what with the kids piling in for their after-school snacks. We didn't expect the rush.'

'Cuppa?'

'Wonderful! Coffee please!'

As the mothers convened in the lounge, Sharon collapsed on the settee and waited with bated breath for Michael to detect her arrival. Hazel entered with two mugs and perched herself in the armchair opposite.

'Ooh...that...tastes...great! Thanks for fetching the boys for us. It's a weight off my mind.'

'Well...Peter's still not too keen on the idea of being chauffeured by mummy. He asked again if they could get the bus tomorrow...but I said no straight away. To be honest, Michael doesn't seem that bothered either way. But we don't want any hiccups this early in the term, do we?'

Sharon sampled more of her drink and nodded.

'Dead right! I bet they looked really cute when they came out at half-three, didn't they?'

Hazel laughed and waved her free hand in the air.

'Cute? Our Peter looked as though he'd just been running a marathon! All red-faced and sweaty! Apparently, he tried to pick a fight with a girl at dinner time over a sandwich.'

'You're joking, Hazel? Please tell me you're joking. Not your Peter. He couldn't fight his way out of a paper bag.'

Hazel shrugged her shoulders and gestured to the source of enthusiastic shouting that suddenly began to echo from upstairs.

'Well, according to those two that's what happened, anyway. Oh…and apparently, your Michael's got himself a girlfriend as well.'

Sharon sniggered, almost spitting out a mouthful of coffee.

'My god! They have packed a lot in on their first day. Has either of them actually done anything constructive or have they just eaten and played with the girls all day?'

'I know! God help the teachers when they do settle themselves in!'

Sharon sipped from her mug and glanced at the wall clock.

'What time is David due home?'

Hazel checked her watch.

'Oh…any time around six. He'll not be long now.'

The conversation was interrupted as both mothers listened to the sound of heavy and frantic footsteps descending the stairway.

'Take cover, Shaz! I reckon we're about to get stampeded.'

Sharon set her drink on the lounge table and stood up, waiting impatiently for Michael and Peter to make their highly audible entrance.

The unequivocal joy she felt at seeing them in their uniforms once again forced a remarkably uncharacteristic shout of maternal celebration as the boys peered tentatively through the doorway.

'HELLO, MY BABY! COME HERE!'

With practised reluctance, Michael sauntered across the living room carpet and fell into his mother's waiting embrace. Almost squeezing the breath out of him, she cradled his cherubic features in her palms and planted a big wet kiss full on his lips.

'MUM! DO YOU HAVE TO?'

Sharon and Hazel laughed out loud at the ceremonial sufferance, with Peter eagerly joining in on the act.

'Come on Michael! Give your mummy another kiss!'

'Shut it, fool! At least I wasn't nearly sobbing at home-time!'

Sharon looked down at her son with an expression of disapproval.

'Oi! There's no need to snap back. You must be tired if you're acting grumpy. Peter's only teasing. Now give me another kiss!'

Without being given chance to escape from his mother's clutches, Michael was forced to endure another bout of affection whilst he studied his best friend's grinning form perching itself on the settee.

Hazel sat next to her son and reassured Sharon that the first day's arrangements had been a resounding success.

'Same again tomorrow then, Shaz?'

'Oh…if you don't mind? Just for a week or two to settle them in to the routine.'

Peter's alertness announced itself with typical reliability.

'Then after two weeks can we get the bus, Mum?'

'Yes, Peter…maybe. But you need to agree with Michael on this. At least while you're together I know you'll both be okay.'

'Hear that, Michael? She said 'yes'!'

Sharon grabbed her coat and handbag.

'Come on then, matey! Thank your Auntie Hazel for bringing you home and cooking your tea. Let's get off and leave these people in peace.'

'Ha! Fat chance of that, Sharon! The husband's home in a minute! When's your Jim finish work?'

'Six. He'll be home for half past.'

'Long days, aren't they?'

'Well, that's what I tell him. But he says the money's worth it. So it's up to him, isn't it?'

'Okay. Pick you up tomorrow morning at eight, then Michael.'

'Okay. See ya! And thanks for pizza!'

'You're welcome, love. I think I'll do the shopping before I collect them tomorrow, Sharon. The supermarket was total bedlam at four o'clock. Looks like every other mother in Shireheath had the same idea as I did today. See you all in the morning.'

*****

'Hello boy! How you been? You missed me today? Yes, I bet you have!'

James Tompkins had only been in the hallway a couple of seconds when he was accosted by a furious yet affectionate combination of rough tongue and wet nose. With Wallace firmly contented that he had been the first to greet the man of the house, Sharon was then allowed to embrace her husband and offer him a kiss as he lowered his workbag to the floor.

'And what about you, darling? Have you missed me, too?'

'What do you think, love? Tea or beer?'

‘Erm…tea for now. Beer for later, thanks. Where’s Michael?’

‘In the lounge. Watching TV. He’s tired out bless him! He’s hardly said a word since we got back from Hazel’s.’

James kicked off his work boots and dropped his coat onto a hook at the bottom of the stairs. Quietly pushing open the lounge door he observed the studious expression of his son watching the screen. After a few moments of paternal admiration had elapsed, James announced his presence with a soft whisper.

‘Hello, Michael. You okay?’

Immediately jumping to his feet, Michael rushed to his father and threw his arms around his waist.

‘Crickey! I have been missed, haven’t I! School alright then, was it?’

‘Yes, Dad…I’m knackered out, though.’

‘You look it, lad! Told you it would be a shock to the system, didn’t we?’

‘Dad…can I come with you when you take Wallace out?’

‘Yeah…of course…I’m going to have a cuppa with your Mum first and then we’ll go, okay?’

‘Yep! We’ll go after Hollyoaks has finished, then?’

James laughed as he re-joined his wife in the kitchen.

‘Hollyoaks! Bloody Hollyoaks? Christ…he must be growing up fast if he’s watching that tripe!’

*****

David Leavesdon pulled on the brake handles of his mountain bike and came to a stop outside the back door of number thirty-nine, Cromford Road. Hazel greeted his arrival with a wave from the kitchen.

Her amused expression soon evolved into a giggle at the sight of her husband on such a contraption, who was rapid with his protest.

‘It’s alright you laughing! I must be the only I.T. executive manager this side of the bloody river who gets to go to work on two wheels! Even public transport must hold more street credibility than this.’

Still consumed by her amusement, Hazel offered a positive comment on the issue.

‘Yes love…but you will get there a lot faster on a bicycle. And it’s more environmentally friendly. And your temporary sacrifice of the car is for a very good cause.’

David dismounted awkwardly and removed his helmet.

‘Bloody thing! Suits and bike clips just don’t go together! And this damned hat! Feels like I’m wearing a toaster on my head! Anyway…how’s Peter?’

Just about managing to reply through her chuckles, Hazel took her husband’s bike and leaned it against the shed.

‘He’s fine. He’s upstairs…playing on his X-Box…as usual…’

‘Good. How’s his first day gone?’

‘Oh…not bad…fairly…interesting…as you’d expect, with those two. I think they’ll settle in pretty quickly to be honest. He hasn’t said a great deal about it. All the excitement’s worn him out.’

‘Well…he needs an early night then! And he’s not the only one, either! What’s for tea, love?’

*****

Un-hooking Wallace, James hung the lead in place behind the front door and observed Michael remove his jacket to the accompaniment of a protracted yawn.

‘You need to be up bright and early for your mum tomorrow, mate. No racing around like she said you were this morning. If I can get up at four-thirty then I’m sure you can manage to rise for seven!’

Michael yawned once again as his mother entered the hallway.

‘Hello, boys. Enjoy your stroll?’

Wallace led the way back through to the kitchen and continued onwards into the conservatory where he primed himself on his bedding as James shut the door behind him.

‘Yes. Relaxing. He’s had a good hour’s run as well. Hopefully he shouldn’t need another poo trot. Might just let him go in the garden!’

‘James! That’s disgusting!’

‘Alright Sharon…well you take him out at midnight when all the bogeymen are about!’

‘As if you’re worried about that, James Tompkins! You’re just getting lazy in your old age!’

Michael studied the humorous exchange between his parents before making a suggestion.

'Mum…before I go to bed…can I take Wallace out again?'
'No love. You'll be asleep by then. Plus, it's not safe after dark!'
Michael looked at his mother with a stern glare of sincerity.
'I'm not afraid, Mum. Bogeymen don't scare me. Not one bit.'
'Well, Michael…its now nearly eight o'clock. I want you tucked up in bed for nine. Get your school bag ready for tomorrow, then you can watch telly. And make sure you fold your uniform.'
'Brilliant! Then can I take Wallace?'
'NO! Go and get your bag ready!'
James closed the fridge door and cracked open a can of lager as he watched Michael trudge out of the room. A look of bemusement befell his face as he turned to Sharon.
'What's with this fancy for Michael wanting to take the dog for a walk all of a sudden?'
'I don't know. He has spent a lot of time with Wallace over the summer, though. Must have missed him today, I suppose.'

*****

Peter pulled the covers under his chin as he heard his mother's footsteps ascend the stairway to wish him goodnight. She entered his room and in turn flicked off the television, X-Box and bed-side lamp.
'No wonder my electric bill's gone through the roof! Sleep tight, Peter. And no secret midnight gaming. Okay? And no more picking fights with girls in the morning, either. There's a kiss from me. And there's another one from your dad. I'll wake you about seven, okay? No doubt you'll be up anyway playing soldiers on that thing!'
Hazel moved to the bedroom door before her son's muffled voice carried a polite request through the semi-darkness.
'Mum…'
'Yes, my love?'
'Can you leave the landing light on, please?'
'Of course, love. Sweet dreams.'

*****

'Sharon! Did you do my sandwiches?'
James Tompkins averted his gaze from the fridge and called upstairs to his wife, who squirmed under the duvet as her husband's

voice resonated softly up the stairway. A muffled admission of failure was the only option as she huddled in her own warmth.

Although, whilst sensing a pang of guilt at foregoing her loved one's packed lunch, it was far too early in the morning to lose any more sleep over the issue.

Eventually after James had repeated his question in lowered tones through the bedroom doorway, Sharon finally felt compelled to respond.

'No…sorry…I forgot. There's some money in the top left kitchen drawer. Take that to the canteen for your dinner. And stop shouting…you'll wake up Michael!'

A few moments of peace allowed Sharon to nestle her head back into the welcoming cradle of the pillow. But her slumber was interrupted once more a few minutes later by the scent of her husband's aftershave as he leaned across the bed to kiss her goodbye.

'I hate the canteen slop, love. I've made my own sarnies so the money's still in the drawer. I'll see you tonight.'

The sound of James' voice was comforting, but Sharon worried about the amount of time he was spending at work just lately. Lifting her head from the soft down, she squinted at him through the murk with blurred vision and a sense of concern.

'Twelve hours again, today?'

'Yes, love.'

'Oh, darling. You were bloody knackered all last weekend. Can't you try and finish a little earlier?'

He sighed lovingly into her neck, causing goosebumps to form on her arms, legs and shoulders.

'Look…while the moneys on offer, I've got to take it. The bills won't pay themselves. Anyway, I've got to go. It's a quarter to. Give Michael a kiss for me when he wakes. See you both tonight.'

*****

Ninety minutes of blissful slumber seemed like ten seconds as Sharon's mobile phone alarm shrieked in her ear. Reaching across to the bedside table to engage the snooze function was a bad idea but infinitely preferable to getting up at that moment.

The sunshine streamed a filtered passage through the curtains, encouraging her to prise open her eyelids and face another day.

The oddity of beginning the school term in midweek had thrown her routine somewhat. It felt like it should be Saturday and did not feel like a Thursday in any way.

Contemplating her minor confusion, she bolted up in bed and scrutinised her phone display.

'SHIT!'

Drifting in and out of semi-consciousness had cost precious minutes.

According to her mobile phone, it was twenty past seven.

Adorned in just her underwear, Sharon bounded gracelessly from the bed to dash across the landing. Tripping over a damp towel, she pushed open her son's bedroom door to find him completely dormant.

'COME ON…GET UP MICHAEL! WE'RE LATE AGAIN!

Shoving him roughly by the shoulder she promptly yanked his duvet from the bed, dropped it on the floor and descended rapidly down the stairs to be greeted by a very hungry and feisty German Shepherd.

'Come out of the way, Wallace! What are you doing out of your bedroom, anyway? We haven't time for walkies this morning! Here…this will shut you up for a bit.'

Pouring some dog munchies into his bowl, she then re-entered the hall and hollered back up the stairway.

'OY! LAZY BONES! YOU WERE SUPPOSED TO SET YOUR ALARM AS WELL AS ME, YOU KNOW! SHIFT IT!'

To her immense surprise, Michael had immediately risen at the first attempt, partly dressed himself and was already commencing his move from the bedroom toward the landing.

Centring her attention back into the kitchen, Sharon laid out some cereal and milk before entering the outhouse to rummage for a clean work tunic.

Michael duly yawned as he shuffled into the kitchen and pulled Wallace's wagging tail as the oblivious canine continued to clean up the contents of his food dish. Sharon blustered through the back door and held her blouse up to the light to check for stains.

'Are you taking me to school today, Mum?'

'No love. Same as yesterday. I'm at work for eight-thirty. Well…I'm supposed to be! Hazel and Peter will be here soon. Come on…get your breakfast down you.'

Dropping himself into a chair and dropping some Cheerios into a bowl, Michael reached across for the milk.

'Aren't we taking Wallace to the park, then?'

Sharon re-examined her tunic on the work surface to assess the potential need for ironing it.

'No, love. Not today. We haven't time.'

'Mum, can I have the telly on?'

Without answering him, Sharon flicked on the kitchen portable and delved under the sink for the iron. Swearing under her breath before re-emerging, she plugged it in before letting Wallace into the garden as she issued him with a firm instruction.

'You'd better not do a big one, either cos I'm not cleaning it up!'

Paying precious little attention to the warning, the family dog trotted contentedly toward the bottom hedgerow.

Frantically recalling her next task, she turned to observe her son who was transfixed by the seven-thirty news bulletin.

'Michael…hurry up and eat your breakfast or I'm turning the TV off again! Peter and his mother will be here soon and you're not even washed yet!'

The youngster defiantly ignored his mother whilst adorning a knowing smile. It was the previous custom that every morning before junior school he would wilfully test her patience. Of course, he was well aware that even if Peter's mother did knock at the door, they would simply have to wait.

In Michael's view, mornings were not invented for rushing about.

'It's not my fault, Mum. We're late for everything anyway!'

It was no coincidence that Michael's father was never around to witness this daily charade of delaying the inevitable. He always left the house well before his wife and son were even awake.

But Michael knew better than to try such daring tactics with his father, anyway. James Tompkins was not a man to suffer fools gladly and was certainly not a soft touch like his wife. Watching television was a ritual for Michael on a weekday morning and even secondary school had no chance of competing with old habits.

Then again, Michael's father would not readily entertain the idea of interrupting the morning routine with such a visual distraction. He liked things to run on time and without disruption. Michael knew he would not have such a free reign to indulge himself if his dad was in charge of the early morning schedule. All the better then that his father always had to be at work for six o' clock and hence the organisation was left to his rather less stringent mother.

The Cheerios were now totally sodden. Only now was it the perfect time to eat them. Michael had long held the belief that cereal cannot be consumed whilst still crunchy. It is unlawful and indecent. Besides which, every child holds the mandatory right to wait for a few minutes after pouring the milk into the bowl to allow the slushing process to evolve fully.

'Michael! That's it! Telly's coming off...right now!'

Okay, time to start eating.

Michael's mother moved towards the TV but didn't switch it off. Glancing back to the kitchen dining table, she was mildly appeased to see her son finally sampling his breakfast. She said nothing for fear of distracting him and instead ventured upstairs to don her newly pressed workwear.

The minutes passed until finally, right on cue as there was a vigorous knock at the door, Michael emerged from the bathroom, pulled his jumper over his head and applied a handful of hair gel in the hall mirror.

'Your hair's greasy my lad! Needs a good wash. A bath for you tonight, I think. I bet you haven't brushed your teeth either?' Sharon proclaimed.

Michael pretended to sulk at the criticisms as his mother opened the front door to greet Hazel, who bobbed on the doorstep in her typically expectant manner.

'Morning all! Are we ready, then?'

'Just about...I think. Hang on Michael...have you still got the ten pounds I gave you yesterday for your dinner money?'

'Yes, Mum.'

'Good lad. Okay. Have you checked your bag? Got everything you need?'

Michael simply nodded, his expression indicating a current reluctance to meet with the day ahead.

'Thanks again for taking them, Hazel. It's a big help. I just can't get organised at the moment! I will get some sensible hours at work, eventually. I'm seeing the boss today. Hopefully I'll be taking my own son to school soon!'

'We'll be taking ourselves soon, Mum.' claimed Michael as he tied his shoelaces.

Peter's mother smiled and placed her hand on Michael's shoulder as he stood up wearily next to her in the porch-way.

'It's not a problem, Sharon. I've got to pass the top of the street, anyway! I'll pick them up at three-thirty as usual. You need a lift to work?'

'No, I'm nowhere near ready yet. I'll get the bus to town. I'll just have to be late again. See you all about five thirty-ish. Hopefully it won't be for much longer!'

Hazel looked at Michael, whose enthusiasm seemed to have lightened having spotted his partner in crime leering back at the throng through the rear window of his mother's Focus.

'Nonsense, Shaz! That's what friends are for. We'll see you at teatime, then. I'll give them something to eat again.'

Sharon folded her arms and watched her son amble towards the waiting silver car.

'Bye, Michael! Don't I get a kiss goodbye, then?'

Her son scampered back toward her and planted a kiss full on her lips.

'See you later, Mum!'

'Have a good day at school.'

Sharon rolled her eyes at Hazel before chuckling and closing the front door. With her shift at the bakery imminent, she supposedly had only fifteen minutes to get ready. The breakfast pots would have to wait.

After hastily applying some make-up and pulling a brush through her hair, she checking the house was secured and that Wallace was back inside the conservatory.

Locking the front door behind her, she hoped the rest of the day would not prove to be as stressful as its beginning.

*****

The crowds gathering around Riverlands Secondary seemed even denser than yesterday. With no available spaces to station the car nearby, Hazel reverted to parking in St John Street once again.

Peter willingly kissed his mother goodbye as they reached the school entrance. The solemnity of their parting seemed a little diminished compared to the previous day.

'Behave Peter. Okay? No fights! And no asking for other people's dinner! Have a good day, boys.'

Peter's only response to the warning was a thought concerning events after school.

'Mum…don't forget, will you?'

'Don't forget what?' asked his puzzled mother.

'We want burgers and chips for tea, tonight.'

'Yes, yes alright…off you go greedy guts! See you later.'

Ushering the boys along through the white painted iron gates, she checked her watch. They would get into assembly just in time. Hazel remained at the entrance as she watched her son and his friend file along the pathway toward the brimming playground. The random hollering from scores of other pupils carried across the landscaped gardens of the school grounds and over the rooftops of the nearby houses.

Making sure she saw the boys merge with the bustling throng, Hazel turned away from the school and made her way back to the car.

With her mind now fully occupied by thoughts of impending housework and the shopping trip, she did not notice the two occupants of a white van observing her departure as she strode quickly past.

She would never be aware that her reflection remained under scrutiny as she reached the halfway point along Friar Road before turning into the side alley toward St John Street.

Completely oblivious to the spectators, Hazel Leavesdon started the engine of the silver Focus, turned up the radio and headed for home.

CHAPTER 6

Thursday; two-fifty p.m. Plenty of time.

Hazel shut the boot of the car which was laden with the weekly groceries. Checking the views front and rear once buckled in, she engaged gear before turning up the radio to allow Mercy by Duffy to blast through the speakers, as she glided through the supermarket car park, out of the exit and on towards home.

*****

Peter nudged Michael as the class was issued with a written exercise to be performed in total silence. Making sure that the maths teacher was oblivious to the exchange, he held up a piece of paper on which was written a simple message that caused Michael to nod in affirmation.

THIRTY-EIGHT MINUTES TO GO TIL FREEDOM!

*****

The silver Focus pulled onto the driveway of thirty-nine, Cromford Road. Applying the handbrake and releasing her seatbelt, Hazel noticed that her hanging baskets either side of the front door were in need of a drink. She glanced at the numerical display above the steering wheel.

Three o'clock; exactly.

Time was on her side.

Unloading the boot, she proceeded to march several shopping bags through the hallway and into the kitchen. Having bought fresh minced beef quarter-pounders for the boys' tea, she placed them on the draining board alongside a small bag of potatoes which were Peter's undying preference concerning chips. Hazel had always insisted on cooking her own chips as opposed to the strips of frozen fat that feebly passed for French Fries these days.

Emptying each carrier bag in turn, she methodically located each and every comestible with time-honoured precision and speed.

Another glance at the kitchen wall clock.

Nearly three-fifteen.

Time was still her friend.

Filling the watering can she ventured to the front porch and doused the limp-looking flower baskets until they overflowed onto the concrete below.

Back inside, a quick visit to the toilet was followed by a thorough washing of hands and obligatory make-up check. Retrieving her keys and handbag from the kitchen work surface, she then made her way back out through the front door and locked it behind her.

Slipping into the driver's seat, Hazel inserted the key into the ignition and turned it in the barrel, only to be greeted by a shrill repeating beep that emanated from the dashboard.

According to the car's computer, a door was not closed properly.

Then she saw the source of the problem in her wing mirror.

She had not pushed the boot-lid down far enough to latch it, allowing it to subsequently rise up a few inches in its housing.

Mumbling to herself, she hopped out and secured the rear of the car then once re-positioned behind the wheel, she tried the ignition again.

There was no warning noise, yet still the engine did not respond.

Again and again the turn of the fob produced the same result.

'What the bloody hell's up with this thing?!' she quietly fumed.

Whilst avidly scanning the dash panel for any indication of a further technical hindrance, varying profanities leapt forth from her lips, to remain unheard by the outside world.

Removing the key again and inspecting it with customary mechanical ignorance, Hazel sighed with frustration and slipped it forcibly back into the barrel whilst glancing at her watch.

Twenty-two minutes past three.

Time was now seemingly working against her.

Several more fruitless efforts and further cursing only served to increase her bemused anger as the clock ticked onto twenty-five past the hour.

Finally surrendering to the problem, she grabbed her handbag from the passenger seat and left the car with a resounding slam of the driver's door.

'Pissing thing! A mind of your own now, have you?'

Another glance at the watch.

Time was now decidedly in opposition.

Consigning herself to walking to school, she reluctantly embarked on the route through the housing estate with a gradually quickening step and an increasing sense of vexation.

There was no alternative, she surmised.

Plan B would need to be executed.

The boys would just have to wait for her at school.

Their taxi had apparently taken umbrage for the afternoon.

An inner smile gradually emerged on her face as a thought occurred regarding Peter's consistent and recurring wishes.

It looked as though they'd be getting the bus home after all.

*****

'Okay boys and girls...please make sure you leave your chairs tidily and safely on top of your tables. Remember...your homework is to solve all the problems in the second section of chapter one. You've all written it in your diaries, I hope? Okay...stand quietly.'

Miss Doherty observed the bemused faces of the Year Seven maths class. A two-hour introduction to algebra had left most in the room with distinctly ashen hues and one or two with minor headaches.

'We will go through the answers together in the next lesson which I believe is on Monday morning. If anybody has any problems with the homework, we'll discuss it then and iron out any confusion. The important thing is...don't worry about it! Just have a go and see how you get on.'

Michael and Peter had managed to keep their youthful comedy act under wraps for most of the day, but Peter's natural zest was beginning to brim to the surface as home-time beckoned.

Sporting a rosy and mischievous grin, he lightly punched Michael in the ribs as his friend struggled to haul his rucksack into position.

'Hey, fool! You'll pay for that!'

Peter giggled at his friend's mildly fierce vocal retort.

As the welcome final bell of the day shattered the temporary silence of the classroom, Peter immediately received a firm shove into the table which capably alerted the attentions of the teacher as she stood with arms folded by the door.

'Erm...boys...you're holding everybody else up by not standing still! Personally, I can wait here as long as it takes but I'm pretty sure everyone else is ready for the off.'

Michael and Peter stood to blatantly feigned attention fully aware that their fellow pupils were now offering intermittent glances of disapproval. The warranted scrutiny didn't prevent another broad smirk from growing under Peter's nose which in turn encouraged Michael to chuckle.

Eventually satisfied that the room was going to be left in an acceptable state, Miss Doherty announced the end of the lesson.

'I'll see you all next week, then. Class dismissed.'

*****

Just after three-thirty.

Time was the undisputed victor today.

Hazel was still at least twenty minutes from Riverlands at her current pace.

Scanning the hands of her watch as the zebra crossing allowed her right of way, she again cursed the uncooperative cause of the delay under her breath.

'Fucking Ford fucking Focus. They're alright while they're alright!'

That's what Hazel's late father always used to say about cars and despite his lifelong occupation as a mechanic it always surprised her to hear him announce his sometime lack of faith in the combustion engine.

How she wished her parents were around to help her now.

Skipping across the road she made egress along the main route out through the estate as beads of perspiration began to form on her forehead due to the warm September sun. The mile or so distance from front door to school gate was by far the furthest she had walked for a good while.

She checked her watch again.

Twenty-five to four.

Time had definitely beaten her now.

*****

Peter and Michael joined with the buoyant and very vocal crowds out in the main corridor and followed the flow of the heaving congregation through the building toward the main double doors.

A crescendo of conversation echoed around Michael's ears as he shuffled steadily towards freedom. The late summer climate was blessing them yet again and he was keen to get out into the open air and feel the welcoming heat on his face after what had felt like a very confining day in the classroom.

Although temporarily separated by the swaying mass of bodies, once the boys were through the exit doors and onto the landscaped walkway, Peter sharply flicked Michael's earlobe from behind as the precursor to a game of tag and began to make his escape along the path.

'Hey, you idiot!' Michael blasted. 'Come here!'

Laughing loudly, the pair streamed some distance ahead of the swelling body of pupils that heaved behind them. Michael caught up with his friend as the white painted gates to liberty honed clearly into view.

'Peter! Stop running! This rucksack weighs a frigging tonne!'

The boys ceased their sprint and conferred on the plan for later that evening.

'What are we playing tonight?' panted Peter. 'Weapons of War, again?'

'Oh no! Can't we go on the football game? I'm sick of soldiers and tanks'

'But I don't like football, Michael! What about Sims, then?'

'Maybe… I don't know. You must have something else?'

As Peter executed a deftly directed karate kick towards his friend's midriff, Michael's ignored the feeble assault as his attention became slowly drawn to the smattering of parents that awaited the oncoming army of schoolchildren.

He studied the intermittent gallery of adult heads and faces on the other side of the boundary wall as they stared back, toward and beyond the pair.

The realisation quickly dawned on him that Peter's mother was not among the group.

Peter flicked out at Michael's cheek with a stinging forefinger but quickly registered with the distraction. His gaze soon followed that of his friend, and they confirmed their mutual suspicions.

'I don't believe it! Mum's not here! Again!'

Michael studied the minor gathering of grown-ups and declared another notable observation.

'There aren't as many mums and dads here as there was last night, either.'

Peter's attention centred fully on the faces waiting by the school entrance and expressed his disapproval.

'No! Looks like most other kids can be trusted. But my mum doesn't trust us though, does she?'

Both boys reached the white-painted metal gates and scrutinized the small throng of adults.

Resigning himself to another possibility, Peter enthusiastically offered a suggestion.

'I know! I bet she's trying to park! Perhaps she's still in the next street like last night? Come on!'

Michael became aware of his friend's suddenly determined stride and proclaimed his reservations about searching for Hazel.

'Hey! We can't just wander off. Your mum said we must wait inside the school gate if she's not here on time! You'll only get into trouble if she knows you've been looking for her! What if she turns up after we've gone?'

With his thumbs hooked into the straps of his backpack, Peter turned to his friend with a look of total disdain.

'Michael! We are eleven years old you know…we're not babies! Come on! If she bought me a mobile phone like I asked then we could just ring her, couldn't we? But no…not old enough, yet…can't be trusted…'

Michael smiled inwardly as he watched Peter's bouncing trudge along the street, audibly grumbling with frustration under his breath.

It seemed that the decision had been made and that Michael was left with little choice but to comply.

Wherever a friend went, then a friend was deemed to follow.

They walked slowly along Friar Road, looking both ways up and down the pavement and across the carriageway. However, the expedition quickly took on a rather static turn.

Michael and Peter stood together, now fully bemused by Hazel's evident absence from the scene.

The former unexpectedly found himself succumbing to the latter's original plan.

'She's obviously not here, yet. Okay then…let's try your idea of looking in the next street. The alleyway is only just up there. We haven't strayed all that far from school.'

Now united in their mission the pair strode purposefully toward the half-way mark along Friar Road. With his brain now assimilating the puzzle, Michael gradually noticed the silhouette of a tall, lean figure leaning against a lamp post about twenty yards ahead at the alley entrance.

As the boys gained closer proximity, Peter vaguely thought he recognised the man from somewhere. They each continued to walk toward the stranger with a determined gait.

Now passing within arm's reach of the man, both youngsters instinctively glanced up to face him.

His gnarled, gaunt gaze had in turn now firmly centred itself on the pair of eleven-year-olds that had wandered into his realm.

The boys had little inclination to speak to the man and had almost passed him by when his deep, harsh tone startled them. Michael halted his youthful momentum and engaged with the figure, whose outline dominated the pure blue-sky backdrop that framed him.

'You lads after your mum, are you?'

The friends looked dubiously at one another before Peter took the cautious honour of responding to the seemingly innocent question.

'Yeah...she should be here by now, though. She's late again.'

The man drew heavily on a cigarette that was cupped in his palm and stared straight ahead, back toward the approaching swell of departing schoolchildren.

His uncertain yet steely eyes then focused directly back into Peter's.

'Silver car isn't it? Focus? Short woman? Long brown hair?'

Peter again jumped in with his rapid response.

'Yeah! Have you seen her?'

With his cigarette now clamped between forefinger and thumb, the man gestured along the alleyway with his free hand. His tone of voice again caused Michael to be somewhat wary, but he could not be sure as to why.

There seemed little further need to deliberate on the matter.

'I'm not completely certain, lads...but I reckon she might have just parked up through there in the next road.'

Before Michael could absorb the conversation, Peter was grinding through his gears and heading in the direction dictated whilst issuing a conclusive yelp.

'Come on! I told you she'd be down here!'

Michael found himself transfixed by the wild stare of the stranger, who said nothing further and continued to draw on his smoke.

Thanking the man seemed somewhat inappropriate.

Michael's instincts were sending wildly conflicting signals.

Then he gazed toward the alleyway that Peter had now entered in his hurry to confront to his mother.

In turn, Michael began to make his own move, noticing as he did so the man reaching into his pocket and retrieving a mobile phone. Deciding to give the stranger no further thought, he followed his friend's lead.

The boys walked together along the overshadowed cut-through, their pace quickening with each step as they looked tentatively at one another.

'Do you know that guy?' whispered Peter.

'No. Never seen him before. I take it you don't, either?'

Halfway along the alley, they simultaneously glanced back over one another's shoulders alley toward Friar Road before bursting into fits of nervous giggles.

In the midst of their misplaced mirth, Peter noticed another tall figure standing ahead of them at the St John Street junction of the alleyway. The person appeared to be talking to somebody as they approached but no one else seemed to be around.

It soon became evident that the figure was female and was speaking into a mobile handset.

As they neared, she slowly lifted her head and stared intently at the boys.

Firstly at Peter; then across to Michael.

Her attention swiftly moved to the activity behind them, causing Michael to glance back once more along the path they had just trodden.

The tall male stranger from Friar Road was now following the boys and judging by his gangling speed and manner, appeared to be in something of a hurry.

With his heartbeat now beginning to increase with slight trepidation, Michael noticed the man was still talking into his phone.

Having nearly caught up with the trio, he replaced the mobile into his jacket pocket and discarded his cigarette butt on the floor. A confusing hand signal directed Michael's interest back to the woman, who had now moved position to stand next to the pair of bewildered youngsters.

'Are you sure you've seen my mum?' enquired Peter.

The woman smiled giving exhibition to her stained teeth before offering a reply as she glanced around her.

'Yeah…come on, lads. This way!'

Eagerly obeying her reference, Peter traipsed after the woman to the end of the alley. Michael opted to follow, fully aware that the man from Friar Road was also close behind.

Michael watched Peter's blond head reflecting the shafts of September sun as he emerged into St John Street. Gazing up and down the road, a further puzzled query was presented to the supposedly assisting strangers.

'Where is she, then? Where's my mum?'

No sooner had Peter uttered his question than a long-fingered hand was clamped over his mouth and nose, instantly causing him to fret wildly.

Michael watched in dumbfounded shock as his friend's arms and legs kicked out against the woman's unyielding restraint. She forcefully dragged Peter's flailing form toward the open rear doors of a stationary white transit van parked adjacent to the alley entrance.

Now becoming fitful, Peter's stifled whines began to penetrate the primitive yet restrictive mask that had been applied.

The unfamiliar resonance of skull thudding against metal was followed by a deathly silence as Peter's muffled squealing immediately ceased.

As a transfixed Michael studied the incredulous episode play itself out in slow-motion, the encroaching horror of circumstance suddenly began to rain down all around him.

Instinctively taking a breath in order to supply the necessary power to his desperate scream for help, the entire scene was shrouded in darkness as Michael's face and mouth were similarly assaulted by the hands of the male stranger that had followed them down the alley.

Like his best friend, Michael was rendered completely defenceless in the trap. He began to identify the piercing stench of nicotine on the man's fingers as they clasped his nostrils tightly shut; the vice-like grip ably keeping the mouth and jaw from moving.

Yet Michael did not struggle as he briefly detected the feint whimpers of his friend. Roughly hauled backward along the pavement and lifted from his feet, Michael was taken to the open doors of the van.

Easily wrestled into the back, he then received a hard smack across the back of his head which instantly dazed him.

Then the last shafts of sunlight were completely eclipsed. Sudden surrounding darkness descended as their capture was signified by a resounding slam of the van's rear doors.

With the murk in the van enclosing them, the woman's seething voice ordered for quiet as she squatted beside the boys in the rear of the vehicle, hitting out with her bony fist at the slightest sound of resistance.

Michael struggled to visualise the figure in the shadows as he detected the vehicle ignition being engaged and the chassis beginning to rumble beneath him.

He heard the crunch of the gearbox and the employment of the clutch, followed by acceleration along the road.

But he did not hear his friend.

His best friend: now crouched in a supposedly protective foetal position, stunned and in pain, pressed against the wooden headboard of the van.

And then the overwhelming, terrifying truth descended as Michael subconsciously acknowledged that he may never again see the world he knew and loved.

Perched on his haunches and intermittently burying his face from possible further harm, he dared to visualise the ghosts which had manifested themselves in his mind during the past seconds.

Elusive and taunting; bringing the very real premise of noxious harm.

The sharply applied brakes of the van brought it to a halt at the main T-junction causing the occupants in the rear to be shunted forward.

Naturally eager to join the flow of traffic, the driver edged out into the main road but not before giving a certain consideration to a female pedestrian heading in the direction of the school grounds and who appeared to be in something of a hurry.

He afforded her the right of way with a wave of his hand before breaching the white lines and departing the scene.

In turn, the woman nodded to him in thankful appreciation whilst carrying the vein hope that she would not be overly reprimanded by her son for her lateness as she approached the junction of Friar Road.

But time had not been destined to be her ally on this day.

And with every passing, critical, lost second, as her son and his best friend were taken further and further away by their assailants, the imminent future would bear its own inevitable wrath.

Indeed, time would now only allow the excruciating, gradual privilege of understanding just how the seemingly innocuous delay in her arrival would serve to betray Hazel Leavesdon for all eternity.

CHAPTER 7

Hazel marched determinedly along Friar Road and began to study the distant outline of the school building.

Smatterings of pupils remained at random junctures along the street, with the great majority of the three-thirty leavers now having departed the area and followed their individual routes home.

As she approached, Hazel purposely observed the faces of the small groups of older schoolchildren that loitered around the doorway of the sweet shop. They briefly returned her curious gaze without cause for suspicion before reverting to their own general business of texting friends, exchanging cigarettes and playing music from their mobile phones.

The thought occurred to her that it would not be long before Peter would be divulging in such activity. Yet at that moment the scene seemed a different world away from the arena of her innocent junior, and much closer to that of fringing adulthood.

The throng of teenagers seemed to increase in density as she neared the school grounds, but no one offered her more than a glance of casual interest as they milled, swore, and threw various objects at one another across the road.

Hazel navigated an unobtrusive path among the disinterested groups until the front gates of the school came into full view. Expectant of being greeted by her son's wry, rose-cheeked smile, she became instantly alerted to the fact that neither he nor Michael were anywhere in sight.

It also became abundantly clear that she was indeed the only adult in the vicinity. Clutching her handbag nervously she hesitated at the gates, looking along the school driveway and around its neatly manicured surroundings.

Not a single soul interrupted her study of the tranquil scene.

Cursing the failing car under her breath once again, Hazel switched viewpoints and scanned her attention back over her shoulder to Friar Road. Many of the pupils had now begun to leave the scene. The familiar sight of tightly double-parked cars now appeared far less compacted.

Empty spaces dominated the picture as her inner anxiety stirred.

The thought repeated in her head that she was indeed too late.

Annoyingly…consequentially…too late.

Confirming the time on her watch to be five minutes to four, Hazel began to plague herself with notions of possibility and probability.

The thought prevailed that it would maybe prove a futile exercise to question the schoolchildren that remained outside the shop doorway. After all, two eleven-year-old boys in Riverlands uniforms would barely stand out in a crowd of hundreds and would still be unknown to almost all of their fellow pupils.

But real concern was quickly beginning to add to the disgruntlement that had accompanied her march to school.

Hazel moved tentatively toward a remaining group of girls who were huddled around a mobile phone and giggling audibly.

'Excuse me…I don't suppose any of you know Peter Leavesdon? I'm his mum…I've come to meet him…but…he's not here. And his friend…Michael Tompkins? Have you seen them?'

All four adolescent faces glanced up to face the inquisitive mother. They studied the evident worry that had begun to etch itself into her features yet showed little concern for her quandary.

'Sorry…never heard of them.' came the eventual damning reply from one of the gang, before all four reverted their energies back to studying the mobile phone.

'Okay…thanks.'

With her heart now pacing a little faster by the second, Hazel turned disconsolately and trudged back toward the white painted iron gates.

The next logical step emerged as she again cast her eye over the school building. Holding hopes high, Hazel entered the grounds and walked slowly along the pathway. She observed one or two teachers making for their cars in the segregated staff parking area. She made sure to scan the areas in between the trees that would have undoubtedly presented themselves as a wondrous hiding place for her son.

A game he was well attuned to playing.

Yet as she stared into the void of greenery, not a flicker of movement could be seen, or a solitary sound heard. Indeed, the sinister thought briefly occurred to her that without its customary inhabitants, the silent playground resembled a graveyard without headstones.

Hazel's nervous frustration was now evolving into deep maternal apprehension as she stood rooted to the spot in her seemingly hapless mission. The words deriving from such annoyance plundered from her mouth before she had chance to prevent their emission.

'Damn you, Peter! If you've gotten on that bus! After all I said! Wait until I get hold of you! Just you wait!'

Her whispered mutterings were carried away on the light afternoon breeze and disappeared without trace. Now becoming distinctly angry with her son and his friend for deserting their presumedly trusted agreement, she began to increase her stride once again and moved to the edge of the playing field.

She checked the time again.

Nearly five past four.

The period of lateness wasn't even an issue, now.

Her mind was becoming reluctantly adjusted to the fact that the boys were not on the premises and had probably not been for at least thirty minutes.

The thought brought her to the point of brimming vexation.

Why couldn't they do as they were told?

Then a distant voice shattered her furious contemplation.

She switched focus back toward the school building to see a figure in a red peaked cap and luminous green vest waving his arms to attract her attention.

She heard him shout once more but could not decipher the message. Then the inflating thought slammed into her conscience.

It was the caretaker.

He might well know where the boys were.

Relief cascaded over Hazel as she made her way quickly back across the parched grass to the man, whose genuine smile indicated he may hold some positive news.

'Hello there! I'm sorry for wandering around aimlessly like this, but I'm here to collect my son and his friend. I was a little late. Car trouble, you see...'

The man was of Indian descent and cast his strikingly white eyes to the face of his watch. They then rested gently back onto the vision of the evidently worried parent standing before him.

'Well…I can assure you…there are no more children on the premises, Madam. I'm on my final checks now. Even most of the staff have gone home.'

Hazel's heart sank at the declaration, her expanding desperation emerging to the fore as she pointed in vain.

'What about those side doors? Could they have got out that way?'

The caretaker turned to source the area in question.

'No, madam. They are safety and utility exits. They are alarmed. Plus, there are two fire doors which are linked to the main alarm. I tell you what...let's get you to reception. Joyce will still be here. They may have left you a message. Don't worry. We'll find them.'

Contrary to his order, worry was now the largest singular emotion as she followed the caretaker through an access door and along through the main hall of the school. The emptiness of the hall was accentuated by the sound of her heels on the polished wooden flooring. Her footsteps echoed around the chamber as a pressing reminder of the unwelcome predicament.

The caretaker leaned into the receptionist's window and highlighted the problem, leaving Hazel standing by to observe the arrival of several contract cleaners adorned in navy blue tunics. She watched the assortment of ladies organise their equipment in the corridor before being jolted by the voice of the caretaker once again.

'If you would like to give Joyce some details, I must get on with locking up. I'll keep my eye out for them.'

'Thank you. What is your name?'

'My name is Asif.'

'Thank you for your help, Asif.'

'No problem, Madam.'

Hazel watched him disappear out beyond the front main doors before turning her attention to the grey-haired be-spectacled lady behind the window, who smiled with what appeared to be only a partial degree of sincerity.

'So, you're here to collect your son and his friend, are you? Which registration form are they in?'

'Mrs. Gray's...I'm Hazel Leavesdon...Peter's mother. His friend should be with him. Michael Tompkins.'

The receptionist swiftly clicked through the class register on the computer screen.

'Well...they both claimed a mark at one-thirty, so it's only fair to presume they left the premises at three-thirty.'

Hazel became puzzled by the insinuation.

'What makes you think they wouldn't have stayed until home-time?'

'Mrs. Leavesdon…truancy is far from a thing of the past, you know. Quite the opposite, in fact.'

'What? Even for first years?'

The receptionist peered over her spectacles with a smug grimace.

'Especially…among Year Sevens. Yes.'

Now feeling mildly offended, Hazel avidly fought her son's corner.

'Well…I can assure you…Peter would not play truant! This is only his second day here! There's no way he'd try such a gamble with me!'

Still smirking sarcastically at Hazel's rebuke, the lady behind the window seemed unconvinced by the likelihood of the boys' innocence.

'You'd be surprised what kids get up to these days, Mrs. Leavesdon. Even the good ones aren't too bothered about what their parents think, anymore. Are their phones switched off, then? That would be the quickest way to reach them, don't you think?'

Now feeling somewhat naïve, Hazel reluctantly explained her policy on youngsters and mobile phones.

The need for such self-justification was beginning to grate with her and she was quickly becoming tired of the futile exchange with the hindering clerk.

'Can you just tell me where Mrs. Gray's room is please? Can I speak with her?'

The receptionist pointed over Hazel's left shoulder.

'Right behind you…but she'll be in the staff room, now. She's probably ready for going home, actually.'

Now Hazel's patience was being tested to the full as her tone became mildly frantic.

'Well, can you go and check for me…and if she is in there…can you fetch her? If it's not too much trouble…please?'

Hazel waited nervously as the receptionist sighed, vacated her seat and ventured from reception and away along the corridor. Poised in wait, Hazel stared blankly at the white-washed walls of the school foyer.

The hiatus seemed to last forever.

She watched as the cleaners began to disperse with their mop buckets and automated sweeping equipment. She also glimpsed the caretaker through the distant windows of the main hall as he finalised the security checks for the evening.

Her temper was slowly beginning to get the better of her as she checked her watch for what felt like the thousandth time that afternoon.

Nearly half past four.

An hour had passed since home time.

And the boys were still missing.

Her boy.

Her encroaching sense of dread was interrupted by the voices of three women approaching from the staff room. The receptionist returned to her chair behind the window whilst the other two confronted Hazel out in the corridor.

The smaller teacher smiled and offered a hand of greeting.

'Mrs. Leavesdon? I'm Mrs Gray. Pleased to meet you. This is Miss Doherty. She taught Peter and Michael during maths this afternoon just before home-time.'

A little relief now diluted Hazel's feelings of intensive trepidation.

'Oh…good…so they didn't just bunk off then?' Hazel sneered loudly, glancing through the reception window for a reaction which wasn't forthcoming.

'Oh no! They were here, alright!' interjected Miss Doherty. 'In fact, they wouldn't stop talking when the bell went. They held everybody back pushing and shoving each other. Lovely lads, though.'

Hazel smiled as a wondrous vision grew in her head.

'Sounds just like them.' she quipped, nervously.

Mrs. Gray laid a supportive hand on Hazel's arm.

'Don't panic yourself, Mrs. Leavesdon. The chances are they're kicking a ball about somewhere or more likely hiding from you on purpose. Or maybe they're out looking for your car right now.'

'Well, they won't find it! I've had to walk from the other side of Shireheath because the damned car wouldn't start. That's why I'm late in the first place.'

Mrs. Gray glanced at her younger red-haired colleague before further attempting to offer some rational approach to the issue.

'Do they know their way home, okay?'

'Oh yes! In fact, Peter's been nagging me to let them come home on the bus!'

'Well, there you are then! I bet that's what they've done! They've seen you're not here and hopped on the bus! I bet they're at home waiting for you even as we speak!'

The very plausible theory didn't register convincingly, and Hazel immediately shook her head to quash the optimism.

'But Peter wouldn't do that. He hasn't even got a key to get in. We would have organised things if that was what we agreed to do. I don't think they'll have gone home alone, anyway. Some boys would, I grant you. But not my boy. Not Peter.'

Miss Doherty presented another suggestion for the trio to digest.

'Look. It's only half-past-four. If you want…I'll drive you back home now…just to check? It seems to be the most logical idea.'

Hazel was overwhelmed by the unwarranted generosity of the maths teacher.

'Would you, really? Would you mind? Honestly? It would speed things up a lot, wouldn't it?'

Mrs. Gray again calmed Hazel with a hand of reassurance.

'I'll talk to Mister Ford the Headmaster and put him in the picture. We'll wait here until Miss Doherty comes back with some news. Please…and I know it's easy to say it, Mrs. Leavesdon…but please…don't fret. They'll be fine!'

Hazel nodded timidly as Miss Doherty went back to the staff room for her handbag. With the bemusing analysis of events having now been shared, Hazel felt slightly more at ease with the scenario.

Miss Doherty returned promptly, and the pair made their way from the main building and toward a metallic blue Corsa parked just behind the school canteen.

'Hop in! You'll have to give me directions to your house, though. I'm a little bit useless when it comes to navigation!'

Now fully consumed by confusion and uncertainty, Hazel slid in beside the teacher and buckled up. She felt like screaming inside as her heart twitched at a rate of knots. But the anxiety at that moment was not sourced by undue upset or concern for the boys.

Moreover, she felt an intensive disgust at her own inept contribution to the whole episode.

The journey back to Cromford Road seemed to take an eternity as the rush hour masses built steadily. Every crawling minute in the car felt like an hour. Every meter they covered seemed like a mile.

As the Corsa finally manoeuvred away from the main thrust of traffic, they entered the fringes of the housing estate. Everything beyond the window that had seemed so familiar for so long now seemed completely unrecognisable to Hazel as her mind intermittently toiled with a furious combination of outrageous possibility and feeble self-assurance.

Miss Doherty attempted to make light conversation, but Hazel's answers were short, humourless, and sharp due to her blinding preoccupation.

The sight of one or two loitering children in Riverlands' uniforms along the route made her veritably jump from her seat with hopeful anticipation, but alas the intermittent repetition of school colours did not belong to her son or his best friend.

Eventually turning into Cromford Road was a disquieting experience.

Hazel's heart was now thumping like a bass drum at the prospect of seeing the boys standing outside the front doorway of number thirty-nine.

Similarly, the likelihood that they may well not be there left her shuddering with a cold, creeping dread.

The frontage of the house came into full view as Hazel strained to assimilate the scene from the passenger seat.

The silver Focus remained on the drive; exactly where she had left it at three-twenty-five.

The hanging baskets; still dripping slowly onto the floor from their earlier drenching.

And finally, the stark, painfully obvious absence, of her son and his best friend.

Miss Doherty's car pulled to a stop and Hazel leapt out. With a frantic sense of urgency, she checked the front door which remained locked. She peered through the lounge window. The interior of the house was untouched and empty. Retrieving the keys from her handbag in a fit of hopeless, frantic frustration she then unlocked the Focus and jumped in behind the wheel.

Hazel attempted to start the engine.

It purred into life at the first time of asking, leaving her even more disconsolate for the fact, as the sympathetic maths teacher crouched beside the open driver's door.

'I don't pissing believe it!' bemoaned Hazel. 'I *do not* pissing believe it! Why will it start now and not a bloody hour ago when I needed it to?'

Miss Doherty thought carefully for a moment before volunteering yet another option.

'Does his friend Michael live far from here?'

'No! Its only five minutes by car! I suppose they could be there, couldn't they?'

With a nod of inspiring affirmation, the young maths teacher rose to her full height.

'You lead. I'll follow.'

Both cars made the speedy journey across the estate to Basford Lane and came to a halt outside number twelve. However, the home of the Tompkins appeared just as deserted as Hazel inspected the exterior, peered through the front window, and explored the side path to the locked back gate.

Wallace had detected the untimely presence of the mysterious visitors and began to bark loudly in response from the muffled confines of the conservatory.

Hazel shook her head as the shadow of her despondency rapidly began to lengthen.

Feeling completely helpless she became upset as Miss Doherty moved quickly to embrace her.

'Hey…come on! They'll be around, somewhere. Kids are kids. They are never where they should be, are they? Listen…the best thing to do…you go back home…make a drink…and I'll make my way back to school to inform the Headmaster. What time is Peter's father due home?'

The gradual tipping of emotion now avalanched unashamedly as the thought of David coming home to the apparent dilemma fully immersed Hazel in a deep well of upset.

Then her thoughts instantly switched to Sharon and James.

All three were so pivotal in the scenario, yet at that inglorious moment in time were still so blissfully ignorant of the increasingly fraught situation.

Hazel wiped away more tears of desperation as the teacher's voice resonated softly once again.

'Mrs. Leavesdon. Please. Go home. So that you're there waiting when the boys do eventually turn up. I'll go back and alert the school. We do actually have a contingency plan for this sort of thing.'

Peter's mother nodded slowly before engaging with the gaze of the pony-tailed young teacher.

'Tell me…Miss Doherty…has the school ever had to employ the contingency plan before now?'

Contemplating the earnest query before slowly shaking her head, Miss Doherty could only respond with honesty.

'Not so far as I know…but then again…I've only been at the school for a year. Go home and wait. It's all you can do for now. I think I can find my way back to Riverlands from here.'

The two women ventured back to their cars.

Hazel watched through a moistened gaze as Miss Doherty's blue Corsa veered away from the kerbside and eventually vanished from sight around the corner.

Now beginning to feel physically and emotionally sick to her core, Hazel started her own engine and headed back to Cromford Road.

CHAPTER 8

The van swayed from side to side as it navigated an indeterminable route at what felt like reckless speed.

With his vision having steadily attuned itself to the darkness that had encompassed the journey, Michael could still only vaguely identify the outline of the captor that sat facing him with her back to the vehicle doors.

Sitting cross-legged and guarding over the defenceless quarry, the expression on her face was difficult to ascertain. Michael thought he glimpsed her frowning intermittently whilst she maintained a particularly close vigil on Peter, who had slowly begun to rouse himself from the drowsiness caused by her aggressive efforts to apprehend him.

Michael silently observed his friend idly rolling over towards him. Peter rubbed his forehead before hauling his form upward onto his backside. The faintest strains of light within their travelling cell reflected off his blond head, giving a welcome glimmer of familiarity to the frightened figure that now started to mumble with mildly confused realisation.

'That hurt! Michael! That woman in the street hit me! Did you see her? What did she do that for? Where are we? And where's Mum? Did she come for us? I'm telling my Mum! That woman in the street hit me!'

Michael wanted to respond to the quivering voice of his best friend, but the honour was quickly taken from him by the shrill bark of their abductor.

'Quieten down! Don't start whining, sonny! You'll be out of here soon enough.'

A momentary pause ensued before Peter responded.

'Who is that? Who are you? And where's my mum? Are you the woman who hit me?'

A roughly administered movement across the void suggested to Michael that his friend had again been violently struck by the woman.

'I said SHUT IT! And I mean…SHUT IT!'

Michael jumped involuntarily in response to the unnecessary increase in her volume whilst feeling himself becoming increasingly angered by the situation.

An attempt to calm his friend was understated and ineffective.

'It's okay, Peter…we'll be alright. Don't worry.'

Another few seconds of stillness elapsed as Michael's thoughts centred on their circumstances. However, his friend was not willing to tolerate the unwarranted order for silence.

'Michael…where's Mum?'

The hiatus in Michael's reply was short and pained.

As were the words he eventually spoke.

'I…I don't know, Peter. I don't know.'

'Where are we going? Is Mum driving us?'

'I'm not sure where we're going.'

And still Peter persisted with his questions as Michael anticipated another fist to fly unexpectedly in his friend's direction.

'But…is my mum driving?'

'No, Peter. I…don't think so.'

'So…who is driving? And where are we going, then?'

Michael felt a sharp jab of the woman's knuckles into his ribs as a repeated warning was hissed at the boys through the jolting murk.

'Stop talking to him! I don't want to hear another peep from either of you! You'll be told when you can talk.'

Michael's sure belief that his friend would not oblige was soon satisfied. Indeed, Peter's response had attained a tone of resilience that served to increase the overwhelming anxiety.

'You can't tell us what to do! You're not my mum! I want my mum! Where is she? Why are we in here?' exclaimed Peter with youthful defiance.

Michael again sensed a rapid movement as the woman reached across and employed what sounded like a hard slap across Peter's face.

'Now will you shut up, you fucking little shit?'

Peter's body began to twitch with renewed discomfort which was overpowered by a reaction of anger as his emotions now rose uncontrollably to the fore.

The untamed weeping threatened to betray Michael's own fragile sense of self-imposed bravado and furiously wiping his own eyes he desperately fought the onset of tears.

Yet Peter was now in the harsh grip of a fearful upset and wailed unashamedly. His deafening cries echoed around the rear of the van, in turn incurring a further vocal wrath of the woman.

'You little fuckers won't see another day if you don't fucking button it! Stop crying you mardy little bastard! Stop it…or I'll stop you fucking crying once and for all!'

Michael wanted so to protect his friend but adamantly kept his instinctive responses in check. He watched the unmoving outline of their nefarious escort as she perched on her haunches in readiness to strike out again.

Peter's relentless whimpers continued to haunt the journey, until eventually Michael felt the van slowing down. He could hear a grating sound under the wheels which sounded as though they had left the tarmac road and were travelling across gravel or stony earth.

He lurched forward due to clumsy application of the brakes before the van was brought to a final stop. There was the click of a latch as the driver's door opened, immediately followed by crunching footsteps.

The knock on the rear doors of the van was loud and furious, quickly compelling the woman to open it from her side and leave the boys alone for a moment. The blinding flash of late summer daylight was immensely relieving if frustratingly temporary.

Failing to accurately assess the view of the surroundings outside or the faces of the kidnappers, Michael listened very carefully over his friend's moaning to decipher the man's seemingly angry voice, which issued a muffled instruction to his female accomplice.

Fewer than ten seconds had elapsed before she was climbing back inside. The taunting glimpse of sunshine had completely confused Michael's vision again. He then heard Peter's warbling voice continue to accompany his physical pain for a few moments and then there was an absolute, unholy period as Michael heard Peter fighting for breath.

Michael wanted to retaliate with all his might, but sensibly retained his composure that belied such tender years.

Believing his best friend to now be gagged, the journey would continue without arousing any further audible suspicion from the outside world.

The driver's door slammed shut with a damning resonance.

The clutch was clumsily engaged before the vehicle skidded from the scene carrying its cargo ever further into unknown territory.

Now fearful of their immediate future, Michael's unprecedented policy of self-analysis began to intertwine with horrendous imaginary waves of thought and vision.

Feeling distinctly alone in the darkness, he tightly clutched the top of his school rucksack with the hope that the prevailing nightmare was to end as inexplicably as it had begun.

*****

Hazel entered number thirty-nine and closed the front door behind her as the weight of immense distress hampered her every move and thought. Retrieving her mobile phone from the zip pocket of her handbag, she furiously selected David's number and pressed the green call button.

The ring tone was accompanied by the competing sound of her thrashing heart as it thudded relentlessly against her chest wall.

Wandering into the kitchen as she impatiently awaited David's response, Hazel noticed the potatoes and burgers she had left out earlier.

Her gaze unravelled beyond the back window and to the gently swaying scenery of the garden. The golden image of serenity contrasted greatly with the deep-rooted anguish she was now being compelled to accommodate.

The seconds passed and still she longed for her husband to answer his phone.

Swearing nervously under her breath as his voicemail activated, Hazel cancelled the call and immediately redialled. Disturbing David at work was not a preferable course of action, but she ascertained that on seeing his wife's number on the display he would know that the likely cause would be nothing if not important.

Yet despite the seemingly critical nature of the matter at hand, a significant part of Hazel did not want to report to him that the boys had not been seen since half-past three.

Nearly ninety minutes ago.

It seemed totally surreal to have to disclose an absolute loss of contact with their son and his best friend.

Sheer disbelief adequately fogged the fact that, under her charge, they had seemingly vanished without trace.

It was a potentially terrifying announcement; one that she had not even begun to formulate into words although she would need to very soon.

How she wanted to hang up once again.

How she wished for the boys to knock on the door at that very moment and allow her the overwhelming, relieving luxury of hearing their mischievous, wonderfully charming voices disclosing their elaborate yet misguided hoax.

Yet her intensive pangs of human instinct suggested that this was no joking matter.

Hazel's mind continued to toil with immense foreboding as the ring tone continued to reign unanswered. But although bound by maternal duty, Hazel still did not want to worry her husband unnecessarily.

Yet the starkness of possible truth was now unavoidable. David needed to be aware that the situation had quickly accrued a level of dreadful priority.

Churning the nature of the revelation over and over in her head, she could still not ascertain any appropriate way of phrasing the disclosure. Her attention briefly focused on a blue tit that perched itself on the guttering along the outhouse roof.

It was a pleasantly brief diversion from the business at hand.

And only a temporary respite from inevitability that rained down all around as David finally responded to his phone call.

'Hello? Hazel?'

Jolted back into immediate reality, she concentrated her energies into maintaining a semblance of composure.

'David?'

'Yes. Of course…you okay, love?'

Another lapse; another breath; another chance to be deafened by the crescendo of rhythmical thudding that swelled within her.

'Look…I…I think…you should come home…'

Now David paused with registration; his justified silence echoing agonisingly back to her.

He was fully entitled to know the motive for her unusual request.

'What's the matter, love? It's about five now, isn't it? I'll be home for half-six at the very latest. What's the rush?'

Now her features twitched randomly with the renewed onset of thrusting emotion. Now the consuming mental and physical distress pressed against her very threshold. But Hazel stayed firm as she issued her demand once again.

'David…please…come home…now. I'll fetch you if you want. But you have to be here…*now*.'

Another, longer, more contemplative hiatus in the exchange ensued before his reply.

Now her husband was understandably bound by husbandly duty.

Now his wife had off-loaded just a little of her personal burden.

And now the questions would surely come back at her.

'Hazel? I can't just leave. I've got a meeting with the head of department in a few minutes.'

Now a wife's patient resolve would fail, and she would surrender entirely to her upset.

And now the husband would listen again.

And now he would hear her.

'DAVID! PLEASE! YOU NEED TO BE HERE! *NOW*! COME HOME! PLEASE!'

The disturbing quietude that followed from her husband was perhaps in bemused acceptance of the distraught command. Standing in his shirt and his tie and his two-piece navy suit in the middle of his office, David Leavesdon found himself rooted in pure bewilderment as his wife unleashed an unbridled torrent of emotion across the airwaves.

And it was the worst sound he had heard in his whole life.

'Right! I'm coming now then! I'll be twenty minutes!'

And then the signal connecting them went dead.

Hazel turned off her own phone and returned to the lounge. Slumping dejectedly onto the settee she began to chew the skin around her fingernails as she gazed helplessly and hopelessly through the bay window and into the street beyond.

Her mind fuelled itself with thoughts of her dearest only son and his best friend.

And now nothing could eclipse the barrage of horrendous thoughts that invaded her desperate search for solace.

*****

In considerably less time than his twenty-minute forecast, David Leavesdon rode into Cromford Road in a state of perspiring confusion. It had been a long while since he had heard his wife cry.

Let alone emit such a genuine, shredding display of raw despair.

In fact, to his memory, such an affliction had never had reason to previously occur within their relationship.

The cause for her grievance remained a mystery as he pulled sharply on his bicycle brakes and jumped off beside the silver Focus parked on the driveway.

Scanning the body work of the car it dawned that at least there had been no traffic accident, which was one of the theories cursing his mind during the frantic pedal homeward.

Removing his safety helmet, David pushed the bike through the side gate and checked the scene at the rear of the house. He leaned the bike under the kitchen window and peered through in expectation of observing his wife preparing dinner.

She was not in view, but aside this, all seemed normal.

Then, on entering the kitchen, the untypical stillness of the house greeted him like a cliff face.

No radio.

No television.

No cooking.

No talking.

No wife.

No children.

The lounge was vacant, forcing David's search upstairs.

He called out to Hazel on his ascent, but there was no audible reply.

Standing on the landing, he noticed that Peter's bedroom door was wide open. His son's television and X-Box were also switched off.

This was, indeed, far from typical.

Into the main bedroom, he finally discovered his wife.

Hazel's back was to him as she perched on the edge of the bed staring beyond the window toward the adjacent rooftops and overlying curtain of azure sky. He sensed her evident discomfort, yet she would still not turn to face her husband.

And somehow, he felt he already knew there was a serious dilemma at hand.

Something distasteful lay ahead; and it was telling him of her plight.

Despite the expectation that froze his emotions at that moment, his tone was soothing yet demanding.

'Hazel...what's going on? Where are the boys?'

He moved to stand behind his wife, watching her head shake slowly from side to side as she continued to stare into nothingness.

He could hear her steady whimpering as she tried desperately not to shed her concerns.

'Hazel? What's happened? Where's Peter?'

Now she finally confronted her husband.

The father of their son.

Their only son.

Their only child.

Staggering up from the bed, she turned into him and buried her straining release deep into his embrace, shaking violently as he involuntarily held her tight and close.

He whispered softly to her as she trembled.

'Talk to me, Hazel. Please…talk to me. What the hell is wrong?'

Eventually lifting her face to engage with David's now pulsing concern, she again surrendered to monumental waves of crashing emotion before slumping back onto the bed.

David crouched beside her, cradling her quaking hands in his.

Her words were clear and defiantly, horrendously concise as they overrode her mental contortion.

'I…don't…know…where…the boys…are…'

David observed her tormented grimace further etching the drastic symptoms across her face.

'I don't understand, Hazel. What do you mean…you…*don't know*?'

She gazed quickly to the floor and then reluctantly met with his eyes once more. Her tone lowered in volume and quivered helplessly with damning recollection.

'I…I…went for them…as planned…at half-past three.'

'Yes? So, what happened then?'

Shivering under the strain of remorseful fear, she battled to convey the story through gritted teeth.

'But…the…fucking…the fucking…car wouldn't…fucking start! So, I was late to school. I had to fucking walk. I got there as soon as I could.'

Now completely baffled by the honest simplicity of the account, David struggled to dissect the implication of earlier events.

Still holding her hands tightly, he pressed for more answers from his wife.

‘Hazel…they must be around somewhere. Did they not wait for you at school as arranged?’

She shook her head rapidly as the premise of a further outpouring verged.

‘They weren’t there. I…I informed the schoolteachers. I think the Headmaster is still at school now. Their new form tutor, Mrs Gray. I spoke to her. And Miss Doherty their maths teacher. She brought me home. Mister Ford is the Headmaster. Perhaps you should talk to him. Maybe…he might have some news…’

As he studied the evident searing torment in his wife’s crushed demeanour, David decided the time was appropriate for rational thought and checked his watch.

Five-twenty-five; exactly.

‘Right. Do you want a drink?’

Hazel shut her eyes and declined the offer in a strangled refusal as David pulled her up from the bed.

‘Come downstairs with me. I’m going to phone the school. See what the Head has in mind. It’s not that long ago. They can’t be far away. Not in two hours, they can’t.’

Reluctantly joining her husband in the lounge, Hazel sat on the settee and watched with throbbing trepidation as David picked up the handset and filed through the phone memory for Riverlands’ reception number.

Quaking under the might of her own sorrowful guilt, she shamefully covered her face whilst listening to her husband’s voice as he introduced himself to the receptionist and requested urgent contact with the Head.

As the receptionist put the call through, the subsequent pause seemed to last for a lifetime.

Then David’s authoritative tone commandeered the room as Hazel listened to him exchange current details of the emerging crisis into the mouthpiece.

‘Hello, Mister Ford? Yes…David Leavesdon. Peter’s father.’

‘No…not yet. Nothing this end.’

‘I’ve just come home from work. Hazel’s told me the basic facts.’

‘No. I understand. But surely we will need to inform the police at some point this evening?’

‘Yes. Of course.’

‘Twenty-four hours.’

'No. I know they won't.'

'Is he? That's brilliant! Thank you.'

'So, you want us to stay here?'

'Okay. If you're staying at the school for a while, then there's no point.'

'Yeah…sure…no it's a good plan for the time being.'

'Seven o'clock.'

'Okay.'

'Yes. Then we phone the police and inform you?'

'Fine.'

'I hope so too.'

'Thanks for your help, Mister Ford.'

'Okay…yes.'

'Speak to you soon.'

'Bye.'

David gently replaced the receiver in its cradle and joined Hazel on the settee. Putting an arm around her only served to encourage her sense of isolation even further.

She shook untamed in his empty embrace as he briefly conveyed the plan of action in a voice of hopeful condolence.

'Mister Ford and the caretaker are staying on the school site for the time being. Hazel…please…calm yourself down. He's told me to ring the police at seven if there is still no sign.'

She looked deep into her husband's eyes, searching beyond them for the resolution she so craved at that moment.

'But that's over an hour away, Dave! Another whole fucking hour away! What are we supposed to do until then?'

David firmly gripped his wife's shoulders and squared up to her terrified gaze.

'Listen to me! I tell you what we do! We wait here! What more can we do? Sharon and Jim still need to be told, yet. We must act together on this. Not start getting all stressed up and squabbling.'

Having wrestled herself from David's grasp, Hazel stood defiantly to her feet and moved to the lounge window to face the street.

Their street; their road; Cromford Road.

A neighbourhood once so familiar; now so utterly alien.

Her impulsive reactions to the situation were now becoming random and wild.

‘JESUS FUCKING CHRIST, DAVID! WHAT WILL SHARON SAY? THIS IS ALL MY FUCKING FAULT! SHE’LL BLAME ME! SHE’LL BLAME ME, DAVID!’

‘Blame you for what, Hazel? We don’t know anything yet, do we? Stop being so fucking melodramatic until we know some more information.’

Hazel turned to face her husband; her features now contorted into a mask of elemental fury as she conveyed her reply.

‘Melodramatic? Fucking…melodramatic? Our son has disappeared…and you want me to take it easy? What fucking planet are you on? Don’t you watch the fucking news? You want information, do you? We’re not likely to find any fucking information by sitting around here on our fucking arses, are we?’

David raised a hand to gesture for some civility.

‘Hazel…please…stop…swearing at me. I’m trying to keep a clear head over this. Don’t take it out on me. It’s not fair. I want those boys back as much as you. But this doesn’t happen to people every day. There’s no rulebook for this stuff! I think Mister Ford’s advice is pretty sound. Like he says…this could all resolve itself within the next hour.’

Hazel had now stopped crying and her attention had again centred to the static scene beyond the front window.

Static, that is, until Sharon Tompkins appeared from around the corner to collect her son.

A stoical facade was suddenly adopted by Hazel.

She spoke in a more considered tone, but the persistent sense of terror had laced itself far too deeply now as a familiar knock at the door resonated throughout the eerie silence of the house.

‘Oh my God! Sharon’s here to pick Michael up! She’s here for her son and he’s not fucking here. And I don’t know what to fucking say! Jesus David! What do I fucking say to her?’

Taking Hazel forcibly by the elbows once more, he pushed her back toward the settee.

‘I’ll go to the door. You sit there. I’ll bring her in to you once I’ve put her in the picture. Stay…there! Do you hear me?’

Hazel nodded solemnly as David departed from the lounge.

The next agonising sound was that of her husband tentatively unlatching the front door.

Hazel strained to listen to the usual display of attractive easy charm that Sharon always exuded in conversation.

Then she heard Michael's mother enter the hallway.

The sound of the front door being closed was followed by the downbeat and muffled tone of David's voice.

Then Sharon Tompkins was told of what had transpired.

Hazel listened through the open lounge door as Sharon's typically jovial mode of greeting was quickly reduced to a resolute silence. She heard each exchange as her husband quickly relayed the afternoon's events.

The revelation endured for only half a minute before Sharon entered the lounge on the verge of tears and met with the wilting figure of her lifelong friend.

The two looked forlornly at one another and simultaneously broke down. The union of mutual comfort was warm and tender, leaving David to depart into the kitchen to fill and switch on the kettle.

He listened to the tearful disclosure between the two mothers as the scant details of the mystery were conveyed once more. Grateful to be away from the arena for the moment, he tried not to think too much about the looming shadows of possibility.

Busying himself with the task of preparing coffee, he didn't hear Sharon enter the kitchen behind him.

Her face was now a portrait riddled with raw shock.

Yet her voice remained calm; her words and manner collected and cautious.

'Tell her it'll be alright, Dave. She thinks I'm going to hate her for this. But it will sort itself out. Please…put her right. She's a bit of a wreck.'

'I will do. What about Jim?'

'He'll not be home from work yet. I might take Hazel round to ours. She's working herself up into a right state. I need to be there to tell Jim myself.'

David handed over a steaming mug of coffee.

'Of course. Do you want a lift?'

'No. Thanks. We both need some air. I just need to be at home now. Just for now. Just until I've spoken to Jim. We'll have this drink. Then we'll go.'

*****

An hour had elapsed since David had watched covertly from the front door as Hazel and Sharon wandered slowly in the direction of the Tompkins' home on Basford Lane. The women linked arms tightly in support of one another; their heads were bowed in apprehension of the imminent future.

He had observed the sorrowful sight until the women had disappeared from view around the corner; hoping that the unprecedented chronicle of the day would bring forth a positive outcome.

The premise of any other possible revelation was still unthinkable and utterly unbearable.

Resigning himself to the uncertain whim of fate, he opened a can of cold beer, slumped into an armchair, and checked his wristwatch.

Six-forty-five; exactly.

Now James Tompkins would surely be home from work.

By now the other father involved would have been informed of his son's disappearance.

His only son.

His only child.

And as David Leavesdon contemplated the rapid onset of his own emotional frailty, he maintained a determined eye on the lounge wall clock.

Soon the police would have to be told.

Soon the time would be upon both families to unite in surrendering their sufferance unto the hands of the authorities.

Soon enough, David feared that the marked, heart-wrenching absence of two eleven-year-old schoolboys would evolve into a process. A search for clues and maybe, perhaps, in the worst-case scenario - a hunt for perpetrators.

And as David vainly drew hope from the depths of his very core, the vaguely optimistic thought flickered in the back of his ailing mind that soon enough, their sinister ordeal might be at an end.

Yet little could he know that, for the two truly innocent victims of this unholy scenario, the ordeal had barely commenced.

CHAPTER 9

Immersed in his own train of thought, David was startled by the sound of the front doorbell. Peering furtively through the lounge window as diminishing daylight darkened the backdrop beyond, he was acknowledged by James who gestured with a subdued thumbs-up.

Opening the door to his friend was typically pleasurable, but in the current circumstances the task seemed unpredictably difficult and riddled with angst. Angered concern was mirrored in the features of both men as they convened in the lounge.

The stuttering discomfort between them was finally broken.

'What we gonna do, Jim?' murmured Peter's father through trembling strength.

James' customary ease in offering an opinion was stunted by a sudden, uncanny inability to decide how to reply.

Finally, he made a tentative enquiry.

'When are we going to tell the police, Dave? How long do we wait?'

David sighed heavily and conveyed the earlier proposal from the school Headmaster. James stared hopelessly at the carpet around his feet as he absorbed the plan.

'Okay, Dave. Yeah. That sounds good. Fancy a drive around town first? We've perhaps got an hour's decent daylight left. I can't just sit around waiting for the coppers to turn up. I've got to do something. We'll have a scout about and then go back to our house. I'll call the police from there. Okay?'

Peter's father stared blankly at Michael's.

'Yes. Okay. Let's go. We'll take my car.'

David grabbed the keys to the Focus from the kitchen table and accompanied James outside into the early evening air. Securing the house, he felt a little easier at knowing his friend was now with him. It was time to work together, and the sense of unity was strangely comforting.

Even if their random journey should garner little in the way of any positive conclusion, at least they would temporarily satisfy the yearning to go and seek out their absent loved ones.

Gripping the wheel as James slid in beside him, David looked to his friend with a mournful grimace.

'How's the wives doing, Jim?'

James looked at the florally decorated frontage of the Leavesdon's house beyond the windscreen and rubbed his tightening forehead.

'They're...well...they're in pieces between them. As you'd expect, I suppose. And to be honest, mate...I'm not far behind them. Come on. Let's just drive. And keep your eyes peeled.'

David tentatively steered the car along Cromford Road once more as both men avidly studied the passing views without word. The local estate seemed deserted and almost echoed with the ghostly calls of the two missing schoolboys.

As the minutes and miles passed, the fathers' spontaneous dalliance with hope was quickly proving futile.

Through junction after junction; around corner after corner.

Glimpse after tantalising glimpse of youngsters in the streets caused intermittent excitement at the possibility of sighting their sons.

Indeed, the identities of many youngsters were analysed en route.

But not Peter's.

And not Michael's.

Not their two missing boys.

The exploration ventured beyond the fringes of the district and accessed the three main B-roads that dissected Shireheath.

Back they cruised through the middle of the town.

Skirting the supermarket and the church; the leisure centre and the Town Hall.

Not a single glimmer of inspiration presented itself as two desperate fathers rankled heavily with their own inevitable fears.

Not a syllable was exchanged as the dawning realisation cut into both men that they were indeed about to endure their worst nightmare.

They had travelled for over thirty, fruitless minutes.

In conceding to his parental resignation, David eventually stopped the car in a lay-by and bravely stemmed the flow of tears.

'Jim...let's give in. It's nearly eight. Light's fading. Let's go back to yours and phone the coppers. There's no alternative now. You agree? This is pointless.'

James simply nodded as his mindset became similarly diluted by emotion. He could not bring himself to speak for being wary of allowing his customary male composure to wane.

Instead, both fathers opted for a suitably soothing peace as the Focus crawled back towards number twelve, Basford Lane.

A silence that, within its own natural dignity, also carried a prayer for the safety of their offspring.

*****

Sharon and Hazel greeted the ominous appearance of the silver Focus as it came to a stop against the kerb outside.

How they both wished to see the vibrant, enthralling vision of their sons in the back of the car. How their hearts sunk beyond retrieval when it was obvious that only two adults occupied the vehicle.

Both men hauled themselves dejectedly from their seats and wandered wearily to meet their wives who had moved quickly from the lounge to the edge of the driveway next to the Tompkins' green Astra.

Hazel had managed to compose herself to some degree and ventured to ask as to the success of the search, even though the conclusion was painfully evident for all to behold.

'No good. Total waste of time. We don't really know where to start looking, do we?' declared David. 'Come on. We have no choice now. The police have to be told.'

James looked deeply into Sharon's tear-blackened eyes. He placed an arm around her which quickly evolved into a tight embrace of reassurance. All four parents retreated into the comparative sanctity of the house, yet all knew that there would be no effective refuge from their current torment.

As James entered the kitchen to fill the kettle, Wallace offered a shrill bark of confused enquiry as he wandered in and among the group. With his tail wagging in curiosity and nose twitching as it detected every aroma present.

His shining bright brown eyes darted from adult to adult for even a scant clue as to the whereabouts of the very notable absentees.

'Hello, boy!' James whispered as he ruffled Wallace's neck. 'I know what you're asking. If only we could tell you. I'd give anything to take you to Michael now. You know he's gone missing don't you, hey? Yeah...you know. Good boy! Sit down then! I'll take you out in a bit.'

The German Shepherd duly obliged as Sharon entered the kitchen and stood next to her husband as he observed the disconsolate-looking canine curl up in the conservatory.

'Jim…will you…be the one to ring the police? Now that…we're all here…all together? We need to phone the school as well. The Headmaster will still be there. He rang whilst you were out to see if there was any news.'

James nodded as he pulled four mugs down from the shelf.

'Yeah…in fact…I'll do it now.'

Hazel, David and Sharon watched in admiring yet fretful anticipation as James entered the lounge, picked up the handset and dialled the number nine three times.

The subsequent hiatus was unbearable for all.

The knowledge that they would now be disclosing the scenario to officialdom offered little crumb of comfort.

On the contrary, the harshness of their ordeal was now only being fortified with a searing sheen of reality.

James Tompkins' voice dispersed the unwelcome deliberation of minds.

'Yes…the police please.'

'Thanks.'

Another pause.

Another few seconds of pained reflection for four, yearning parents.

Another few seconds without their children.

'Yes…hello?'

'James Tompkins.'

'Twelve…Basford Lane.'

'Yes…Shireheath.'

'Erm…I erm…I need to report the apparent disappearance of my son…and his friend.'

'Yes…they've…they've both gone missing…'

Both mothers looked at one another as James' confession cut far deeper than they could ever have imagined. Trying desperately to retain a fragile composure, they were assisted by David, who sat between them on the settee and placed an arm tightly around each woman's shoulder.

All three stared at James as he continued the damning declaration into the handset.

‘They both attend Riverlands secondary. Both in Year Seven.’

‘Yes…both were at school today.’

‘Half past three.’

‘Yes…they were definitely there.’

‘No. Not since then.’

‘My son…Michael Aaron Tompkins.’

‘His friend…Peter David Leavesdon.’

‘Okay…thank you.’

‘Yes. Bye.’

With his heart beating almost beyond control, James gently replaced the phone into its cradle and mournfully faced his wife and friends.

He observed the expectant expressions of the trio.

Yet the hope in their hearts was betrayed by the evolving fear in their faces as he revealed the outcome of the call.

‘The police will be round…as soon as they can.’

Hazel interjected with the obvious query.

‘When will they be here, exactly?’

‘Should be within the hour…so the sergeant said.’

James slumped against the kitchen door frame.

The deed was done.

Desperation and a need for assistance had forced the issue into the hands of others.

His attention was diverted to the activity beyond the conservatory doorway, as Wallace sat bolt upright with ears flicking avidly for any new scrap of information or sign of his human brother.

He also offered James an opportunity to temporarily escape from the stifling cauldron of foreboding that number twelve had suddenly become.

‘Look, you guys…Wallace…he needs a walk. I won’t be long.’

David stood up and joined his friend.

‘I’m coming with you, Jim. I need some air too.’

James cast his sorrowful gaze to his wife.

‘You’d better get hold of the school, Sharon. Tell them we’ve spoken to the police…tell them…we’ll probably go there in the morning. I don’t know what to tell them, really. And thank Mister Ford for his concerns. There’s nothing more he can do, now.’

The family's German Shepherd returned from the hallway with his leash clamped between his jaws.

'Come on, Wallace…let's get you out of here for a bit.'

Sharon faced James with an earnest request.

Rarely had she spoken to her husband with more damning sincerity.

'Jim…don't be too long…I want you back here…with me.'

As the wives blessed their husbands' temporary departure from the scene with a tender kiss apiece, the diminished daylight had begun to cast ever-lengthening darkness across the surrounding estate.

With a bemused Wallace hooked to his lead and trotting steadily between the two adult figures, the male trinity of faithful defiance became evermore enshrouded in the steady onset of dusk.

A dusk that would soon evolve into the blackest night that four parents could ever experience.

*****

The sun had long completed its retreat beyond the rooftops of Shireheath leaving the sky a shade of distinctive deep blue, when the police car made its inimitable appearance outside number twelve, Basford Lane.

David checked his wristwatch as the four adults nervously stood to attention in the lounge. Each offered extremely wary glances through the window toward the two officers that departed the fluorescent yellow and white vehicle before promptly adorning their hats.

'Half past nine. Just over an hour. Not bad I suppose.' he remarked, as the other three shuffled indecisively about the room.

James placed a hand on Sharon's waist.

'Check the dog's secure, love. I'll get the door.'

Sharon observed the stern glint in her husband's expression. Always one to favour with the lighter side of situations, it was painfully evident that he was now under real duress with matters.

In the hallway, James rubbed his eyes and squinted through the circular portal in the front door. He hesitated, fighting with a raging heartbeat as the shadowy silhouettes made their approach under the yellow porch-light and produced a firm series of raps on the wooden panelling.

With hands now shaking, James pulled down on the handle and greeted the acutely ominous vision of the two police officers: one male and one female.

With stony authority accentuated by a narrow face and pencil-thin black moustache, the male officer did not hesitate in beginning his introduction.

'Good evening. Mr. Tompkins?'

Struggling for breath, James entire body squirmed as he relayed confirmation of his name before welcoming the visitors inside.

'I am Police Constable Rhodes. My colleague is Police Constable Coombs.'

James glanced at the young female officer who offered a brief smile of sympathy from beneath her peaked cap.

Once into the lounge, James introduced the police to the trio of parents who all stood to attention with their arms folded tightly around their chests.

Declining the offer of a drink, both officers removed their headwear and assumed the offered seats. Hazel and Sharon squatted on the floor in front of the sofa between their husbands' legs.

An atmosphere of torturous trepidation rapidly descended on the room as P.C. Rhodes removed a notepad from his jacket and commenced his initial questioning.

'Okay…so present here are both sets of parents. The Tompkins? And the Leavesdons? Good. And the boys' names are Peter and Michael? And both are Year Seven, so they are eleven years old? You say that the boys have not been seen since being discharged from school at the official finish time of three-thirty this afternoon?'

Hazel intervened with her recollection.

'Yes. That's correct. I was due to meet them. But my car wouldn't start. So…I had to walk and was pretty late.'

The officer eyed her with interest.

'And you had arranged to meet them at home-time, Mrs. Leavesdon?'

'Yes…and they were expressly told to wait inside the school grounds if I wasn't there. It's only their second day at Riverlands, you see…'

'And what time precisely did you eventually arrive at school?'

'Oh…I'd say about a quarter to…no…perhaps it was nearer four. I can't be exact.'

P.C. Rhodes scribbled intermittently on the pad as he spoke.

'Does either of the boys own a mobile phone?'

An indicative pause proceeded Hazel's answer.

'I...we...I...don't think boys should be given such things until they are responsible enough to use them properly.'

Sharon supported the mothers' standpoint.

'We've said they can probably have one when they become teenagers.'

Neither police officer responded to the evidently old fashioned and frustratingly obstructive revelation.

James again briefly engaged with the understanding gaze of W.P.C. Coombs as her counterpart continued with the informal inquisition.

'And you reported the matter to the school immediately?'

'Yes...after I spoke to the caretaker. He was very helpful. He and the Headmaster have only just left the school now, actually. They thought it best to wait until...well...until we told them otherwise.'

The male officer nodded at Hazel's summary and offered a fleeting glance to his female counterpart.

'Yes...that's fine. We'll likely be going to talk to the school tomorrow, anyway. So...there's no chance the boys could have gone home with say...some other friends...or gone to other pupils' houses in the local area?'

Again, Hazel's anxious interruption re-cemented events in the minds of all in the arena.

'NO! Absolutely not! They hadn't really had time to make any...to make any new friends, I mean...'

The male officer rubbed his chin as he cast a discerning stare across all four parents.

'What about any nearby relatives?'

'No! There's no one from either family living close by. There's only me available to collect them as David, James and Sharon all work full-time.'

Hazel's insistent responses crumbled steadily as rising emotion threatened to strangle her words. David offered an arm of reassurance as he took up the mantle of chief communicator.

'Jim and I...we've searched the local estates in the car before the light went. We...couldn't see anything...well...we didn't truly expect to...'

The enveloping futility of his declaration resulted in a knowing nod from P.C. Rhodes, who tapped his pen repeatedly onto the notepad.

'The school should have some form of CCTV, Mister Leavesdon. We hope this will disclose any possible initial leads. For now, we shall put the call out to the relevant units and keep close vigil overnight.'

Sharon opted to offer a curt contribution to the discussion.

'What? That's *it*?'

The male officer replaced his pad into his jacket pocket, seemingly in expectation of Sharon's reasoning.

'At this moment in time, Mrs. Tompkins...we can log the reported incident and put all duty officers on alert.'

The husbands and wives looked despairingly at one another.

'But they've been gone for six hours! SIX BLOODY HOURS! Anything could have happened to my boy by now. Anything!'

Sharon's anger began to froth as the policeman attempted to allay her concerns.

'Yes...exactly...Mrs. Tompkins. Anything could have happened. And, as yet, we have no procedural course of action to follow.'

'What do you mean? You're just going to do nothing?' barked Hazel in support of her friend's dismay.

'Officially, absent persons are not classed as missing until twenty-four hours has passed since the last quantifiable sighting. In this case, possibly the schoolteacher who dismissed them from their final class. After that time has elapsed, an investigative officer will be assigned, and the incident will become an official police matter.'

Aghast at the apparent tardiness being presented, the four adults gazed at one another in helpless disbelief.

Yet Sharon was not prepared to let the officer's explanation stand.

'Well...they're not bloody sitting here with us, are they? So, I'd say they were classed as bloody missing? Wouldn't you, officer?'

P.C Rhodes gestured for his colleague to join him.

Both officers replaced their hats whilst scanning the expressions of the disgruntled throng.

'Mrs. Tompkins...I fully understand your reaction. But despite your naturally worst fears, I can amaze you with some reliable statistics.'

Sharon stared intently without word in abject demand of some further conviction.

'In many reported incidents such as these, the absentees make an appearance well before the twenty-four-hour threshold has elapsed. That is why the threshold is in place. It can save a lot of time and trouble for all involved. Especially with minors…they always turn up somewhere.'

Hazel gestured toward the lounge window and the unappealing scene beyond the glass.

'Yes…in most cases. But I don't really think they're still out there playing hide and seek or football, do you? Its pitch black! It's a bloody long time for two eleven-year-olds to be out playing, don't you think?'

P.C. Rhodes did not reply, instead producing a contact card from his wallet.

'On there is a number to call if anything occurs between now and tomorrow morning. We shall be visiting the school in due course. All that can be done…at this stage…is being done. Rest assured. Please refrain from panic. It does nothing to help the issue.'

Hazel fell into David's embrace as tears forcibly returned to the fray.

Sharon looked blankly at her husband.

'I don't believe this, Jim! I cannot believe they think the boys are just going to appear by magic and this will have a happy ending.'

James watched as the police officers shuffled back into the hallway before whispering a guarded response to his wife.

'Sharon…they don't know what is going to happen! That's the whole point! They're at the same starting position as us.'

P.C. Rhodes and W.P.C. Coombs stepped out through the front door and turned to the discontented group hovering in the semi-lit hallway. The male officer commended their actions.

'You can do nothing more than you are doing. You've done the right thing by letting us know this early. Please let us do our job. Someone will be back here tomorrow. Obviously, we will call you with any news. I suggest you all take the day off work tomorrow and stay together.'

The police began to make their way along the drive back to the squad car, their black uniforms merging ominously with the shadows of early night-time.

James offered one last suggestion as their outlines were almost subdued by the encroaching darkness.

'It's worth us going out again and looking though, isn't it? If we want to go and look, that is? We're not interfering with anything are we?'

The doom-laden hiatus in P.C. Rhodes' reply was coldly significant, as were the words that followed.

'If it helps you at this moment, sir...then yes...please look everywhere you can think of. It may just assist us in our process, too. I bid you all good evening for now.'

*****

It was nearly midnight when the two sets of parents reluctantly opted to separate to their own abodes.

The Leavesdons pledged to keep in touch with the Tompkins throughout the early hours should any development be forthcoming, yet such a premise felt devoid of potential.

'I'll fetch the car tomorrow, Dave. It will be okay at yours, I'm sure.'

'No worries. Try and get some kip, mate.'

Sharon solemnly waved to Hazel as David lifted the clutch of the Focus and guided them back to Cromford Road.

Quietly shutting the front door on the tranquil scene beyond, she then slumped to her haunches in the hallway and sobbed without restraint.

On hearing her outpouring, James was not long in joining his wife. Crouching beside her, the pair found a certain sense of solidarity and even solace in finally sharing their shattering concern in private.

A few minutes of impassioned release gave way to a welcome tranquillity within the house; yet that same serenity quickly began to send shudders of horror through Sharon.

She did not want to be alone with her thoughts; all of which were determinedly centred on her little boy and his best friend.

'Do you want a bite of anything, love?' whispered James.

Sharon shook her head and blew her nose into a tissue. James let his gaze rest on her suffering form for a moment or two.

'I'm thinking of taking Wallace out again. He must be going nuts in the conservatory. Do you think you'll be okay for ten minutes?'

Sharon wiped her eyes and smirked wryly.

'Do you think dogs can sense trouble like this, Jim?'

'Oh yes! He knows alright! He's being very good about it, though.'

Sharon hauled herself to her feet as James retrieved the lead from the hook behind her. Departing back through the passageway, he promptly returned with Wallace, whose unusually lethargic manner was also now fully in evidence.

'I don't think he's that bothered about walkies, Jim. He looks bloody fed up to me.'

'I know…he probably is, bless him. But it's a chance for him to go to toilet. Do you want to come with us or stay here?'

Sharon contemplated the offer for a moment before suggesting an alternative.

'I tell you what. I'll sit outside on the step and wait for you. Just in case…well…you know…just in case.'

James' mind focused on the lingering kiss exchanged with his wife as he trudged dejectedly along Basford Lane with his faithful canine companion.

There was no bounce in the stride of either man or beast as they alternately flitted among the amber hues of the streetlamps before being immersed in shadow.

As he walked, James eyed every nook and cranny of the bleakly strewn scene ahead.

Every movement and every sound alerted his senses.

Every rustle encouraged by the nocturnal breeze made him instantly alter the target of his attention.

The world suddenly seemed a more savage and unforgiving place without his little boy around.

James Tompkins hardly felt like a husband and father at all at that moment in the blackness.

In truth, he barely even felt himself to be a man.

What he would give to have his son returned.

As the minutes passed, it was obvious that Wallace would be content until morning, prompting James to re-direct them quickly back toward home.

*****

Sharon had maintained her vigil on the front step for the best part of an hour. She scanned the lifeless vista of the street beyond, completely oblivious to her husband's presence behind her in the hallway.

'It's half-one, love. Are you coming to bed?'

His wife did not look at him, instead, concentrating fully on some indeterminable pinpoint of silver light in the sky.

Finally, she whispered in response.

'No, Jim. I won't sleep. Not until my boy is home.'

Nodding without response, James left Sharon with her solitude and retreated to the lounge where he curled up on the settee.

Morning was not far away.

And unbeknown to four desperate parents, with that painful sunrise would evolve the onset of unthinkable events.

CHAPTER 10

Friday; eight oh seven, a.m.

The Leavesdons' silver Focus pulled to a stop at the kerbside that fronted number twelve, Basford Lane. David and Hazel shut their doors and sidled towards Sharon and James who both stood disconsolately just beyond their front door.

Sharon offered a weak smile as her friends approached.

'Heard anything?'

Hazel and David simultaneously shook their heads without word.

James watched the growing activity in the street, totally envious of the daily normality he witnessed around him. The early shift starts had long deprived him of observing such little pleasures.

Neighbours commuting to work for the day.

The postman on his round.

The local village bus service winding its way through the estate.

Other schoolchildren from Riverlands and the other nearby schools meandered past. Smiling laughing and shouting. Never giving the gathering of adults on the driveway of number twelve a second or even first glance.

'I haven't slept a wink.' Hazel confirmed as she shivered feebly in the early morning air.

'Me neither.' yawned Sharon

'Coffee anyone?' enquired James.

The conversation was stunted by a mutual and deep-rooted disbelief at the circumstances that had transpired during the previous hours. The entire episode had now acquired an unreal, other-worldly sensation.

The parents gathered in the lounge just as the crucifying weight of expectancy was disturbed by the piercing resonance of the house phone. James looked at his wife and friends as he let it ring four times before plucking up the courage to grasp the receiver and pull it from its cradle.

The other three adults looked on in suspended hope that the caller may be about to reveal some positive news, yet such hope was increasingly being countered by negative expectation.

James swallowed a solid lump of trepidation before opening the exchange with the caller. He breathed deeply before placing the handset to his ear.

His side of the dialogue trembled across the room to the others; his voice laced with a combination of paternal anxiety and wavering optimism.

'Hello?'

'Yes…speaking.'

'Oh…hello, again.'

'Yes…we are all here.'

'Okay. No problem.'

'No…not yet…but we can do.'

'Yes…sure.'

'Okay. Ten o'clock.'

'See you soon.'

James gently replaced the receiver and reluctantly met with the stern expressions of his companions. With their rabid anticipation bearing down upon him, he attempted to sate their burning curiosity without prompt.

'That was the police. They want us to accompany them to school this morning. They'll be here at ten. We all need to attend. We have to ring work and tell them what's happening. Dave…can you take me back to yours for the car.'

Within minutes, James, David and Sharon had all informed their places of employment as to the developing situation.

Thankfully, all responses were avidly sympathetic, yet this gave minimal comfort as a prelude to the unpredictable day that lay ahead.

*****

It was exactly seven and a half minutes to ten when James finally prised his eyes away from the lounge wall, as the brightly daubed orange and yellow squad car pulled up behind the Leavesdon's silver Focus.

The same officers who had visited twelve hours earlier alighted their vehicle, donned their hats and moved tentatively toward the frontage of number twelve, where James duly greeted them at the front door without the necessity for knocking.

P.C. Rhodes removed his cap and hooked it under his arm.

W.P.C. Coombs offered her customary smile and greeting.

'Good morning, Mister Tompkins. How are you all?' asked the male officer.

James forced a half-smirk and nodded awkwardly.

'Okay…bearing up, I think. Just about. I take it the school are expecting us?'

'Of course. We've informed the Headmaster at Riverlands, Mister Ford, that we will be visiting to speak to him and assess the school security footage. He's expecting us.'

The officers were duly ushered through the hall into the lounge.

Sharon glared at the unwanted visitors with renewed angst burning through her veins.

'Has anything turned up?' she barked.

The male officer shook his head slowly.

'No…Mrs. Tompkins. Not as yet. A local neighbourhood enquiry will be commenced today. As I have just relayed to your husband, we're going to accompany you all to the school this morning to try and assess what may have happened to the boys after they vacated the school premises.'

Hazel rubbed her eyes before making a half-hearted plea.

'Do you have any suspicions as to what could have happened to them?'

P.C. Rhodes glanced at his colleague as he compiled a tactful reply.

'Not as yet, Mrs. Leavesdon. You must understand that our inquiry is barely in its infancy. Until we progress further and continue thoroughly with our procedures for a sustained period of time, we have no way of knowing what clues may arise.'

David held Hazel's hand as he dutifully expanded on his wife's query.

'But what do you think is the likely scenario?'

'Please…Mister Leavesdon…it's far too early to say and would be wholly inappropriate for me to try and speculate. You're asking me questions to which I can provide no discernible answer. The answers we need will hopefully present themselves over the next few hours.'

Sharon interrupted again with a more enforced demand.

'But these cases of missing children have occurred before, haven't they? You must have a gut feeling?'

P.C. Rhodes raised a hand to halt the onset of any further futile discussion on the issue.

'Please. Personal opinion is not in my remit. We're doing all we can. When you're all ready…let's get ourselves to the school.'

*****

James opted to drive Sharon, Hazel and David in the green Astra. Tightly gripping the wheel as he guided the car through Shireheath, the occupants barely noticed the surrounding traffic of the dispersing morning rush hour.

The attentions of all four parents focused firmly ahead on the police car that guided them toward Riverlands Secondary School.

A route through the town that had become so familiar during previous years; yet this particular journey was enshrouded in clogging apprehension, especially as the distant roofline of the school became fully visible.

Unusually, both cars managed to find parking spaces in Friar Road.

Nobody uttered a word as the two groups departed their vehicles and commenced the dreaded walk toward the school premises.

The white-painted gates and uneven architecture provided a stark and menacing motif of recent events.

The throng passed quietly through the gates and along the pathway to the main double doors. Adjacent classroom windows framed varying curious young faces observing the approaching visitors. Faces which were instantly called back to attention by their respective teachers.

Standing nervously in the foyer, Hazel could smell the scent of disinfectant on the floors. She glared at the receptionist on the other side of the glass as the police introduced themselves and announced the motive for their call.

In turn the stern-faced bespectacled woman behind the window rang to inform the Head and diverted her attention to the four parents positioned beyond the two officers.

Hazel continued to observe the clerk, whose increasing expression of concern needed no vocal accompaniment.

Within seconds Mister Ford had emerged from his office and beckoned the group to join him whilst making a request to the receptionist.

'Joyce…could you please ask for Mrs. Gray and Miss Doherty to come to my office? Just send them straight down, please. They've arranged temporary cover for their classes. It's all in hand.'

On entering the Headmaster's domain, Sharon immediately noticed the placards, certificates and awards that decorated the grey-painted walls. Four chairs had been assembled around the large desk as the Headteacher gestured for the parents to be seated.

James moved to the seat nearest to the window before offering it to W.P.C. Coombs.

'No, please...Mister Leavesdon. The chairs are for you. We'll stand.'

Within seconds, the congregation had convened in the now cramped office. Soon to join them were Mrs. Gray and Miss Doherty whose wary complexions appeared distinctly ashen in the face of such unusual company.

Teachers and parents shook hands and introductions were quickly meted. A discomforting silence was bestowed upon the room as P.C. Rhodes brought all present up to speed with the situation.

'Obviously, at this point we wish to confirm that the boys were in fact at school until three-thirty yesterday and then to analyse your security camera footage to try and establish where they may have gone afterwards.'

Mrs. Gray placed a hand to her mouth as the scenario quickly adopted an air of pure menace.

The Headmaster displayed a similar mask of concern which all four parents noticed immediately. His following statement offered little in the way of inspiration for those present.

'We do have closed circuit television, yes, but it may not be any use for the purposes of this situation. I can retrieve it here on my computer monitor. The camera is just outside reception, but only spans the foyer area. There is a second camera that covers the car park. But we don't have any adequate coverage beyond the main doors or entrance gate.'

Quickly selecting the relevant file on his lap-top, Mister Ford beckoned the police officers who moved closer to watch the grainy section of recording as the Headmaster continued with his explanation.

'You see, this is only really to monitor visitors. We don't really see the need to concern ourselves with any activity beyond the school premises. Well...there's never really *been* any need...not until now.'

Mister Ford's gaze cast itself somewhat guiltily at the two sets of parents perched opposite. All four held a mildly hopeful light in their eyes, yet somehow felt none the worse for hearing that their absent offspring may not be identifiable on film.

The police officers carefully scrutinised the screen as the Head utilized the mouse to search for the precise section of recording.

'Aah! Here we are. This is it!'

'This is yesterday at home-time, is it?' asked P.C. Rhodes.

'Yes...but...as you can see...it just looks exactly like what it is...a mass of moving pupils. They all look the same really, don't they?'

The Tompkins and Leavesdons scanned the unimpressed faces of the police officers as they in turn studied the grey and grainy images on the monitor.

P.C. Rhodes began to shake his head and fingered his moustache.

'This isn't much use. You're right. No one pupil is particularly distinguishable from another at the rate they're moving. I have to say, Mister Ford, that this coverage is pretty inadequate for a school of this size. Woefully inadequate, in fact.'

The Headmaster defended his position lamely.

'To be honest, the local authority has never considered such a facility to be a priority. They won't provide funding for expensive equipment if it isn't deemed absolutely necessary.'

Hazel broke her silence through trembling tones.

'If those boys don't turn up soon, Mister Ford, the local authority will have little option but to revise its school security measures. It's a bloody disgrace in this day and age. Unbelievable!'

David and James looked briefly at one another in a mutual plea for a way forward. Finally, James disclosed his feelings.

'So...what do we do now?'

The police officers shifted to a more suitable position in order to address the room. P.C. Rhodes folded his arms and paused before revealing his thoughts.

'We will continue with our enquiries and send copies of this footage to the station for re-analysis. It is highly likely that this afternoon I will be submitting the matter to my superiors with a request that setting up a missing persons' enquiry is the next stage of the procedure. A more intensive search and investigation of the local area will then be administered. At home time this afternoon officers will be despatched around the school gates to talk to anybody who may have seen anything unusual yesterday and then initiate a local door to door enquiry. To be honest, the school can help us little further at this stage and as such must not divulge any details or speculation at this moment.'

Mister Ford placed a hand on the shoulders of his female staff, both of whom had begun to wipe their eyes as P.C. Rhodes turned his attention to them.

'Ladies…is there anything you can think of at this point that might assist us? Did the boys mention anything during the day yesterday? Anywhere they might be going after school? The home of a classmate, perhaps?'

Both teachers shook their heads slowly in complete helplessness.

Miss Doherty tried to recall the previous day for the group.

'They seemed fine. Happy…messing about…just normal boys. But you have to understand that it was only the second day of term. I'd only just presented them with their new exercise books, yesterday. It's difficult to spot anomalies in kids that you don't even know.'

P.C. Rhodes nodded and offered a final glance of concession to the computer screen.

'Mister Ford…this discussion is totally confidential at this moment. We don't want a panic on our hands. This is a big school. Rumours can cause unrest and severely hinder any investigation.'

The Headmaster nodded with avid sincerity.

'Yes, yes of course. This situation will be treated with the strictest discretion. It goes without saying. We await your orders.'

Mrs Gray interrupted with a need for some urgent guidance.

'But what happens when the other pupils begin to ask questions? It's bound to happen? What are we allowed to say to them?'

'Be honest with them. You don't know where the boys are. It's as simple and truthful as that.'

P.C. Rhodes stark tone continued in his closing address to the four distraught parents.

'I need to assess the immediate plan with my superiors back at the station. I suggest that all of you go home and wait for instruction. It's highly likely that when you see the police again, it will be the investigative officer in charge of the search that will be speaking to you.'

*****

Departure from the school was intensely emotional and cloaked in immense despondency. All four parents conveyed their gratitude to the teachers before leaving the premises.

The journey back through Shireheath was coldly silent.

Hazel and David collected their car leaving the Tompkins to fester alone at Basford Lane.

At number thirty-nine, Cromford Road, Hazel entered the kitchen to make a drink, her entire mind and body increasingly tormented by constricting apprehension.

Filling the kettle, she gazed at the scene of the late summer morning in the back garden. She was already finding it a little easier to try and eclipse thoughts of her lost son.

To behold pleasant things; just to forget her inner pain for even a second or two.

But just as she managed to inject herself with a sense of calm, another sight brought the fear and emotion erupting back to the fore.

The small bag of potatoes and packet of beefburgers from the previous afternoon remained on the draining board.

Untouched.

Uncooked.

Unnecessary.

Dropping the kettle into the sink, she sank to her knees and cried out in an agonised wail of wrenching desire for her offspring, as a creeping possibility painted its increasingly desolate picture.

HELL

CHAPTER 11

It was impossible for Michael to ascertain the time of day as he tentatively peered through the shadows of the room. The aroma that assaulted his nasal passages comprised an unfamiliar mix of septic ingredients.

He hardly dared move as his vision slowly acquitted itself to the strange environment. Certain objects gradually conveyed a strain of normality. He identified a single wooden chair and bedside cabinet. An oval-shaped rug was strewn unevenly over the floorboards. A solitary framed painting hung on the wall near to the door, but its image was too vague for him to accurately decipher.

Having partially assessed his surroundings it was only then that his attention fell to his friend.

His best friend in the whole world.

Curled up on the bed opposite lay Peter; scared beyond constraint and staring wide-eyed back across the stench-filled void to meet with Michael's curious gaze.

The boys simply looked at one another as mutual, fearful confusion further embedded itself. The foreboding silence continued as very recent events began to relay themselves in Michael's mind.

Forcing himself up onto his elbows, Michael blinked as shafts of shredded light tantalised him from beyond the doorway and crudely blacked-out window. Peter remained with his head positioned into the pillow. He did not vocally acknowledge Michael, who quickly opted to pull himself upright and stand to his feet.

He was still dressed in his school uniform, but strangely his shoes had been removed and placed under the bed.

Listening intently for any sound from beyond the door, he advanced stealthily toward the bed that cradled his friend and crouched down to afford his voice to carry in a lowered tone.

Still Peter's gaze remained fixed firmly into the uncertain space beyond; his eyes did not respond to Michael's cautious approach.

Despite the semi-darkness, his blond hair still shone brightly, contrasting against the utter greyness of the room. Yet still he did not move a muscle as his friend finally broached an exchange.

'Hey…Peter…Peter…you okay?'

Michael's heart began to lurch as he endeavoured to encourage some form of response from his most favoured classmate. He glanced inquisitively around the small, dank space, looking for any indication of their location.

The very real probability struck him that the pair could be anywhere in the world at that moment.

Again, Michael's mind toiled with the time previous.

Yet the past few hours were fogged in his memory.

Leaving school yesterday - if indeed it was yesterday - had retained only brief elements of clarity.

Yet their subsequent movements remained confused and vague.

'Peter…talk to me…can you remember what happened?'

Then Michael himself suddenly recalled the man and woman in the alley as pieces of the puzzle came to the fore.

A white van with open doors.

A struggle.

Pain.

Puzzlement.

And now, a disconcerting, empty, nothingness.

Rising to his full height once again, Michael tip-toed across the threadbare rug to the solitary window which was shuttered from the outside.

A quick test also confirmed the window to be locked.

A closer inspection unveiled that it had actually been nailed shut.

His contemplation of their immediate predicament was interrupted by a sniffling sound from Peter's side of the bedroom. Michael resumed his former position and placed his head close to that of his pal.

Peter was now weeping gently into his pillow. Tears trickled down across the bridge of his nose and resided in a damp circular patch that grew under his right cheek.

'Peter…please…come on…talk to me…do you know where we are?'

Michael's chest continued to thump wildly as he laid a comforting hand on his friend's moistening face. Any communication was kept to minimal volume so as not to arouse their supposed enslavers.

Then another memory came back to life.

The woman; cracking his friend's skull onto the door of the van to dampen his vigorous defiance.

'Peter…is your head alright?'

Finally, Peter's eyes trained themselves away from the far wall and looked desperately into the piercing gaze of his school friend. With youthful terror etched into his expression, he summoned a simple request through bloated, reddened lips.

'Michael…I want my Mum.'

His tears resumed and began to gather audible momentum by the second. For some unknown reason, Michael began to adhere to an instinctive sense of security and a need to stay calm.

'Peter…ssh…try not to cry. I'm here. I'll look after you. Please don't cry. Please. I need you to be strong.'

Eventually succeeding in temporarily abating his friend's upset, Michael's attention was suddenly drawn to an unusual noise emanating from the adjacent room.

Initially it was a definitive feminine tone and the sound resembled nothing he had heard before in his life. A dull thudding accompanied the woman's intermittent wailing, which increased in volume and intensity by the second. Continuing to try and locate the source, Michael concluded that the thudding was an object making repeated contact with the wall behind Peter's headboard.

'Michael…what's that banging…I want my mum.'

Peter's repeated statement was ignored as Michael found himself intrigued by the dubious activity in the next room. And then as the competing noises seemingly reached their peak, an unsteady quiet prevailed once more.

Puzzled by the potential events elsewhere, Michael resumed his attention back to his friend.

'I don't know where your mum is just now, Peter. I don't know where my mum is either. I don't even know where we are.'

Peter slowly sat up and looked solemnly down to the bedclothes that lay strewn across his midriff.

'But …I need her. I need her…to change me.'

Michael stared into the cowering expression of his friend.

'What do you mean…change you?'

Peter diverted his attention back to the wall over Michael's shoulder and mumbled a confession.

‘Because…she’ll be angry…because…I think I’ve…I’ve…wet the bed…’

Urging his friend to move position, Michael quickly helped Peter out of the damp sheets and placed him to the middle of the room. Feeling the legs of his school uniform confirmed his friend’s shameful admission.

‘Okay, Peter…you’d better take off your trousers. I’ll look in those drawers over there for some more.’

Both boys were halted in their intentions by the sound of approaching footsteps from outside the room. Astutely observing the ominous shadow that danced at the illuminated crack under their door, Michael found himself transfixed by the impending visitor.

The boys were afforded no time to respond as the bedroom door was promptly unlocked from the outside and a menacing silhouette paraded itself before them.

The woman entered the room, switched on the light, and laid down two porcelain bowls on the bare floorboards.

‘Here. There’s no milk. We don’t want to hear a fucking peep. You understand? Uncle Tim won’t like it if he hears you whining.’

Adjusting to the sudden illumination, Michael’s blinking gaze bore into the skinny female figure that seemed to tower above them. She was attired only in black, lace underwear that hardly left anything to the imagination. Her bony structure was improved little by way of such decoration. Indeed, it only served to heighten the overly lean appearance of her shoulders and hips.

The obvious alarm and posture of her captives as they perched in the middle of the rug compelled the woman to press for some answers.

‘What the fuck you two doing out of bed anyway? Why are you crouching there…like that? Like a couple of fucking puppies?’

Peter’s embarrassment forced him to look down to the floor, yet Michael’s resolve only hardened in the face of such aggressive scrutiny.

He considered his options before revealing Peter’s accident to the scrawny woman.

‘My friend…he needs…some…some…clean clothes…’

Rapidly coming to her own conclusions as to the motive for the boy’s request, the woman’s tone altered dramatically as she moved to the bed that Peter had vacated. Swiping an open palm across the mattress, she turned to face her quarry with an expression of amused disgust.

'Dirty…little…bastard! You dirty…little tramp! Wait until Uncle Tim finds out! He'll go up the fucking wall, he will! Dirty…smelly…little…fucker…'

Now afforded closer proximity, Michael studied the display of her yellowed and uneven teeth which may have sometime counted as a smile but more often only a grimace of displeasure. Stomping her way past the boys, she switched off the light, exited the room and slammed the door behind her before turning the key in the lock.

Peter and Michael gazed at one another through the resumed semi-darkness in growing wariness of what was to follow.

'She's angry at me isn't she, Michael? But I didn't mean to do it. Honestly. I didn't mean it. I haven't wet the bed for ages! Please tell her Michael! Please tell her!'

Placing his hands on his friend's shoulders to steady him could not allay the onset of more distress. Peter sobbed as he wrestled to remove his trousers.

Seconds later the sound of footsteps could be heard to approach the bedroom door once again. This time the imprint was heavier and more determined than previously.

This time, the visitor was Uncle Tim.

The door was unlocked and duly pushed open with such force that it collided into the adjacent wall. The tall man walked into the bedroom with a leering swagger; a cigarette hanging from between his lips.

Michael recognised him immediately.

It was the man from outside the school.

The man at the end of the alleyway.

The man on the mobile phone.

And a subsequent realisation then cemented itself in his head as his memory gradually recalled the skinny woman who was also in the alleyway.

Michael's confusion had now ceased.

His mind was capable and clear.

Despite all the warnings and precautions that had been administered for as long as they could recall, the two boys had been taken against their will. Their Mums and Dads were quite right.

Bogeymen did exist after all.

And for the first time in their young, innocent lives, Michael and Peter found themselves in the company of a fully grown living specimen of such a creature.

'SO WHICH ONE OF YOU LITTLE CUNTS HAS PISSED HIS SELF? IS IT YOU?'

Michael did not reply to the imposing aggressor who stood swaying unsteadily before them in his boxer shorts. He noticed the man's thin and gangly frame.

His long fingers.

The hooked nose and snarling mouth.

The image of physical repulsion that he studied carefully had now been ingrained in his mind.

For eternity.

'WELL? WHAT ABOUT YOU...FATBOY? HEY? SPEAK TO ME! ARE YOU THE DIRTY LITTLE LAZY BASTARD?'

The man's scathing tone forced Peter to nod with reluctance. Cowering in his underpants, the eleven-year-old began to shake with fright as the acidic tirade continued.

'DO YOU KNOW WHAT MY DAD USED TO DO TO ME IF I EVER PISSED MY SELF?'

Peter's shake of the head as he tried to restrain further tears only invited a severe slap across the face. The impact sent Peter reeling off balance. Michael stood and watched through gritted teeth as his vulnerable friend succumbed to the man's ensuing wrath.

'HE WOULD MAKE ME WEAR GIRL'S CLOTHES! YES! THAT'S WHAT THE CUNT DID TO ME! MADE ME WEAR A FUCKING DRESS! AND DO YOU KNOW SOMETHING, FATBOY? IT FUCKING CURED ME! I NEVER PISSED THE BED AGAIN! SO, I RECKON THAT'S WHAT YOU NEED! A FROCK! YOU...FUCKING...DIRTY...LAZY...LITTLE...GIRL!'

Peter's uncontrolled wailing forced him to curl up once again into a feebly protective posture. But the verbal hurricane continued as Michael registered every single derogatory word said against his best friend.

'SHUT UP THAT FUCKING GIRLY SOBBING OR I'LL CUT YOUR FUCKING TONGUE OUT! NOW...GET YOUR CLOTHES OFF! AND I MEAN FUCKING EVERYTHING! DO IT! NOW!'

With terror clawing at his every nerve, Peter trembled as he slowly discarded his uniform and underwear as their ferocious captor stood by and grimaced inanely at the display.

The man flicked cigarette ash onto Peter's naked form before gathering up the garments and moving back to the doorway.

'RIGHT! EAT YOUR FUCKING BREAKFAST! AND IF THERE'S ANY LEFT OVER I'LL FUCKING FEED IT TO YOU MYSELF!'

Uncle Tim left the boys in the room.

The door was duly slammed and locked once again.

Michael's futile yet warranted inner anger was now brimming.

He watched his quivering, naked best friend striving to cover himself with a bed sheet before reaching for one of the breakfast bowls.

Michael followed suit, quickly realising that the vessels contained nothing more than dry cereal. As he studied his shaking friend attempt to eat a handful of cornflakes, further footsteps were heard returning beyond the door.

The familiar click of the latch was followed by the entrance of the woman carrying a short length of dark material.

She grabbed Peter and easily wrestled him to the floor after thumping the back of his neck as he ate. Resistance would prove totally ineffective as his weeping eyes were blindfolded.

Michael so wanted to help his best friend yet felt utterly powerless. Any aggressive reaction to events on his part could place them both in severe jeopardy.

The odds were totally against them and mounting beyond retrieval.

He could do little but stare in disbelieving shock as Peter was then pulled to his feet by his blond hair and, still completely naked, vigorously ushered from the room.

'MICHAEL! HELP ME! MICHAEL! NO! MICHAEL!'

Peter's departing plea was ended with the slam of the door and the click of the latch. Michael listened intently.

Then another distinctive cry for help could be heard from outside the building. Moving quickly to the window Michael tried to glimpse the developing episode through the narrow slats. To his amazement, Peter's punishment was available to view in the full.

Squinting into the shafts of sunlight, he watched as his friend was escorted across a gravel yard surrounded by green fields. Unclothed and now blindfolded, he was ordered to stand still.

The woman re-appeared in frame, perched herself next to him and set down what appeared to be a bucket containing water. The man also entered the fray.

Standing to one side with hands on hips he gave her the order to begin.

Retrieving a scrubbing brush from the bucket, she ruthlessly set about Peter's body.

Peter's immediate reaction was one of screaming agony as the woman utilised the brush across every section of his tender, defenceless skin. Completely unable to view the incoming punishment, Peter could only succumb to the torture with regular shrieks of intense pain and numerous feeble attempts to belatedly deflect any assault.

His flesh slowly began to redden and sore as he writhed under the merciless attack.

And all the while, Michael simply watched.

And digested every sickening moment of his best friend's indeterminable, agonising sufferance.

Then in conclusion to the display, the man finally moved across the yard to join the pair and proceeded to hold Peter's arms tightly behind his back by his elbows. The woman in turn then concentrated her efforts to supposedly cleanse Peter's groin.

Both adults visibly shouted at Peter as the penalty was administered but their words were muffled by the sealed bedroom window.

So vigorously did she apply the brush, that Peter's visible crescendo of tears was now reduced to mere whimpers of submissive agony.

Michael wiped his salting eyes as the savage ritual thankfully found its end. He slowly backed away from the window and contemplated the unflinching horror just witnessed.

And a theory gradually began to manifest itself in his young, capable mind.

Peter had supposedly offered them a reason for their despicable actions.

In wetting the bed, he had apparently flagged up a motive to inspire them into engaging such brutality.

Maybe having learned such a theory would stand the boys in good stead for the immediate future. Perhaps without provocation, the aggressors would have no motive.

As he perused the logical flashes of thought, the door was pushed open and Peter was returned to the bedroom with his blindfold removed.

Thrown to the floor, he flailed before Michael. His flesh was rendered crimson, in places bleeding and raw. Open sores were visible along his legs and arms. Exposed new skin glistened painfully scarlet.

Michael crouched on the oval rug as his best friend quietly wept before him.

Then the final insult was thrown onto proceedings.

The man tossed a pair of white cotton socks and a blue chequered dress towards Peter's limp and ailing form. Michael instinctively looked up at the man, who simply smirked and lit another cigarette.

His tone was now calmer having seemingly sated his sadistic appetite.

For now, at least.

'Tell fat-boy to get dressed when he's through with whimpering. Any more accidents like that and he'll get dragged outside for a wash again.'

Peter buried his head into the rug and issued a resounding, desperate plea into the floorboards. His weakly formed fist of fury landed repeatedly into the underbelly of fate.

'I WANT MY MUM! I WANT MUM!'

The man simply drew on his smoke and offered some menacing assurances as he swayed in the doorway.

'Believe me, girls…mummy ain't fucking coming! You've seen the last of her! And she's seen the last of you!'

Michael continued to stare at the man; ensuring to further ingrain the features of a monster deep into his memory.

The bedroom door sealed once again with a resounding slam, leaving two eleven-year-old boys alone to contemplate their future and the nature of the peril that had encompassed them.

CHAPTER 12

Friday; twelve-forty-five p.m.

Four extremely nervous adults awaited the arrival of the squad car and lost within the maelstrom of their individual thoughts, each stared without word, desperate for any inspiration that might materialise from beyond the lounge window. The Tompkins and Leavesdons had been contacted by the police an hour earlier and required to convene at number twelve, Basford Lane for one o'clock.

When the officers finally arrived, Hazel and Sharon offered one another brief glances which conveyed both deep reservation and fleeting hope.

James opened the door and solemnly nodded to the visitors.

'Afternoon again, officers. Please…come through.'

P.C. Rhodes and W.P.C. Coombs moved determinedly through the hallway and politely declined the offer of a drink. They took the seats that had been vacated for them and settled themselves among the cautious parental throng.

Unlike their inaugural visit to the Tompkins' home nearly fifteen hours earlier, neither officer displayed a facade of even mildly positive interpretation.

Two mothers and two fathers watched under the strain of shredding anticipation as the policeman and policewoman removed their headwear and in a cold tone of authority, proceeded with an update on the matter at hand.

P.C. Rhodes eyed his audience tentatively before commencing the latest disclosure.

'Mister and Mrs. Tompkins…Mister and Mrs Leavesdon…the current situation is this. As yet, we have had no concrete sightings or any thread of a tangible lead regarding the possible whereabouts of Michael and Peter. We have spoken to local residents this morning who could add nothing to what we already know. After further scrutiny of the CCTV footage, we are now discounting this piece of potential evidence. The boys certainly left the premises at home time yesterday, but no one can confirm seeing either Peter or Michael after this point.'

Hazel immediately began to panic and did not hold back in venturing her concerns.

'What? Nothing? Nobody in the street saw *anything*? I cannot believe it! Someone must have seen them! It was school kick-out time! It was broad bloody daylight for Christ's sake! There were people everywhere, surely?'

P.C. Rhodes nodded before tracing his moustache with a forefinger as he contemplated his next words.

'Mrs. Leavesdon…our units are preparing to begin more in-depth house to house enquiries around the immediate neighbourhood. You must understand that people's memories can be unreliable in situations such as this. When asked to recollect certain periods of time, aspects that are not presently deemed important may well arise to the individual at a later date.'

Sharon was not about to be blinded by the apparent attempt to convey excuses.

The passage of time was now becoming a critical factor.

In growing desperation, her voice began to falter as she pleaded for more decisive action.

'But…my boy…our boys…have been gone for nearly a whole day, officer! Nearly twenty-four hours! How long do we wait for the memory lapses to end? Another day? A week? A year? More needs to be done now! This minute! We're all going stir crazy just sitting here waiting!'

The two officers eyed one another before P.C. Rhodes continued to clarify the scenario.

'Please…Mrs. Tompkins…let us all try to understand one vital factor to this. Any strand of information may fall into our hands at any time…for any reason. We cannot predict what it will be or when it will happen. We just have to continue with our current procedure and hope that a significant breakthrough is on the cards. Believe you me…when a breakthrough is uncovered…events will quickly accelerate.'

Wallace peered tentatively through the conservatory doors as he observed the mysterious meeting unfold on the other side of the glass.

James glanced back toward the ever-curious German Shepherd before intervening with a query of his own.

'What is being made of the boys' whereabouts at this time?'

The policeman appeared confused by the question.

'In what respect, Mister Tompkins?'

James paused for breath before explaining in simpler terms.

‘I mean…what is the usual police reaction to such a situation?’

P.C. Rhodes hesitated momentarily as if his response was about to cause an increase in the families’ rapidly growing consternation.

Shuffling in his chair, he conveyed a surprising disclosure.

‘I am duty bound to inform you that my superiors are now actively involved in this case and are becoming increasingly concerned for the welfare of the boys. Firstly…because there is…as I have said, no discernible clue that might suggest where they may be at this time. With many similar cases these days we would begin by tracking their mobile phones…this is obviously out of the question. But CID is particularly curious because they have disappeared simultaneously.’

James grimaced at the officer’s scant reasoning whilst pressing for expansion through a tone of paternal alarm.

‘Well…we know this already, don’t we? They left school together. It surely stands to reason that they are still going to be together somewhere. Well? Doesn’t it?’

W.P.C. Coombs continued to remain silent, keeping due vigil on the parents as her male colleague tactfully responded to the justified barrage of scrutiny.

‘Yes…Mister Tompkins…we can logically assume that the boys are still in direct contact with one another. But there is also a distinct possibility that they may have become separated at some point.’

Hazel snapped again at the officer’s apparent lack of urgency.

‘So, what are you saying? That they could have run away together as some kind of plan? That this is a stupid game they dreamed up as some kind of a sick joke?’

P.C. Rhodes again shifted uneasily in his chair; discomfort dressed his features as he elaborated.

‘Mrs. Leavesdon…we have assessed the very minimal evidence involved. What I am about to suggest is going to sound unavoidably blunt but is a necessary possibility for us all to consider.’

All four parents gave the officer their full attention as he carefully deliberated on his choice of words.

‘C.I.D. is becoming persuaded to the possibility that Michael and Peter were taken against their will. The strange thing is…taking one child is far easier than taking two. It is quite possible, if they were abducted, that it occurred very close to the school and from there the boys have since been transferred to an unknown location.’

Hazel placed a hand to her mouth as a shroud of shock began to descend in the room.

Sharon squeezed James' hand tightly as emotion recommenced its steady eruption.

David opted to try and understand the theory just conveyed.

'So…is that the suspicion, officer? That the boys have been taken? Why should you think so? You must have some evidence to suggest this?'

Yet again P.C. Rhodes attempted to maintain his composure despite the upset that was gathering momentum before his eyes.

'If the boys found trouble at any distance away from the school it would likely have found interruption from witnesses, and we would be dealing with a very different scenario. In other words, someone would have seen something. However, at the moment, Mister Leavesdon…this is only a theory. But…without any substantial evidence to suggest otherwise…we are treating this as a worst-case scenario. Now…because of these concerns, we have decided to escalate our normal mode of operation. As you are all aware, the school security footage has offered little scope. CCTV in the nearby area has been checked and has also revealed nothing unduly suspicious.'

James cradled Sharon as she limply coiled into his embrace.

With his own voice now quaking with dread, Michael's father demanded more answers.

'But Officer Rhodes…the public aren't even aware that Peter and Michael are gone? I'm really confused. I want to know what your men are going to do to find our boys!'

P.C. Rhodes paused for breath before detailing the brief he had been given.

'C.I.D. will be imminently fully involved, sir. For the moment, as I have said, this is being treated as possible abduction. They are aware that the boys are potentially extremely vulnerable and as such…may well come to some harm. A team of forensic officers will be located at the school tonight once the children have been dismissed. We have been granted authority to close the school until next Tuesday at least. That gives us three whole days in which to examine the area without disruption and help minimise any undue panic.'

Hazel shook her head as the tears fell relentlessly.

David held his wife tightly into his chest as she rocked and wept in a spiralling void of helplessness.

'Oh God! Not my Peter. Not my baby! God no! I want my baby back! David…bring my baby back! I can't do this. It's not happening! Not to us. David…find my Peter…'

Hazel's descent into a pit of utter despair caused Sharon to follow-on with her own submission to inevitable distress.

As the scenario rapidly dissolved into a swollen tide of raw grief, both police officers stared respectfully to the floor as the two sets of parents searched in vain for some strand of comfort.

Several minutes elapsed before the Tompkins and the Leavesdons retained their composure and offered their full attention back to the officers sitting patiently before them.

James eventually summoned the strength to demand what possible role they could play as parents.

'I have been informed that the official search will begin today. A superior officer has been assigned and will need to take official statements from all of you before he can commence a wider inquiry.'

Hazel wiped her eyes and engaged with the stoic expressions of the officers seated opposite.

'There must be something more we can do?'

P.C. Rhodes nodded and invited his female colleague to speak.

Swallowing a solid lump of jagged reservation, Police Constable Stacey Coombs addressed the parents.

'It is highly likely that the assigned D.I. will request recent photographs of the boys. I suggest you find the latest images you have to hand. These portraits can then be immediately circulated to other county constabularies.'

David sat up and stared directly at the female officer through his diluted gaze.

'What…what do you mean…nationally? Up and down the country, you mean?'

W.P.C. Coombs nodded in reluctant confirmation as she expanded on her instructions.

'Yes…Mister Leavesdon. The D.I. is also likely to request that you all attend a media conference to make a plea to the regional public on the boys' behalf. Knowing D.I. Woodley…he has already made arrangements for this.'

Four parents gazed in pure bewilderment at one another.

‘You’re…you’re really…concerned about the boys…aren’t you…?’

The male officer’s reply did not directly answer David’s question.

‘We are treating the situation with extreme urgency. Priority number one…yes. Those boys have disappeared, and it is our job to find them. We need to utilise every means available to trace their whereabouts. This…as my colleague has just explained…will directly involve the four of you in the initial stages.’

The two police officers stood to their feet and replaced their headwear.

‘We are going back to school now to administer the request for closure in order that the pupils can be notified before they leave the premises this afternoon. We shall leave you to sort out the photographs. Someone will collect them this afternoon. Rest assured we’ll be back in touch very soon.’

*****

One forty-eight pm; precisely.

Two squad cars pulled up in Friar Road outside the white painted gates of Riverlands Secondary School. A pair of escorting male officers stood by the entrance as P.C. Rhodes and W.P.C. Coombs strode along the landscaped pathway just as they had done a few hours earlier.

Requesting an urgent communication with Mister Ford, the officers waited at the reception window whilst the bespectacled lady behind the glass rapidly obliged their order.

Occasional curious glances from passing pupils and teachers alike were unacknowledged. P.C. Rhodes’ stern glare along the brightly lit corridor did not falter as the Headmaster briskly approached and offered a hand of greeting.

‘Hello, again. No news is there?’

‘Not as yet, Mister Ford. May we speak in private?’

In the Head’s office, the trio seated themselves and the intentions of the police were conveyed.

Mister Ford checked his watch.

‘Right. I’ve got an hour and a half. I’ll get Joyce to type something up quickly and get the letters distributed to each classroom a.s.a.p.’

‘Yes, of course.’ replied P.C. Rhodes. ‘We greatly appreciate your assistance. As you can now rightly assume…this matter is steadily becoming critical.’

The Headmaster sat back in his chair and slowly shook his head.

‘How are the parents holding out?’

W.P.C. Coombs was offered the chance to respond.

‘They are predictably emotional and confused. Shock is typically the major reaction. But the reality is that the complete lack of information is a real stumbling block at this moment in time. It’s rapidly going to make the situation increasingly desperate.’

With an expression of sorrow, the Headmaster leaned forward and rested his elbows on the desk.

‘And you will need statements from whom on the staff roll?’

P.C. Rhodes checked his notes before confirming.

‘Mrs. Gray. Miss Doherty. And the caretaker. But once the investigative officer is on the scene I can take those. They are just formalities. It will give the enquiry team a solid base to work from. The facts are sparse at the minute, but this is exactly why C.I.D. need to know absolutely everything there is to know at the outset.’

A prolonged silence enveloped the room before Mister Ford broached the necessary requirements of the letter to pupils.

‘Just inform the parents that for Monday at least the school will be closed for say…inspection…and should be re-opened as normal on Tuesday morning. There is nothing more we can reveal at this moment that won’t encourage unwarranted speculation. Let’s get the kids out of here happy. We don’t want to set the seeds of concern just yet. After all, those boys might just turn up by the weekend.’

The Headmaster offered the pair of officers a knowing glare before clarifying another strand of the plan.

‘Which streets are your team going to be searching?’

‘Well obviously they’ll be utilising portable flood-lamps overnight, so we aim to keep it thorough and pretty short range. Friar Road…Clumber Street and St John Street to begin with. It’s not preferable for them to wait until daylight tomorrow, although they will re-check all areas again in the morning.’

The Head grimaced as another thought crossed his mind.

‘Do you believe there is the chance somebody has taken the boys off the street from under our noses?’

The steely glint in the eyes of both officers suggested they were now dedicated to such likelihood.

'If our worst suspicions are proved correct, the boys' possible abduction could not have occurred too far away from the school grounds. Peter's mother is convinced she was here at the school gates by four o'clock at the latest. Somebody would have seen something obvious if they had strayed to the main road and beyond.'

The Head was not convinced.

'But officer…nobody is actually aware that the boys are missing, yet?'

'No. The parents have made that very same point. That is correct. But as I have explained to them, if there was a very visible fracas or any kind of accident or incident then any potential perpetrator would likely have been deterred from their intentions. You might find this surprising in this day and age, but we still tend to find that witnesses will invariably report anything that appears unusual.'

An empty silence accompanied the Headmaster's growing sense of foreboding.

All three stood to their feet and shuffled uneasily from the room.

Just before leaving the building, the officers turned back toward the foyer and conveyed one final piece of advice.

'Mister Ford…one more thing…inform your key colleagues only of the current situation. They have the right to know what is happening if only for the sake of discretion. But do not court their natural speculation. Inform them of the facts and tell them to stay at home until Tuesday morning. Hopefully…by then…this matter may well have been resolved anyway. D.I. Woodley will be here shortly to brief you fully on what is to happen later today.'

The Head found he could add nothing more to uplift morale in such dire circumstances.

Through the double glass doors of the school entrance, he watched with sincere disbelief at unfolding events as the police hurriedly left the school grounds and made their way back to their cars.

*****

Four-thirty-one; exactly.

Euan Ford entered the bustling staff room which instantly ceased its typical rumble of chatter. With an unsteady peace quickly prevailing, the Headmaster stood before the twenty-four teachers present and swallowed dryly as he began the announcement.

'Ladies and gentlemen…thank you for attending this rather belated extraordinary staff meeting…but events of the past hours have in themselves been distinctly extraordinary by nature.'

A wave of confused whispers drifted across the room before quiet descended once again.

'As you will now be aware, the school has been requested to close tonight…and re-open for normal business on Tuesday morning. I apologise for the short notice…but this request has been ventured by the police.'

Further grumblings emitted from the pack as the Head prompted for their attention. His eyes fell to two teachers in particular, whose expressions of sheer despair would remain with him for the duration of the evening and beyond.

'I need to inform you fully of the circumstances at this time. I have been authorised by the police to give you all the facts. Please do not ask me questions…as sadly…I have no answers to give you…at the moment.'

The Head waited patiently to ensure that everybody's concentration was poised on what he was about to reveal.

'Peter Leavesdon and Michael Tompkins…two of our Year Seven influx…were reported missing by their parents yesterday evening. Now, I am well aware that these boys will be unfamiliar to the great majority of you. We are absolutely certain that they left these premises at three-thirty yesterday…but their current whereabouts is causing increasing concern…especially for the police. Hence, there will be a thorough search of the surrounding streets which will commence as soon as possible this evening and will no doubt eat into much of the weekend.'

Mister Ford halted his speech due to the cutting resonance of upset that had crept into the room.

Miss Doherty and Mrs Gray had tried in vain to contain their emotions, but the harsh reality of the announcement had defeated them whilst leaving their colleagues completely dumbstruck.

As a welcome counter to the ensuing distress, an enquiring voice raised itself from the rear of the room.

'What do they think has happened to the boys, Euan?'

Another prolonged period of mutterings emitted until silence resumed. The Headmaster struggled to compose himself as his staff anxiously awaited the reply.

'The police are very concerned…as there has been no trace of the boys' movements after leaving school yesterday.'

The same voice sounded again; this time pressing for some expansion on the supposed truth.

'I'm sorry to convey such downbeat suspicion, ladies and gentlemen…but due to the complete mystery surrounding the boys' apparent disappearance at this time…the police are treating this matter…as a possible abduction investigation.'

The staff room suddenly choked on inherent fear and cautious reservation as Mister Ford closed his statement.

'Any more questions will now be pointless. You now know…as much as I do. And please…do not confer this information beyond these walls until I am given clear permission for you to do so. I suggest that you make your way home. I shall wait for the police unit to arrive back here imminently.'

Another female tone of alarm emerged from the middle of the worried throng.

'There must be something we can do, Euan? This is awful news for all of us. We must be able to help in some way?'

The Head waited for hush to prevail once again and attempted to offer his fellow teachers a word of reassurance.

'There is only one present course of action for anyone connected with this school at this time. Let us all be united in the hope that this horrible situation is brought to an end quickly, and that those boys are back in the classroom with us as soon as possible. Good evening, to you all. I'm sorry to send you all to your weekends with such negative news. I'll see you again…all being well…on Tuesday morning. By then…hopefully…there should be some more information available.'

The Headmaster departed the renewed murmurings of the staff room and returned to the now tarnished sanctity of his office.

Moving across to the large window that overlooked the white painted entry gates, he could not help but succumb to the mindset that had also befallen two sets of distraught parents.

The simple humane concern for the safety of two, absent, eleven-year-old boys; and the soul-numbing realisation that events were possibly adopting an ever more sinister slant with each passing minute.

CHAPTER 13

Friday; six thirty-five pm.

Michael stared intermittently through the slats whilst studying the half dozen or so dead flies that lay strewn along the windowsill. Dusk was slowly approaching washing the late summer blue sky with a slightly darker hue.

His mind constantly toiled with the reasons for his presence in that place.

The boys had been left to their own devices for much of the day, which looked as if it had been relatively sunny, although the view through the shutter offered minimum vantage.

The aroma that occupied the bedroom had become more potent as time had elapsed. Far from becoming accustomed to the acrid stench, Michael had endeavoured to identify its increasingly offensive concoction and possible source, concluding that perhaps a drain was blocked somewhere.

Aside from his nose and eyes working overtime, his ears had become readily attuned to the silence that they had endured during the previous hours. Now even the faintest movements beyond the bedroom door served to alert his attention.

Then a feint and pained voice carried across the room to disturb his meditation.

'Michael…it hurts…it hurts me bad. And I'm hungry.'

Michael turned slowly to watch his friend walk unsteadily across the room. Peter had lain in bed for much of the time since the assault at breakfast. His skin still throbbed scarlet and looked intensely raw. But much of the stark evidence had been concealed by the clothing that he had been forced to wear by way of a supposed remedy for his nocturnal accident.

For a best friend, it was indeed a pathetic image to behold.

Peter's adolescent and chubby frame, adorned in a navy-blue chequered school dress and white ankle socks. The fact that he winced with each and every step across the threadbare oval rug exemplified his continuing physical plight.

'Michael…I want to take this off. It feels silly! Why are they making me dress like a girl, Michael? Why did they hurt me?' he whimpered.

Michael looked his friend in the eye and conveyed a learned warning.

'It's a test, Peter. To see if you'll do as you're told. Keep the dress on. If you don't, you'll make them angry again. Then they'll hurt you again.'

Peter glanced across to the bedroom door and whispered a venomous declaration under his breath.

'I hate them! I hate both of them! Wait 'til my dad gets here. They'll see who kicks ass, then. Won't they?'

Michael did not reply as he contemplated the jarring visions of home life that had suddenly flashed across his mind.

Images that were symbolic of the loving family comfort that he had rightly taken for granted over the eleven years of his entire young life.

The abiding sensation of domestic security that customarily enveloped his being, now felt so alien and so detached from their current circumstances. Gazing at his favourite pal's destitute and desolate appearance once again, Michael then observed his own attire.

Still in his brand-new school uniform worn only for two days, he recalled his mother giggling mischievously whilst taking photographs of him before the first day at secondary school.

Thoughts of his parents encouraged a swell of piercing emotion which threatened to disperse his purposely nurtured inner calm.

Instead, Michael fought the tempting lure of self-pity.

Despite the fearful confusion in which the boys had been immersed, another glance to his friend confirmed at least one factor of their predicament.

Peter was infinitely the more vulnerable of the two.

And as Michael watched his blond-haired pal reluctantly urinate into the over-spilling plastic bowl that had been unceremoniously provided, he wondered whether he might afford to offer any defence should the demons beyond the door return to haunt them.

And then, as if his mind had been read, Michael's quiet contemplation of the next stage of their nightmare was instantly shattered as footsteps approached from outside.

As per the recent custom, the latch clicked and the bedroom door swung forcefully open.

Her stick-thin silhouette framed by a yellowish half-light; the woman staggered in the doorway as though drunk.

Both boys turned and observed the figure and waited in silence for the next ordainment.

Stumbling across the floor toward them, she clasped each boy at the back of the neck and applied enough pressure to incur mutual expressions of discomfort.

Her command hissed above their heads as she pushed and pulled them.

'Okay girls…time for tea! Uncle Tim's got something really special lined up. You can eat with us tonight! Now shift your fucking arses!'

Forcibly escorting her captives from the bedroom and along a narrow passageway, the woman continued to walk with an unsteady stride. To accompany the march, she cackled whilst administering intermittent forefingers into each boy's back to usher their movement.

A small window in the passageway presented a brief and blurred view of the scene outside. Michael tried desperately to identify the image, which was a blurred mixture of green landscape and greying skies.

The thought was reaffirmed in his head that he and Peter could have been taken anywhere in the world.

A door coated in flaking brown paint was half open and emitted the welcoming sound of a television set. Stopping her quarry in the passageway, the woman poked her head through the gap in the doorway and murmured something inaudible to the occupant.

In turn, the response she received was similarly muffled but evidently accommodating as both boys were pulled by their upper arms and deposited into the room.

As Peter's emotions began to stir once more, Michael registered the unappealing sight before him.

A sparsely furnished kitchen was denoted by a metal stove thickly coated with soot. A filth-laden sink-top sat inside an unwashed section of work surface. The portable colour television was perched on a chair in the corner beneath a window which was loosely lined with lace netting.

In the centre of the kitchen, a large rectangular wooden table was flanked by three chairs.

Upon one of which perched the gnarled figure of the man who had supposedly orchestrated proceedings together with his female accomplice. He sneered at the flickering TV screen as a cigarette drooped lazily from between his lips.

Adorned only in his underwear, he swivelled position in the chair to greet the unwitting guests and smirked.

'Hello, girls! Sit yourselves down! You're just in time for dinner! My glamorous assistant will serve you your heart's desires. By the way, porky…that dress don't half suit you!'

The man and woman laughed heartily at the humourless quip. Michael looked at Peter and saw his eyes beginning to well with the combination of embarrassment and fear.

The fury was now burning so deeply for his best friend.

But Michael would hold true to his theory on the despicable captors that snarled and swooped before his eyes.

Neither boy opted to speak as they were sat opposite one another and stared down at the grime-lathered tabletop. The woman moved around and behind them before depositing a large glass jug of what looked to be water into the middle of the table. Next came two bowls of what Michael could only barely identify.

The man removed the cigarette from his mouth and held it between thumb and forefinger. The toxic rasp of his voice alerted both youngsters to the next round of entertainment as he flicked ash onto the floor.

'Eat your oats girls. Make you grow big and strong. Just like your daddies!'

Again, the man chortled and drew deeply on his smoke before continuing with the taunts.

'I'm sure it's not your favourite…but mummy hasn't been shopping yet…SO IT WILL HAVE TO FUCKING MAKE DO!'

Peter and Michael jumped simultaneously in their seats as the man's voice violently altered in pitch.

'Now…be good little girls and eat up all your food. I want those bowls emptied! The water might just soften things up for you both a little…make it go down easier.'

Still laughing, the man rose to his feet and floated toward the woman. Placing an arm around her waist and a kiss directly on her lips, he turned back to his young prisoners and displayed a crazed, lust-fuelled grin.

'We'll be back in half an hour, girls. Remember what I said about those oats. I want them all gone…OR ELSE…'

The kitchen door slammed shut behind them and the sound of footsteps gradually diminished.

Peter looked solemnly at the bowl of beige coloured powder and centred his gaze across to his friend.

'Why… why are they doing this to us?'

Michael's inert state of shock regarding events had not allowed him the clarity of mind to analyse their situation too deeply up until that moment.

Searching vainly for the elusive answer to his friend's innocent query, he succumbed to simple stark honesty.

'I don't know, Peter. I…just don't know…'

Peter left his chair and moved around the table to join Michael. His whispers gamely fended off the trepidation that laced his next question.

'Why are they doing this to *us*, though? Have we been naughty? Did our mums and dads send us here? I can't remember being naughty. Can you?'

Bravely fending off his own verging upset, Michael placed two hands on each of Peter's shoulders and embraced his friend's naivety.

A quick glance at the door confirmed it was safe to continue the conversation.

'They are very nasty people. They are real life bogeymen. Did your mum and dad ever talk to you about stranger danger?'

Peter's eyes widened as he nodded.

'Well…these are the kind of people that we were warned against. They have brought us here, Peter. They've kidnapped us. Mum and Dad didn't want you to come to this place. Our parents are probably looking for us now. And they'll find us, Peter…believe me…they'll find us.'

The conversation was interrupted as the kitchen door flew open and clattered into the conscience of the two captives.

'CAUGHT YOU! YOU LITTLE FUCKERS!'

The man ambled into the room carrying a can of beer in one hand and a fresh cigarette in the other. Placing both items onto the work-top next to the sink, he turned to face his startled prey.

'What did I say about the food? Must be eaten by the time I'm back? Well…here I am…and there is the food. TUT-TUT-TUT! Naughty little girls…'

Michael could do little to prevent his friend from supplying a typically instant retort.

'You said half an hour! It hasn't been half an hour! You're too early! You cheated!' volleyed Peter in anger.

The man's expression altered from one of sly amusement to a mask of abject distaste. Michael clenched his fists under the table as he sensed Peter's increasing vulnerability about to be exposed once more.

In a split second, the back of Peter's head was clamped by the man's vice-like grip and he was hauled back around the other side of the table. With his free hand, the man emptied some of the water into the bowl of oats and swiftly mixed the concoction with his dirt ingrained fingers.

Peter vainly attempted to struggle but it was obvious that the physical battle was only ever to have one victor.

Michael stared in distressed silence as Peter's shouts for mercy were instantly ceased by the man's grimy fist which rammed a handful of porridge into the youngster's mouth.

The man then forced Peter's head down into the bowl, completely submerging his face and quickly cutting off his air supply. Strands of blond hair breached through the man's bony fingers as he towered over his drowning, flailing victim.

The torture endured for second after relentless second, with Michael torn between direct intervention or maintaining his steady composure so as not to exacerbate matters.

A full twenty seconds elapsed as Peter's defensive responses gradually weakened against the infinitely stronger opponent.

And then the most damning sight of all was revealed, as Michael looked directly at the perpetrator; the aggressive smile of twisted pleasure that returned to the man's face as he stared directly back at Michael and offered a stark warning.

'THIS LITTLE PIGGY'S HAD HIS OATS! NOW…YOU GONNA EAT YOURS WITHOUT ANY TROUBLE, GIRLY?'

Michael nodded slowly as he observed Peter's overdue release from the shackles. His friend gasped for breath and began to sob in between bouts of spluttered coughing. The tears cascaded down his rosy-hued face and mixed with the congealed globs of oats and water.

'NOW THIS NAUGHTY LITTLE PIGGY'S GOING INTO THE TOY CUPBOARD FOR A LITTLE WHILE TO BE TAUGHT

A LESSON. STOP CRYING, PIGGY! IT MAKES UNCLE TIM VERY ANGRY!'

A resounding smack around the back of Peter's skull dazed the boy once more, rendering him completely helpless and at the full mercy of the man's next sadistic whim.

Michael shifted his weight to the edge of the seat as rage now frothed from within his soul. He could not let Peter endure any further punishment.

The unwavering instinct for rebellion was now pulsing through Michael's mind and body.

He could no longer stand by and do nothing.

The decision had been made.

And such compulsive loyalty finally found its voice.

'HEY! LEAVE HIM ALONE! HE'S HAD ENOUGH! HE'S NOT A GIRL! AND HE'S NOT A PIG! HE'S MY BEST MATE! PUT HIM DOWN! NOW!'

An uneasy hiatus rapidly descended on the arena of battle.

The man finally released his grip on Peter's whimpering form, shoving him back into his chair. His hateful glare attempted to bore into Michael's, but he sensed the boy's unusual courage and duly became aroused to the unexpected challenge.

'Oh? So…you want to take his place, do ya…girly?'

Again, Michael's attention was drawn to the pathetic figure of his friend across the table. Inner resolve demanded that he react to the situation.

And now was the moment.

'Leave him alone. Take me on instead…if you dare.'

Now the man's uneven pout evolved into a broad thin line of agitation that spread from ear to ear. His eyes widened with a sick sense of joy and his cries carried beyond the kitchen.

'OH! A LIVE ONE! SHEILA! SHEILA! I'VE GOT A WILLING PARTNER! A REAL LIVE ONE! I'VE GOT ME A WILLING PARTNER! WOW!'

The woman duly appeared in the doorway again now dressed only in a t-shirt. Waiting for further instruction, her menacingly cold eyes alternated focus between the boys as the scrawny man began to jig with evident delight.

Finally, a decision was called.

'Take the porky squealer back to the bedroom. This other little girl fancies a go in the toy cupboard, apparently.'

His heart beating like a drum, Michael observed his friend's murmuring exit before engaging with the man's disturbing visage once again. Through pursed lips he issued the next demand.

'Okay…you…little…fucker…move it.'

Following the direction indicated, Michael was escorted from the kitchen and back out into the passageway. Pushed along the creaking floorboards of the corridor, a hand eventually landed heavily on his shoulder, effectively stopping his stride.

'In here…go on. In you go. In you go.'

A small unpainted hatch was duly opened by the man and Michael was promptly shoved inside. A naked light bulb was illuminated and swung steadily due to a puzzlingly shrill draft.

The only contents of the tiny utility room were a solitary chair which was perched under a small table. Michael flinched as the hatch was shut, enclosing him inside with his captor.

Looking around to ascertain the new environment, Michael then eyed another item; a large cardboard box in the corner, into which the man delved excitedly.

'Right…sit down…girly.'

Tentatively taking the seat, Michael watched as the man produced some rope which he looped over his forearm several times before facing his young prisoner.

'Okay…little piggy…get your top half stripped off.'

Natural embarrassment initially discouraged Michael from compliance, but there was precious little choice in the matter. Removing his school pullover and white shirt, Michael shivered as he allowed the ogre to weave the rope in and around his bare torso several times until he was unable to move.

Then a piece of rag was wrapped tightly across Michael's mouth with some of the material gagging into his throat lining. Its oily taste and aroma made him want to vomit.

Now enclosed and bound, the eleven-year-old retained his sense of stoicism and remained silent as the opponent continued to chuckle.

The man retrieved a packet of cigarettes from his boxer shorts and lit one, never averting his gaze from Michael's. Then his eyes wandered over the boy's bare skin. His neck, shoulders, stomach and back all came under scrutiny as he drew ever closer to his victim.

‘Now then…girly…because of your big mouth…you’re going to get what your piggy friend was due. I’m going to leave you a little mark. A calling card…so you keep quiet in future. Something you’ll always remember me for. Now…little piggy…this might just pinch a little…’

*****

A short distance away in another room that may as well have been in another world, Peter stirred alone in his own unwarranted pit of misery.

Then something unfamiliar disturbed his momentary respite from the personal torture.

A piercing sound; a definitive yet also muffled scream of agony.

It repeated.

Not once.

Not twice.

But several times in the ensuing minutes.

Each call for mercy was separated by a period of deathly nothingness.

Peter continued to analyse the din.

And then finally he identified the mysterious wails of devastation that echoed from that other, now not so distant room.

It was the resonance of his best friend in the whole world enduring unyielding torment at the hands of their nefarious keeper.

And those echoes would continue to haunt evermore unbearably as night gradually cast its shadow over their sufferance.

CHAPTER 14

Friday; seven-fifty-four p.m.

Detective Inspector Kevin Woodley stood in contemplative silence in front of the white painted iron gates, observing the activity around the grounds at Riverlands Secondary as it became the temporary base of operations.

Despite his hardened experience in such matters, the discomforting white-amber glow reflecting off the windows of the main building symbolised an increasingly necessary practice in police procedure.

The employment of flood-lamps usually indicated that individuals at the centre of the given investigation had come to some harm, and as such an overnight commencement was imperative.

He sighed in resignation that the particular business at hand had so far produced nothing in terms of evidence to guide him in any given direction. With no single trace of a scent to follow his task was currently nigh on impossible.

The air was turning distinctly chillier as dusk gradually evolved into darkness. Placing his hands into the pockets of his long black overcoat, he turned away from the school and scanned a similar scene that was in development along Friar Road.

Local residents had been questioned again by several officers since the school's closure at three-thirty.

Then the perturbing thought regarding how much more time had been lost ricocheted around his mind, leaving him suddenly disconsolate and feeling both starved of hope and desperate for progress.

These were his naturally negative emotions that always seemed to accompany him when faced with such depressing scenarios.

A familiar voice resonated in his ear, distracting the inspector from his unenviable quandary.

'Guv…we've taken the three initial statements from the teachers and caretaker. Are they okay to leave?'

D.I. Woodley paused before responding to the fresh-faced young constable, who watched with learned respect as his gruff-looking superior lifted a hand to gently rub the greying whiskers around his chin and jaw line.

After a few seconds of purposed deliberation, the inspector acknowledged the concerned officer, although he continued to stare avidly into the midst of the activity beyond.

'Okay, Smithy. Yes. Thank them for me. They can go home. They have done all they can for now.'

P.C. Liam Smith departed to convey the message of appreciation whilst two large navy transit vans manoeuvred into position adjacent to the school entrance gates.

From the interior of each, two teams of four forensic officers adorned in pale blue overalls emerged and began to assemble various pieces of equipment.

One of them, Detective Sergeant Neil Griffin, instantly spotted D.I. Woodley and acknowledged the superior's presence with a query.

'Ready to begin yet, sir?'

Again, the detective inspector appeared preoccupied with something taunting and elusive. His eyes followed the movements of a nearby resident who had been asked politely to move his car to allow the police to access the alleyway leading to St John Street.

'Yes, not long now. The locals have been requested to keep a low profile for the next twenty-four hours. Should give you enough time to double check all three roads, shouldn't it?'

'No problem, sir. Hopefully we'll pick something up quickly.'

D.I. Woodley flicked his wrist and affirmed the time.

'Okay. It's nearly eight. I'll leave you to it then, Neil. Make sure the top end of each road is cordoned off and marshalled, first of all. We can do without nosey buggers tonight. Is Stacey Coombs still here?'

The officer in the overalls glanced back toward the school building.

'Yes, sir. I can see her just outside the reception with P.C. Smith. She's seeing off the teachers by the look of it.'

The inspector turned and ventured through the gates toward the school's main doors. He gestured back to the forensic officer with a forefinger as he neared the glass frontage of the foyer.

'Right...you get anything at all, Neil...and I mean *anything*...I need to know a.s.a.p.! I'm off to see the parents now to fill them in about tomorrow.'

The forensic specialist confirmed the order as he closed the side door of his van.

'Okay, sir. Hopefully speak to you soon.'

D.I. Woodley nodded before making for the reception in order to intercept W.P.C. Coombs.

'Stacey…you still pulling in the extra shift tonight?'

The female constable smiled politely at her superior.

'Yes, Guv. Fourth in a row this is! I'm knackered!'

The inspector displayed not a flicker of sympathy.

'Good! Come with me. I want you to act as liaison for the parents. You've been with this from the off, haven't you?'

'Yes, Guv…with Tony Rhodes.'

'Fine. At least the families will feel a little more assured with a familiar face around. You okay to spend the night with them?'

'Yes…but I'll need relieving for a few hours after six am. That will be my sixteen hours up.'

'Thank you. I'll sort your relief. We'll drive to Basford Lane now so I can convey the plan to both families.'

The two officers left the school premises and quickly headed for a silver Mercedes parked toward the other end of Friar Road. The female officer found herself jogging to keep astride with the long legs of the inspector, whose ever-determined focus rarely wavered from matters at hand.

She could instantly tell by his demeanour that the situation was now being viewed as increasingly desperate. He did not feel the need to speak again as the car was unlocked from a short distance by remote.

Sliding behind the wheel, the D.I. garnered one last view of the demoralising undertaking on display in his rear-view mirror. A brightly lit picture of purposed dedication, which only briefly belied the severity of its motive.

The thought crossed his mind that such an operation would maybe not prove itself to be a completely futile exercise. As he turned the key and engaged the gearbox, something instinctive gnawed at his conscience.

A nagging, conflicting sensation that had had been present since he had first been associated with the case and still would not abate.

It felt like a subconscious recognition of some underlying wish.

Perhaps the wish that this torrid tale he had only just started to apply himself to would have a rapid and happy ending.

And the similarly aching recognition that it would probably not.

*****

James Tompkins entered the hallway and observed the rough-edged silhouettes in the porchlight.

Dejectedly turning the latch, he was greeted by the sight of W.P.C. Coombs and an older, male, plain-clothed officer he did not recognise.

The man who had been designated to lead the hunt for two missing schoolboys spoke with harsh sincerity.

'Good evening. Mister Tompkins, I presume?'

'Yes. The others are in there. We were told to expect you both.'

The D.I. held out a firm hand of introduction.

'Detective Inspector Kevin Woodley. I've been assigned to lead this investigation. You are already acquainted with Stacey Coombs, I believe?'

'Yes. Hello, again, Stacey.'

Her genuine smile was visibly constricted by sympathy as she stepped into the hallway of number twelve.

'Hello again, Mister Tompkins.'

James nodded out of courtesy as all three moved into the lounge where David, Hazel and Sharon were waiting. They exchanged pleasantries with the officers before D.I. Woodley removed his coat to reveal a black suit and tie.

He stood in front of the mantelpiece, which ironically boasted a framed image of Michael at nine years of age. He addressed the group with a tone of commandment, yet the presence of authority was strangely comforting for its audience.

'I shall endeavour to make what I am about to reveal crystal clear to you all. I am absolutely determined to find your sons...but this is a very early stage of the investigation and from your naturally very uneasy perspective...patience must be the key. Obviously...from my point of view...things cannot happen quickly enough.'

None of the parents responded verbally. Instead, they hung onto every word of the higher-ranking policeman who they hoped would bring them what they were praying for.

'A team of forensic officers is currently assessing the residential area around the school. This thorough examination will go on through the night and into tomorrow when my teams will re-check the area in daylight. The teachers concerned have made their statements and I will need confirmation of the accounts you have already submitted. I apologise for this, but it is a procedural formality.'

The detective's words were continually soothing considering that the subject under discussion was painfully raw for all to endure.

'I believe you have supplied recent photographs of your boys to my team?'

James squeezed Sharon's hand as she looked deep into her husband's eyes for the slightest strand of solace.

She nodded to him with some reticence, as if to give him permission to confirm the D.I.'s query.

'Yes…two officers collected them at teatime.'

'Those images will be the backbone of this operation. So far as I am concerned those boys' faces now need to be seen and their names known. They now need to be in the public eye…and soon. Those photographs will now be in the hands of our search unit back at the station and will have been despatched to every regional constabulary in the country.'

Hazel began to shake as the significance of such a drastic development descended around her like an exploding thunder cloud.

'I can't believe this, David! This can't be happening. My little boy…oh my God…'

Offering a momentary respect for the parental struggle, D.I. Woodley continued with due caution.

'I am placing W.P.C. Coombs here as your liaison officer for the foreseeable time. Anything you need to know from us…you can go through her. And likewise…anything we need to know urgently…she will be here to coordinate on our behalf.'

Two mothers and two fathers were now at a complete loss for words.

Passage of time had erased the scant possibility of the scenario being nothing more than a childish game that could have been drawn up by two eleven-year-olds. Many hours had elapsed since such a theory had retained any likelihood to hold water.

Now, with their disappearance over twenty-four hours ago, circumstances were increasingly dire.

And the unwavering expression on the face of Detective Inspector Kevin Woodley only served to reinforce the urgent nature of the business at hand.

A seriousness that was dramatically compounded by his next revelation.

'Mister and Mrs. Tompkins…Mister and Mrs. Leavesdon…you need to consider something very carefully. And you haven't too long to make up your minds.'

Absolute quiet prevailed in the lounge as the investigating officer shifted his weight discomfortingly from foot to foot.

'I have arranged a media conference for tomorrow at noon at Shireheath Town Hall. I wish for you to make a collaborative, considered statement on camera. This will bring events into the public arena and hopefully flush out any potential leads that might be clinging to the shadows.'

James was the first to offer a response to the officer's wholly unexpected proposal.

'Who will be at this conference?'

'At this moment…local radio, TV and press. But if I feel it appropriate…the plea can go national with an hour's notice.'

Sharon was the next parent to interject.

'Why not go the whole hog from the off? Why wait?'

D.I. Woodley clasped his hands behind his back and considered every responsive word.

'Because…Mrs Tompkins…things may develop overnight which deem it unnecessary to bring it to national attention.'

James supported his wife's curiosity and squeezed her hand tighter as he quizzed the inspector.

'Such as? What kind of developments?'

'Well…if our forensic team uncovers anything for a start. A lot can happen over the next few hours. The lie of the land could alter rapidly by morning.'

Hazel had calmed herself sufficiently to contribute to the debate.

'Do you think that the boys might turn up by then? Do you think it's really possible, inspector? That they could be back home by morning?'

D.I. Woodley was immediately alerted to the misplaced sense of optimism and attempted to keep a lid of the remaining reservoir of positive thought that the parents had nurtured during the past hours.

'I cannot say, Mrs Leavesdon. What I am certain about is this. If, in twelve hours' time, we are no further on with the search…then I strongly suggest that your plea goes national. We have the wherewithal to arrange such things very quickly. You must understand...your media statement could encourage the vital link we're looking for.'

Sharon relinquished James' grasp and stood to her feet, wrapping her own arms around her shoulders as if to deflect the inevitably chilling speed of events.

Scanning the desperate faces of those present, she decided to squash the natural reticence that suddenly reigned within the group.

'I'll do it! I'll speak for us all! It can happen as soon as possible for me! I want my son back. We've got nothing more to lose. We need to help them come home. It's horrible to admit...but they might need us to do this!'

Hazel rose to join her friend in a hesitant admission of maternal agreement.

And then, two husbands stood by their wives as they opted to confront the unavoidable predicament of taking part in something they had only believed ever happened to other, terribly unfortunate souls.

D.I. Woodley silently applauded their united courage and nodded in grateful appreciation of their assistance.

'Okay. One more important thing. If any of you have any close relatives that are currently unaware of the situation...tell them what is happening...and tell them as soon as I leave. Letting them discover such news on television is unthinkable. Put everyone close to the boys in the picture. The more the merrier. This may sound harsh to acknowledge...but you are doing exactly the right thing for this investigation. I must now return to the station. Stacey here will stay here with you as I've already said. I'll see myself out. I'll be in touch very soon.'

*****

An hour had passed since the inspector's visit.

With the female occupants of number twelve, Basford Lane musing over matters in the lounge, James and David stood together in the hallway.

The tears had flowed freely during the previous minutes as they informed grandparents, aunts and uncles of the detestable panic that had invaded their lives without invitation.

Holding on to one another for mutual comfort, with Wallace waiting patiently at his master's heel, the fathers had listened in loving agony as two doting mothers took turns to convey the situation to their friends and immediate family.

Emotionally rocked to the core, James could not deflect the impact of his wife's unrelenting upset as she stammered weakly into the telephone.

Having submitted himself to the horrendous monologue for nearly a minute, he pulled on the front door handle. Led by a faithful German Shepherd and accompanied by his best friend, the two men walked the confused yet loyal canine into the increasingly menacing shadows of evening.

CHAPTER 15

Friday; two minutes before midnight.

Michael turned over in bed and instantly winced with physical distress as the permanent reminders of his recent encounter throbbed open and raw.

Sitting up and resting his back against the headboard, he glanced across and observed the unusually peaceful image of his best friend, still adorned in the girl's dress.

Rolling up the sleeves of his school pullover and shirt, he squinted through the semi-darkness at the weeping sores that had been administered by the cigarette.

With tentative caution, he explored each section of his upper body as the memory of the earlier torture remained pertinent.

There were deep circular burns to his inner arms.

Blisters across his chest.

Sores on each of his shoulders.

Even his armpits had been marked by scorching red hot ash. But the most vivid remnant came to the fore as Michael reached to feel the left side of his throat just under the jawbone.

Without a mirror to confirm the detail, he could only vaguely assess the wound with delicate fingertips.

It seemed to gape wide open to his touch; totally susceptible to further irritation and the possibility of infection.

Laying himself gently back down on the mattress he proceeded to study the naked light bulb that hung overhead. The bright orange element contained in the oval of glass seemed to flicker intermittently as his vision begun to play tricks.

And then he finally conceded.

Curling himself up against the incessant shooting pains that enveloped his torso, Michael buried his face into the pillow and wept unashamedly.

He grieved for himself; for his friend; for his parents.

And as he finally relinquished to his inner plight, he also remained consciously adamant that he would strive absolutely to conceal his torment from the aggressors beyond the locked door.

No matter what it took, he would show them no weakness.

Only strength.

CHAPTER 16

Saturday; eleven-twenty-one am.

The Tompkins and the Leavesdons had been afforded police escort from their homes to the grand Victorian-built council complex situated in the market square. The centre of Shireheath had adopted a typically modern High Street sheen over the years that detracted from its historical splendour.

Yet today, in such an auspicious arena, there was little to rejoice upon.

Never in all of their shopping trips over the years did Sharon and Hazel forecast that they would be frequenting the Town Hall for such a purpose.

The unwavering trepidation felt by all four parents was mutually tangible as they alighted from the squad cars and vainly huddled together for comfort.

Despite the rattling unease within the group, all acknowledged that the police had been most considerate in their approach to matters so far and indeed supremely urgent in their responses.

Even though the scent of truth had not yet been detected, the rapid intervention of the authorities had garnered the families some loose renewal of faith.

Despite the relatively short period that had elapsed since the last sighting of Michael and Peter, all involved sensed that the time was nigh to actively assist their two young boys.

Yet the vibrancy felt by the parents in embracing such an undertaking was temporarily stunted as they observed the vision of several different television and radio units and their logo-wrapped vehicles, that only served to bring the raging horror back to haunt them.

The business of the hour became ever more poignant as they climbed the stone steps and were ushered through the large, tinted glass entrance doors.

The motive for such an unholy congregation pricked sharply at the minds of all at the scene and the principal factors involved resonated around the high corners of the greeting chamber.

That two eleven-year-old boys were still missing.

That their whereabouts was still unknown.

That their possible sufferance at that moment was unthinkable.

The investigative team now leading the search had provided the media platform from which two mothers and two fathers could make their own plea for the safety and return of their offspring.

And as they convened privately behind a large navy-blue curtain in preparation for the public announcement, the tears fell unabated once again among the foursome.

Hazel could barely maintain her fragile composure as both James and David struggled to stand firm and adopt a mask of empty bravery.

Yet contrary to the agony etched into the faces of the others, Sharon had willingly employed a sense of deep determination regarding the imminent conference.

All told, it was a wholly necessary and deeply unpleasant task for everybody present.

An unavoidable deed that she would never have wished upon herself or indeed on any parent.

But for the sake of two absent sons, there was no remaining scope for any deliberation on the issue.

Seated nervously on chairs behind the protective blue screen, all four watched and listened as D.I. Woodley offered some conveyance of calm whilst waiting to be given the signal to introduce the four parents to the incoming throng of journalists, broadcasters, and cameramen.

Together with W.P.C. Coombs, who had volunteered to extend her shift further, he perched himself opposite the four; a stern glint of assurance helping his words carry extra weight.

'The choice of phrasing is ideal. Very direct and touching. Just try and stay composed...especially you, Sharon. This will be broadcast live on several channels. Other networks may choose to replay it during their own bulletins. Rest assured...nobody is going to ask you any questions. They are here to listen. I will be sitting right beside you and will add a few words of my own at the end. Any queries will be addressed directly to me. The Press knows the rules. Aside from this, the podium will be yours and yours alone.'

James wiped his eyes and ventured a final, hopeful question.

'Do you think this will do the trick? Do you think the investigation can begin to move on after this?'

Detective Inspector Kevin Woodley strived to find an appropriate response which ultimately did not materialize. It was impossible to provide a concrete answer to sate the families concerns and he considered it wholly inappropriate to fabricate hope.

Inner relief diverted his gaze from the floor as another police officer appeared from stage front and spoke quietly into his superior's ear.

The D.I. nodded and turned his attention to the distraught parents.

'James...Sharon...David...Hazel...they're ready when you are.'

*****

The man lit a cigarette and reclined on the chair nearest to the television. He scanned the kitchen surfaces impatiently for an ash tray but soon surrendered to laziness and began to flick his deposits on the grubby linoleum-tiled flooring around his seat.

Straining for the remote control, he idly hopped through the minimal selection of channels, becoming mildly frustrated at the lack of entertainment on offer.

With twelve stations to select from, his appetite for something even vaguely interesting was quickly beginning to fade.

The man swallowed dryly and hauled his lean frame upright to make himself a drink. Standing at the worktop next to the stove he filled the kettle whilst glaring through the unwashed windowpane.

The familiar musical intro to the midday news bulletin hummed from the screen, still doing little to stimulate his curiosity in proceedings.

Spooning coffee granules and sugar into a dirty mug, he paid little attention to the opening patter of the TV broadcasters.

As the water slowly began to boil, he reclaimed his chair, retrieved his cigarette, and continued to draw heavily on the smouldering filter tip.

And then, as his eyes gradually focused themselves back to the television, they beheld a vision that immediately caused him to jump back to his feet and shout at the top of his voice through the open kitchen doorway.

'SHEILA! SHEILA! GET THE FUCK IN HERE! NOW! YOU'VE GOT TO SEE THIS! WOW! FUCKING AMAZING!'

Within seconds the tall thin woman hurriedly entered the kitchen and joined the man at the table. With heads close together they leered at the screen which portrayed the apparent commencement of a press conference.

The accomplices studied the movements of four parents and two police officers, who emerged from behind a blue canvas screen to be paraded in front of a large backdrop that boasted expanded photographic images of two missing schoolboys.

Without word, both abductors were now completely transfixed by the scenario playing out before them; with both becoming rapidly fuelled by their perverted sense of elation.

They listened enthusiastically; and sniggered intermittently.

They grimaced and snarled to each other as the back-story to the conference was unveiled by a doom-laden voiceover.

And then it was revealed by the main newscaster that the bulletin would be imminently transferring live from the Town Hall at Shireheath.

The man adjusted the angle of his head and conveyed a whispered request to his female associate.

'Sheila…get them two fuckers in here! They've got to see this! We're all going to be famous by tonight! Get the girls in here now…and be fucking quick about it!'

Obeying her partner's demonic command, the woman quickly exited the room to the sound of her own raucous cackle.

In no time at all she returned with Michael and Peter, whose confusion and learned reservation caused them to stand attentive and quiet before their squirming enslavers.

With his attention partly centred on the screen behind them, the man remained reclined in his chair and declared the reasons for requesting their company, as his female counterpart stood ominously by the door.

With events on the screen still to begin in full, he made his opportunistic intentions perfectly clear to the cherubic young faces that stared straight back at him.

'Hello again, girls. Now then…I think it's time for another little game.'

Neither boy responded aside a reactive flexing of fingers.

And neither boy averted their gaze from the man's distorted expression as he continued with the riddle.

'The game goes something like this…I spy…with my little eye…something beginning with 'm'…and I spy with my little eye…something beginning with…'d'. Now…can you guess what they are?'

Still the eleven-year-olds engaged with the man's wild glare as he became increasingly enthralled by the pending revelation. He looked around to offer an affirmative wink to his leering associate across the room. His brow furrowed as he reverted attention back to his fearful subjects.

'Well, girls…actually…you don't really have to guess…because I'm going to fucking *show* you the answers! If you turn around…you'll see 'm'…and 'd'…together! Go on then girls…look at the telly! Don't be afraid. It's only just behind you!'

The man again grinned recklessly as his frail looking counterpart moved to stand closer to the table; her arms folded and her own smile of insane pleasure broadening.

As the inner euphoria reached fever pitch for the tormentors, the boys overcame their initial sense of reluctance.

In turn, Michael and Peter slowly faced in the opposite direction and were ordered to watch the television screen as their antagonist merrily disclosed the damning solutions to his strange conundrum.

A cold chill seemed to occupy the room as the boys gradually digested what was being shown to them.

Neither responded as their attention settled to the spectacle playing out before them.

'Yes! You've both got it now, haven't you! Yes…you little fuckers! 'M'...and…'D'. YES! YOU'VE GOT IT NOW HAVEN'T YOU!'

Still the boys endeavoured to concentrate as the story unfolding on the screen gained awful clarity.

'It's…'M'…'D'…MUMMY…and…DADDY! Hey girls? How fucking cool is that?'

Clapping inanely as he writhed almost uncontrollably on the chair, the man could not immediately visualise the rapidly altering expressions on the faces of his two young prey.

To remedy this, he altered position and squatted next to them in front of the screen. The volume was increased with a crooked finger whilst he hissed the next malevolent instruction.

'Now…be very quiet…because it looks like mummy wants to say something very important! By the way…whose mummy is that?

Which one of you ugly girls fell out from between her stinking legs, then?'

A deathly hush descended as Peter and Michael engaged with the starkly transmitted figure of Sharon Tompkins, who paused momentarily to consider the opening statement of her desperate plea.

The boys exchanged brief glances of desolate acknowledgement.

Michael shook his head at his blond-haired friend as if to prevent Peter's impending natural response. He flexed his jawbone tightly to stave off bubbling emotion, which also served to remind him of the weeping open scold to his upper neck.

Little could Sharon know as she strived for composure in that room crammed with its fully attentive media representatives, that at that precise moment, the very reasons for her presence on the screen were about to witness her harrowing plea in its entirety.

The tears fell slowly from Peter's eyes as he watched the various cameras pan at different angles and occasionally rest on the solemn features of his own parents.

Instantly recognising his own mother and father, Peter felt Michael instinctively reached over and grab hold of his trembling left hand.

The enlarged and imposing junior school photographs of them both formed a chilling indication as to the nature of what they were about to endure.

Now the boys were becoming slowly accustomed to the fact that their whereabouts had been ably concealed from the rest of society. And as such damning knowledge registered, Michael felt he wanted to scream out loud and disclose their location to an ignorant world.

But of course, he did not even know himself where their dank, damp, diseased confine was situated.

He and his best friend Peter had seemingly been completely and permanently stranded from the life they knew and loved.

And from the people that knew and loved them

The only option available to both boys at that moment of torturous enlightenment was to listen to a frenzied mother as she rubbed the traces of intense upset from her cheeks and finally began to address the eager congregation.

'Nearly forty-eight hours ago, our son, Michael Tompkins and his friend, Peter Leavesdon, left school at home time and promptly vanished. Treating this as a matter of utmost urgency, the police are now launching a full-scale investigation as to the boys' whereabouts… but as yet have uncovered absolutely no evidence that might suggest where they may be, or indeed, who they may be with.

I, together with Michael's father, James, and Peter's mother and father, Hazel and David…have decided to accept police advice and make this public plea, both as an aid to the police effort and maybe…just maybe…as a direct token of assurance to our boys.

If anybody watching this broadcast has seen, or thinks they may have sighted, our two boys during the past two days…please…please come forward and tell the police whatever you saw and where you think you saw them.

Any strand of information will be considered confidential and at this moment may just prove to be invaluable.

As loving parents, we are now desperate to find our children. If by some miracle our boys are sitting somewhere, watching this broadcast, then I can say only this:

Michael…Peter…wherever you are…whoever you are with…you must know that you have done nothing wrong and that your mummy and daddy are looking for you. If you have run away for any reason…then please…please come home and we can sort this out.

If somebody has taken you away and is now preventing you from coming back home…then you must believe our word that those responsible will soon be captured, and you will soon both be back safe and sound with us.

As for the members of the public that are viewing this plea…I repeat again…anything that you recall as being strange that occurred soon after three-thirty on Thursday afternoon… probably in the Shireheath district…the police need to know immediately.

It goes without saying that as time passes…the public contribution to this investigation will become ever more vital.

Michael…Peter…we love you…we hope that you are safe.

We will see you soon.

Love Mummy and Daddy.'

The man's raucous laughter dispersed the concentration of the two eleven-year-old boys standing beside him.

They continued to observe the screen as the cameras randomly scanned the distraught features of the four parents.

The volume was quickly decreased to obscure the subsequent speech of the police investigator who responded to the evident concern among the eager gaggle of flashing press photographers, scribbling journalists and voracious news anchor-men.

Both youngsters were now fully aware that they were in serious jeopardy.

But as Peter's resolve weakened once more, Michael turned to confront his nemesis.

The man who had committed this sin of all sins.

The man who now simply sat on crossed legs beside them and smirked at the stranded, helpless juveniles in his presence.

'Told you! Didn't I tell you? Famous you two are, now! Your faces on the telly! Real fucking superstars you two are! In fact…there's a good chance you might be recognised now if we decide to take you out anywhere as a treat! SO THAT'S FUCKED THINGS UP FOR YOU A BIT…WOULDN'T YOU SAY?'

Neither boy offered a hint of a reply as the man rose wearily to his feet and conveyed a request to his female assistant now hunched back in the kitchen doorway.

'Do you think you could be a love, Sheila…and go and fetch me the clippers? A change of appearance is called for here, methinks!'

Within the minute, the woman returned and plugged in the appliance. The man's unforgiving scowl was accompanied by a loud hum as he played with the switch.

The electric shears ably concealed the volume of the television as they groaned.

'Okay…who wants to go first? What about you, squealer? Want a haircut? You're well overdue by the looks of that girly blond thatch. Come here, then! I can't reach you if you dither about over there, can I!'

Peter remained fixed to the spot as he eyed the scrawny interrogator with earnest hatred.

Looking briefly to his best friend, he found no alternative but to remain rooted where he stood.

'I don't want a haircut!' mumbled Peter under his breath.

The statement fell on deaf ears as the man gestured with his free hand.

'I say, Sheila. I reckon porky needs a bit of a nudge this way. Do the honours please?'

The woman moved to position herself behind Peter and grabbed his arms above the elbows before forcing them up high and tight behind his back. He yelped in agony as the woman quickly rendered him totally defenceless.

Despite his initial attempts to struggle against her physical will, he quickly relented and conceded defeat. The man utilised the shears quickly and roughly.

Swiftly enough, Peter's thick head of blond hair lay shorn and scattered at his feet.

Michael studied the disturbing vision of his best friend.

Peter looked ravaged and spent; every inch the unwilling, terrified victim.

With scalp completely shaven; and still attired in the chequered dress.

Wounded and helpless.

And now it was Michael's turn as the man continued to play idly with the on-off switch of the shears.

'Come on, sunshine…don't make me wait all day. We can't have folks recognising you now, can we? It's for your own good! Now get the fuck over here before I start to get mad!'

The woman applied the same restraining grip on Michael's arms and escorted him toward the demon barber with the droning clippers.

The fury was now burning within Michael's heart and soul as he was manoeuvred ever nearer to the demented aggressor.

Ever nearer; to again be forced to encounter humiliation and discomfort beyond his wildest imagination.

Ever nearer; to considering his first chance to strike out.

To retaliate; to exact his own personal wrath.

And then, once in suitable proximity, Michael opened fire with the most convenient weapon in his armoury at that moment.

The most unpopular childhood habit that had never, ever appealed to him, until that split second of decisiveness.

Michael ejected the mouthful of saliva from the closest possible range and immersed himself in the moment as it impacted and splashed across the man's pointed, dirty features.

A shiny, sticky, satisfying solution to the quandary.

And the sense of partial retribution was all consuming and pleasurable for its young executive.

Even if in practice, the act was only briefly disarming and would now incur an inevitable heavy consequence.

Dropping the electric shears to wipe the globules of spittle from his face, the man then grabbed Michael aggressively by the lapel of his school shirt.

'You little fucking bastard! Right! So that's your game, eh? Time for a dunking methinks! Sheila…get that fat squealer back into his pen. This one here needs a drink before lock-up!'

Michael was punched to the floor and veritably dragged out into the passageway by his ankles. He thought he briefly heard his name being called by Peter from the kitchen.

But there was no opportunity to contemplate regret for his actions.

Once into the bathroom, he felt another sharp rap on the back of the skull which instantly rendered him nauseous.

He was then shoved across toward the filthy toilet bowl in the corner and duly up ended. With one hand holding Michael's arms in place up his back, the boy was bent over the man's knee and his face forced into the turgid water.

Michael struggled for breath as the germ ridden liquid filled his nostrils and entered his mouth. Being held upside down over the stench-laden vessel, he was powerless to resist against the strength that the assailant employed.

His head repeatedly banged against the grimy porcelain as he was dunked unceremoniously several times and for several flushes.

'NOT SO SMART NOW, ARE YOU? FUCKING LITTLE BASTARD!'

Yet Michael's inner resolve would not be erased by such so-called punishment.

He simply held his breath and withstood the barrage.

Michael patiently endured his penalty until the man's enthusiasm and energy for the task eventually waned.

Now sodden and gasping for air, Michael was eventually righted and smacked across the face for his wilful dissension before being thrown forcibly back into the bedroom to re-join his best friend.

And then the door was locked once again.

Leaving the two boys to contemplate their ever-worsening plight.

But also leaving Michael to reflect on the satisfying accuracy regarding his previous thoughts.

A purely personal theory on the fragile nature of his keepers that had so far proved fully founded. Despite their air of menace, Michael had sensed that Uncle Tim and Sheila were weak and afraid.

And ripe to be exploited for the fact.

CHAPTER 17

Sunday; eleven-thirty-five a.m.

D.I. Woodley ignored the vibrant gathering of journalists and cameramen that had surrounded the entrance to number twelve, Basford Lane as he parked the Mercedes.

On departing and locking his car, he was enveloped by the group as he walked the short distance to the front driveway. A crescendo of queries simultaneously erupted concerning the families and the missing boys.

Professional duty compelled the D.I. to display learned patience with the eager throng and their thirst for information.

'Please…ladies and gentlemen…not now. I might be able to make a more in-depth comment at a later time. At this particular moment the parents are my priority.'

Failing to abate the jostling curiosity, he simply turned his back on the group and walked toward the house. James Tompkins conveniently pulled the front door open and ushered the detective inside, noting the very vocal crowd bustling for position at the gate.

The instant chatter of camera shutters and two dozen simultaneous questions encouraged James to quickly allow the visitor entry and shut out the unwanted scrutiny.

'How long have that lot been out there?' enquired the D.I.

James appeared nonplussed and shook his head.

'To be honest…I didn't even know they *were* there. Nobody's come knocking that I'm aware of.'

'Well…rest assured…they won't be bothering you any more than they are doing currently. Trespassing is still illegal…even if they do want a front-page story out of you.'

Entering the lounge, the senior policeman was greeted by the now familiar sight of its temporary resident occupants.

Despite offering a courteous smile, he immediately sensed that the atmosphere and disposition of the parental vigil had become decidedly more downbeat since the televised speech the day before.

The offer of a coffee was politely accepted, with D.I. Woodley perching himself in the armchair next to the mantelpiece. There was a tangibly awkward atmosphere in the room. He briefly glanced at the photograph of Michael above the fireplace before taking the drink from Sharon, who was the first to request an update on the investigation.

The detective paused, sampled some of his drink and commenced the current report.

'So far…there has been little in the way of public response to yesterday's broadcast I'm afraid…apart from the collection of headline scribblers outside. But…as I said…patience is vital…it is still very early days.'

A tired looking Hazel rubbed her palms together in nervous anticipation and put the next question to the policeman.

'What about the forensic search around the school? Anything come up?'

The D.I. was fully prepared to supply answers although he virtually whispered a carefully worded reply.

'Yesterday our units performing house calls were given a statement by one resident of Friar Road that claimed he definitely saw two boys in Riverlands' school uniforms making down the alleyway that connects the road with Clumber Street. However, the timing of the sighting remains vague…he only passed his landing window by chance and he also claimed that many other kids use that alley at the same time each day. So…despite him seemingly being a reliable witness…his account doesn't give us a great deal to go on.'

David sat forward in his chair and stroked the growth of blonde-brown stubble that was gaining density around his jaw and mouth.

'But…the witness's description fits in with Michael's and Peter's…doesn't it? Is this what you're telling us? Or am I misunderstanding the situation?'

Tasting some more coffee, the detective inspector shook his head.

'Sorry, Mister Leavesdon…he couldn't positively identify the boys he saw to be yours. It was a chance observation which came and went without him deliberating on the matter. This is what I mean when I say that people's brains don't fully absorb what they have seen. He saw two boys in the alley. That is not in dispute. But they could have been any two boys in the school and the lengthy process of eliminating them from the enquiry won't take us any further on with the search.'

Sharon interjected with frustration in her tone.

'So why get him to give you a statement if it doesn't mean a damn thing?'

'Mrs. Tompkins…I don't know for certain if it means anything or not. As I say…it's the early days of the jigsaw. At this stage we are trying to uncover the pieces…never mind attempt to try and assemble a picture. The point is that the witness statement compelled me to order another examination of the alley in question…just to fine tooth comb an area that had been flagged as potentially important.'

Hazel's impatience was now beginning to overpower her as she demanded some expansion on the detective's linear train of thought.

'So…assuming your men checked the alleyway again properly…did you find anything relevant second time around?'

The detective partially drained his mug and clasped it between both hands.

'The on-site forensics team have collected a few items from the scene…yes. But please bear in mind that even though we are sending the retrieved articles for checks…they might well turn up nothing.'

'What kind of checks? What items have you found?' barked Sharon, impatiently.

D.I. Woodley emptied his mug as the tone carrying the conversation became ever more alarmed.

'General items of litter. A crisp packet. Chocolate bar wrapper. A discarded cigarette end. All these items will carry identifiable prints or perhaps strains of DNA.'

Still Hazel did not sympathise. Her perception of the police operation depicted nothing less than disinterest.

'But anybody could have dropped these things! Probably half the school kids on their way home for Christ's sake! Most of them smoke these days as well! In fact, our Peter was one of the few that didn't…I can assure you of that much! How pointless is all this!'

D.I. Woodley raised his hand to request a little calm.

'The point is…Mrs Leavesdon…these days we can quickly disregard any futile lines of enquiry by quickly comparing any discovered DNA traces to our records. We have forensic history of every convicted criminal that has been released back into civilian life during the past twenty-five years. Offenders are often released only to repeat their crimes. If anything found at the scene matches up to a name on our file…then…well…we've practically got him in the palm of our hand! Or indeed…her…'

*****

Peter finished his meal and placed the cutlery in an orderly, practiced fashion on the plate.

The woman removed the crockery from the kitchen table and dropped it noisily into the kitchen sink. Her tone of voice was unusually polite.

'So...did you enjoy your fish fingers and chips? A nice treat, wasn't it?' she enquired.

Peter's gaze dropped to the tabletop and across to the plate opposite. It remained filled with food.

'Yes...thank you. What about Michael? Why isn't he here at the table? Why isn't he eating his dinner?'

The woman shifted position and promptly slid the other plate under Peter's nose.

'He decided he'd rather play up than eat. In a bit of an awkward mood is your friend. Uncle Tim doesn't like awkward little boys. They get him very angry. So...your friend is going to have to learn to do as he's told in future.'

Peter was about to reply when a scream from a nearby room silenced him.

It was a shrill yelp; unrestrained and yet quick to pass.

A pathetic cry for mercy emanating from somewhere too close for comfort; from a young boy whose fate lay in the hands of an unseen, merciless tormentor.

CHAPTER 18

Sunday; ten-seventeen p.m.

Hazel and David had barely shifted position from the settee since returning home after D.I. Woodley's uninspiring visit to Basford Lane.

Now back in the distinctly unwelcoming fold of number thirty-nine, Cromford Road, they felt anything but at ease beneath the unrelenting black clouds of continuing devastation.

Hopelessly transfixed by the stream of television news clips and repeated displays of Sharon's stoical plea for the boys' return, it seemed that the only remaining option left for four desolate parents was to sit and wait.

Wait with growing impatience and inflating despondency.

And believe with wavering, only half-hearted defiance.

Time and time again the Leavesdons would glance across to the lounge telephone with the sincere expectation that it was about to ring and bring them the message they so longed for.

Wild anticipation compelled them to watch the continual hourly media coverage in the vain knowledge that it might just bring some positive news, aside from the avid speculation and media activity which both families were already fully aware of.

The sole known facts of the story remained undisputed.

That the boys were still gone.

And that the police search intending to uncover their whereabouts had not progressed any further forward since three-thirty last Thursday afternoon.

*****

A few streets away, the Tompkins were trying to handle matters with similar perishing dignity, but an unpleasant physical fracas involving James and a newspaper reporter had also reached the television networks as being repeatedly newsworthy in the absence of any more important developments.

Subsequently, the police were made aware of the assault which occurred when James tried to exit his property with Wallace to take him for his afternoon walk.

A resulting broken camera accompanied by its owner's broken nose did little to serve the cause for Michael and Peter, nor did it encourage peaceful relations between the Tompkins and the constant press vigil beyond their front gate.

In truth, the incident served only to temporarily distract the media from the main story.

It had been a long, strenuous afternoon.

Sharon sat alone in Michael's bedroom. Perched on the edge of her son's neatly made bed, she observed the array of glossy posters that adorned the walls. Steven Gerrard faced off Christiano Ronaldo, whilst large prints of Batman and Bart Simpson battled one another for the minimal display space.

She glanced down with diluted vision and let her eyes wander over his collection of super-hero comic books.

Retrieving his shiny silver-belled clock from the top of the bedside cabinet, she noted the alarm hand which was still set for seven a.m. in readiness for schooldays.

She turned to look across to the floor which sported his television cabinet, DVD's, X-Box and ever-expanding collection of console games.

Standing to her feet she set the clock down on the dresser and gently pulled open his chest of drawers. Respectfully browsing for nothing in particular, she eventually removed two pairs of Michael's socks and a set of clean pyjamas.

Cradling them in her hands, she buried her face into the soft linen and detected the soothing scent of fabric conditioner.

The aromatic memory of her missing son.

As the tears readily dispersed into the clothing, her heart began to beat rapidly as a foreboding question loomed at the back of her mind.

It was a thought that attempted to fully eclipse her slowly fading hopes.

A fearful wonder that had emerged from nothing suddenly gnawed at her conscience like a thousand tormenting ghosts, rapidly assaulting her temporarily peaceful train of thought.

Her immediate surroundings began to beg questions.

Would she ever see her son wear his clothes again?

Would he ever be able to lie on his own bed and read his own comic books?

Could he ever have the chance to watch his own television whilst sitting up eating toast and raspberry jam as he so regularly did on a Saturday morning?

Would he ever be allowed to return to the loving arms of his mother and father; to sleep soundly in the knowledge that they would protect him forever and always?

And then, as the persistent issues reigned down like acidic darts to scar her mind and soul, an ultimate realisation occurred.

The devastating certainty plagued her.

That, as parents, they had allowed their son to become vulnerable.

They had effectively permitted him to be taken away from them.

To be possibly imprisoned against his young will.

To God knows where.

And by God knows whom.

And yet another excruciating possibility thrashed untamed within her as she again relented to overwhelming grief on her son's bedroom floor whilst clutching his all-time favourite teddy bear tightly into her chest.

A mother who now wailed helplessly under the might of her scornful release, as a very real monster crawled steadily over the horizon of her psyche with the intent to destroy everything she ever thought she knew and held so dear.

Everything she had ever and could ever love was suddenly crushed to dust.

A foretelling that should Michael be returned to them, that he might be fully armed with the awareness that his parents had indeed failed in their duty to protect him.

And the potentially unthinkable prospect that he would never find it in his young heart to forgive them for such failure.

CHAPTER 19

Sunday; ten minutes to midnight.

Michael stirred during a fitful sleep, sensing that something lurked in the darkness behind him.

Indeed, a demon was calling.

He turned over in his bed and squinted through the shadows.

And then he focused on the uncertain shape of the presence.

Two wild, white, staring eyes that glimmered with dubious intent from the other side of the unlit bedroom.

The silhouette moved ever closer; ever nearer.

The eyes of the monster became ever wider; ever whiter; ever wilder.

A significant weight nestled onto the edge of the bed.

And then the man leaned toward Michael's ear; his presence emitting definitive traces of stale tobacco and alcohol that remained hanging in the air.

A hand touched Michael's shoulder.

Surprisingly gentle; yet firmly purposed in motive.

A chill of confused anticipation ricocheted through the boy's core.

His suspicions of what was to come were vague yet borne out of a wary and youthful intelligence.

And in confirmation of the boy's instincts, the visitor declared his intentions through a low, poisonous hiss.

'Move over, son. Uncle Tim wants you to do something for him. Now be a good lad and don't make a sound. This won't take long.'

CHAPTER 20

Monday; eleven-twenty-three a.m.

D. I. Kevin Woodley had again requested that all four parents be present at the Tompkins' house in Basford Lane.

In the lounge, Sharon nervously distributed the customary drinks around the room. The leading figure of the investigation, loyally assisted by W.P.C. Coombs, briefly went through the phrasing of his impending revelation with the female officer in the rear garden.

As ever, Wallace studied the bemusing episode from the glass walled arena of the conservatory.

With two mothers and two fathers now sitting and ready to listen, they watched with trepidation as the two police officers returned to join them.

Hazel quickly noticed the distinctly uneasy demeanour of the inspector and ventured to ascertain his mood.

'It's not good news…is it?' she demanded.

With the female constable reliably beside him, the detective set his coffee mug down on the small lounge table and standing to his full height, he clasped both hands behind his back.

'At the moment it isn't particularly good…Mrs. Leavesdon…no. But…it's not totally bad news, either.'

The adults gazed in woeful apprehension at one another before the D.I. continued.

'At precisely nine oh five this morning, our forensic team stationed at the school declared their inspection to be fully completed. They have searched all relevant areas thoroughly. Subsequently, they have granted me the authorisation to re-open the school as planned tomorrow morning.'

Hazel buried her face in her hands as David clutched for further information.

'What? Nothing's turned up at all? Absolutely nothing? What about the articles that you sent for checks? The litter and stuff? Was all that a waste of time as well?'

Opting to sample some more drink if only to delay the reply, the D.I. sighed heavily.

Reluctant resignation displayed itself across his features as he swallowed.

‘Most of what was found was attributed to simple public refuse. There was no positive match-reference with anything on our files. There was a cigarette butt which has been confirmed as recently belonging to an adult and judging by the condition of the un-perished tobacco…it could have been discarded around the time in question.’

James interrupted with sharp desperation that caused his voice to carry a hardened edge.

‘Don’t tell me…no link to anything on your record. So, it could have been anyone’s fag end, then? Just like we said!’

The inspector simply shook his head in frustrated sympathy.

‘I’m sorry. Of course, I am. I am now going to contact the school Headmaster. So far as I can see…there is no reason to keep the premises closed any longer. Obviously…we shall continue to press on with our enquiries along other lines.’

Sharon felt the need to satisfy one yearning query.

‘The TV speech I made. That’s been a waste of time as well…hasn’t it?’

The police officers could not have expressed their sorrow any more explicitly as they offered the group strained hope.

‘Please…all of you…you’ve no idea how immensely untypical this investigation has become. Yes…we as a team are currently struggling for a breakthrough. And as time goes on…we are increasingly at odds to find other avenues to explore. I’m incredibly sorry for the distress this is placing you all under. But I shall…as I say…carry the hope that someone comes forward with some information soon. At this time, I can only apologise for the lack of any positive progress. I’ll see myself out. It goes without saying that I will be in touch with any new developments.’

*****

Monday; three-forty-one p.m.

Michael and Peter felt the ropes being pulled around them and the gnarled bark of the trees subsequently digging into their backs.

Tied individually to separate trunks, the boys were positioned facing one another although with their sight totally impeded, they knew nothing of their location.

They heard the man moving around them and detected his now familiar scent of nicotine and booze.

Foul tasting rags had been stuffed into their mouths. Michael did not resist the infringement, but Peter began to scream silently in protest.

A sound that was cut dead in customary violent fashion by the man who volunteered an explanation to their current predicament.

'We've brought you out for the afternoon, girls. Thought it might be a nice change! Oh…suppose I better take those blindfolds off! Not much point you coming otherwise! By the way…trust me…those haircuts look great!'

The sound of the adults laughing together caused Michael to twitch in anger as his vision and airway were suddenly cleared. Having eventually been forced to have his head shaved too, the sensation of being outdoors was quite acute against his scalp.

As far as he could behold as his vision cleared, the pleasantly sunlit view consisted of nothing but heathland for miles around.

Barren; featureless, bleak.

Isolating.

The only area of interest on the landscape was the large group of trees that were situated around them. He studied the distant horizon, wondering if liberty might just be waiting for him beyond that elusive, distant point.

The man's arresting tone quickly halted Michael's momentary indulgence.

'Now then…me and Aunty Sheila have got a little business to attend to. But if you're very good and behave yourselves, we might just have a little surprise in store for you both afterwards!'

The boys watched as the man and woman held hands and ventured a few yards away behind another large tree at the edge of a clearing.

Peter's brow furrowed in innocent bemusement, but Michael sensed the imminent act that was about take place. A minute or two of silence prevailed before the woman's pleasured groans begun to carry on the late summer breeze.

Enduring the increasing resonance of sickening pleasure that echoed around the area was most discomforting for the two eleven-year-olds.

Yet the captors did not restrain their illicit cries of joyful, physical relief, nor did they go to any great lengths to fully conceal the action from such young, impressionable eyes.

Michael opted to stare directly back into the horizon which was supporting a late summer sun. Peter remained seemingly oblivious to the unsavoury display not thirty yards away from him.

Michael wondered deeply about the future, considering if their ordeal would ever find closure in some way.

In any way.

Still the low-pitched moaning of the woman penetrated his conscience as he contemplated the very uncertainty of the situation. So embellished was he in his train of fantasy, that he failed to notice Peter's vigorous attempts to wriggle free from his restraints were becoming successful.

Only when his best friend had totally dispensed himself from his poorly applied shackles did Michael's heart begin to jump with a rush of anxious euphoria.

Suddenly, the closure wished for only seconds ago was seemingly upon them as Peter stood to his feet and bounded in pain across to Michael's stake. His roughly shorn head did not detract from the expression of undiluted excitement that paraded across his worn and fatigued young face.

Yet the smile was back; the crimson features framing this unexpected moment of opportunity.

A side of Peter Leavesdon that had not surfaced for several days.

And the sincere visage of his best friend was more than enough inspiration for Michael. Peter crouched, checked he had not been spotted, and proceeded to try and loosen Michael's bindings whilst conveying his whispers of adrenaline-fuelled ambition.

'We are going to escape, Michael! I'm going to untie you…and we are going to escape!'

The whining backdrop of adult fornication confirmed that the man and woman were still fully occupied with sating one another's immediate needs.

And this was the instance that the two young prisoners had longed for.

Yet as Michael tried to assist his friend's efforts in detaching himself from the tree trunk, a sudden thought pulsed through his brain.

An inspired insight that evolved into an unwavering command.

'Peter…leave me! Go! Run for it! Quickly! Now! You must! Just run like your life depends on it! Don't worry about me! This is your chance to save yourself! Take it, Peter! For God's sake go! Hurry! Before you're discovered!'

Two lifelong companions engaged uncertain stares for a few seconds.

Peter stopped his efforts to loosen Michael's ropes, completely baffled by his best pal's selfless request. His innocent and confused mind toiled with the unexpected proposal.

Friends were supposed to help one another.

Friends weren't supposed to desert one another.

Yet Michael's insistent determination was unbalanced by the storm of emotion that Peter was struggling to contend with.

'I can't leave you, Michael! I can't! We've got to go together!'

Peter frantically resumed the attempt to free Michael's torso and arms as the writhing conspirators continued their mutual indulgence. But unlike Peter's shackles, the rope around Michael was fastened true and tight.

The plea was repeated firmly.

'No…don't stay with me…run away you idiot! Find some help! Find out where we are! Peter! Listen to me! You must leave me and find help! Quickly! This might be the only time we get!'

Still Peter grappled with the knots.

Still Peter wept as he tugged and yanked in vain.

And then, to Michael's full, disappointing horror, the opportunity for escape had passed them by as the man appeared from the clearing adorning a satisfied grin.

Pulling up his trousers from around his ankles and securing his leather belt, the captor leered at the vision of two desperate little boys that thought they might be so bold as to seek respite from their incarceration.

The beastly expression on his face that suddenly developed suggested he even found pleasure in the fact that his most prized possessions had exercised their right to make a bid for freedom.

But the grimace of irony carried a sinister undercurrent.

'Oh? Almost ready for the off are we, girls? A bit rude of you not to wait for us…I told you we wouldn't be long.'

Peter looked briefly at Michael before finally leaping to his feet and then sprinting as fast as his legs would take him.

Away down the gently sloping hill.

Away from the cluster of trees.

Away through the calf length grass that swayed gently in the late summer breeze.

He dared not look back as tears of frustration poured from the young boy's eyes.

And away he kept on running as his lungs throbbed under the most unusual duress.

Fleeing from the monstrous keepers as his heart threatened to burst with the effort.

Running away from his best friend; and thinking of home.

Yet unknowingly, charging a gauntlet that would bring him straight back into the maw of purgatory itself.

Michael's voice had attempted to convey the warning to Peter, but the predator had already commenced pursuit and effortlessly re-apprehended his quarry.

Promptly returning to the scene with his catch, the man reminded the boy of his mistake with a consequential procession of punches and kicks to the body and head.

Michael watched helplessly as Peter's dire figure was wrenched to the edge of the clearing.

'So…try it on will you…you little fucker! Sheila…get his mate untied and bring him along. It seems Uncle Tim has got to turn teacher again!'

The boys were escorted through the tree line toward a trickling brook. The woman was ordered to restrain Michael again some yards away as Peter was forcefully thrown to the ground near the water's edge. The man then knelt astride his victim and stared down at the adolescent's terrified face.

Now trapped between the man's knees and unable to move beneath his weight, Peter felt the coldness of the running water as it began to douse the skin on the back of his recently shaven head.

'Now then little piggy…we were going to treat you to something nice to eat this afternoon. But as you've been naughty…again…you'll have to make do with an alternative.'

Michael struggled to maintain his gaze on the ensuing scene. From a short distance, he could not see Peter's face, but he saw his friend's legs begin to kick out in fruitless resistance as the latest chapter of their ordeal commenced.

The man appeared to grab a sod of damp earth from the bank of the stream and force it into Peter's mouth. There was no further wail of rebellion as more grass and soil was wrenched out and stuffed unceremoniously into the cavity of Peter's throat.

The woman began to cackle in Michael's earshot as Peter's legs continued to flail wildly against his torturer. More weed was yanked out by its mud-clotted roots and thrust into the defenceless, desperate victim.

The man began to laugh as Peter began to choke violently and swing his fists upward, narrowly missing the man's jaw several times.

Swivelling his position, the sinister torturer eyed a much larger source of intimidation. Still positioned with his might clamped across Peter's chest, he clutched at a large rock about the size of a football which was half nestled in the flowing water of the stream.

Slippery in his grasp, the jagged stone was held unsteadily aloft, directly above Peter's sobbing, fitful, suffocating form.

Michael wanted so to help his friend; yet felt nothing but total, desperate hopelessness as he watched Peter continue to writhe and splutter under the man's far superior physicality.

A raucous laughter again resonated around the clearing as the beast continued to parade the rock above Peter's head like some kind of trophy.

His venomous tirade of amusement gathered volume and gradually caused the woman to again giggle mercilessly in support of the despicable feat.

'Scared now are you, girly? You promise not to run out on me again? Are you sure? Because this thing is mighty heavy! Could do some real damage to that cherub little face of yours! You convinced now piggy? You had enough grass now? You gonna toe my line now…you little fucker?'

Peter's legs kicked out harder than ever in reply to the taunts.

Indeed, the boy's youthful resistance seemed to be growing in power as opposed to naturally weakening.

Still the boy's hands grasped wildly at the man's upper body.

'Oh! Trying to take me on again are you piggy? Want a wrestle do you piggy? Hey…Sheila…the piglet wants to fight me all over again!'

Still with the weighty stone held overhead in his clutches, the man turned and smirked at his female counterpart.

In turn, Michael's gaze lifted to engage with hers.

As Michael examined her complete ugliness, he observed her prolonged expression of perverted pleasure.

And he continued the study of her face as it then altered in an instant from twisted amusement into a blackened mask of utter dread as she speculated upon the dastardly episode playing out before her.

Michael became momentarily puzzled and continued to be curious about the sudden evolution in her features.

But he had not seen what she had just witnessed.

Unlike her, Michael had failed to behold Peter's final, exasperated effort to free himself from a monster.

A hefty punch that had landed squarely in the man's midriff, as his tormentor's attention focused on the gleeful audience behind him.

And whilst that blow was barely enough to significantly pain the monster, the second consequence would be damning to that defenceless eleven-year-old.

The rock that hovered precariously above Peter's head was instinctively released as the holder flinched against the unexpected blow to his rib cage.

The stone landed down on Peter's face without any sound.

Instantly cracking the jawbone, the heavy weapon remained in place as the broken remains of the boy's head fell back into the gentle waters of the brook.

A crystal-clear, peaceful passage of nature now became slowly polluted with scarlet.

The colour of a boy's prolonged sufferance that now also represented the finality of that same plight. Five seconds of inert silence followed as Michael unfathomed the mystery for himself.

And eventually, the woman screamed out in horrified disbelief.

'OH MY FUCKING GOD, TIM! WHAT THE FUCK HAVE YOU DONE? OH MY FUCKING GOD! FUCKING CHRIST! NO! YOU CAN'T HAVE! YOU STUPID BASTARD! YOU STUPID FUCKING BASTARD! YOU STUPID BASTARD!'

Michael turned to see the man staggering from his knees to his feet, leaving Peter's prostrate, lifeless form half submerged in the flow of water.

The woman's highly pitched fear continued to pierce his focus.

'FUCKING HELL TIM! FUCKING HELL TIM!'

The man stood above the body of the boy.

The boy no longer kicking out against his constraints.

The boy no longer fearing the unpredictable.

For that boy, Peter Leavesdon, was dead.

And the man's realisation of his woeful miscalculation soon came rushing to the fore.

And an almighty argument ensued.

Michael listened to the explosive exchanges but was quickly blindfolded once again and pulled to his feet. Having been marched for a few minutes, he felt himself being hauled into the back of the van.

The adults continued to scream at one another as the engine started and the unholy carriage began to pick up speed away from the clearing.

Back to God knows where.

It seemed only minutes before Michael was returned to the unsavoury surroundings of the dank, foreboding bedroom. He was left alone as the violently vocal conflict continued in the next room.

He could not make full sense of what had transpired back on the moor. It was almost too excruciating to recall.

The relentless crescendo of raised voices eventually caused him to cover his ears, shut his eyes and transport himself elsewhere.

For now, at least one thing was certain.

He was rendered alone in his nightmare.

Peter was gone; permanently erased from the scenario.

The victim of a terrible misfortune.

The target of grievous horseplay; that had turned irretrievably awful in the blink of an eye.

The victim of a sadistic being.

And as he closed his mind off to the furore in the next room, he would not have heard the eventual conclusive slamming of a door and the instant, elementary silence that followed.

Unbeknown to that solitary eleven-year-old, as he desperately cowered into the crevices of his own conscience to hide away from the inevitability that awaited him, he need not have concerned himself any further.

For Michael Tompkins, the ordeal was nearly at its end.

CHAPTER 21

Tuesday; three-twenty-six a.m.

The air felt strangely cold around him as he began to stir.

In the cool shadows, Michael's vision began to acclimatise to the darkness of the early morning hours.

Daring to move no more than his eyelids, he attempted to try and identify his surroundings.

For five days he had been abandoned to the wilderness of an alien land in an unknown time. Cut off from all he knew. Nothing had appeared familiar. There had been no recognisable sign of the life from which he had been unwittingly extracted.

Yet he felt a curious semblance of safety as the amber glow of a nearby streetlamp cast its guiding presence across the concrete floor and brick walls that enclosed him.

Tilting his head one way and then the other, he began to try and assess his location. No longer was he in that cell of a bedroom.

Another thing was momentarily clear; he was alone.

There was neither sign nor sound of his captors.

Gingerly rising to his feet, he scanned the rows of rooftops that flitted with the early morning skyline. Looking down at his attire, he shivered whilst vaguely analysing his school uniform and new shoes.

Now dirty, stained, torn and tattered.

The harsh cry of a distant bird caused him to twitch nervously.

Then his legs began to move of their own accord.

One tentative step at a time.

Along the paved alleyway.

Out into the adjoining street.

And then, as if in subconscious relief, Michael stopped his stride.

He faced right towards the silent junction with the main road in the distance.

Then his focus turned one hundred and eighty degrees to embrace a most welcome and familiar vision.

A glinting silhouette that had become the motif of recent troubled history, and yet now supplied his mind with a feeling of absolute sanctuary.

The windows reflected orange-tinted patterns as the bell tower in the centre of the roof touched the black sky above.

At the frontage of the ensemble; a set of white-painted, iron gates.

With uncertain purpose now forcing him onward again, Michael began to make for the symbol that enticed him fully.

Riverlands Secondary School beckoned him ever closer as guiding stars looked down from once enraged skies.

And it quickly became clear to the eleven-year-old that the ruthless demons that had once emerged from that same sky, had now apparently vanished.

CHAPTER 22

Tuesday; 7-20 a.m.

D.I. Kevin Woodley slammed the door of his Mercedes and checked the display of his mobile phone. He rushed past the ambulance and two squad cars and stormed through the gates of the school entrance causing them to clang heavily into the adjacent brickwork.

He found himself to be almost running with the overriding sense of joyous anticipation.

He was greeted by the sight of two police officers who patrolled the entrance to the main foyer and landscaped surroundings. The expression on their faces was difficult to assess. He did not speak to his lower-ranking colleagues as his concentration became centred fully on the activity inside the building.

Yet the demeanour of those inside would seem to be neither happiness nor sorrow.

The Headmaster, Euan Ford, opened the double glass doors and allowed the detective inspector access.

'Which boy is it?'

The Head looked sternly into the eyes of the senior police officer.

'It's...Michael. Michael Tompkins.'

'Where is he?' snapped the D.I. impatiently.

'He's in the First Aid room. The paramedics are checking him over now.'

Kevin Woodley nodded as he brushed past the Headmaster and strode purposefully down the corridor.

In the bright artificial light, he stopped and pointed to a closed door.

'In here?'

Following closely behind, Mister Ford offered a gentle warning.

'Inspector...he's...he's alone. There's no sign of Peter. He...he hasn't spoken a single word since the caretaker found him.'

'When?'

'Asif would have arrived...oh about...about six-thirty.'

The inspector temporarily refrained from opening the door of the first aid room as he contemplated his secondary thoughts.

'Where was the boy found, Mister Ford?'

‘Right outside the school gates…huddled up against them. Asif said he was very cold and disorientated. He still had his school uniform on. A bit worse for wear…but seems physically okay. I arrived here soon after I got the call from Asif at about seven.’

D.I. Woodley pondered his next query.

‘Where’s the caretaker now?’

The Head pointed tentatively to the door that contained the subjects.

‘In there…with Michael. The boy wouldn’t let go of him. He becomes very distressed when Asif tries to move away.’

‘And…you’re sure? You are absolutely certain it’s Michael Tompkins?’

Euan Ford grimaced with more than a hint of remorse cursing his tone.

‘Yes. Lord only knows where his friend Peter might be.’

The detective opted not to interrupt the uncertain scenario beyond the door and began to walk slowly back toward the school’s reception area.

Once in the foyer, he beckoned one of the guarding officers at the entrance to come inside.

‘Smithy…we need to get the lad to hospital for a thorough physical. And as soon as you get hold of that uniform he’s wearing send it to forensics. Let’s see what comes up this time. I need to get hold of Stacey Coombs. Is she still encamped at Basford Lane?’

‘Yes Guv. Do you want me to contact her?’

‘No…I’d rather do that. You go with the boy and the medics to Shireheath General. Oh…and you might need to let the school caretaker go with you. We will get another statement from him today at some point. Don’t worry. It’s fine. It’s a comfort thing…the youngster’s obviously in deep shock.’

P.C. Smith appeared puzzled by the instruction but did not venture for explanation.

In any case, the D.I. had refocused his attention to the Headmaster who had begun to pace up and down the corridor with growing uncertainty.

‘Mister Ford…I know that school is due back open today. But there’s no chance…possibly all week now. My forensic unit needs to cordon the whole area off again as soon as possible. This is pretty damned unbelievable and very unusual. But there may just be that vital scrap of new evidence lying around. It might just help take us to the Leavesdon boy.'

The Head nodded in avid agreement.

'But what about letting the pupils know about the development, officer?'

'Not your responsibility. My units will deal with the pupils and public alike today. You need to get something in the post to every parent explaining basically what's happened. But we'll talk about the details of the letter later.'

The leader of the investigation did not give Mister Ford further chance to respond.

In a split second he had gone back outside to re-brief his men and then continued onward beyond the school gates and back to the Mercedes.

Pulling open the driver's door, he retrieved his mobile phone from his coat pocket once again and frantically searched the number list and pressed dial.

A deep sigh of trepidation was exhaled as he waited for the call to be connected.

He paused as the familiar sound of a female police officer answered swiftly.

'Hello? Stacey? It's Kevin. I'm on my way around there. The Tompkins boy has been found and is on his way to the hospital. Say nothing to anyone. I'm ten minutes away.'

CHAPTER 23

James Tompkins suddenly experienced a restrained sense of expectancy as he stared beyond the lounge window. He was fully aware that the families' liaison officer, W.P.C. Stacey Coombs, had taken a phone call only minutes earlier.

Her subdued reaction after confirming the brief details of the call suggested nothing untoward.

Yet despite the urgent requests of both mothers, the female constable had dutifully followed the order to disclose nothing of the reported development until her superior officer had arrived.

After the longest ten-minute duration of the entire investigation so far, it was with not a little relief that she spotted D.I. Woodley's silver Mercedes pulling to a stop outside and she quickly moved into the hallway to intercept the inspector.

Surrounded immediately by the persistent throng of journalists, the D.I. was politely adamant that he would have an announcement for them in due course as he forced his way through the melee.

The scene beyond the front driveway and the seemingly determined approach of D.I. Woodley suggested to James that the news about to be revealed was progressive at the very least.

Eventually closing the door to activity on the pavement, the two police officers requested a couple of minutes alone.

All four parents sat impatiently in full attentive mode, trying desperately to decipher the mumblings from the adjacent passageway.

They knew instinctively that the officer had come to report a significant piece of news, yet the compounding emotion of the previous days was sufficiently suppressed as Detective Inspector Kevin Woodley finally entered the lounge and began to address the room with an appropriate air of authority.

All eyes settled on the police as they stood before the parents.

'There has been news. Please listen carefully. I have just left Riverlands Secondary School. I was called by Mister Ford to attend there at approximately seven o' clock. At six-thirty this morning, the caretaker and his assistant arrived to open the school premises as agreed with the police last Friday. Huddled against the entrance gates…alive and seemingly well…was one of our missing boys.'

David and James jumped to their feet simultaneously as W.P.C. Coombs discreetly joined the bewildered mothers on the settee.

The atmosphere altered in an instant, switching from inert anticipation to euphoric, cascading relief.

'Which boy? Which of our sons has been found?' demanded David.

The inspector glanced at the source of the query almost shamefully. He noticed that Hazel Leavesdon had already placed her hands over her face in dreaded expectation of the name about to be revealed.

D.I. Woodley slowly cast his gaze toward James and then Sharon.

'Mister and Mrs. Tompkins…it was…your son. We've found…Michael…'

With positive emotion now dictating reactions to the disclosure, both couples moved to embrace one another in a somewhat uncomfortable display of abject commiseration and earnest pleasure.

'Oh my God!' cried Sharon into her husband's embrace. 'Oh my God I don't believe it! Oh thank God. Oh my boy. Oh my poor boy. Oh we've got him back, Jim. We've got him back!'

The D.I. patiently watched the dramatic responses play themselves out, fully expecting the next painful enquiry from Hazel as her fraught features pleaded for some similar news about her own son.

'Inspector…where is my Peter? What has happened to my Peter, then? Where is he? Why didn't Peter come back as well? Why just Michael? It's nonsense! Oh Jesus…DAVID! WHERE'S PETER?'

The Tompkins were taken swiftly into the kitchen by W.P.C. Coombs who explained further details of the current situation, as D.I. Woodley tried to establish the known facts to Peter's mother and father.

From the disturbed sanctity of the conservatory, Wallace pressed his ever-inquisitive nose to the glass and watched silently as the mouths of the adults discussed the incredulous development.

Officer Kevin Woodley's professional and sympathetic manner implied that whilst the news was infinitely positive for the Tompkins, the business at hand was far from concluded.

Despite their distress, David and Hazel listened fretfully as the imminent scenario was relayed to them in a respectful whisper.

'Michael hasn't said a single word about what happened to Peter. I haven't yet personally spoken to him. The Headmaster initially identified him. He's in the care of the paramedics at the moment. We hope in a very short time that he'll lead us straight to your son. I believe the search is nearly over. This investigation is finally moving forward in the right direction. I am about to ask Michael's parents to attend the hospital. You may come if you wish.'

Hazel's overwhelming relief for her friends could not eclipse the jagged pill that she and David were being made to swallow.

The situation carried no logical explanation to anybody at that moment.

A miraculous, if wholly unsatisfying turn of events had only served to stir the mix of emotion between the four parents.

The Leavesdons wilfully followed the leader of the investigation into the kitchen to join with the others.

Sharon instinctively held open her arms to offer her condolences.

'I'm so sorry, Hazel. I don't understand this at all. I don't see why they haven't been found together. This is beyond real. It's just not fair. Like some twisted game. I just don't get it. They'll find Peter…don't worry…they'll find him now.'

James and David exchanged glances of mutual puzzlement. There had been a partial solution, yet the major aspect of the mystery remained unanswered.

The D.I. checked the time and proposed the next stage.

'Okay…the team will be at hospital by now. We can go now and wait there. Or you can stay here until I get the call for you to follow me there.'

Sharon was not prepared for any further hiatus in being reunited with her son.

'I want to go now! I want to see Michael now! Why the wait? What's going on?'

W.P.C. Coombs relayed the procedure that Michael would be undergoing.

'Michael needs to be placed under observation for a little while as well as undergo some simple tests. When the doctors are happy with his state of physical and mental wellbeing, then you will be allowed to see him.'

James felt a sudden pang of alarm at the worrying insistence on hospital checks.

‘Tests? What exactly are you testing him for?’

The female officer tried to soften the phrasing, yet the blunt nature of proceedings made such an attempt appear futile.

‘Just general clearance tests, sir. His bodily appearance. Blood and urine samples. Reflexes. Eyesight. Weight. Basically, just a standard physical. If there is any irregularity with Michael’s health, then we need to ascertain the symptoms and source immediately in order to administer remedial treatment to fight any infection that may be present.’

Sharon raised her voice in growing consternation.

‘Infection? But what kind of infection?’

Stacey Coombs remained calm as she explained to the increasingly agitated parents.

‘We are never sure, that is why the test procedure is in place. To be truthful, Mrs. Tompkins…any irregularity will be quickly detected. We need to establish that your son has not been in contact with anything, shall we say…unpleasant. Toxic materials, for example. Drugs, perhaps. It is much better to be safe than sorry.’

The D.I. quietly observed the debate yet was running out of patience with the unfolding drama.

‘Can we have a decision please? Are you all coming to Shireheath General? If so…I’d like to move forward with things. I need to talk to Michael promptly. His friend is still missing.’

*****

The four parents travelled in the Tompkins’ Astra behind the D.I.’s Mercedes as the journey snaked rapidly through the local estate and towards the city centre.

In the back seat, Hazel and David held hands tightly as they observed the increasingly frenetic rush hour traffic.

Eventually passing the junctions with Friar Lane and St John Street on the way, all four stared wide-eyed at the daunting picture beyond the car windows. The police had already sectioned off both roads and were diverting any approaching cars away from the scene. Scores of uniformed children were amassed, most carrying expressions of confusion as they were ushered back toward home.

Two mothers and two fathers would exchange no words.

The imposing sight of the hospital grounds instantly caused Sharon's entire body to tingle with reserved excitement. The Mercedes came to a halt at the security control barrier.

From behind the wheel, James watched avidly as D.I. Woodley imparted their business upon the parking attendant who promptly allowed provision for both vehicles to be stationed in the forecourt normally reserved for hospital staff.

Sharon's heart began to race uncontrollably as James applied the handbrake. Quickly alighting from the car, she stared up at the impressive old hospital building and its unsightly array of progressive extensions.

And the wondrous thought entered her mind that somewhere inside, was her son.

Although reunification was imminent, the moment had not yet gathered clarity for Sharon or indeed the others present, including the two police officers that led the group quickly and quietly to the paediatric ward.

James simply held his wife's hand again and looked into her eyes as the group walked swiftly into the busy entrance foyer.

Words could not be summoned to describe the inner elation felt by Sharon at that moment. She squeezed her husband's fingers tightly as they marched.

For the Tompkins, the remaining mystery surrounding Peter's whereabouts had been dispersed to the background momentarily.

This was Michael's time.

This was their time.

And if truth be known, despite the unsolved quandary, all four parents were equally relieved to see that at least one of the boys had been found. It was hoped by all that time would quickly bring matters to a positive conclusion.

D.I. Woodley instructed his female colleague to fetch some drinks whilst the four were stationed in a briefing room just outside the children's ward. He spoke quietly with a stern mask accompanying his instruction.

'I am now going to consult with my second in command and the hospital's police advisor. The tests will now be underway. I'll be back as soon as I can, but I may be a while. Please be patient. This is a critical time for the investigation. I need to establish the next stage of the search. Michael's responses to being back with us may not yet be rational but I need to talk with him first if possible.'

Hazel looked the detective in the eye and picked up on the sinister implication.

'So...you definitely believe that a third party is involved? That somebody kidnapped the boys?'

The inspector grimaced solemnly before trying to appease any further worry.

'Please...this is not the time for me to speculate. My job now is really only just beginning. I shall come back to you when Michael is ready to be seen.'

Sharon began to weep quietly in front of the Leavesdons, whose heads dropped in silent support for their friends.

'I want Michael now! I want to see him now!' she murmured.

James and David glanced up to the vacant doorway and then across to each other.

There was no opportunity to ask further questions.

The Detective Inspector had left the room.

*****

Three hours and twelve minutes had elapsed since the parents had arrived at hospital. With the time pushing toward midday, all four were becoming agitated at the lengthening hiatus in communication.

W.P.C. Coombs had tried to reassure them that such a situation was normal, yet she knew through her own relatively limited experience in such matters that events so far had proved far from typical.

It was also inevitable that imaginations were now naturally beginning to work overtime for some.

Whilst Hazel's mind toiled over her missing boy, Sharon's initial elation had slowly evolved into deeply rooted concern for her own child's welfare.

'What if he's not...very well...you know, Jim? What if they have found something wrong with him? What if something horrible has been done to Michael?'

Hazel responded to her friend's maternal trepidation with a surprisingly dispassionate claim.

'It's just standard procedure, Sharon. He'll be absolutely fine. They're just doing right by Michael. That's all. Making sure that he is returned to you exactly as he left you.'

The minutes ground slowly onward.

James watched every single person pass the row of windows that flanked the length of the briefing room, just as he had done for the past three and a half hours.

Sharon's concentration assessed the floor at her feet as she reflected on the excruciating pain of the previous five days.

The random impulses of frantic fear; the unrelenting terror of where her son might be or what he may be encountering.

The utter helplessness of the entire scenario had rocked the worlds of two families to their foundations.

It had almost been too much to bear.

Even now, sitting in the hospital briefing room, she could not fully register with the events that had turned her life upside down and very nearly threatened to tear it apart.

But now, the worst was seemingly over for at least two parents.

And then a voice emanated from the open doorway to disturb her unwelcome contemplation.

A familiar and welcome tone that spoke words of purest gold.

Stacey Coombs smiled broadly as she spoke.

'Sharon…James…Michael is ready to see you now.'

With legs instantly quivering as if made of jelly, Sharon pulled herself upright whilst tightly gripping James' arm, digging into the flesh of his shoulder for support.

The moment had arrived.

Finally, they would see their son again.

And in her subconscious, she hoped that the relentless remorse that had ever so recently infected her mind had now retreated once and for all, never to darken her days ever again.

'I'm thinking of you, Sharon.' whispered Hazel, through a tear-strewn gaze as she held her friend tightly.

'Brilliant. It's just brilliant.' whispered David, as he offered James a similarly warm gesture.

A mother's smile of overriding empathy emitted a parting promise.

'We'll come back to you, Hazel…in a bit…you know…when…'

Sharon's pledge could not find completion as she stuttered in anticipation of the imminent, overwhelming encounter.

The Leavesdons could only watch in envious suspense as the Tompkins were slowly led out of the room and hovered along the row of windows that lined the corridor.

Hazel and David watched until their friends finally disappeared from view, before they reluctantly reclaimed their seats.

As Sharon and James walked hand in hand behind the female officer, the sound of their own footsteps echoed around the stark white walls, bringing to bear the stifling proximity of their surroundings.

Following W.P.C. Coombs led them ever deeper into the workings of the city's hospital.

Through into another ward; down another corridor; around another corner.

The excruciating walk seemed to take forever.

Finally, Sharon and James were led to a door in which was a small window offering a view of a brightly lit room beyond.

Officer Coombs smiled with genuine elation and offered a suggestion as all three convened outside.

'This can be a very difficult moment for parents. If you want, you can try and catch his attention through the glass. Save causing him to jump. He is still in some shock as you can imagine. I think he's watching TV at the moment by the looks of it.'

James looked to Sharon for a sliver of guidance.

'Well? Do you want to take a peek at our son first? Or shall I?'

She nodded tentatively.

Nerves rattled her bones as a mother's gaze focused on the eye-level square of glass in front of her.

Moving tentatively toward the tiny window, she continued to intermittently engage with the encouraging stare of her husband.

And then finally, Sharon Tompkins succumbed to all-consuming maternal temptation.

Peering studiously through the small pane of glass, she let her eyes absorb the interior of the room beyond.

A young male nurse tended to the television set as Sharon's eyes scanned the room until they rested on the most uplifting sight of her life.

Sitting on a small settee, with a Rupert Bear annual in hand, was Michael.

Her whole body lurched with emotion as more tears quickly followed and the sensation constricted her throat.

Struggling to speak, she retracted from the window and pointed with a forefinger to guide James' viewpoint.

In turn, a father finally looked upon his son once more.

And the natural love of a parent came brimming to the fore.

'It's him...Sharon...it's him, isn't it! It's...Michael...our Michael...'

Both of Michael's parents nearly succumbed to the simultaneous release of their bewildering relief and instantaneously strived to suppress it.

Finally, they made the decision to enter the room together.

W.P.C. Coombs nodded gently in agreement and opened the door for them.

The boy's innocent gaze gradually became alerted to the fact that he was about to receive two unexpected visitors.

From the doorway, his parents saw the face of the child they believed they had lost. Both were quietly aghast at the drastic change in his appearance.

Yet after a mutual, prolonged, taunting silence, they then heard the pleasurable yet infinitely heart-breaking sound of his slightly quaking yet greatly soothing voice.

A resonance they earnestly started to believe they would never be privileged to hear again.

Words from a son they never thought they would ever see again.

His wide blue eyes engaged with the two adults standing only five yards away, as the infecting moment of recognition rapidly eclipsed their initial cautious wonder. Michael's lips trembled as he spoke.

'Mum...Dad...I'm sorry. I didn't want my head shaved...'

A tidal wave of glorious release swamped the moment, drowning the occupants of the room in its wilful, cleansing swell.

A mother, a father and a son were joined once more in blissful reunion.

And as they wallowed in the healing joy, they hoped the monsters that had ever so recently begun to crawl over their distant dark horizons were now banished for all eternity.

HAVEN

CHAPTER 24

Sharon felt at that moment that she did not want to let go of her son ever again. She forced her eyes tightly closed for a few idyllic seconds, both to absorb the proximity of Michael's physical being and ultimately to confirm that the scene would not reveal itself as some tormenting dream.

She immersed herself in the aroma of his exposed scalp and adjoined with the warmth of his body.

The irony was brutal; it was pleasure beyond imagination, yet derivative of such abominable events.

When finally she submitted to the maternal desire to once again embrace the vision and behold her boy at arm's length once more, she looked across to James who had momentarily withdrawn from the reunion to wipe away the release of joyous relief from his face and absorb the immersion into delirium.

Now, at last, it was the time.

Gently placing a palm on each of his shoulders, Sharon crouched lower and engaged directly with the sumptuous image of her son.

In turn he simply stared back, with his own features visibly stressing with emotional contortions caused by recent atrocious experience.

Sharon did not wish to speak at that moment; merely to look.

To allow herself to love Michael completely once again.

She observed again his face with its light tan, which now appeared somewhat paler under the clinical lights of the hospital ward.

Dark rings around his eyes suggested significant lack of sleep.

And she briefly contemplated the thoughts that might lay behind those young eyes; thoughts that would perhaps remain with him for a lifetime. Although she dearly hoped not.

Whilst declared physically intact by the doctor, the possibility pummelled her; that Michael's mind was now probably in turmoil, his juvenile psyche having perhaps been transposed to a very dark place where an untold chronicle of misery would surely unfold from his memory banks to haunt him.

But not now; not at this time of tender reunion.

Now was not the time for analysis or reflection.

But for jubilation.

Sharon pulled her son closer again and duly squeezed his frail form until she dared exert no more pressure for fear of hurting him. Michael's eager surrender in response to the maternal gesture mildly concerned her considering his customarily coy reaction to such displays of affection.

Unusually, he stood still and wilfully let himself be held firm and fast. Feeling his arms link around her neck exhibited his vulnerability to Sharon. Michael drew away again and kissed his mother on the lips. His resulting smile confirmed an inner happiness, yet the soft, almost infantile tone of his voice conveyed concern as he began to visibly fight his own emotional impulse.

'Mum…and you…Dad. And Wallace? Is he here? Have you brought Wallace with you?'

Again, his mother gently pulled away and cradled Michael's face in her palms as James knelt by his family's side and let his tears run freely with fatherly relief.

'We've missed you, darling. Oh my god, Michael…we've missed you. Wallace isn't here, no. But we'll take you to see him soon. We promise. Get you back home, eh? Back to your bedroom? Sound good, yeah?'

The crystalline eyes of the innocent child declared nothing less than pure love for his parents as Michael transferred his gaze between mother and father.

'Yeah! I've missed my television, too!'

Sharon's amusement was a welcome antidote to the pain of the previous days. Still in partial disbelief at what had transpired in the last hours, her eyes began to wander up and down and over her son once more.

She observed the slippers and Spider-man pyjamas that the hospital had kindly provided. They were a little large in size, but the notion was warming and fully appreciated. His shorn head would soon recover, and he would soon be applying his gel again in the mornings.

Then she unavoidably uncovered an unwelcome physical memento, giving a harsh clue as to the ordeal she could only imagine her son had endured.

Tentatively prising a forefinger underneath the thick cotton dressing, Sharon recoiled at the wound underneath as Michael cowered slightly with discomfort.

'OH NO! OH MY GOD! Your neck! Jim…take a look at his neck…my God what happened to you, Michael? Jim…look…at the marks on his neck! Oh, my poor baby…'

Michael's father drew closer on his knees and tentatively pulled open the collar on his son's pyjama top.

Michael's reaction to the discovery was simply to cry.

He wept at seeing the revulsion in his mother's sorrowful expression and the fermenting anger that began to prise itself into the stoic features of his father.

Engaging fully with her son's upset, she asked the rightful and justified question.

'What happened, Michael? Please tell me. Who did these things to you?'

Constrained by an inappropriate sense of guilt, Michael did not answer the question. He looked to the floor as potent memories suddenly revived themselves.

The most discomforting hesitancy was quickly relieved by another small group of visitors that had convened in the corridor beyond the door.

Led by the male nurse that was on supervisory duty, D.I. Woodley entered the playroom, also accompanied by an elder man with spectacles and a bald head which sported a skirt of grey hair. His white tunic suggested some medical connection, which was quickly confirmed by the detective.

Sharon, James and Michael offered their full attention to the entrants as the D.I. offered an introduction.

'Please…take a seat all of you. Hello Michael. So relieved to see you all back together again.'

The D.I.'s sentiment was met with a subdued silence which prompted him to continue with a gesture to the bespectacled man beside him.

'This is Doctor Graham Peterson. He is the hospital's leading paediatrician and has been treating Michael since his admission this morning. He specialises in criminal trauma and works in official conjunction with the local constabulary. Needless to say, his input over the past few hours has allowed him to draw some conclusions which you as parents now have the right to know.'

Sharon placed her arms tightly around Michael's waist and pulled him closer into her before begging the question. A protective palm cradled her son's shorn head which felt strange to the touch.

'You mean *now*? Do you want to speak to us right *now*?' she quivered.

'Yes…if that is agreeable. Time is now absolutely vital.' replied the superior officer. 'You can delay if you wish. We can talk elsewhere if you want to. Or we can stay in here. Here might be better. For everybody to remain as we would be the convenient option. We won't be disturbed.'

The group settled itself around the large table positioned at the end of the room. Sitting opposite the nurse, doctor and policeman, Michael perched between his parents, casting a wary and somewhat embarrassed glance over his strange inquisitors.

D.I. Woodley recommenced the conversation.

'Obviously I will need to talk to Michael in due course about the specifics of what has happened. But his health and wellbeing are the immediate priority at this time. Doctor Peterson has a full resume of the procedure that he authorised before you arrived. Most of it is just standard health checks. There is no cause for alarm.'

The physician shifted position in his chair and peered over his spectacles across the table with a certain sense of sorrow in his demeanour.

His expression altered to mildly sympathetic as his attention darted between the page on his clipboard and the expectations of the two parents sitting opposite.

'Mister and Mrs Tompkins…I am so glad to meet you both. I am very happy to report that Michael's general physical faculties are in normal functioning mode. He was extremely cold when admitted to the ward, but his temperature had recovered and now shows stability. His heart and respiratory functions are fine…as are his reflexes, hearing and eyesight.'

Sharon breathed a reserved sigh of relief as the doctor continued with the disclosure.

'Of course, his change in appearance may have startled you at first sight but I assure you his scalp has been examined and all is in good order. Blood and urine samples uncovered nothing more than a significant trace of mild sedative, akin to the potency of a common prescription sleeping tablet. By my reckoning it was administered into his system as little as four or five hours before he was discovered outside the school.'

James' glance diverted to D.I. Woodley, whose immediate expansion on the doctor's findings made some logical if disturbing sense.

'It is my belief that Michael was drugged before being returned to Shireheath. That way, he would be oblivious to any potential clues either to his surroundings or indeed the person or persons that brought him back. This theory lends itself to the probability of abduction.'

James again glared at the police officer with a demand for answers.

'But…I don't understand how Michael could have been just dumped at the school gates without anyone seeing anything. You've had police units around the place for three days, for Christ's sake.'

The D.I. nodded and was quick to reply.

'We've already checked local CCTV. Nothing shows up. Whoever was involved is either very shrewd or very lucky. Their timing was perfect. A three-second stop in the dead of night. Then they're gone as though they were never there at all. I'm as puzzled and frustrated as you, Mister Tompkins. Believe me.'

The doctor continued.

'The sedative would have greatly reduced your son's heart-rate, thus inducing a deep drowsiness and drop in body temperature. However, due to the limited potency of the drug he was given, he will make a full recovery and the substance will be completely out of his system within twenty-four hours.'

Sharon wiped her eyes and held Michael ever nearer.

Still her son remained silent as Sharon raised her major concern.

'What about his neck? What are the marks on his neck?'

The doctor studied the notes on his clipboard for a few seconds before the briefing continued.

'Michael's fine internally. However, as you have discovered for yourselves, he does carry some external injuries.'

James leaned forward as he struggled to contain his paternal fury.

'Some injuries? You mean…more than one? Such as? What has been done to my little boy?'

Doctor Peterson swallowed the natural despondency that always enshrouded such situations.

Despite his wealth of professional experience, it was never easy depicting the sufferance of a child.

Especially to the parents.

'Michael has some areas of severe bruising to his shoulders, arms and legs. They are not marks pertaining to a kick or any kind of an acute impact. It's more likely to have been caused by extremely aggressive physical handling.'

Sharon buried her face in her hands as James pressed for more answers.

'And his neck? The wound on his neck. What is that?'

'I believe the damage to the soft tissue on the region of his upper throat was caused by direct contact with an extremely hot implement. Some of the tissue is now dead and will be naturally dispensed in time. Other, more raw areas have been less severely harmed, and the blood vessels have self-cauterised. This tissue may well survive, but I'm afraid that the eventual disfigurement will not be fully reparable without surgery. Even then, there will likely be a scar. Thankfully there is no sign of infection.'

Both consumed by a prevailing sense of desperate anger, James and Sharon observed the composed reaction of their son, who now stared straight ahead as though transfixed by some distant, unknown distraction.

The doctor stood to his feet and shook the hands of the adults opposite.

'That is my report in its entirety. I am very pleased to say that Michael will be back to full health within a matter of days. I am happy for him to go home when it is deemed appropriate by the consultant. I do suggest however that you refer Michael back to the family GP. He can then liaise with my ward on any concerns. I'm certain it would prove beneficial to have a more familiar secondary opinion on matters and would provide subsequent peace of mind for you both.'

James shook the hand of the paediatrician and bore deeply into the elder man's eyes.

'Doctor…'

'Yes, Mister Tompkins?'

'Thank you…from the bottom of our hearts. Just…thank you…'

Graham Peterson nodded quietly, wished them luck, and left the room.

D.I. Woodley clasped his hands and offered the family a wide smile of earnest relief as his attention fixed to the eleven-year-old across the table.

'He hasn't much to say for himself. Is he normally this quiet?'

Sharon nodded sarcastically.

'Yes. He rarely speaks unless he feels the need...which is normally every twenty seconds. I can't believe you would make such a stupid comment, Officer Woodley. You believe he's just been kidnapped and you're wondering why he's a little bit subdued.'

'I'm just making observations, Mrs. Tompkins. This search isn't over yet. Peter Leavesdon is still missing. It might be perceived as tactless, but I need help. Your son is the only link I've got at this time. I need Michael to start talking to me...and quickly.'

James presented a more understanding appraisal of the larger picture.

'Yes...of course. We understand. Jesus! What must Hazel and Dave be going through back there?'

The tone of the exchange reverted to a more amiable level.

'My team is dealing with them appropriately. They have been taken home. I am still the officer in charge of this case and am obliged to keep you up to date with developments. I have sent Michael's school uniform to our forensic department. It would appear from what Michael told the nurse that it remained on his person for the entire duration of his disappearance. There should hopefully be a DNA match with what we have already collated.'

Sharon's moistened gaze suddenly widened with acute fear.

'Are you saying that if no more evidence comes to light, then Peter's whereabouts hinges directly on information from my son?'

It was unpleasant for D.I. Woodley to confirm such a damning scenario.

'That...is exactly the circumstance that I might be facing come this time tomorrow. However, considering the trauma and upset that you've all been through, I shall allow you time to recuperate until then. But please bear in mind...I need some answers from Michael. Anything at all that might help me to locate Peter. I know my current standpoint seems very untoward and callous...but a child is still absent. I'm charged with that responsibility. It's my job to find him.'

Sharon Tompkins looked directly into the piercing gaze of the detective inspector with her consternation increasing by the second.

‘And what if Michael *can’t* help you? What if he can’t remember anything? What if he doesn’t *want* to talk? What if he doesn’t *know* anything about what happened to Peter? What do we do then?’

The D.I. rose quickly to his feet and moved toward the door.

‘Quite frankly…Mister and Mrs Tompkins…I haven’t bargained for such an eventuality. Without assistance from your son, my search is currently rendered at a standstill.’

James tried to inject a strain of optimism into proceedings.

‘But Michael was found where he was last seen! Surely that must instil some form of hope for you. Don’t you think…perhaps…the same will happen to Peter?’

D.I. Woodley pulled down on the door latch and sighed with foreboding suspicion in his response.

‘Yes…I agree…it was an incredible twist of fate that brought your son home. The question I must ask myself now is…why? There must be a valid reason for the act. Frankly…I’ve never seen anything like it. Returned to the probable location that he was first abducted from? Its baffling to say the least.’

A puzzled silence remained in the room as the detective stepped into the corridor.

‘I shall leave Officer Coombs here with you. She will escort you out to your car and follow on when you are allowed home. I will see you all tomorrow. By the way…I am actually overjoyed for your family. It makes a change to get at least half a result that falls into my lap for once. Enjoy the reunion. But bear in mind there is still work to be done.’

*****

It was another hour before the Tompkins family was discharged from the ward. Sheer euphoria accompanied Sharon and James’ departure as they sat with their son in the family Astra.

Yet the journey home did little to lighten Michael’s inner darkness.

He persistently averted his gaze from the passing scenery and positively curled up in retreat on the back seat when the car travelled adjacent to the area by the school.

He was still in his Spider-man pyjamas when James lifted him from the rear of the car and lovingly cradled his son to the front door of number twelve, Basford Lane. It was also of great relief to see that the hungry press pack had been completely dispersed by the police.

'That was nice of the nurse to let you keep those pyjamas wasn't it, Michael?'

Sharon's loving whispers carried little weight of provocation as Michael simply smiled and nodded.

Unbeknown to his parents, the youngster's anxiety to enclose himself at home was overbearing.

Once back into the hallway, the Tompkins were each given hugs of congratulations by W.P.C. Coombs, who allowed the family to settle in the lounge before departing.

Sharon followed the female officer back to the door.

'Thank you, Stacey. For everything. You've been brilliant. A real rock.'

'No problem, Sharon. It's my job. I just hope his friend turns up, now.'

Michael sat on the edge of the settee, allowing himself to become familiar with surroundings once more. His concentration diverted across to his father calling from the kitchen.

'I know somebody who has really missed you, Michael. In fact, I can see him from here. Can you see him? He's peering at you now!'

Michael stood to his feet and turned slowly to gaze through the kitchen toward the conservatory door. The large furry head and pointed ears of Wallace formed a welcome sign of home. His exuberant barking was symbolic of a return that all had begun to believe might never happen.

James moved aside to allow the German Shepherd out of confinement and the dog's nose took him immediately to his human brother who resumed his perch at the end of the sofa.

Whilst Wallace sniffed, whined, and licked, Michael simply held his hands clasped between his knees and maintained his attention beyond the lounge window.

Everyone in the room was present except, it seemed, for the eleven-year-old.

His focus was fully occupied elsewhere, dealing with other, infinitely more sinister scenarios

As his family moved around him and cast him tokens of their parental love by the minute, Michael's demeanour remained aloof from his immediate surroundings.

Through the glass of the bay window, he watched the darkening azure of the late-summer sky; his mind now spinning helplessly through fathomless depths of tragic misunderstanding and unyielding deliberation.

Over his shoulder in the kitchen, his mother and father intermittently yet subtly celebrated the end of their nightmare.

But for Michael, the true ordeal had only just commenced.

CHAPTER 25

The following morning heralded a sense of great uncertainty for D.I. Kevin Woodley. Having been summoned to his superior's office for an urgent briefing at nine o'clock, he could not help but wonder what the higher-ranking policeman would offer as a plan, once his most prolific investigative officer had again declared a complete absence of current leads aside the re-appearance of Michael Tompkins.

Chief Superintendent Joseph Barnes remained seated behind his desk as the D.I. knocked and entered the room.

'Morning, Kevin. Please…take a chair. I'm sure I don't need to inform you what this discussion will be about.'

The detective shuffled uneasily into the seat opposite.

'No, sir. The missing boy…I presume.'

The Superintendent eyed Inspector Woodley with anticipation, sincerely hoping that some form of positive development in the search would be conveyed.

'You would presume correctly. So, Kevin? Any news on the other victim…Peter…I forget his surname…?'

The D.I. rubbed his eyes in frustrated fatigue. His last useful night's sleep had seemed to belong to another lifetime. His body and mind ached for respite as the Chief waited impatiently for a constructive response.

Whichever words were chosen, it was not going to be an easy revelation.

'Leavesdon, sir. Peter Leavesdon. The other lad that was found yesterday…Michael Tompkins…he has now been discharged from hospital and is back at home with his parents, sir.'

The Super slightly shifted his not inconsiderable bulk and leaned his elbows on the desk. He scrutinised the police detective with narrow-eyed expectation.

'So…when will you be talking to him properly, Kevin?'

'Today, sir. Hopefully…this afternoon…at the very latest. The family have been informed that their presence is required.'

'That boy has the answers, Kevin. You do know that…don't you? He is vital. He'll talk to you if you're decisive enough. If you probe him directly, I am certain this matter will resolve itself.'

'Maybe so, sir. It's difficult to say at this time.'

'What about the physiological report?'

‘Nothing at all on his body sir, besides a lot of severe bruising and some areas of temporary scolding from what we believe likely to be cigarette burns. His head was shaved, too sir. Very odd. However, there is certainly nothing incriminating with regard to toxins. His clothing is still with forensics. Judging by the state the school uniform was in I’m hoping to uncover a definite match pretty soon.’

Finally, the Chief compelled himself to rise to his full height and began slowly pacing the room. Placing his hands in his pockets, he gazed through the window behind his chair and deliberated on the impending scenario.

‘Yes…there’s a lot of hoping and wishing going on, isn’t there. Far too much, for my liking. It’s a strange one this, Kevin. No evidence. No witness. No trace. Yet a schoolboy has been taken and shoved back under our noses within the blink of an eye? How the hell could we not have seen this?’

Kevin Woodley began to lightly perspire as he formulated a mildly argumentative reply.

‘Well…actually, sir…let’s remind ourselves of what we actually know about what has transpired.’

The Superintendent swivelled his squat form toward the inspector.

‘Explain yourself, Kevin.’

‘Well…put quite simply, sir…every theory is still open to scrutiny at this current time. We have no evidence to even suggest abduction took place yet.’

‘But that’s what we’ve been touting to the media and public, isn’t it? Or are you telling me you’ve got it wrong?’

The D.I. was becoming increasingly agitated at the accusatory slant in the Chief’s tone but having to defend his corner from superiors was not unfamiliar territory.

‘I’m telling you, sir, that I am not prepared to speculate. We checked the local area very thoroughly. All weekend I had two units stationed inside the school grounds and the surrounding residential estate. Those same units are doing it all again now the boy has re-appeared. As you yourself have just this minute intimated…it’s a complete puzzle for sure.’

Now the debate began to gather its own natural energy.

‘Come on Kevin…there must be something? What about the CCTV? They don’t miss a trick nowadays, you know!’

'Nothing from either the school security monitors or the town cameras. It's as though the boys simply vanished into thin air last Thursday afternoon.'

Joseph Barnes stopped his somewhat laboured stride around the desk and rubbed his protruding jowl as an expression of frustrated curiosity formed itself into his features.

'I'm afraid that is not an acceptable conclusion…Detective Inspector. The public and press will be demanding some answers. Let alone the parents of the Leavesdon boy. They will expect us to be hot on the trail now…as we speak…right on the scent…'

Kevin Woodley gestured with open palms as his voice became laced with annoyance.

'Sir…there is no trail…there is no scent…I am not too proud to admit that this search is still currently beyond my control. I've got nothing.'

The Super pointed a stubby forefinger toward his colleague and grimaced.

'Well…being as you are currently clueless…you'd better adhere to my immediate tactic. As soon as possible, inform the parents of the Tompkins boy that they must address another media conference. And stick your oar in as well! Try and at least give the impression that the police are on top of things, eh?'

The D.I. shook his head and smiled cynically.

'With all respect, sir…I'm not playing your stupid political games…you can't fool the masses. Most of the public are actually intelligent beings, you know! Plus, I don't think that the Tompkins family will appreciate being shoved in front of the cameras again quite so soon.'

Now the Chief's demeanour carried more than a hint of dissatisfaction.

'Kevin…whether they like it or not…the Tompkins family are still part of an official police investigation…now more so than ever! They are legally obliged to partake on our say so!'

Despite the Chief's evident stance in the matter, the D.I. stood his ground.

'I'm sorry, sir. At this moment I'm far more interested in finding Peter Leavesdon. His parents and the public expect me to perform my duty. Something which I believe I have not yet been able to fulfil.

Your plan of giving the police a pat on the back is hardly appropriate, is it?'

The Superintendent calmed himself a little as he again turned to gaze at the view beyond his office window.

'It would convey the right impression to the right people, Kevin. That's all I'm saying. Those behind this crime are mocking us. A positive word or two from you would maybe suggest we are achieving something to eclipse that.'

Now Kevin Woodley began to lose his temper.

'But…with respect…that's total bullshit, sir! We have no idea who is behind this! You know as well as I do that I'm no further on with this now than I was five bloody days ago and things don't look like altering in a hurry! There's a top team behind me on this and we've been dead in the water from the word go. That's a fact I can do nothing about until some clues start to fall into my lap!'

Joseph Barnes turned to his most revered detective and stared at him with a discerning glint of insistence.

'I suggest that you don't sit about waiting for the clues to appear, Kevin. Go out and find them. They are there if you look hard enough…I'm sure. Get the Tompkins parents on camera. ASAP! Let's tap into the pool of positive morale while it's there. Which is now…at this minute…today! By this evening, once you've spoken to the Tompkins boy…we should be getting somewhere fast. You mark my words.'

The detective felt nothing less than exasperation at what he was being forced to listen to. As an officer of over twenty years' experience, it went against the grain to be patronised about his professional instinct and technique.

'Sir…the lad is eleven years old. I can't even guess what he's been through. Or where he's been! Or with whom! He's still very scared and I would assume in deep shock. This isn't a time for putting the big boots of authority on! It's not as though he's some accomplice with form who is choosing to keep his mouth shut. It's not even as if I can try and jog his memory with any bits and pieces.'

The D.I. watched disconcertingly as Joseph Barnes jabbed another fist his way.

'BUT SO FAR, HE'S THE ONLY BLOODY WITNESS TO THIS SO-CALLED CRIME THAT WE'VE GOT, KEVIN! SO

PLEASE NAIL DOWN SOME BLOODY FACTS WILL YOU! AND DO IT QUICK!'

Unlike his frothing Superintendent, the D.I. maintained a sense of emotional control as he attempted to argue with earnest reasoning.

'But he's a child, sir! A mere child! How much of what he recalls is going to be reliable? Pushing this issue could cause the entire case to explode on us…even though we have nothing anyway! For the time being…I ask you to trust my judgement. This situation needs a little TLC at the moment…don't you think? For everybody concerned! Especially for the constabulary?'

The Chief sighed as he again scanned the slow-moving rush-hour traffic beyond the glass.

'Alright! Have it your way. Kid gloves, it is. I'll leave the tea and sympathy to you, Kevin. Let's just get this thing moving and get the other boy back with his family. I'm not so concerned about finding any suspects just yet. They'll crop up in due course. We'll pop 'em when they crawl out from their hole. Just give this thing some visible momentum. That's all I ask.'

The D.I. could not help but feel less than enthused regarding his superior's somewhat naive overview of matters.

At a loss for any further personal contribution, he vacated his chair and sullenly moved to the door.

'Do you want to use the Town Hall for the media conference again, sir?'

The Chief turned and spoke with misguided confidence.

'No! Outside their house will be fine. The press hacks will put the word about quickly enough. And get the whole family on the thing if possible. Then get the Tompkins boy back here for questioning.'

D.I. Woodley shook his head in disbelief once again but did not offer any further question as to the motive and strategy of Chief Superintendent Barnes.

'Right, sir. I'll call the Tompkins' house now. I'll arrange both the conference and station interview.'

Closing the door quietly behind him, Detective Inspector Woodley could not help but sense that events had already moved beyond retraction.

There was a tangible, hopeless menace about the entire case.

A gnawing feeling, that from the moment the boys disappeared, any police attempt to solve the mystery would prove to be futile.

Despite his conscience plaguing him with such a tormenting notion, orders were orders, however transparent, feeble, and desperate.

With little other option on the table, he made his way back to his own office and prepared to organise arrangements for the day ahead.

*****

'Stacey…how are they?'

W.P.C. Coombs quickly checked her watch as she greeted the D.I. at the front gate of number twelve, Basford Lane.

'I haven't really spoken to them that much this morning. It's a bit of a private time just now as you can imagine.'

'Well…you've done a great job. Did you discuss the media call with them?'

'Yes, Guv.'

'Are they okay with it?'

'The father says he will come outside and say a few words. He's very concerned about the reaction of the Leavesdon family. But he's agreed in the hope that it will finally get rid of this lot once and for all.'

The inspector turned to glance at the gathering throng of journalists and cameramen that had re-assembled in the last hour. He simply stared through them, whilst ignoring the repeated requests for a statement.

'Yes, hopefully, Stacey. To be honest, there will be little more reason for them to stick around after today, anyway.'

The female constable noticed a definite sense of discomfort in the D.I. His typical assuredness in dealing with daily business was alarmingly absent.

In its place was an aura of disdain and she felt obliged to enquire as to its source.

'I know it's not really in my remit, Guv…but how did you get on with the Chief Super this morning?'

There was a momentary pause as the detective carefully considered his response. It was difficult not to openly criticise his superior in front of a constable, but professional courtesy quickly came to the fore.

'Barnes wanted this conference today, you know! Not me! I think it's a badly judged idea. But he feels our units are not being seen as active enough. He thinks that the return of one of the boys should entitle me to soften the fact that the other lad is still missing whilst I conjure him up from behind my back.'

W.P.C. Coombs screwed up her face in bemusement.

'So, what does he expect you to achieve with this, then?'

'Apparently I've got to tell the media that the police are on the case and things will be okay.'

'But how can he expect you to do that? We've had nothing to go on. Absolutely nothing!'

The D.I. moved slowly along the drive toward the front door of number twelve.

'I know, Stacey. Don't I bloody know it! It's all fucking politics at his level though isn't it! He's forgotten what the reality of the job is like. I've tried to tell him…this entire episode could make us look a laughing stock if I make even the vaguest promises that aren't kept. Plus, I need to take the Tompkins boy in for questioning this afternoon. It goes without saying that I'm not looking forward to that! I just hope he comes up trumps without too much pressure. Anyway…it's nearly midday. Let's get this over with.'

*****

An hour passed whilst Sharon had covertly watched the scene unfold below from the sanctity of Michael's bedroom window. Through the gap in the curtains, she had observed James talking to the swollen gathering of media reporters. Most had subsequently vanished to make their phone calls, write their emails, and prepare their headlines.

James remained at the front gate talking with the D.I. and W.P.C. Coombs, but it was impossible for Sharon to decipher what exactly was being discussed.

She diverted her gaze to look down at Michael, finally resting peacefully in his bed. Still adorned in the colourful pyjamas donated by the hospital, he had only submitted to sleep a couple of hours earlier. His hair was showing signs of soft re-growth which was pleasing.

Sharon on the other hand had not slept at all. She had remained fixed by her son's side ever since his return.

Never once had she dared to leave him out of her sight.

She found herself ever eager to tend to his every possible whim.

Yet the strain of guilt was now beginning to grind within her soul; already to disturbing levels of tormenting persistence.

Guilt for her self-imposed sense of maternal failure.

Guilt for the untold sufferance of her only child.

And guilt for her friends, whose son remained beyond the reaches of their loving, desperate grasp.

Michael had been requested by the D.I. to attend the police station with his parents at three o'clock.

It was already time to wake him and get him ready for his appointment.

As she moved across the landing to the bathroom, she heard James enter the hallway and close the front door. He was alone.

Sharon peered over the top rail of the stairway and caught her husband's attention.

He instantaneously looked upward to her and offered a weak if affectionate grin.

'You alright, love?'

Sharon nodded avidly.

'Yes…you?'

'I think so. To be honest though…it's felt a long while since I felt alright about very much. But we'll get there again, won't we?'

His wife acknowledged her agreement with a smile.

'What's happening now, Jim?'

'The police are going to wait for us at the station. I said we'll make our own way.'

'Okay. Fine. I'm just about to run Michael a proper bath. He still smells of that hospital shower!'

James ascended the stairs to meet Sharon at the landing balustrades. Their conversation evolved into a whisper as he gazed toward Michael's open bedroom door.

'How's my son doing?'

'He's doing great, Jim. Not long nodded off. He watched a bit of telly. Had a bit of toast earlier, too.'

'And how's my wife doing?'

Overcome by a rush of love for the man standing before her, Sharon cradled his face in her palms and kissed him gently on the lips.

'Your wife's also doing fine. I've made an appointment for Michael to see Doctor Davies tomorrow morning at ten. I thought it best to get all the unpleasant stuff out of the way sooner rather than later.'

James nodded as his expression altered to adopt a rather more downbeat demeanour.

'Good thinking, love. Listen...what do you reckon we ought to do about Dave and Hazel? We haven't spoken to them since we left them at the hospital, yesterday. It's really beginning to bother me.'

It was an unpleasant situation with no obvious remedy.

The continuing heartache felt by the Leavesdons would not be easily appeased.

Unfortunately, the police had offered no credible suggestion, either.

'I think we need to keep ourselves as the number one priority...just for now, Jim...don't you? They'll be fine about things. They'll be okay with us. I'm sure of it. I'm sure Peter will come back to them.'

James kissed Sharon once more and began to descend the stairs back down to the hallway.

'Right...if you say so. God this is a nightmare. Listen...the coast looks clear outside...looks like the press have got bored. I'll take Wallace out for a walk while you get Michael ready. I won't be long.'

*****

One o'clock p.m.

The news bulletin ran its opening titles whilst overwhelming dejection shrouded Hazel and David Leavesdon as they huddled together on the sofa.

Neither parent felt compelled to utter a single word as the stiff-suited broadcaster introduced the programme and listed the main featured items.

Yet there had only been one story to capture the attention during the past days. The issue of the two missing boys had anchored itself into public psyche.

Their images still formed a stark backdrop to the announcer's fabricated display of concern.

But now the situation had altered dramatically.

Now only one boy remained missing.

The painful fact was confirmed by the sudden appearance on the screen of James Tompkins, standing outside his own house, thanking the police for their efforts, and praising the gentlemen and ladies of the media for their patience and understanding.

It is a time for reflection; he says.

A time for reassessing values and priorities; he says.

A time to spare a thought for two other parents who's loved one had still not been returned to them; he says.

And despite the subsequent pledges of the by-standing Detective Inspector that he will continue in his endeavours to locate Peter Leavesdon, the titanic struggle just became mightier for the parents in question.

Wrapped in a brittle unison on the settee, they found little hope to be derived from the vision and words emitting from the television screen.

Despite the plea from the police, Hazel had refused to perform a secondary press conference to bolster the effort to find Peter.

And as a loving mother suddenly doubled up with the agonised intensity of her continuing loss, a loving father held back his own wave of helpless release, just long enough to reach over and switch off the damning TV set.

Then together, as man and wife, and as mother and father, in the piercing silence of the family home, they wept relentlessly for their absent offspring.

*****

Sharon swished the water around and added some bubbles.

'Michael! Are you awake yet? Your bath's almost ready.'

As the tub gradually filled, Sharon studied the patterned tiles on the wall around the bathroom. So many times she had sat and studied them in Michael's absence during the recent days, wishing dearly that her agony would soon relent.

How she now relished the fact that she could appreciate their pastel motif with her son by her side once again.

To once more feel at liberty to enjoy her home as a safe and carefree environment.

Her concentration was broken by the appearance of Michael at the door. He looked tired, pale, and disinterested.

A cleansing soak would surely rejuvenate him.

'Hello love! Take your pyjamas off and get in. It shouldn't be too hot. Put some cold in if it is. I'll go down and get you a clean towel.'

'Mum…I'm hungry. Can we go to Macdonald's later?'

'Of course we can, darling. I won't be a minute.'

Elated by his presence in the house and his renewing appetite, Sharon bolted downstairs and into the outhouse. From the tumble drier she retrieved a large, soft peach-coloured towel and jubilantly embarked on the return trip up to the bathroom.

At the top step, she discreetly enquired as to whether Michael had yet taken to the water. She was cautious not to embarrass him by intruding on his youthful nakedness.

Just beyond the door her wishes were confirmed by the welcome sound of splashing. She entered the bathroom and glanced at her son as he sat tentatively in the soapy water.

'It wasn't too hot, Mum.' he smiled.

'Make sure you use a little shampoo on your head, as well. You know how to do it. And wash everywhere! Armpits too! All your bits and bobs! Your clean towel is on here love, okay?'

Turning away from the vanity sink, her attention switched back to Michael as he asked another question.

'Mum…why am I going to the police station?'

Temporarily distracted by disbelief at the dark bruising on his body, she stared intently at her son's bare skin, which had been rendered black and blue across his back. She recoiled quietly at the burn marks and concentrated on responding to his question.

Her answer was simple and to the point.

'The police need to speak to you. They need to find out what happened to you and Peter.'

With emotion gathering force from deep within her core, she moved closer. Crouching down beside him she took the opportunity to indulge in a more definitive assessment of his injuries. Deep purple patches on his shoulders and torso caused her throat to tighten with fretful maternal instinct.

Again, Michael's mind ventured for information.

'Why do they need to know what happened, Mum?'

She gazed into her son's innocent eyes as she replied.

‘Because they want to know who caused these bruises and burns, Michael. So they find them and send them to prison. And…and because Peter hasn’t come home yet.’

The lint dressing around his throat had been discarded as per the hospital’s instruction. Sharon would apply a fresh disinfectant pad once Michael had bathed. Yet the wound glistened back at her, instilling an astonishing sense of revulsion.

Revulsion at his injuries.

And of her supposed incompetence.

And abject hatred for the unknown administrators of such a detestable crime.

Michael sensed he was under scrutiny and attempted to conceal the physical reminders of his experience.

Pulling his knees closer under his chin, he evidently did not feel comfortable in displaying himself as a testament to such brutality.

The atmosphere between mother and son became suddenly terse as his voice adopted an unusually ominous tone.

‘Mum…I will remember. I will remember who did it. I won’t ever forget who hurt us.’

And then it hit Sharon squarely between the eyes.

The full, unflinching horror of what the two boys must have endured.

Torture.

Pain.

Suffering.

Repeated.

Repeated until they could probably take no more.

And as Michael cowered from his mother’s concerned observations, he stole a brief glimpse of her faltering expression.

Her exaltation at his return was to bound be short-lived in such circumstances.

Words and feelings could not even begin to heal the hurt she nurtured inside her soul.

The utter remorse of a mother; sourced by the fact she had ever allowed her child to be harmed.

A mother who believed she had failed her offspring in the worst possible manner.

A mother who had not upheld her responsibilities.

And as she combatted her relentless conscience, that same mother's tears ran from her eyes, splashed down her face and into the bath water.

As in turn, did her son's.

CHAPTER 26

Michael watched his father through the car window. James Tompkins pulled open the rear passenger door of the green Astra and offered his son a warm smile of reassurance.

'Okay, Mikey. It's time to meet the nice policeman again who helped try to find you.'

Sharon quickly moved next to Michael and firmly held his hand as the trio began to walk steadily toward the tinted glass frontage of Shireheath Police Station.

He squeezed on his mother's fingers with increasing pressure as they entered through the sliding door and approached the reception desk.

A concerned mother turned to her son with a whispered enquiry.

'You alright, darling?'

Michael nodded vacantly as the surly looking reception officer greeted the trio.

'Good afternoon…may I help?'

James firstly observed the sergeant's pristine white shirt and then his attention cast upward to absorb the distinctly unwelcoming expression.

'Yes…we're here to meet with Detective Inspector Woodley.'

The officer instinctively glanced down and eyed Michael carefully before picking up the phone handset from the ledge behind him.

'I take it he is expecting you? He is a busy man, you know.'

James did not respond to the disinterest of the sneering desk sergeant.

With the arrival of the Tompkins family communicated, they were asked to be seated across the other side of the foyer.

Both parents quietly observed the interior of the building as they waited. It seemed such a daunting environment for parents to bring their children. Bare grey walls offered little in the way of character or even mildly positive inspiration to be in such a place.

Starkly illustrated posters warned of the penalties for various crimes.

James and Sharon each read the grimly depicted collage of modern society with increasing depression.

Then again, both supposed, the station was hardly designed to act as a place of pleasantry.

Sharon heard the sounds of angry raised voices in the corridors beyond, causing her to wonder what dastardly deed they may have endeavoured to accomplish before being encouraged to revolt against their temporary custody.

Her gaze again fell to Michael. It may have been because of his shorn hair, but for some bizarre reason he looked far more grown-up than before. Despite her maternal bond with him, she certainly believed that the child-like essence in her son had faded away many months ago.

Indeed, he was very mature and formed for his tender years.

Yet never more so had he displayed such maturity, than now.

Her concentration was broken by the sight of a familiar figure.

All three centred their attention on the oncoming figure of W.P.C. Stacey Coombs.

'Hello, again! Hello Michael! Would you all like to follow me?'

The Tompkins family stood as one and they followed the female officer into the depths of the station with an accompanying inner fear.

Fear derivative of two sources.

A fear of the unknown.

And fear of the known.

The day would yet decide whether the monsters hiding beyond the horizon would remain undiscovered or be openly turfed out from their shadowy domains.

Sharon held Michael's hand tightly whilst they walked as if it might be for the last time. And after the past days, she had indeed been forced to learn only too abruptly how such bleak desperation could manifest itself.

Turning several corners and navigating a flight of stairs, D.I. Woodley was eventually located leaning against the grey plaster-skimmed wall outside the interview room as he scanned a report.

Quickly standing straight to greet the Tompkins family, his jovial facade was received as genuine yet could only truly convey a mere semblance of warmth to the oncoming visitors.

'Good afternoon, James...Sharon. How are you feeling today, Michael?'

The son looked innocently to his mother before answering.

'I'm alright, thanks.'

‘Would anybody like a drink?’ enquired the D.I.

Michael paused before affirming the invitation.

‘I’d like coke, please.’ he answered.

‘One coke. What about you two? Anything?’

Sharon and James simultaneously shook their heads as James confirmed.

‘No. Not yet. Thanks all the same.’

With W.P.C. Coombs despatched to the drinks machine, the detective invited the Tompkins family inside the interview room and tactfully positioned Michael between his mother and father across the table, ensuring that his own chair would be directly facing the eleven-year-old.

Shutting the door, he set himself down, loosely clasped his hands together and rested his forearms on the hard wooden surface of the tabletop. A notepad and pen were positioned in front of an empty chair at the end of the group.

Sharon noticed for the first time that the detective carried a kindly yet battle-hardened air about him.

He spoke softly, yet his professional motives were quite clear and authoritative as he addressed the nervous adults.

‘Okay…of course I know that this has been the most difficult of times for the three of you. But as I am sure you are all aware, this police investigation is far from over. In fact, since your son’s return, it has only escalated in priority. I need to ask Michael some serious questions about what happened. And I’m hoping for some honest cooperation. I’m going to be totally frank, Mister and Mrs. Tompkins. As things stand, without Michael’s help, Peter Leavesdon’s current whereabouts are going to remain a complete mystery for the foreseeable future.’

As his parents dutifully nodded their alarmed acknowledgement of the scenario, Michael remained calm and appeared almost aloof from the scene. It was almost as though the severity of the matter at hand had not yet registered with him.

At that moment, the door opened and cracked the unwelcome growth of apprehension.

W.P.C. Coombs placed Michael’s can of drink and a glass on the table before him whilst beckoning her superior to attend to some activity outside the room.

‘Please…excuse me for one moment. Stacey will remain here with you.’

Mildly frustrated by the intrusion, the D.I. left his seat and ventured quickly into the corridor.

He suddenly became excited to be greeted by Detective Sergeant Neil Griffin, the leading forensics officer assigned to the investigation.

However, the dour introduction to the conversation rapidly dampened the inspector’s enthusiasm.

‘Kev…you’re not going to believe this.’

D.I. Woodley was sure to close the interview door behind him and the pair began to walk slowly along the passageway.

‘What is it, Neil?’

‘I’ve now fully analysed the boy’s school uniform. I’m sorry for the delay but we did a thorough job.’

‘Not a worry, Neil. I understand. So…what have you got for me?’

There was a short and determined hiatus before D.S. Griffin disclosed the news.

‘We’ve found a link with some evidence we retrieved from the scene.’

Both officers stopped their stride and indulged one another in expectant silence.

The inspector’s eyes widened with feint hope.

‘Go on…’

‘The cigarette end…taken from the alleyway dissecting St John Street and Friar Lane. DNA lifted from that matches exactly with DNA on the boy’s shirt and pullover. Hair fragments on the clothing also match with the DNA strains on the cigarette filter.’

It was hard for D.I. Woodley not to jump with a reasonable sense of accommodating euphoria, yet experience tempered his initial response to the news.

‘What about records, Neil? Have they got me a name?’

The forensics officer shook his head in sympathy.

‘Sorry, Kevin. Of course, we got it straight over to them as I always do. Not one single candidate cropped up.’

The conversation had ultimately proved to be tremendously disappointing.

‘Fuck…fuck…fuck!’ declared the D.I. under his breath. ‘That data match really was my last hope up to now.’

The forensics specialist placed a hand of support on the inspector's shoulder.

'No, Guv…your last and best hope is sitting in that interview room.'

The police officers eyed one another with long held mutual respect.

'Thanks for your efforts, Neil. I'm sure the Chief Super will be delighted with your contribution to proceedings!'

'Yeah…right! See you soon, Kev. And…best of luck.'

The D.I. promptly returned to the Tompkins family and asked W.P.C Coombs to remain with the group to take notes as she sat next to the trio.

He observed their natural apprehension and attempted to quash any uncertainty about what was about to ensue.

'Mister and Mrs Tompkins…I wish for the business of this meeting to remain as informal as possible for the time being. Your son is not going to be asked to confirm any kind of a statement today. I just want him to try and feel confident in attempting to recollect some key events. That's all. He is free to leave whenever he wishes. You have the right to legal representation of your choice, or we can appoint a solicitor on your behalf.'

James nodded his head in pleasant satisfaction.

'No problem, inspector. Please…do what you need to do. The audience is big enough, for now. You have our full cooperation. My son will help you if he can. He's a good lad.'

The focus shifted quickly to Michael, who simply stared back without word as the D.I. addressed him in a softer, less intimidating tone.

'I really appreciate your visit today, Michael. We're all really pleased to see that you're back safe and sound with your family. The thing is…your friend, Peter…is still missing. And I need your help to find him. Do you understand what I'm saying?'

Michael's gaze did not waver from the detective for a second.

'Yes…I understand.'

With a sharp intake of caution, the inspector continued.

'Let me take you back to last Thursday. The last time you went to school. Can you remember? Do you recall the final lesson you had that day?'

There was no hesitation in Michael's reply.

He engaged completely with the police officer's commanding aura.

'Maths…with Miss Doherty. She seems nice…for a maths teacher.'

The expression of the D.I. lightened with amused surprise.

'Yes. Good! And after the lesson…do you remember leaving school at home-time?'

Again, Michael spoke with supreme confidence and immediacy.

'Yes. Me and Peter left school together. His mum was supposed to be there to meet us. But she wasn't at the gate.'

On hearing the details of the account for the first time themselves, Sharon and James alternated their transfixed attention between the interviewer and their son.

Michael's cool compliance was to be admired.

The enthusiasm of the four present adults to hear more increased by the second as the inspector pressed onward.

'What did you do when you discovered that Peter's mother wasn't there to collect you?'

'Peter walked off to try and find her. I didn't think we should leave the school, though. Mrs Leavesdon told us to stay inside the school gate if she wasn't there on time. But Peter couldn't wait. He never did as he was told.'

'Did you tell him to stay with you at school?'

'Yes…but he just walked off.'

'Did you follow him?'

'Yes, eventually. He wouldn't listen to me when I told him we'd probably be in trouble.'

'What happened next?'

The D.I. watched as Michael's juvenile façade of strength began falter ever so slightly.

The eyes of the boy flitted from his parents to the tabletop as his memory searched for the correct answer.

Michael reached for the drink of coke and took a sip before cradling the can between his fingers.

'We…we reached the alleyway…the one just opposite the sweet shop.'

'Yes…and then what happened?'

'A man…standing in the street…said he'd seen Peter's mum parking her car…'

Adrenaline began to pulse through the veins of the Detective Inspector. Not in his wildest imagination did he hope to be confronted with such a concise account from the eleven-year-old considering his suspicions regarding what the boys had endured.

The shroud of mystery surrounding the timeline was clearing rapidly.

Then the infuriating thought briefly crossed the inspector's mind that the Chief Superintendent may well have been entirely correct in his strategy that Michael would be the willing key to the whole case.

'The man who spoke to you and Peter…what did he actually look like?'

There was a pause as Michael attempted to assimilate the vision in his head.

'Tall…thin…ugly…he smoked…he had a phone…'

'What happened next?'

'We went both down the alleyway to look for Peter's Mum.'

Now Sharon's attention was completely captivated by Michael's unfolding story. She squeezed James' forearm for support as her mind raced with distressing anticipation.

Still the detective pushed for answers.

'Is that where the man directed you to go…down the alley?'

'Yes. Well…sort of. We just did it anyway, I suppose. He didn't exactly tell us to do it.'

'And what did he do then?'

'He followed us.'

The inspector sensed the raw emotion now emanating from the adults across the desk. He observed Michael's parents as they wiped their eyes, struggling to retain composure whilst listening to their son's torrid chronicle.

For them, Michael's stunningly frank recollection was as painful as it was intriguing.

The detective continued.

'Were you scared by this point, Michael?'

'Not really…scared…but I knew something seemed wrong.'

'How did you know something was wrong, Michael?'

'Because at the other end of the alley a woman was standing…just…waiting.'

The officer's eyes widened with aroused determination.

'Can you describe her?'

'She was like the man, I suppose...tall...thin...ugly...with a phone as well...and she was talking into it.'

'Talking? Talking to the man that was following you?'

'I don't know. I'm not sure.'

'Okay...and what happened next?'

The stony atmosphere of the interview room was disturbed by the sound of quiet weeping.

Michael looked across to his mother. He studied her renewed display of open remorse and watched as his equally distraught father attempted to console her.

The D.I. intervened with due consideration for their reactions.

'Mister and Mrs. Tompkins...we can take a break if you wish?'

Both Sharon and James shook their heads and pleaded for the interview to continue.

Yet Michael himself remained completely unmoved by the responses of those around him and willingly turned back to the D.I. in order to answer the previous question.

'They put us both in the back of a van, I think. The woman hit Peter around the head. They didn't hit me. They just shoved me inside. Then we drove off.'

'What colour was the van?'

'I'm not sure. White...I think.'

'How long do you think you were driven for?'

'I don't know.'

'Did you not recognise the eventual place you were taken to?'

'It was dark. I couldn't see. I might have been blindfolded. I can't remember. We didn't see outside that much.'

'That's alright, Michael. What happened when you were eventually let out of the vehicle?'

'We were both inside a house. We woke up in a dirty smelly bedroom...with a pink plastic bowl to wee in. And the windows were bolted shut from the outside.'

The next query from the D.I. followed a considerate pause.

A deathly cold silence descended upon the room.

'What happened inside the house while you were there, Michael?'

The instantaneous replies of the eleven-year-old suddenly ceased their pattern of regularity.

Michael again glanced over to his parents, for whom the intensity of the revelations was now way too much for them to hear.

Yet understandably, the D.I. was not willing to let the momentum of the conversation drop.

'Michael…please…please…tell me…what happened to you both when you were trapped inside the house? What did the man and woman do to you?'

Again, the young victim did not respond.

The inspector rapidly altered his question to retain the welcome flow of information.

'How did you get the marks on your neck and the burns and bruises to your body? How did they happen, Michael?'

Michael did not answer; his attention falling to the tabletop again as he listened to his parents crying.

'Did the man and woman go in the house with you straight away?'

'Yes…I think they were there all the time.'

'Did they call each other by name?'

'The man was called Uncle Tim. I don't know about the woman. She had a name, but I can't remember what it was.'

The inspector was temporarily content to pass over the sordid minutiae of Michael's ordeal.

For now, it seemed far more important to try and unveil the possible location of his friend.

'Can you tell me why they brought you back here, Michael? Back home…here to Shireheath? Back to the school gate? Can you tell me why they did that? Did they say anything to you? Do you know why they brought you back here without Peter?'

Michael's pained memory had now been effectively tapped into.

Now the schoolboy's inner fury began to rage inside.

Silent, untamed, and so far, undetected.

Yet no one in the room was aware of the boy's overwhelming vexation at that precise moment.

Yet his successful act of indifference was upheld for the increasingly pensive spectators. Finally, after a minute or two of careful deliberation, Michael opted to continue with the disclosures.

'I think they brought me back here…because of Peter.'

The D.I. shifted uneasily in his seat as W.P.C. Coombs frantically scribbled her record.

‘What do you mean, Michael? Why…because of Peter? What did he do? What happened to him?’

Michael swallowed back his carefully guarded remorse and again considered his response.

‘Peter tried to run away. He tried to escape…but…only because I told him to. And…it was all…all my fault. He would never have made it. There was no chance. And now…’

The pause was again unbearably protracted, forcing the detective to actively press for the fuller picture.

‘And now, Michael? And now…now what?’

The boy’s gaze focused on each adult in turn before he felt ready to make the declaration.

‘And now…because of me…Peter is…Peter is dead.’

Emitting a long deep sigh that had seemingly been held for hours, the D.I. reclined fully back into his chair, folded his arms, and determinedly studied the face of the young boy sitting opposite.

The boy, whose last words had effectively shattered any fragmented hope that had been nurtured during just a few inspiring minutes of encouraging reflection.

James and Sharon looked to one another through their mutual veil of emotion, begging one another for some sliver of guidance.

Even the slightest comprehension of their son’s plight seemed well beyond their grasp as Michael continued to sit and stare across the table at Detective Inspector Kevin Woodley.

Composing his thoughts, the superior police officer carefully broached the subject once more, whilst simultaneously fearing the potential answer.

‘Michael…you say Peter is dead. How…how did Peter die?’

There was no hesitancy from Michael this time.

‘It doesn’t matter.’

‘It does matter, Michael. It matters very much. I need to find the people that did this to you and your friend. You’ve been really helpful so far. Please…can you try…try to tell me how Peter died?’

Michael’s sudden growing reluctance to indulge the policeman was becoming slowly more evident as the seconds passed.

‘I didn’t exactly see how he died. I just know that he’s dead.’

‘But what makes you know he’s dead, Michael? Why do you think that Peter is dead?’

‘Because the man and woman were blaming each other after we got back to the house. They were arguing.’

Instinct halted Kevin Woodley’s vocal stride.

Something told the detective he had listened to enough.

Indeed, the childish sincerity of the revelations left him with pangs of deep insecurity.

A subconscious notion began to bother the D.I., leaving him feeling that quite possibly, he had just about heard all there was to hear.

‘Michael…you’ve been a brilliant little boy, today. Your parents can be so proud of you. Is there anything else that you think would help me find the people who took you and Peter?’

Michael did not look at the officer.

He did not look at his parents.

Instead, his gaze centred to the far wall.

To an undisclosed point of personal focus unknown to anyone but the boy himself.

Then he emitted a stunning declaration of intent.

‘I don’t want anyone else to find them…’

The D.I. furrowed his brow at the innocuous request.

He exchanged bemused glances with Sharon and James.

Eventually, it was his mother that offered the obvious question.

‘Why not, Michael? What do you mean? Why don’t you want the police to find the people that took you and Peter?’

With a steely-cold glint of ambition in his eye, Michael’s mask of assuredness never averted from the point on the wall.

Then, without prompt, his next words would seem to bring down a symbolic curtain on the entire investigation.

‘Because…one day…when I’m older and bigger…I’m going to find them myself.’

The adults looked to one another in bemused horror.

Sufficiently alarmed by the boy’s declaration, the D.I. quickly opted to call a close to the meeting with the Tompkins family, although it appeared to have reached a conclusion of its own accord anyway.

Escorting them from the interview room and down the stairs, the D.I. pledged his support.

'I appreciate you all coming today. I will probably need to talk with Michael again, but for now I think that's enough. He seems a little overwrought with recalling certain things. It's natural.'

James and Sharon seemed thankful for the opportunity given to Michael but were infinitely more relieved to be leaving the station than they were to be arriving.

Their son's direct and unflinching response to questioning came as a relieving surprise to everyone whilst it was generally felt that in time more detail would emerge.

None of those present in the room truthfully accepted Michael Tompkins final, totally unexpected sentiment.

Right on cue, just as D.I. Kevin Woodley bid the Tompkins family a good day and re-entered reception, the desk sergeant informed him that Superintendent Barnes wanted to brief him.

'Probably just wants an afternoon chat, Guv! A tea and biscuits, job!'

'He never wants a bloody chat…it's always only a moan. Thanks anyway, Phil.' exclaimed the D.I. as he wearily began to ascend the stairway back to the Chief's office.

He pondered the details of the previous hour, turning possibilities over in his mind as he walked. Yet his concentration on the search for Peter Leavesdon was interrupted as he strode along the carpeted top landing towards his superior's domain.

The door was open.

The Chief Super was immersed in a read-through of some files on his computer.

'Come in, Kevin. Park yourself down. Well…how did it go with the Tompkins lad?'

The D.I. shut the door behind him and perched himself opposite Joseph Barnes who sat back in his chair and grinned.

It had already been a long day for Kevin Woodley.

He was certainly not in the mood for another stand-off with the head of the station.

'It went…surprisingly well, actually. I got a clear account of how the boys were actually abducted. The Tompkins boy was excellent. We need to talk to the residents near to the school grounds again, just to check whether they might be able to give a description to our suspects.'

'Good! Anything else of interest arise?'

It was with a sincere sense of regret that Kevin Woodley shook his head.

'A name was used…Uncle Tim. Vague isn't the word. I'll run it through records but I'm not hopeful. Neil from forensics has just drawn a big fat blank on any DNA database matches as well. The boy's account was fine…if unyielding of relevant detail.'

'What do you mean? You're not making sense, Kevin.'

'Well, sir…we still don't have any single lead on the culprits. All we know is that they were a male and female. Michael Tompkins also seems convinced that Peter Leavesdon is dead but doesn't know how or where this might have taken place. I'm not sure whether to give that line too much credence. Or whether to begin an all-out national police hunt.'

As was his usual manner, the Chief Superintendent rose to his feet and encircled the inspector with more questions.

'Yes…I see. Well…going national isn't really feasible, is it at this stage. What about vehicles involved? Any description?'

'He doesn't know any details, sir. Not even a colour, really. He said possibly a white van. A CCTV double check is going to be arranged imminently. He does however recall the struggle beforehand.'

The chief's eyes narrowed as his curiosity deepened.

'Does he know which direction they were taken?'

'No idea.'

'Was any possible destination mooted at all?'

'Again…he's no idea, sir. He says they were inside a house. They were kept locked in a bedroom, apparently.'

With hands clasped behind his back, the Chief stared impatiently at the inspector.

'Any details of what was done physically to the boys? How they sustained their injuries? Any motive as to why his friend was supposedly murdered?'

The D.I. was becoming angered by the futile necessity for the Chief's wilful intrusion on matters.

However, for the moment, he maintained a cool head and continued cordially.

'Michael says he blames himself because he advised his friend to try and make a run for it. Things got out of hand. There was an argument between the man and woman. If Peter Leavesdon has been killed it doesn't make sense to deposit the one solitary witness back into the centre of the investigation, does it? There was certainly no obvious motive for murder. Not from what Michael has said, anyway.'

The Chief turned on his heel with fury in both expression and tone.

'Kevin…these animals don't need a motive for anything! They certainly didn't have a motive for taking the boys in the first place, did they?'

The D.I. felt his policy of colleague diplomacy being breached.

'Sir…with all respect…far more worrying for me is what Michael said right at the end of our chat, sir. It had left me feeling like this whole damned thing is now already possibly out of our hands.'

'Go on?'

'He claimed it wasn't up to the police to find those responsible…almost as if it's way too late in the game now. He seemed almost…apathetic about his friend's current situation. Almost gave me the impression that we're wasting our time, in fact.'

The Chief Super was less than satisfied with the resume.

'He's eleven years old, Kevin! For crying out loud! Eleven! It's not up to him how this operation proceeds or concludes!'

'I know, sir. But it kind of brought an end to things for me today. I've never felt this way about any investigation before. Something just doesn't add up.'

'I agree with you…for once! You're damned right it doesn't bloody add up! But obviously you'll need to speak to him again. There's a lot more to come out, Kevin. I'm sure of it. It's just the shock talking at the moment. Youngsters are unpredictable. You know that as well as anyone.'

D.I. Woodley rubbed his weary eyes and sighed heavily.

'Do you want me to interview him back here again, sir?'

'No…not until something concrete un-earths itself. Perhaps you could make an impromptu call to their house tomorrow? Try and dig a little deeper? In more familiar surroundings he might feel a little more open about things.'

'Okay…though I'll perhaps leave him for a day or two to relax. I don't know. May I go now, sir?'

'Yes. I think that's all for now, Kevin.'

The D.I. had rarely felt more eager to leave the Chief Super's office than at that moment.

'Oh…by the way, Kevin…'

'Sir?' the inspector sighed.

'Top marks for the media job this morning. I'm very impressed with the solidarity we've shown. I would say the public and press are onside. Well done.'

Confusion and despair combined making the detective feel nauseous.

'But we've done nothing! A boy is still missing, sir!'

'Mere detail, Kevin…mere detail. Kids go missing all the time. Don't forget…like you just said…without further evidence…we've nothing suspicious to address yet. We can't be seen to handle things badly if there's nothing to grab hold of…can we?'

'WHAT?'

'Thank you…Detective Inspector Woodley.

Now evermore bemused by the evolving standpoint of his Chief Superintendent, the D.I. closed the door behind him and ventured wearily back to his office.

CHAPTER 27

It was just after eleven am the following morning when the Tompkins family returned from the doctor's surgery.

The family GP Graham Davies had settled Sharon's natural consternation regarding Michael's condition. His words of comfort were deemed most welcome by both James and Sharon as they sat opposite the man who had becoming something of a trusted mascot over the years.

'I've studied the progress of your little boy ever since you came to me and told me you were expecting, Mrs. Tompkins. I am more than happy with the hospital's report on Michael's physical status but considering the potential emotional response that must still reside within him…I suggest at the outset that he receives large doses of relaxation and plenty of cuddles from mum. Any problems…please see me without hesitation. By the way…without wanting to dredge up the recent awful experience…I must say how absolutely thrilled I am for you all.'

The diagnosis from Doctor Davies confirmed that Michael was indeed in latent shock and would benefit from at least a couple of weeks residence in the comfort of home.

It was also affirmed that prescribing medication was not a preferable option until future signs became determined such practice as being vital, but this course of action was suggested to be highly unlikely.

Both parents agreed that their son's return to school was an issue that would probably best be left for Michael to decide for himself.

James unlocked the front door of number twelve as a couple of pertinent thoughts reigned down upon him.

'Glad those press-men have scattered. Thought they'd camped out for the year! I'd better ring work, Sharon. They'll want to know how things are. I'll see how much more paid leave I can have.'

Michael darted through the open door without word and up to the sanctity of his bedroom. His wordless departure encouraged a noted response from Sharon.

'Not very sociable today again, is he, Jim? Though, he looks to have a little more colour in his cheeks than yesterday.'

Halting his progress toward the lounge, James stopped to kiss his wife on the forehead as she closed the front door behind them.

Holding her close, he sewed some seeds of reassurance.

'Leave him be, Sharon. You said it yourself to the detective yesterday. He's probably quite happy in his own company for the time being. It's going to take a while for him to come to terms with what has happened. It will be slow going to adjust back to the life he knew.'

A mother's eyes did not divert from the top of the stairway.

'But he seemed so…cold…and so…distant yesterday, Jim. Especially at the police station. It was as though he felt no unease about the situation at all. It's as though Peter never existed. Yet they've been like brothers for their whole lives.'

'He's going to feel very confused and strange about things, Sharon. Give him space. He's only eleven, love.'

'I know…I know…but it's like he's not bothered. It's almost as though nothing's happened. I don't want him to bottle things up. It's not healthy.'

James ushered his wife from the hallway and tried to offer perspective.

'There's little more we can do about the investigation, Sharon. The matter is entirely in the hands of the police. I suggest we let them get on with it and try to get our lives back to normal. If Michael wanted to say anything else, then I believe he would have said it. We can't force him.'

Sharon nodded in very reluctant agreement as James suddenly leaned toward the telephone to check the display. The flashing red call light indicated that someone had tried to make contact whilst the family were at the surgery.

James pressed the call history confirmation and turned to his wife with raised eyebrows.

'It's Dave and Hazel. They phoned whilst we were out. What do you think we should do?'

Sharon scrunched up her nose as she quickly joined her husband's side and confirmed the number displayed on the cradle.

'Shit…bloody hell…I've been dreading this to be honest, Jim. We've got no choice really, have we? We'd better see what they want…if they perhaps want to come round. Do you want to call them back?'

The hesitancy in his response seemed to amplify the cruelty of what had recently occurred to both families.

'Jesus…yeah…I suppose I should. But what do I say?'

Sharon did not deliberate any longer.

'I tell you what. You ring work. Sort that out first. Then I'll ring Hazel. It'll give me a minute or two to get a plan together.'

In actual fact, it took less than one minute for James to confirm a return date to work. Thankfully his manager seemed most sympathetic. Letting the handset slip back into its cradle, he turned to smile at his wife.

'Okay. I'm back in next Monday. I'm more than happy with that. I'll be ready by then. They sound like they'll be pleased to see me. The gaffer sends his love. Right then! That's the easy one done. Now it's your turn!'

Designating thirstiness with her usual hand signal, Sharon gestured for her husband to take himself away to the kitchen and make them both a coffee. She retrieved the handset, dialled in the Leavesdon's number, and listened as her heartbeat thumped in rhythm to the foreboding click of the connection.

James could only stand back and listen to the adopted tone of wary gentility in his wife's voice as she commenced the overdue re-opening of communications with their best friends. As the kettle begin to hiss into life, he re-positioned himself back to her side to hear clearly.

A deafening silence preceded her words, which veritably jumped from her mouth as Hazel answered.

'Hello…Hazel? It's Sharon! We missed your call earlier. We were at the doctors with Michael.'

'Yes, hopefully. We think so. Yes he is…thank you…yes…he's doing okay…considering…you know.'

'No no…school's going to be out of the question for at least a couple of weeks.'

'Yes…of course you can.'

'Is David still off work with you?'

'Okay. Great! I'll prepare some lunch for us all if you want.'

'No…it's not a problem at all.'

'See you in about an hour then.'

'Bye!'

Sharon listened as her friend hung up before clumsily dropping the receiver back into its housing. She engaged with James and displayed a half-smirk that signified an uneasy combination of relief and trepidation.

He husband looked at her in response, anxious to learn what had been planned.

'That was quick and painless! Well? Are daggers drawn, do you think?'

Briefly glancing at the clock above the mantelpiece, she folded her arms in wonder about what the next couple of hours might bring.

'Hazel and Dave will be here about twelve. I said I'd do us all some dinner.'

James moved toward her and embraced his wife once again with a considerate word of support.

'Well done, love. That was pretty damned brave. Don't fret. I'm certain they'll be amiable with us, Sharon. We're only doing the right thing here, you know. Imagine if they were in our shoes. How would they react? What would they be thinking and doing?'

Sharon rubbed her moistening eyes and strived to retain her suddenly brittle composure.

'I know, Jim. I know. I'm just pissed off with it all. I want the life back that we had before!'

'That's going to take a good while, Sharon.'

'I know! It just doesn't seem real any more…all this…all this fucking… pain. What have we ever done to ask for it?'

'Nothing whatsoever! Just you remember that! But we'll get through it. Michael's back home now. Back with us! That's the main thing…isn't it?'

'It's not fair though, Jim! Not bloody fair! I've just spoken to someone who has been my best friend for over thirty years…yet…to listen to her voice…how cold she seemed in talking to me…you'd think we'd never met before in our lives.'

James moved away from the sitting room and into the kitchen to finish making coffee.

'Why? Was she a bit funny with you?'

'No…not at all…not really…but somehow…I don't know…I just think that maybe they ought to feel a bit resentful, at least. I think I probably would in their position. I just don't know. Just ignore me. I'm talking rubbish.'

Wallace peered through the conservatory door both in readiness for his morning escape and typical canine curiosity as to the reason for the conversation beyond the windowpane.

'No, Sharon…you're not talking rubbish at all. I sense the difficulty, too. You feel like this because you're a caring person. Hazel's been like a sister all your life. It's because you want your friend to be happy. And all this fucking horrible shit has chucked a spanner into the works.'

Again, Sharon struggled to hold her emotions in check.

'I just want things to be how they were a week ago! Fucking Hell, Jim…I just can't imagine even looking her in the eye at the moment. Never mind making fucking lunch for them both! It seems pathetic even to think about it. You know the worst thing…since Michael came back…I've completely forgotten about poor Peter. Jesus, Jim. Poor darling Peter. Where the hell is poor Peter?'

The frustrated German Shepherd began to whine in sympathy at the sight of his owner's tears beyond the closed glass door of the extension. He scratched lightly on the pane with his paw which encouraged James to let him out to fetch the lead from the hallway.

'Listen, love…I'm going to have to take Wallace for a walk. You think about what we're having for dinner. I know it's really hard…but try and take your mind away from the negative stuff. Things will be alright. Believe me.'

His wife's upset barely relented as she continued to convey her instinctive guilt.

'But how am I supposed to concentrate on anything when their baby Peter's still missing? God knows what they're going through now.'

'I've told you, Sharon. There's nothing more we can do about Peter. Or any of this mess. That's the job of the police. Now try and relax. Please. I'll be as quick as I can.'

*****

Five minutes after noon, the knock on the front door echoed through to the conservatory. Seated nervously on the plush cane furniture, both James and Sharon jumped nervously to their feet and clambered past one another to greet the visitors.

In the hallway, Sharon offered to let them in, leaving James standing helplessly behind her.

He watched with quaking anticipation as she peeled back the front door and revealed the peering silhouettes of the Leavesdons.

The discomforting pause was pleasingly brief for all.

'Hello, Hazel! Hello, David! It's really good to see you! We're so glad you've called! Please come in.'

Handshakes and kisses were exchanged with seemingly forced warmth as the four adults gathered in the Tompkins' lounge.

Once a room that felt so welcoming to them all as friends.

A place of regular sociability.

Yet it now felt like a cold arena for some dramatic summit.

The sense of alienation between the couples was tangible. It was almost as though four complete strangers had convened for the first time in their lives.

The hiatus in exchange of dialogue was again kept to a relieving minimum.

'I'm making a pasta salad for us!' announced Sharon. 'Would you like some coffee first?'

The offer was met positively from both Hazel and David as they settled uneasily onto the sofa. James quickly provided the required drinks and returned to the living room so as not to leave the duty of forming uncomfortable dialogue solely with his wife.

His opening statement was directed to both of them as he hovered uneasily in front of the fireplace.

'We have to be honest with you both…Sharon and I…we didn't know what to do…you know…about how to start talking to you again. It's been…well…a weird few days to say the least.'

Hazel sipped her coffee whilst eyeing the hosts with disaffection.

Finally, she responded with a very un-typical air of indifference.

'No, of course you wouldn't feel at ease with things…we understand…its difficult…isn't it? As you can imagine…Dave and I are just a total mess. Don't know which way is up. Can't stop crying…glued to the bloody television and those relentless bulletins.'

David glanced briefly at Wallace who peered inquisitively back at him from behind the conservatory door, as he strived to conjure his first comment.

'How is work being with you, Jim? Are they obliging?'

'Good mate. Good. No complaints. I've just phoned them this morning. I'm back next Monday. They're very pleased about the outcome…obviously. You know…everyone's been really supportive. What about you?'

David nodded as he sipped some more drink.

‘The same, really. Though of course…we’ve yet to get the round of congratulations like you two have had.’

Sharon studied Hazel’s deeply furrowed brow.

In the space of just a week she seemed to have aged ten years.

She sensed the atmosphere in the room was already in steady decline.

The suspicion arose in Sharon that the Leavesdons must have had an underlying motive for their visit, yet rather than inflame the matter she decided to let it reveal itself in due course.

However, to her surprise, the revelation was not long in coming.

‘So…how is Michael?’ enquired Hazel, with distinctive angst lacing her voice. ‘Is he here? Can we see him?’

The situation was already escalating rapidly beyond the wishes of the hosts. Remaining calm, Sharon attained a comforting glance from her husband before answering her friend’s demand.

‘He’s looking…and feeling…alright…I think. Some bad bruising and one or two nasty wounds to his neck and arms. He’s quiet though. Hasn’t had much to say for himself today.’

Hazel shuffled forward to the edge of her seat and set her mug down heavily on the coffee table.

Her glare became stern and tone suddenly much more purposed and resentful.

‘He didn’t have much to say for himself yesterday either, so I heard.’

Hazel’s anticipated offensive had now begun in earnest.

‘We…we took him to speak to the police.’ replied Sharon.

‘We know you have! We’ve spoken to the police this morning. The inspector…Woodley, is it? He called round to see us. Not much good came of it, though. They say they are doing all they can. They say that they were hopeful of some clues from Michael. He also said…that the interview Michael gave yesterday…went very well. I don’t see how, myself?’

David said nothing. His wife’s impassioned resume of the situation was stark yet understandable. Sharon and James became agitated with the unbridled course of the conversation.

Hazel continued with her analysis.

‘Yes…apparently there were some DNA traces which matched up…but there is no one on police file to link them to. I take it you two knew about all this already?’

The earlier trepidation regarding current relations between those present in the room were quickly becoming unbearably evident.

James opted to relieve his wife from the role of the unwilling negotiator as the tension attempted to stifle his friendly approach.

'In fairness, Hazel…we only found out what happened to the boys yesterday, as well.'

Peter's mother did not hesitate to snatch for further information.

'So…what did Michael actually have to say for himself at this…so-called…interview, then? I don't see how it could have gone well if the police still don't have a clue where our son is, and that they were told nothing by the chief witness!'

Again, James took the lead in fending off the emerging passage of scrutiny.

'Well…we now know basically how the boys were taken.'

Hazel rolled her eyes dismissively.

'Yes. We were told about that as well. But what about the fucking bastards that did it? Surely Michael can describe them?'

James was suddenly enshrouded in unwarranted guilt.

It was indeed all too easy to forget about Peter.

'No, Hazel…not really…not in…very much detail.'

Hazel snapped back with her reply.

'Well, I find that very hard to accept! And if I was in charge of this search…I'd be more than a little peeved at Michael's mysterious memory lapse!'

Hazel's demeanour was becoming less tolerant by the second as her inherently aggressive temper steadily simmered. She continued to say her piece with her burning frustration more than evident for all to see.

'But even so, guys…come on! He must at least remember where they were taken to. He must surely know where Peter is being held as we sit here talking about it. How can he NOT know these things? He was fucking there! So why is he keeping his fucking mouth shut? Why?'

James gestured for renewed calm as he sensed Sharon becoming upset at the increasingly prickly manner of her friend.

'Hazel…listen…Michael knows just the basic details. It's not enough to help the police at this stage, granted. But D.I. Woodley has stated that Michael will be interviewed again soon.'

‘When? How long do we have to wait for him to remember his best friend?’

Her question was laced with flippancy, yet Hazel was fully justified in asking it. James retained composure to issue his reply.

‘Perhaps tomorrow…when hopefully he can recall some more information. We’re trying not to get him too upset if we can help it. The police believe that if Michael gets pushed into providing answers, then he’ll clam up altogether or worse…make something up. And that doesn’t help anyone either…does it?’

Hazel was blatantly unsatisfied by the theories she was hearing.

Sharon’s earlier suspicions on the fragile nature of their once impenetrable friendship were looking to be correct.

Hazel had determinedly set out to cross swords and her next request was inevitable.

‘So…can *we* see him now? Can *we* talk to Michael?’

James was now struggling to fend off the barrage of uninvited interest.

‘I don’t think that’s such a good idea. He barely wants to speak to us at the moment…let alone anyone else. We’re just trying to let him settle back home slowly.’

Sharon observed her friend begin to gesture with brimming frustration and her manner of address was becoming wilder and louder by the second.

‘And what about us? What about me and Dave? We’d like to settle our fucking son back home as well! But only Michael knows where our son is! He needs to open up! And open up bloody quickly! You have to let me at least try and get it out of him!’

Sharon wiped her eyes and rose to her feet, moving protectively toward the lounge door.

James continued to defend her from the verbal attack.

‘Hazel…please…I know exactly what you’re going through…but you’re not helping by getting mad at us. You can see for yourself what this is doing to Sharon. We were told by the police that patience is the key. Please…for all our sakes…try and let the police deal with it. Falling out over this is pointless. It won’t solve a thing.’

Hazel’s body language suggested that her temper had now frayed beyond retraction. Her eyes were wide and white as she pointed an accusatory finger at the Tompkins.

It was also notable that David continued with the policy of silence as his wife continued with her increasingly desperate tirade.

'WHAT? YOU'VE A BLOODY NERVE, JIM! We've had to sit through you…ON FUCKING TV…telling the police what a great job they've done! Well…that's total crap isn't it! You know exactly what the police have done! Jack shit! FUCK ALL! Without Michael's testimony this search is dead in the water. Your son knows far more than he's letting on. He needs to start helping us. And he needs to start now!'

Ever the eager diplomat, James attempted once more to offer oil onto very troubled waters.

'But he's only eleven years old, Hazel! Try and be reasonable, will you? He's a child for Christ's sake! A mere child!'

Now Hazel stood up; her speech evolving into an erratic rant as her forefingers continued to point and accuse.

'And my Peter's only fucking eleven years old, too! And he's still fucking missing! And without Michael's help, we'll never fucking find him! I'll never see my son again!'

Sharon could cope no longer and began to weep openly as the situation unravelled from everybody's control. With her voice quivering through its emotional stranglehold, she begged for some understanding as she slumped with dejection onto her knees in the lounge doorway.

'I beg you both! Please don't get angry with us, Hazel. I knew this would happen. We've been friends for years. Don't blame us for this. We didn't want any of this fucking mess to happen, either! And please don't blame Michael. I beg of you! Don't blame my son! Please!'

Yet Hazel was unmoved and unflinching.

With hands on hips, she continued to unleash her rage.

'Let me see him, then! I need to talk to him, Sharon! You must understand that! You do understand, don't you?'

'Yes…but just not now! Not today! Just leave it a while. Please. For Christ's sake, David! Say something. Have a word with her, will you? Don't just sit there and let her say these things! We're still your friends…aren't we?'

Hazel's eyes fixed menacingly toward her cowering husband as a welcome cold silence descended on the exchange.

And the reason for the rapid cessation in debate soon became obvious to all.

Everybody's attention suddenly focused on the lounge doorway behind Sharon, where Michael stood quietly by, having heard and observed the latter stages of the ensuing quarrel.

Hazel swallowed in mild trepidation, finding herself temporarily unable to continue talking.

Transfixed by the stare of the youngster, she attempted to present an obviously false if accommodating smile.

Yet unbeknown to all present, his intrusion on the fractious arena was not at all sociable in motive.

'Hello, Michael. How are you?' Hazel asked tentatively.

James and Sharon observed their son, somewhat dumbfounded by his willingness to be present in the room.

'Did you want to join us, darling?' asked Sharon, her emotions quickly regaining a semblance of composure.

Michael nodded and moved position to sit cross-legged in front of the fireplace at his father's feet. The apparent serenity of the youngster was staggering in such circumstances.

His evident desire to discuss the issue of his missing friend had bewildered all four adults.

And then, he spoke with a restful assurance as he focused his attention on the Leavesdons.

'I've told the police everything that happened, Mrs Leavesdon. I can't say any more...because...I don't know any more'

David shuffled further to the edge of his own seat and glared intently at the boy he had known since birth. At last, he uttered a few words of contribution.

'But...Michael...please...for Peter's sake...there must be more.'

'You must remember what these people looked like...where you went with them?' Hazel concurred.

Michael simply shook his head slowly.

'The police think there will be more to come. I know they want me to give them more information. But there isn't any more. They know all that I know. I can't say where we were taken or who took us because...I don't know. They were just...people. A man and a woman. Ugly. Tall. Thin. Smelly. If I drew you a picture of them it wouldn't mean a thing. They were just nasty...horrible...people.'

Hazel visibly struggled to keep her bubbling vitriol under control.

‘But Peter is still with them, isn’t he? They are still holding him, aren’t they? Please…you’ve got to help us try and find him, Michael! Please. He’s your best friend. Please help him! Please help us?’

With incredulous ease, Michael rose back to his feet and moved position to stand between his mother and father.

‘There’s something you should know. I told the policeman this…but I don’t think he believed me. He thought I had imagined it.’

Now the minds of all four adults centred on the imminent revelation from Michael, whose own parents knew what was about to be unveiled.

‘What? What did you tell the police?’ demanded Hazel.

Sharon and James waited for the inevitable fallout to implode as their hearts lodged in their mouths.

‘That Peter is gone. That…Peter…is dead.’

The pent-up emotional storm immediately unravelled itself with a hellish power as both Hazel and David allowed the words of the youngster to register before they collapsed into one another’s arms.

Sharon and James held their son in defence against the unavoidable torrent of decimating turbulence that proceeded to engulf the room.

Hazel pointed at Michael with callous and poisoned desolation pouring from her very core.

‘YOU TERRIBLE CHILD! I CAN’T BELIEVE YOU WOULD SAY SUCH A THING ABOUT YOUR FRIEND! MY BOY CAN’T BE DEAD! HE CAN’T BE! NOT MY BOY! YOU’RE FUCKING EVIL, MICHAEL! EVIL! FUCK THE LOT OF YOU, THEN! WE’LL FIND HIM ON OUR OWN! WE’LL DO IT WITHOUT YOUR FUCKING HELP! AND WHEN WE FIND HIM, WE’RE GOING TO BRING HIM HERE AND MAKE YOU SAY WHAT YOU JUST SAID TO US! YOU SHOULD BE ASHAMED OF YOURSELF!’

Ushered forcibly away from the scene by her husband, Hazel exited the lounge amid an uncontrollable fit of anger that echoed into the hallway and beyond into the street.

‘Hazel! Wait! Please!’

Sharon’s tearful request went unheeded as the Leavesdons left the house and made for their silver Focus. Neither looked back to view the scene outside number twelve, Basford Lane as the car accelerated away.

Michael's mother and father stood arm in arm on the driveway, as behind them, their son observed the Leavesdons' hasty departure from the comparative safety of the front doorway.

As predicted, the black clouds of anticipation had gathered and opened upon the once closely tethered scene.

And it would be some time before the storm would pass.

Yet through all the doubt, the pain, the mystery, and the confusion surrounding Peter's whereabouts, only one person remained resolutely certain about the matter.

He had ensured events were ingrained permanently in his conscience.

Leaving his parents to console one another about a broken and seemingly irretrievable friendship, Michael silently ventured back up to his bedroom and shut the door on the unwanted shadows of reality.

CHAPTER 28

Monday. Four days had passed without incident or development.

James had gone back to work as arranged, feeling that a sense of normality would be more than welcome for the inhabitants of number twelve, Basford Lane.

The police had paid a brief visit out of courtesy, duly informing the Tompkins family that all efforts were still being concentrated to try and retrieve any clues regarding the location of Peter Leavesdon.

Detective Inspector Woodley had opted to defer an official secondary interview with Michael, hoping that the youngster would volunteer information in due course should it arise.

He had casually probed Michael's parents for any sliver of further progression in the youngster's thinking, yet he left Basford Lane empty handed and empty hearted.

The Leavesdons had not been in touch since the debacle of four days earlier, yet unfortunately for all concerned their agony was continually exhibited and analysed on a daily basis through the various television news reels and occasional speculated theories in the national press.

A handful of reported sightings had been documented, yet every single line of subsequent inquiry had drawn a blank. The trail was quickly going cold.

Sharon and James had also maintained a keen eye on the media coverage, which forebodingly had gradually begun to wane due to the lack of any concrete advancement in the investigation.

One positive moment had occurred that morning with a phone call from Euan Ford, the Headmaster at Riverlands Secondary. He declared that the school had re-opened that very day and that they eagerly awaited Michael's return – whenever that might be.

Sharon cordially invited the Head to call round and see Michael for himself should he wish to do so, believing that her son would benefit from knowing that, despite the derisory attitude of the Leavesdons toward them, life would indeed go on and that the adults around him could still be trusted.

The day had passed with Michael offering intermittent conversation about the television schedule and what he had been playing on his X-Box. He had devoured a large plate of spaghetti on toast and taken a bath, during which his mother had discovered the pleasurable sight of his noticeably dispersed bruising.

The dressing to his neck wound had been regularly changed and appeared to be performing its role in the healing process. Doctor Davies pledged to keep a close eye on the area suffering the most tissue damage to administer any necessary future treatment in prevention of infection. On the face of it, Michael looked to be healing slowly and surely.

James had telephoned home at dinner time to enquire how his wife and son were coping in his absence. Sharon chuckled at the revelation that yet again she had opted to take the dog for a quick walk through the park and yet again forgotten to take a depository bag with her.

It was just after four o'clock in the afternoon and warm sunshine bathed the rear garden of number twelve. Sharon had just completed bringing in washing from the line when she thought she detected the sound of a knocking at the front door.

Entering the hallway, she tried to scan the visitor through the frosted window in the door panel. No one was clearly visible, yet a repetition of the light rapping made her jump.

Opening cautiously to greet the caller, Sharon was met with the vision of a schoolgirl of similar age to her son and adorned in uniform. Strikingly attractive, the girl sported a shock of blond-hair which had been randomly streaked with black and pulled back into a short ponytail.

With her wide blue eyes glistening in hope, the girl enquired if she was at the correct address.

A puzzled Sharon stuttered in her response.

'Well…that depends on who you want to see, my love.'

The young visitor smiled sweetly and openly declared her intended target.

'I'm looking for Michael Tompkins…you know…the boy who disappeared. I was told he lives here. I hope you don't mind me calling. I wanted to see how he is.'

More than a little bewildered by the obviously genuine interest displayed by the girl, Sharon finally summoned an expression of pleasure at the evident kindness on display.

'Yes…yes…Michael does live here…please…come inside.'

Needing little more encouragement, the young caller stepped into the hallway.

'Do you know Michael, then?' enquired Sharon as she closed the front door.

'Yes…well…not very well…but he's in my new form class at school. Mrs. Gray's group. I'm Chantelle Burley.'

Sharon found herself smiling, but this time in amused recognition of the girl's connection with her son and the previous mention of a possible girlfriend.

'Ahh…yes…I think you might have been talked about in passing. You're all back at school now, aren't you?'

'Yes…it re-opened today. The Headteacher told us what has happened in assembly. Everybody was crying. Even the teachers. But we all watched the news while we were off school, anyway. They…they still haven't found Peter…have they?'

Sharon had not forgotten about Peter. Far from it. But she had recently acknowledged the fact that it was something of a relief to not be persistently reminded about him every second of the day.

'No…not yet. Do you want to come through to the kitchen, Chantelle?'

The youngster confidently followed Sharon whilst upholding the conversation with obvious concern.

'The police have searched our school and some nearby streets as well, haven't they?'

'Yes, love. Were the police there today?'

'Yes. Two police cars, I think. One at each end of the road. All day. I don't know what they were doing there, though.'

As the exchange ensued downstairs, Michael overheard the voices from his bedroom and crept onto the landing. Seated at the top of the stairway, he listened to his mother offer Chantelle a drink as the two then relocated into the lounge.

'It's ever so nice of you to come and visit. No one else from the school has been to see him yet. Here's your coke, Chantelle.'

The girl nodded and expressed thanks as she gratefully cradled the can of drink, just as an inquisitive pair of ears and eyes appeared through the open kitchen doorway.

'Ahh what a cute dog! Ohh…he's lovely! So big and fluffy!'

The family German Shepherd needed no further encouragement to introduce himself and trotted into the living room to inspect the stranger with a very keen nose.

'Have you got a dog at home, Chantelle?'

'Nah…I always wanted one, but my dad says they smell.'

'He's not wrong, either!' laughed Sharon.

'What's his name, Mrs. Tompkins?'

'Wallace…after Wallace and Gromit…apparently.'

Chantelle appeared most puzzled by the disclosure.

'But *Gromit* was the dog…not Wallace!'

'I know…I know! Michael's dad thought it was funny, anyway!'

Wallace sniffed through his ritual inspection of all visitors and avidly licked Chantelle's hand as she stroked his soft snout.

'It's still a cute name though. Is Michael at home, today?'

'Yes…he's just upstairs. I'll go and fetch him for you.'

Inwardly overjoyed at the unexpected guest, Sharon bounded upstairs and poked her head through Michael's bedroom doorway, just affording him time to retreat into position at his games console.

'Hey you! You've got a visitor! Come on!'

Michael's gaze did not avert from the TV screen.

'Yes…I know.' he mumbled

'Well come down then! Don't be rude. Chantelle's in your class apparently, isn't she? She's come to see how you are.'

Still Sharon was not visually acknowledged by her son as he wrestled with the joypad.

'I don't want to see her, Mum. Not today, anyway.'

'But that's a bit unfair. She's come here especially. Is it the same girl that took an interest in you on your first day, by any chance?'

Now Michael engaged with his mother's gaze and could not help but smile in mild embarrassment at her astute powers of deduction.

'Yes…it is. At least…that's the silly story Peter made up. I know she wants to see me, Mum. But…I don't know…I just feel…silly. My hair…'

'There's no need, Michael. She's very concerned about you. The whole school is apparently. It's just re-opened today. You'll be back with all your friends before you know it.'

The resulting pause was indicative of the harshly downbeat claim that followed.

‘I haven’t got any friends at school, Mum. Not anymore. Not now.’

Sharon felt like crying on the spot as Michael’s words registered oh so heavily. It was the most tragic sentiment she had ever heard her son convey. Emotion bubbled in her throat as she made a plea.

‘Oh no…don’t ever say things like that, Michael! You’ll make Mummy feel so sad. Listen…you’ve got at least one other friend. And she’s downstairs now… waiting just for you. Why don’t you and Chantelle go out and take a walk together? It’s a really nice day outside.’

Her son’s attention focused back to the flickering images at the end of his bed.

‘Please…Mum…not today. Some other time, maybe.’

Finally accepting defeat, Sharon relented in her pursuit with a certain amount of respect for Michael’s cautious standpoint.

She returned to the lounge to find Wallace flat on his back having his tummy tickled.

‘There’s not many that he’ll allow to get away with that! He must like you! I’m sorry, Chantelle. Michael’s fast asleep. Out like a light.’

‘It’s okay, Mrs. Tompkins. I’ll come another time. I hope to see him very soon at school, anyway. I’d better go, then. Thanks for the drink. Bye Wallace!’

A little disappointed at being deserted in his peak moment of pleasured serenity, Wallace flipped back onto all fours and began to whine in protest as the girl hauled her rucksack onto her shoulder. A motion which seemed to trigger a thought.

‘I’ve just remembered. Can I leave these with you? It’s not much. But I thought they might cheer Michael up.’

Sharon watched as Chantelle retrieved a bulky blue envelope from her school bag.

‘What’s this, then? A present?’

‘It’s just some chocolate…and a card. Me and my friend Kim have signed it. She’s been ever so upset today.’

Then another sullen penny dropped with Michael’s mother.

‘Kim? Was Kim the girl that Peter wanted to fight with over a sandwich?’

Chantelle and Sharon chuckled as they reflected on such a scenario.

'Yes! Kim doesn't like boys all that much! Peter knew how to wind her up without even trying!'

Then a frosted silence intruded as current terrifying reality reminded the pair of prevailing circumstances.

The moment of solemn awkwardness remained between them, which Sharon quickly opted to eradicate.

'Well…thank you ever so much for coming. I'm sure Michael will see you soon enough. In fact, if you want to leave your phone number, I'll get him to ring you when he wakes up.'

Chantelle nodded eagerly and proceeded to scribble her mobile number on the bottom of the blue envelope.

'Don't you have a home number, Chantelle?'

'Yes…but I only ever use my mobile. Everybody does! It's cheaper and quicker. Get him to text me when he's awake.'

Left with plenty of food for deep thought, Sharon escorted the girl from the front door and watched her walk slowly away along Basford Lane.

Peeping covertly from his bedroom window, Michael also observed her departure; his hands shaking uncontrollably as he held the curtains almost completely closed to conceal his presence.

Once assured that Chantelle had finally gone, Michael allowed the daylight back into his room and sat quietly on the bed in contemplation of his relentless inner fury.

The moment passed and the demons on his subconscious horizon slowly retreated, but only leaving Michael to quake in fear of their inevitable return.

CHAPTER 29

The boy squirmed violently before emerging from the depths of slumber and unleashed a scream of terrifying resonance.

On either side of him his mother and father responded immediately with a comforting arm of reassurance as Michael awoke from the clutches of his ragged memory.

Struggling to calm himself, he assimilated his surroundings and gradually re-immersed himself within the sanctity of his parents' protective arch.

The nightmares had begun a week earlier around the time of Chantelle's impromptu visit and had readily manifested themselves in varying forms, each and every night since.

Dark, dangerous images polluted the boy's fragile sense of peace, clawing his mind back from a restful conscience and plundering him into the murky chasm of his confused history.

Distortions of the recent truth plagued him, regularly compelling Michael to flee from the perceived isolation of his own bedroom and into the reliable cradle of his parents.

Ugly, surreal visions of sufferance; yet they carried no authentic reference to what had actually transpired in the past.

Sharon and James had naturally questioned the source of their son's evidently dire and ongoing trauma. Seeing Michael under such duress was almost as painful to them as his actual period of abduction.

The police, GP and hospital had all been informed of the alarming evolution in their son's psychology as soon as the interruptions in his sleep pattern had begun to exhibit themselves.

The medical standpoint suggested that such occurrences were the mind diluting itself of shock and the excessive nature of his bad dreams would decrease with time.

Of course, so far as the police were concerned, the scant and erratic details conjured by Michael's nocturnal events did little to assist the continually uninspiring investigation into the whereabouts of his friend Peter.

In secret, Detective Inspector Kevin Woodley had all but relinquished any hope of Michael supplying even the faintest strand of vital information.

Twenty days had passed since his return to Shireheath, yet the boy's standpoint remained firm and un-swayed.

So far as he was concerned, his best friend was gone.

No reason; no method; no motive.

No culprit; no witness…no crime.

Daily media coverage of the case had all but diminished completely, although one major television station had been in touch regarding plans for a possible reconstruction of events to be utilised on their crime programme to reinvigorate the public appeal for information.

The Tompkins family were now relatively assured in the belief they could not foresee any prospect of rekindling cordiality with Peter's parents. The Leavesdons were only too desperate to assist any possible cause in the search for their son and were more than eager to try and piece together the puzzle that remained unsolved to all.

All, that is…but Michael.

The two families had become estranged since their last encounter.

The mutual policy of remaining incommunicado had been incredibly discomforting for both sides at first, yet all concerned had seemingly accepted the upsetting rift having slowly adjusted to the absence of once dear friends.

Consultation with Doctor Davies about Michael's night terrors did encourage a relatively creative suggestion from the GP. Because of his tender years, any form of medication was generally deemed wholly out of bounds and highly unethical in any case.

An alternative method to dissect Michael's quandary was the potential employment of hypnosis to try and unravel the tightly wound fabric of his memory. Professional expertise was at hand should the concept prove tempting.

James had suggested that such a practice, if successful, might just enable their son to recall some further vital details about his ordeal.

Sharon, however, was most distrustful of the proposal and wholeheartedly rejected any possibility that her son should undergo what she considered to be potentially dangerous and unreliable treatment.

Although such a strategy would need the patient's full consent, Michael was not even consulted as a matter of parental principle.

*****

Wednesday the first of October brought better tidings. Having roused himself from a very welcome full night's sleep for once and a much-needed lie-in, Michael eventually ventured down to the lounge in his pyjamas and perched his weary form on the edge of the settee.

He observed the small white box on the coffee table as Wallace appeared next him for a cuddle. Sharon asked what he would like for breakfast and implored him to look at the small box as it was a present.

Michael did not engage with his mother or Wallace as he picked up the box and pulled out the contents. The mobile phone was sold to Sharon and James as being top of the range. Free texts; camera; internet access; I-pod player - the works.

Looking dismissively at the technical wonder held in his grasp, Michael then opted to simply place it beside him on the sofa.

In a further gesture of disinterest, his attention quickly fixed itself beyond the lounge window to the shifting greyness of the early autumn skies.

The dark clouds swirled menacingly around the peaks of the distant roofline, as though gathering energy for another storm.

Without any verbal expression of positive emotion, Michael steadily rose to his feet, moved toward his mother, and kissed her on the cheek. He ruffled the shaggy collar of Wallace, who sniffed at his human brother's bare feet.

'It's a really good phone…but I could have done with one of these a month ago, couldn't I? So could Peter…but it's too late now. Thanks…anyway.'

And with her son's un-typical and damning summary drifting heavily around the room, Sharon could only stand and listen to Michael's footsteps retire back upstairs to his bedroom with thoughts of his absent friend obscuring all else in his mind at that moment.

*****

Two days later, there was another caller to the front door of number twelve, Basford Lane.

The visitor had not officially arranged to meet the Tompkins family at their home but had decided to take up the informal invitation offered a few weeks earlier. However, the caller's trepidation was somewhat tempered by an overriding purpose to his mission.

He displayed an earnest smile as the door was peeled open and propelled a practised and firm hand of greeting to Sharon.

'Hello, Mrs Tompkins…'

Somewhat surprised by the sight of the lean angular figure in the grey suit, Sharon took a second or two to register with the gradually familiar vision.

'Of course, yes! Do come in, Mister Ford. How are you?'

The Headmaster visibly relaxed his posture and duly produced a gift-wrapped package from behind his back.

'Very well, thank you…I do hope I'm not intruding. I've brought a little welcome home present for Michael. There's a card, too. I've gotten as many pupils to sign it as I could. There are a few items in there as well. The kids donated them. A couple of DVDs. Some comic books. Sweets. You know.'

It seemed such an unlikely scenario as Sharon gratefully retrieved the unexpected bounty and closed the front door.

'Oh, that's so lovely! But you shouldn't have! Please come through!'

Mister Ford clasped his hands behind his back as he followed Sharon through the hallway.

'Nonsense! It's the very least we can do. How is Michael, today?'

'He's…getting there…slowly…can I get you a drink?'

'No…honestly…I'm fine.'

'Please…come and sit down in here.'

The teacher entered the lounge and secured himself into an armchair.

'And what about you? How are you and your husband coping?'

It was a question that no one had previously asked so directly yet he held an obvious concern for the answer.

Having hardly had chance to analyse her own state of mind recently, Sharon's found her response was not easy to summon.

'Erm…just about okay…I think…Jim is back at work now…I'm hoping to go back soon. But a lot depends on Michael, really. How have things been at the school?'

The Head's expression became suddenly rather stern as he nodded slowly.

'A very subdued environment…as I'm sure you can imagine. The police seem at a loss for a way forward. They are still making random enquiries at home time but it's difficult with the number of pupils coming and going. The officer in charge of the investigation is under a lot of pressure. But I've addressed the pupils and teachers of the exact situation. I must say they have all responded commendably in the circumstances.'

The next subject jabbed itself into to the forefront of Sharon's mind, compelling her to ask the question.

'Have you…been to visit…Peter's mother and father…at all?'

The Head did not respond immediately. Instead, his visage became rather sorrowful as he fidgeted in the chair.

'Obviously…as you are well aware…their situation is far bleaker than yours…at this moment, anyway. We have tried to make a personal contact…but have had no response to phone calls or a letter of support I sent last week. Have they been in touch with you at all?'

It was a bitter memory that still served to upset Sharon as she attempted to convey recent events.

'Yes…well…we tried…but emotions are obviously running very high. We were best friends with the Leavesdons, you know. I've known Hazel all my life. But…she's…well…let's just say things are very strained at the current time. They seem to think Michael is withholding vital information on purpose. I suppose they've got the right to believe that if they want.'

Euan Ford shook his head in sympathy.

'Yes…it must be so incredibly difficult for you all. Well…I'm not going to dwell on the negative things if I can help it. The principal reason for my visit today is to see how Michael feels about coming back to school.'

The matter had not even been discussed with her husband in any great depth, yet Sharon sensed a certain amount of relief that the resumption of her son's education had finally been placed under the spotlight.

'Personally…Mister Ford…I think the time is definitely coming. And the sooner the better.'

The Head's body language evolved into a more positive position.

He leaned forward with enthusiasm now fuelling his manner.

'Really? That's good news! Has he spoken to you about returning to Riverlands at all, Mrs. Tompkins?'

'No. Not a word as such. He seems content just to sit upstairs watching TV or playing on his console. But I honestly think that going back to school would do him a lot of good, now. What do you think as Headmaster?'

The teacher shuffled further to the edge of the chair. It was obvious that he had Michael's interests at heart and Sharon felt quite confident in disclosing her feelings to him.

'I think...knowing the natural adaptability of children his age...that it would do him no harm at all to at least give things a go. His form tutor, whom you've also met, Mrs. Gray, is quite concerned that he is missing out on familiarising himself with his new classmates especially at this early time of the new academic year. Obviously as a school we don't want Michael's absence to go on indefinitely...mainly for his own sake, of course. We want him to establish himself. Pick up the threads of a month ago...you know? It will all help in the healing process.'

Sharon felt incredibly appeased by the affection displayed for her son. It was the first time in several weeks that she felt her faith in human nature had been somewhat restored.

'No...I agree with you. Definitely. When were you thinking?'

Mister Ford swallowed in preparation to announce his suggestion.

'Well...today is Friday. How about...Monday morning?'

Sharon's protective reflexes responded immediately.

'Oh...oh...I don't know. That's very soon, isn't it?'

The Head was very persuasive.

'There has to be a starting point somewhere, Mrs. Tompkins. We could wait another week...another month? I'm not sure. But I'm pretty certain that if we can help Michael move on from what has happened as soon as possible...then it would be beneficial to all. Don't you agree?'

It was most difficult to disarm the Headmaster when such logical reasoning had been conveyed. He seemed to be a good man at heart and had rapidly commandeered Sharon's respect.

There was little argument against the fact that it would be healthy for everybody to turn the page and begin a normal life again. As such, Sharon found herself struggling to provide any iron-clad diversion from the proposal.

'But...I've not got any new uniform for him. He's got no P.E. kit. I don't know what happened to his school bag.'

'Please…don't concern yourself about such things. Bring Michael along in his normal clothes. I'll get a new uniform ordered for you next week. Anything he needs will be provided. This is all about your son's welfare and state of mind, Mrs. Tompkins. All I'm saying is that we can only be of any real help to him if he actually begins attending school again.'

Still Sharon stirred over the issue.

'But…what if he says no? What if he's awkward about it?'

'Children can be very awkward…I fully agree. What does his doctor say about going back to school?'

'That it's up to Michael, really…whenever he feels fit and able.'

The teacher smiled broadly and placed the palms of his hands and fingers together in a solid gesture of optimism.

'Well then…I think we should talk to him about it, now. Don't you?'

Sharon still felt a certain amount of maternal reticence, yet the abiding notion of doing the right thing for her son quickly erased any remaining doubt.

In truth, the Headmaster had already made the decision for her.

'Yes…okay…I'll fetch him down to see you.'

Sharon trod lightly upstairs and tapped on Michael's bedroom door.

She whispered to him as he stared intently at the enemy soldier on his console screen.

'Michael…you have a visitor. Mister Ford is here to speak to you about school. Do you want to come down and talk to him?'

Michael simply nodded and shifted his weight to the edge of the bed.

'Just finish this section, Mum. I've nearly survived the third level!'

'Erm…Michael…he's waiting downstairs for you…now…'

'Okay…'

With an unexpected enthusiasm, Michael suspended the on-screen warfare and brushed past his mother. Leading her back down the stairs and into the lounge he smiled at seeing the Headmaster standing to greet him.

Teacher and pupil shook hands firmly as Sharon sat quietly by to observe.

'Hello, Michael.'

'Hello, sir.'

'You're looking very well!'

'Thank you, sir. I'm glad my hairs growing back, too!'

Michael avidly eyed the large parcel that the Head was barely concealing behind his back.

'First things first! Here is a present from all your classmates. They wish you well. And they want to see you soon!'

Michael smiled as he ripped open the seal and scanned the contents. The Headmaster didn't waste any time as he offered Sharon a glance of hope.

'Your mother and I...we've been considering your return to school, Michael.'

'Okay.' he replied, still scrutinising his bounty of presents.

'How do you feel about coming back to Riverlands on Monday morning?'

Sharon could never have anticipated her son's instantly enthusiastic and wholly cooperative response.

'Okay...I think.'

'So...Monday morning...is not a problem, so far as you can see?'

Michael glanced up from the box of goodies to fully engage with the Headteacher.

'No...that's cool. I think I want to, now. I'm a bit fed up at home, really.'

Sharon found herself shocked at Michael's ready compliance and felt inflated as the Headmaster expressed his relief.

'Okay, Michael! That's absolutely brilliant!'

The Head's attention switched to Sharon once again.

'Bring him to reception on Monday at about eight-fifteen, Mrs. Tompkins. I'll have a quick chat with him just to make sure he's still fine about things. I'll inform Mrs. Gray this afternoon about what's happening.'

Michael noticed the smile of genuine pleasure adorning his mother's face.

It was a vision he had not embraced for some while and her heartfelt satisfaction with the arrangement was quite evident.

'Great! Wow! That was almost too easy! Thank you, Mister Ford! Thank you...very much. I can't wait to tell Jim! He'll be thrilled to bits, I'm sure!'

The Head stood and raised a hand which rested lightly on Michael's shoulder.

'Believe me…it was totally my pleasure! Michael's a very brave lad, indeed. We'll expect you Monday then, Michael. See you then!'

'Yes, sir. See you on Monday, sir.'

As Euan Ford departed the hallway of number twelve and strode across the road to his car, Sharon held Michael in front of her and placed both arms over his shoulders as they observed from the front door.

In turn, his hands lightly gripped her elbows as a mutual thought entered their heads.

Perhaps, just possibly, the monsters on their individual horizons had been vanquished.

Maybe, just maybe, the future was finally ready to fully embrace their return to normality.

CHAPTER 30

Monday the sixth of October; five-twenty-two a.m.

'All the best. I'll be thinking of you every second of the day.'

Lightly planting a kiss on his sleeping son's forehead, James retreated from the room just as Michael stirred under his duvet and snorted something inaudible into the pillow.

In a second, he was deep in slumber once again.

Thankfully, another evening had passed without any recurrence of the recent nightmares. Michael's calmness of mind may have been in coincidence with the imminent return to Riverlands but nevertheless, it marked his second full night's sleep for the better part of a month.

James entered his own bedroom to find Sharon sitting upright among the covers and drinking the mug of coffee he had prepared for her.

'Right, love…I'm off to work. Have a good day. I hope it goes brilliant for you both.'

Rubbing remnants of sleep from her eyes, Sharon smiled broadly to her husband across the semi-darkness.

'Well, at least I shouldn't be late getting him to school today! I've just got to sort his clothes out and get him up. He hasn't woken during the night, has he?'

James was careful to keep his voice to a whisper.

'He's not been in here…no. Fingers crossed! Look…I'd better be off. I'm going to be late. I'll ring you at dinner time, okay?'

Man and wife embraced, both feeling extremely nervous about their son's return to something like routine.

'Okay, darling…look forward to it.'

'Don't forget…Wallace needs a walk before you go to school! You know how regular he is at the moment!'

Sharon rolled her eyes.

'Yeah…okay…I take it he's my dog again today then, is he?'

James smirked and waved before trotting downstairs and beyond the front door into the early autumnal dusk. Peering contentedly from between the bedroom curtains, Sharon watched the flashing red rear lamp of his bicycle vanish beyond view before dragging herself into her dressing gown in readiness for the day ahead.

*****

'Michael…its seven o'clock, darling! Time to get up! It's time to go back to school!'

Michael did not take long to rouse himself from dormancy and was surprisingly eager to accompany his mother down to the kitchen. Perching wearily into a chair, he filled a bowl with cereal as he felt the alerting sensation of his bare feet being avidly licked under the table.

'Wallace…stop it! It tickles! Stop it!'

The family canine popped his head up next to Michael's waist and observed with typical interest as his human brother poured milk into the bowl. The obligatory hiatus before eating allowed the breakfast to soften a little as Michael's eyes centred his attention on the portable television next to the bread bin.

The sound was barely audible as he began to munch and as such, Michael paid the images on the screen scant attention. Sharon re-entered through the back door with an armful of washing retrieved from the tumble drier.

'Mum…have I got a new uniform to wear today?'

Sharon reached behind the back door for the ironing board.

'No, love. The Headmaster says you can wear your favourite clothes this week. He's going to order you a new uniform. He says it doesn't matter for now.'

Michael shovelled another spoonful of mashed crispies into his mouth before asking the next seemingly inevitable question.

'Mum…what happened to my old uniform?'

Sharon did not really want to answer as she plugged in the iron and set its thermostat. Yet, such an inquisitive mind only deserved some honesty.

Besides which, she felt little justifiable reason to hide the truth.

'It was taken…by the police…when you…you know…when you came home…'

More cereal was ingested.

The next query readied itself for emission.

'What did the police want it for, Mum?'

It was mildly frustrating for her that such an insistent seam of curiosity should arise at such a critical stage of Michael's supposed rehabilitation, yet Sharon obliged once more with a carefully veiled answer.

'They wanted to…to study it…you know…for…evidence…'

She waited and simply listened to the sound of Michael's jaw opening and closing. After many days of relative disinterest in his recent history, the mind of the youngster was suddenly alerted to his circumstances.

'What am I wearing for school, then?'

'I've washed your favourite jeans…plus this shirt and your black jumper. It should cover up the marks on your neck. I thought it would be best…just to stop people asking how you got them.'

Michael nodded whilst gently fingering the scarring around his throat.

'I don't mind people asking, Mum.'

Sharon's discomfort was not obvious for Michael to identify, though it soon became clear why there was a temporary halt to the interview.

She turned to see him staring intently at the TV screen. As her own attention fixed to his source of interest, she was alarmed to see that the seven-thirty news had opened with a story about the ongoing investigation.

The image of Peter that had ingrained itself into the minds of millions continued to perform a foreboding backdrop to the newscaster's forlorn expression.

In blind haste, Sharon snapped the set off at the wall.

'Come on, love! Eat up! We need you washed and dressed. Wallace wants you to take him out before you go to school.'

Another disaffecting silence developed as Sharon completed preparation of Michael's shirt and jeans and let them hang over the back of a chair.

She was aware that his brain was more than active enough to respond to what he had just seen. It would be very unlikely for the subject to be dropped without Michael being content with some form of conclusion.

And of course, he never disappointed.

'Mum. They haven't found Peter yet…have they?'

It may have been a wholly selfish approach to the issue, but Sharon simply did not wish to discuss the events of a month ago. For her, this morning was a major step in the right direction for the whole family. She wanted no undue upset or damning reminders of what may or may not have been occurring elsewhere.

Today was the beginning of a new dawn for the Tompkins household.

Yet his intensive stare would not abate until she relented, engaged, and answered to his demands.

'No, love…they haven't found him. Not yet. Now eat up and get ready for school. There's a good lad.'

For the moment at least, Michael seemed appeased on the issue of his friend's continuing absence. Within minutes, he had complied with his mother's orders, and both were ready to take to the streets.

Wallace duly fetched his own lead from behind the front door and once attached, began to strain with excitement.

In the hallway, Sharon checked her make-up and wiped a forefinger across each eyebrow. Nervous tension racked her body as she prepared to accompany her son into the public arena for the first time in what seemed like an age.

On opening the front door, she was immediately confronted by the sight of a small yet boisterous group of photographers and journalists who had gathered uninvited around the front drive.

Evidently there had somehow been a leak of the Tompkins' plan.

Taking a deep breath, she locked the door behind her and turned to her son who struggled gamely to prevent Wallace from bounding toward the group of media reporters.

'Whatever they ask you, Michael…ignore them…ignore all of them. Don't even look at them. Okay? Just follow me.'

Mother, son, and canine shuffled uneasily through the melee whilst running the expected gauntlet of questions.

'Is it true that Michael is back at school today?'

'Have you spoken to the Leavesdons about this?'

'Are you still friends with Peter's parents?'

'Can you confirm Michael's claim that Peter Leavesdon has been murdered?'

'What do you make of the police investigation?'

'Does Michael know where Peter is?'

The last request rang heavily around the recesses of Sharon's mind as she encouraged Michael to jog along with Wallace's ready canter. The pressmen initially began to follow in their desperate search for a headline, but the conveniently surprising sight of an approaching police car rapidly dispersed their interest and immediately allowed Sharon and Michael the freedom of the public pavement.

Even though she had only discussed Michael's situation with her husband and the Headmaster at Riverlands, it was annoying to think that her confidence had perhaps been compromised by somebody.

However, it was not a priority issue at that moment.

Entering the comparative sanctity of the local parkland, Sharon breathed a deep sigh of relief.

She checked behind to ensure that the vultures had stopped circling.

Assured of some solitude, she began to relax.

That is until Michael, some distance in front, eagerly reminded her of the next imminent hurdle that lay in wait.

'Mum…Wallace is squatting! Did you remember to bring a poo bag?'

*****

On the return to Basford Lane, Sharon was mightily relieved to see that the throng of so-called media representatives had vanished, but the police had remained outside the front of number twelve to affirm that none of the journalists had seriously breached the civil order that ensured the Tompkins' absolute privacy and freedom of movement.

It was a lie, but Sharon's pledge that neither she nor Michael had been asked any questions seemed to appease the concerns of the two officers, who thanked her for her patience and understanding before departing the scene.

Watching the squad car disappear around the corner, Sharon looked down to the faces of her son and her dog, who both appeared confused by the earlier activity outside the house.

Thankfully, both were soon pre-occupied with other matters.

Wallace soon found solace with a bowl of munchies and Michael occupied his mind with the impending return to school.

In the kitchen, Sharon sat opposite her son at the table as she confirmed the time to be just after eight. Still her mind toiled with anticipation.

'You sure you're fine with this, Michael?'

'Fine with what, Mum?'

'Going to school.'

'Yes, Mum. I'm quite looking forward to it in a way.'

His mental strength continued to surprise Sharon, yet it also filled her with immense pride.

Michael was finally declared prepared for his triumphant return. Despite his shorn locks still striving to regain their previous appearance, he added some gel and styled it as best he could. His best casual attire hung itself on his notably growing frame.

Indeed, the thought struck Sharon that her son had suddenly adopted the appearance of somebody a good few years older and was evidently going to be a handsome young man.

'Okay, Mum. I'm ready if you are.'

After securing Wallace in the conservatory, Sharon escorted Michael along the hallway and back out into the open air. A shrill autumn breeze whipped into them as Sharon locked the front door once more.

'I've unlocked the car, Michael. Just check your coat is in the boot would you, love?'

Moving to the rear of the green Astra, Michael lifted the boot lid and pulled out his jacket.

'You'll need a new winter coat for school, my lad. It's going to get much colder than this pretty soon.'

Michael duly slammed the boot shut and joined his mother by jumping into the front passenger seat.

'But I haven't got a school bag or anything.'

Sharon tentatively started the engine and found reverse gear.

'It doesn't matter for this week Michael. Trust me. Mister Ford will look after you. Right then. You know the rules! Belt up!'

'Ohh…Mum…do I have to?'

'Not if you want to get me arrested! Now buckle yourself in! It's for your own safety!'

It was a good while since Sharon had driven the family car but today it was the infinitely preferable alternative to walking. She was very thankful to be at least partially concealed from the eagle eyes of the public as she reversed off the driveway into Basford Lane and set out for the other side of Shireheath.

Her heartbeat steadily increased as they navigated through the estate and out towards town. The unease began to take a firmer hold as they became slowly ever closer to the vicinity of Riverlands Secondary School.

Past the Town Hall and supermarket.

The cinema; the post office; the fire station.

Occasionally she would glance across to Michael, whose idle gaze rested on the passing scenery without him feeling the need to verbally contribute anything to the journey.

Having successfully negotiated the town centre, the main junction with Friar Road soon beckoned and the outline of the school building honed unimpressively into view in the far distance.

Dropping the car down into second gear, Sharon chugged along in search of a parking space.

Her eyes darted quickly from side to side; from pupil to pupil; from kerb to kerb.

It seemed as though the road was typically double-parked along its entire length. Then thankfully, one rather smallish space was eventually located. Sharon wasted no time in positioning the Astra.

Stationing the car, she applied the handbrake and disengaged the ignition. Her mind focused solely on what might lay in store for her son over the next few hours. She gazed up to the white painted metal bars of the school gates at the end of the road and quietly observed the gathering hordes of schoolchildren as they descended on the scene.

Her casual interest in the view beyond the windscreen had momentarily distracted her from Michael.

Yet it soon became apparent that he was in some distress.

Sensing his simmering upset, she unbuckled her seat belt to reach across and comfort him.

Holding him from the curious scrutiny of passers-by, she felt his entire body trembling in her arms. He covered his eyes completely as though to block out all shafts of light.

As she herself panicked inside, Sharon noticed that one or two pupils had possibly recognised the car or indeed its occupants. School children momentarily stood and watched. Fingers of wonder began to point towards Michael's display of upset.

It appeared that the harsh reality of returning to school had suddenly hit Michael as he forced a request from between his lips.

'Mum…don't make me! I don't want to go now! I don't want to go anymore…don't make me!'

Shielding him further from the gathering interest outside the car, she attempted to decipher the source of her son's fears with a loving whisper into his ear.

'But Michael…its only school. You've been here before. You were looking forward to it. You're only a few short steps away. You've done brilliantly to get this far. You've been so brave. You can do this, Michael. I believe in you. You can do it!'

Finally peeling away his fingers, Sharon was horrified to see the genuine fear in her son's eyes.

Indeed, she had never seen him look so frightened in his life.

'Michael…whatever is the matter? You were being so calm! What are you afraid of? Mummy's here to look after you. What is it that's bothering you, darling? Tell Mummy.'

Cowering back into the seat beside her, Michael gingerly raised a hand and pointed back over her shoulder to the scene beyond the driver's window.

Only then did Sharon identify her incredulous faux pas.

The issue of returning school was not the significant problem.

Where she had parked the car certainly was.

'PLEASE! HE MIGHT BE HERE FOR ME! HE COULD BE HERE! HE MIGHT SEE ME! MOVE THE CAR! PLEEAASSEE!!'

The weight of realisation slammed down heavily into a mother's conscience.

'Oh my good God! Michael! I'm so sorry! Fucking Jesus! Of course! Yes! Yes, Michael! We're going! Of course! Mummy is so stupid! We'll park in the school grounds. Jesus, Michael! I'm so sorry!'

Re-starting the engine and quickly crunching the gear box into reverse and then into first, Sharon clumsily guided the car away from the scene.

The place that became the first steppingstone of Michael's ordeal.

Desperate to retreat, he continued to scan the opening to the alleyway where he and his friend had once walked together.

Sharon cursed herself through a veil of instant remorse as she drove back along the road and re-joined the main rush hour traffic.

St John Street would allow her access to the staff car park which was situated at the bottom of the road.

She held Michael's hand tightly as his emotions also slowly began to subside. He did not dare to let his gaze wander beyond the windows; firmly clamping his free palm over his face until the coast was clear.

Only when he felt the car stopping and heard his mother's subsequent distress did he venture to behold his surroundings.

'I'm sorry, baby. Please forgive me. We're okay, here. You see? This is where the teachers park their cars. You're safe here. Mummy is so stupid, isn't she?'

Michael wiped his eyes and carefully scrutinised the cars around him. Finally, he confirmed his upset was over.

'It's alright, Mum. I'm okay. I just…I keep seeing that alley…in my nightmares. It still scares me. It's…where the man and woman…where they…'

Under another wave of overwhelming maternal regret, Sharon placed her lips firmly onto the top of Michael's head and prayed her innocent mistake would not linger in the memory for too long.

The silence that followed slowly brought renewed peace of mind for both.

Finally, mother and son were united and strong once more.

With a renewed sense of ambition, Sharon and Michael left the car and approached the rear doors to the school foyer. With a trace of caution in their stride, mother and son reached the front window of the reception office to be greeted by the vision of the grey-haired bespectacled lady.

Unsurprisingly, her demeanour had altered drastically since the previous encounters.

Her understandable discomfort at the sight of the two arrivals was quickly eclipsed by a ready smile.

'Ahh! Good morning, Mrs. Tompkins! And to you, Michael! Welcome back! I'll accompany you to Mister Ford's office. He's expecting you!'

Politely expressing her gratitude, Sharon inhaled deeply and instantly identified the varying odours that she had previously associated with the interior of the school building.

The latent scent of floor bleach left by the automated cleaners.

The aroma of the kitchen across the assembly hall as ovens were started up in preparation for the day's menu.

The smell of Michael's hair gel remained under her nose from their earlier embrace.

The concoction was most gratifying and followed her as she accompanied her son and the receptionist along the corridor towards the Headmaster's office.

Euan Ford's sincerity as he greeted them spoke for itself.

'Thank you, Joyce. Welcome back, Michael! Wonderful to have you with us at Riverlands once again! Hello Mrs. Tompkins. Please sit down. Can I offer you both anything to drink?'

Sharon and Michael tentatively entered the room as the Headmaster rose to greet them both warmly. She recalled the cold starkness that the office presented the last time she had entered; and the reasons for the previous visit as two sets of parents watched the police study CCTV footage in vain.

But that was in the past.

Now was time for embracing the present.

And the future.

'No thanks. And I'm sorry we are late. I think Michael just wants to get today started, over and then done with, don't you, love?'

Michael simply nodded shyly. Despite his reticence to speak, he found himself quickly comforted by the school environment and immediately began to acclimatise.

'There is one small thing which I forgot to mention last week. I haven't yet informed the pupils that Michael is returning today. I was hoping that the element of surprise would encourage that extra little support he's going to rely on in the coming weeks. I sincerely hope that you are in approval of such a tactic, Mrs. Tompkins?'

Sharon glanced to her son, whose attention seemed anywhere but in that room at that moment.

'No…a good idea I suppose…yes! No…I mean…I have no problem with that. Like you say...it can probably only help him…can't it?'

'Well, I'm all for helping the young man! Mrs. Gray is waiting in her form room. It will be time for registration in about five minutes. So, Michael…you can either be first in the classroom, or you can wait until your form group are all seated and go in last. Which would you prefer?'

He looked to his mother for assistance, but the decision was purely his to make.

The deliberation was careful and considered.

His decision; absolutely.

'I think I want to go in last. If...that's alright?'

'That is absolutely fine, Michael. Anything further we can do to help?'

Another pang of pressing importance descended into Sharon's conscience.

'Oh...dinner money! You'll need dinner money! How much is it a day, Michael?'

The Headmaster raised a hand to halt her concerns.

'Please...it matters not this week. The most important thing is that Michael is here and that he is happy being back with us. The rest is mere detail. We can sort it out at a later date.'

The Head's warming monologue was duly interrupted by the sound of the first bell of the day. As his mother and the Headmaster exchanged details regarding one or two items, Michael, listened carefully as the gradual influx of pupils increased resonance down the corridor.

A thousand shuffling pairs of feet accompanied by a thousand voices; all of them unaware that one of the missing boys was back in school that very day.

And with each second that passed, Michael Tompkins began to contentedly absorb the fact that it was time to make his presence known to them once again.

CHAPTER 31

Once out of the Headmaster's office, Michael suddenly began to sense the gravity of the pending encounter. Becoming uneasy as he followed Mister Ford and his mother along the brightly lit corridor, the foyer area quickly closed him in, barely leaving room to breathe.

He studied the line of coats hanging on pegs outside the classrooms opposite reception. Through the tiny window to his form room, he strained to observe his classmates, wondering if they yet knew of his imminent entrance.

The Head courteously knocked on the closed door and entered room six to inform Mrs. Gray that Michael was now ready.

And in turn Michael's heart raced with a strange brew of excitement.

With sweaty, clinging palms, he retained a desperate grasp on his mother's hand, as though suddenly fearful of leaving her side. Acknowledging his nervousness, she knelt down to her son and kissed him on the cheek.

'Now…remember what we said, Michael. Be brave. And if ever you get worried today…think of nice things.'

A son's courageous features engaged with his mother's.

His innocent eyes; large and wide.

His tormented mind; clamouring for a reliable foothold.

'What nice things? Like McDonalds, you mean?'

'Yes, darling. Just like McDonalds.'

'And Wallace?'

'Definitely! Yes! Just like Wallace! One more thing…did you bring your phone with you?'

'Yes, Mum. Don't worry.'

Swallowing a solid lump of resignation as he eyed the approach of Mrs. Gray and the Headmaster through the porthole in the door, Michael offered one last pledge into his mother's ear.

'I can do this…can't I, Mum? I can do it, can't I?'

Wiping a single tear from her cheek, Sharon smiled broadly at Michael.

'You've nearly done it already, darling! You're almost there! I love you.'

'I love you too, Mum.'

The tender exchange was interrupted by the gentle and welcoming tones of his form teacher.

'Michael! Oh, it's so good to see you. You don't know how pleased I am. How pleased we all are to see you back. I've just this minute told your classmates that they're about to get a surprise. None of them has a clue you're here. Well...I've told a little white lie there...because I have informed just one person in the group. But only just a moment ago. You should have seen the smile on her face!'

Still suffering with his uncertainty, Michael simply nodded and buried his thoughts whilst observing the loving gaze of his mother.

'Well...' exclaimed a buoyant Mrs. Gray. '...we're ready when you are!'

Reluctantly relinquishing his mother's grasp, Michael found himself ushered in front of the form teacher who placed a gentle hand on each of his shoulders in readiness for the grand entrance.

'Mum?'

The mother suddenly became alerted to the call of the son.

'Yes, my love?'

'You'll be here at home-time for me...to meet me...won't you?'

Never had Sharon been more assured of anything in her life.

'You bet! Never ever doubt it, sweetheart. Have a brilliant day, Michael. I'll see you at half past three. Cross my heart.'

Standing beside the Headmaster, Sharon felt her emotions churn once more as she watched her son be slowly escorted to the slightly open door of room six.

Mister Ford thoughtfully ended her maternal struggle and guided Sharon away toward the car park, leaving Michael alone and completely out of her sight for the first time in weeks.

'There is no need to concern yourself about a thing, Mrs. Tompkins. Michael is back where he belongs. Go home and relax. We'll see you this afternoon. One of the teachers will escort him out to you this evening.'

There was nothing more to be said. Michael was firmly back within the realms of normality where he belonged. The Headmaster's parting words were of great solace for Sharon as she walked away from the main school building and reluctantly slid behind the wheel of the Astra. Engaging the engine, her thoughts still lingered on the potential ceremony about to commence back inside room six.

Michael hovered patiently as Mrs. Gray entered the form room first to announce the arrival of the unexpected visitor.

As the seconds ticked by, he listened carefully to the deafening silence beyond as the pupils offered their full attention to the teacher.

Then finally, the kindly form tutor returned and invited him to take his place with his schoolmates.

'In your own time, Michael. There's no rush for anything, today.'

Step by step.

Breath by breath.

Heartbeat by heartbeat.

Michael felt less reticence with each passing second.

The fear within gradually diminished completely as he finally edged himself through the door and positioned himself at the front of the classroom.

Thirty-four young faces stared back at him, united in their awe and in grateful appreciation, as Michael Tompkins inwardly pleaded for immediate re-acceptance to the fold.

And it came as an immense relief for him to discover that the enthusiasm for his re-admission was not long in being conveyed.

The noiseless void of the classroom was suddenly occupied by a gentle sound.

A rippling wave of relieved congratulations that rapidly gathered momentum and volume. He detected his name being whispered in all corners of the room.

And then Michael was awash under the might of a thunderous explosion that could only ever be created by heartfelt applause.

Swaying under the tide of affection, he scanned the different faces behind the tables as they put their hands together.

In turn, every boy and every girl smiled back to him as they clapped, as he in turn acknowledged their support.

Every boy and every girl in the room; secretly, overwhelmingly happy that Michael Tompkins had returned safe and sound.

He turned to look at Mrs. Gray; her own tears at the spectacle being effectively masked by her professional experience. He then returned his attention to the evident sense of companionship that resonated around the room for that full, joyous minute.

Fuelled by his growing confidence, Michael himself began to chuckle at the unanimous and overwhelming greeting, which eventually subsided and afforded him the arena to say just a few words.

All present focused intently on the boy with the spiked – if shortened - hair; all wishing to hear his voice once more.

This boy they hardly knew.

Yet his terrifying ordeal had unfurled itself into their lives during the previous weeks through countless television bulletins and newspaper stories, giving them more detail about him than they could ever possibly wish to know.

And now, at last, he was where he rightly belonged.

Shuffling with youthful embarrassment, he disclosed his feelings to his euphoric peers.

'Thank you…everyone…for the box of presents. And I just want to say…I'm really, really pleased to be back at school again.'

Wavering under the unpredictable whims of emotion, the faces that stared back at him expressed nothing less than pure pleasure as he again allowed his gaze to wander around and among them.

Then, it emerged into view; the point of reference that he had been secretly dreading.

The back table; the middle row.

The table that he and Peter had so recently established as their very own.

Two friends that were once so avid in their adventurous appetite for life and the eternal demands they made of it.

Yet today, sitting in Peter's place, was somebody else.

Attractive with piercing blue eyes; the girl's blond hair was shocked with black and pulled back into a short ponytail.

She tried to smile whilst wiping her eyes on the cuffs of her school pullover, as Mrs. Gray cleared up Michael's obvious confusion.

'Chantelle has volunteered to look after you on your return this week, Michael. If you do not wish to sit at that table, we can move you if you want. Nothing is a problem.'

Again, Michael's eyes rested momentarily on the girl and then in turn back to the teacher.

All in the room waited with bated breath for his verdict.

And once more, unavoidably, Michael's thoughts turned to Peter.

Youthful inner turmoil made itself known only for a split second as Michael fought against the painful throb of recollection.

But in truth, there was no real quandary to solve at that precise moment.

'No…there's just fine. That's my seat. I'll sit there. Next to Chantelle. It's all cool.'

*****

As the week elapsed, Michael began to feel something like a regular eleven-year-old. Chantelle accompanied him whenever he needed her and wherever he sensed loneliness. She also respected the solitude and space that he required on occasion.

She had rapidly proved herself to be a kind and considerate individual and it amazed him how others had also responded positively to his presence. The outpouring of genuine warmth from fellow pupils was something he never knew children could be capable of.

Intelligent and mature for her age group, Chantelle remained firmly guarded against others raising the subject of what had happened to Michael and Peter.

And indeed, so far as they knew, what might still be happening to Peter.

Her role was to augment the future; to allow Michael some clarity on the immediate way forward. And she was his reliable safety net should he falter along the path to recovery.

Dinner times were particularly enjoyable for the pair. They would talk about television; lessons; teachers; pop music; parents and all manner of things associated with adolescence.

Everyone around him including the staff contributed to the protective yet liberating atmosphere, without stifling his personal re-settlement to any degree.

And even though his mother was on hand to greet him at home time each day, Michael himself was beginning to regain a level of personal self-assurance to the point where he believed such cosseting would no longer be necessary.

For Sharon, the sensation of seeing her son emerge happily from the main school gates was heaven itself. For her it was symbolic. He was also emerging from his own personal horror story.

Seeing him mingling with fellow pupils was such a divine and yet simple privilege that she briefly feared could have been lost forever.

Aside from his successful reintroduction into the classroom, there were offers from new friends to call for him after school.

A social invitation to the cinema was tempting but deemed a little too adventurous for the time being.

Time would ordain the healing.

Fate would decide when the mind had accomplished its task of reinstatement.

For Michael, the re-immersion into such familiar territory was more than satisfying for the time being.

By Friday afternoon, the tentative steps of Monday morning had evolved into veritable leaps and bounds of individual achievement.

Despite the natural fears of his parents, that Michael might become overly wary of close interaction with others, it appeared that the opposite motion had very quickly transpired.

And for the first time during this halcyon period of re-acquaintance, number twelve, Basford Lane had re-discovered the loving and zestful daily continuity that the great majority of families took for granted as their right.

But whilst the gods of fortune appeared to once more pour sunshine into the life of the Tompkins family for a short while, the unforeseen was always lurking in the shadows.

The monsters on the horizon were not yet vanquished.

Ever poised to strike; ever ready to make their most unwelcome entrance.

CHAPTER 32

Monday the thirteenth of October; seven-twenty-two a.m.

Detective Inspector Kevin Woodley sampled his first coffee of the day having commenced a conservatively predicted twelve-hour shift.

Finalising details of the assignment to his latest case, the omens for success already appeared bleak.

His colleague and counterpart, D.S. Simms, was the privileged person to make the first phone call of the day to his office to enquire as to his imminent plans.

Wearily reaching over, D.I. Woodley lifted the receiver and muttered a begrudging greeting as he reclined back into his chair and just about injected some grain of enthusiasm into his side of the dialogue.

'Morning, Phil…how are you?'

'Well…a very exciting start to the week in prospect…'

'No…I've got to check up on a knifing over at Littleholt.'

'Part of a gang culture that got out of hand, apparently.'

'Someone with a grudge, obviously.'

'Okay, Phil…ta-ra for now!'

To say the very least, Kevin Woodley was not feeling particularly invigorated about tackling the stabbing investigation. It would throw up the same old conclusions and futile search for eyewitnesses.

The sudden appearance of Chief Superintendent Joseph Barnes hovering beyond the office window did little to lighten his apathy.

Poking his head through the gap in the doorway, the Chief Super offered a discerning smile.

'Are you following up the Littleholt case today, Kevin?'

'Yes, sir. Anything of interest I should know about before I plunder in feet first?'

The higher-ranking officer took it upon himself to enter the D.I.'s inner sanctum and closed the door behind him.

'Well…you might well have a job getting anyone to spill. At the initial response to the incident, we failed to conjure any lead to potential suspects from the area.'

The inspector sighed with despondency and drained the plastic cup of tepid brown water. He threw it toward the waste bin and missed.

'Surprise surprise...nobody saw a thing...another insolvable job.' he muttered, whilst casting another eye on the computer printed report of the assault.

There was even a loosely veiled attempt to evade the case altogether.

'I mean...look at this! Same old story! There's little point in me even getting in the car is there, sir? It's widely accepted that gangland culture administers its own brand of justice in time. It's a cast iron guarantee that no one will be willing to make statements. The unofficial oaths that their ilk swear by prohibit them from subjecting their activities to the scrutiny of the law.'

'We have a duty to serve and protect, Kevin.'

It was the D.I.'s belief that his superior was fully aware of the obstacles they faced in such matters. The hands of the police were already firmly tied, yet the inspector was not quite finished enforcing his argument.

'Organised crime of this nature generates its own in-house remedy, sir. The police invariably fritter away time and money delving into such situations.'

The Chief was not totally convinced.

'Well...have a ride out anyhow, Kevin. See what pops up...you know...without trying too hard and upsetting folk.'

With his feeble conclusion on the issue, the Chief was gone from the room.

Remaining seated behind his desk, D.I. Woodley half-heartedly ensured to organise two mobile units which would accompany him to the estate near to where the attack occurred.

He rubbed his eyes and yawned before phoning down to the duty sergeant and confirming who would be accompanying him to the scene.

'Okay...yes...fine...tell them to hang on for me. I'll be down in the car park in five minutes.'

Standing dejectedly to his feet he moved through the office door and retrieved his keys to lock it just as a familiar voice resonated along the corridor.

He turned to greet the oncoming officer who displayed an expression of distinct anxiety.

'Morning, Josh! Slow down, lad...you'll do yourself an injustice at your age!'

The façade of discomfort displayed by the younger sergeant Josh Hollins only deepened as he reached the D.I. and tried to calm his voice.

'Guv…are you busy? I mean…*properly* busy?'

Listening for the click of the doorlatch, the inspector dropped the keys into his pocket and began to walk toward the top of the stairwell.

'Well…I was just on my way to unearth the mysteries of a stabbing out at Littleholt. Why…what's up?'

Officer Hollins gestured frantically along the corridor.

'Guv…we've just received an anonymous phone call at the front desk. You need to come and listen to this. And I do mean come *now*!'

*****

Seven-forty-three a.m.

'Mum…I want to make my own way home today…if that's alright?'

Sharon took time to respond to her son's completely unexpected request as she pulled the box of cornflakes from the cupboard and set it down on the kitchen table in front of him.

Being cautious in her reply, she looked at Michael and could not help but sense a pang of maternal vulnerability.

'Oh…I'm not so sure that's such a good idea, my love. You've only been back at school a week. Plus, it's getting dark at night now. It just seems a bit silly to take the risk whilst I've got the car.'

Talking over the soundtrack of falling cereal, Michael reinforced his case.

'But it's still light at home time. Chantelle says she'll come home with me. She doesn't live very far away. I can get the bus home with her from school. It's all cool, Mum. And there'll be others from school with me on the bus, won't there?'

'Stop saying that word, Michael. It doesn't suit you.'

'What word?'

'Cool! I don't know where you've picked it up from. It sounds daft.'

The hiatus in the conversation allowed Sharon a little more time for deliberation on the issue.

Naturally, Michael was keen to receive an answer inclining toward the positive. And his insistence was pleasing to hear.

'Please, Mum?'

'Look…let me think about it for a minute. Okay? Just eat your breakfast.'

'But Mum!'

Then the brainwave hit.

Sharon spun sharply in her slippers.

'Right! Okay! I'll do you a deal! If you really feel happy enough to come home without me, you must take your mobile phone to school. Make sure it's fully charged. You've got free texts and credit. If you take that then I can keep track of you after three-thirty. Good idea?'

Michael contemplated the proposal as he chomped on his breakfast.

Wallace sat beside him and alternated his attention between Michael and his mother.

It was more than a tempting offer and above all, seemed like a safe compromise.

'Okay. Deal! I'll take the phone. That's cool.'

Struggling to conceal her inner amusement, Sharon wagged a maternal forefinger.

'Right! I'll fetch it now and switch it on. You can put it straight in your new school bag. I will ring you dead on half-three. You know how to use it don't you?'

'Yes Mum! Brilliant! Thanks!'

'And woe be tide you if you don't answer when I ring!'

Now it was Michael's turn to smirk.

'Woe be tide...?'

'Yes…woe be tide! Now eat your cereal!'

'Woe be tide...? I don't know where you picked that up from, Mum. It sounds daft!'

*****

Seven-fifty-one a.m.

The main C.I.D. briefing room was occupied by several high-profile officers including D.I. Woodley and Superintendent Barnes. The pair eyed one another in bemusement as Detective Sergeant Ian Bannister briefed all present at what was about to be disclosed.

‘Okay…listen up all of you. Josh Hollins was on desk duty when this call came through to reception at exactly oh-seven-nineteen this morning. The message he received is here in its entirety. It was made via mobile phone. We have traced the location of the original signal, though of course the caller will no doubt be long gone by now.’

The room rapidly became fixed under a very pensive atmosphere.

And of all those present, Detective Inspector Woodley was the very last person in the room prepared for what he was about to hear.

‘Okay Josh. Run the call.’ instructed D.S. Bannister.

The recording was promptly activated, and all ears strained to listen carefully to the tape.

The sound of muffled tears formed an introduction to the intermittently crackling monologue.

A female voice broke the silence of the briefing room.

The eyes of the dozen or so senior police officers flitted among one another as the message conveyed itself to the wary throng.

‘This…is a notice…for Inspector Woodley…I can’t hide this any longer…the missing boy you’re looking for…he’s in the moor-lands… situated south of St. Huntswell…on the Yorkshire-Lincolnshire border. Don’t expect to find him alive. And for what it’s worth…I’m sorry. It was never meant to turn out like this. May God forgive me...’

An uneasy silence prevailed as the line went dead.

The woman making the call was evidently racked with emotion and her desperate tones echoed around the room long after the message had ceased to play out.

With his heart and mind now racing, D.I. Woodley felt under immediate pressure to address the eager audience that waited eagerly for his response.

Also having to contend with the typically expectant gaze from Chief Superintendent Barnes, he engaged the attention of the communications team.

‘That was short and sweet. Okay…do we know where the call was made?’

‘Liverpool, Guv. Bootle to be more precise.’ replied W.P.C. Catherine Jenkins.

‘Okay. Inform the boys at Merseyside please Catherine…I want them posted to the exact location. Fine toothcomb the area. Thorough CCTV search…city centre walk…house to house…the works. I also want two local forensics units despatched to the location mentioned in the tape. Looks like our suspect went on the run, leap-frogged the Pennines and then bottled it.'

The Chief Super intervened on D.I. Woodley's rapidly unfolding assessment.

'You off to the site mentioned right now are you, Kevin?'

'Yeah…looks like it. Christ knows where this moorland is, but I'll find it eventually. Unfortunately, some lucky person is going to have to lift the Littleholt stabbing off my desk. I need to get my arse to Yorkshire…and quick. I'll also take two units from here. Ian and Paula…Curtis and Gemma. You okay for a trip to the Yorkshire Dales? West Ridings constabulary can spare a couple of units as back up, no doubt. Can you sort that for me please, Catherine? Thank you.'

The detective's mind raced with professional anticipation. It was inconceivable to think that such a blatant lead had finally landed squarely in his lap.

The final words of his briefing to the crews concerned were cloaked with sincerity as they made their way off their chairs and out to the car park.

'Listen up everyone. This might well turn out to be a sick joke. There are some twisted individuals out there who will make stuff up for fun. Keep in touch. Could all be a hoax.'

Moving toward the door, he turned to Chief Superintendent Barnes with a foreboding proclamation.

'…and for what it's worth, Guv…I bloody hope it is a joke.'

The Super grimaced sympathetically at the D.I.

'Kevin…anything you need…you've got.'

'Cheers, Guv. I hope for the sake of the Leavesdon boy that I won't need a thing. See you later at some point.'

*****

Two-forty-eight p.m.

Number thirty-nine, Cromford Road.

Hazel Leavesdon thought she heard a knock at the door but couldn't be absolutely certain due to the sound of the vacuum cleaner. Switching off the appliance at the plug, she listened again from the top of the stairway.

The repeated rap on the door was indeed sharp and clear,

encouraging her meandering descent to the hallway.

Peering cautiously through the spyhole in the PVC panelling, she was mildly shocked to see the outline of two police officers.

One male; one female.

She recognised the female as W.P.C. Stacey Coombs; the officer who had been a very familiar figure as the chosen liaison when the boys went missing.

With a degree of trembling hesitation, Hazel opened the door and stared intently at the unexpected callers.

'Hello, Constable Coombs. What brings you here?'

Neither officer offered any semblance of pleasantry in their response.

'Hello, Hazel. May we come in, please?'

Now becoming confused by the motive for the unannounced visit, Hazel performed the almost perfunctory custom of offering a seat and some refreshment to the police.

Both officers declined politely as they removed their headwear and settled themselves down on the edge of their armchairs.

Stacey Coombs spoke again; her bleak tone noticeably less inspiring than it was moments earlier.

'Hazel…we need to talk to you. It would be better if you were seated too. Is Mister Leavesdon not at home?'

Now totally puzzled by the unannounced presence of the visitors, Hazel sat opposite the officers, sensing the room becoming colder by the second.

'No…he's at work. What is it, Stacey?' squirmed Hazel. 'Do you have some news? Is it about Peter?'

Stacey Coombs glanced at her male colleague before centring her full attention back to Hazel.

'There has been a major development…yes.'

Ice cold revulsion sliced through Hazel's core.

It was a shattering, debilitating sensation that gnawed aggressively at her conscience.

'What…you mean…it *is* about Peter? Have you found him? Stacey…have you found my son?'

Another pause of professional uncertainty; another maternal pang of increasingly dreadful foresight.

Finally, the female officer spoke.

‘This morning…at just after seven…the station received an anonymous phone message from a female caller. We immediately traced the signal and transaction to Liverpool.’

Hazel’s impatience now overwhelmed her as a perverse quaking excitement began to creep into her tone.

‘Yes? And? Was the call about my son? Did she tell you where Peter is? Did you get her? Do you know who she was?’

W.P.C. Coombs shook her head quickly.

‘We have investigated thoroughly but whilst we identified the precise location of the call, as you can imagine, finding the individual concerned is nigh on impossible.’

Shifting to the very edge of her chair cushion, Hazel began to visibly shake with anticipation.

‘Well? What did she say then?’

Again, the female constable paused to carefully deliberate on her choice of words.

‘Hazel…I have been tasked by D.I. Woodley…with giving you the full and current facts as he reported them to me an hour ago. The caller claimed that Peter was last seen at a location on the Yorkshire border. Since late this morning, D.I. Woodley had been heading a thorough search of the area depicted in the call…it didn’t take them long…’

Hazel’s eyes widened as the spine-chilling truth crept ever nearer.

The monsters had long been over the horizon and were after her.

They were now at her heel; hungry and venomous.

‘…at approximately one-thirty this afternoon…the units at the scene…they…they found a body.’

Hazel began to wilt instantly as instinct crushed her momentary brush with optimism.

With heart and soul wrenching uncontrollably as she collapsed in on herself, Hazel summoned one final query to the officers as she prepared to hear the worst.

‘Is it…my boy…that they found? Is it…my Peter?’

Struggling to restrain her own emotional reflexes, Stacey Coombs reached across and held the hands of an evidently distraught and mentally flailing mother.

‘D.I. Woodley claims that the body…despite its decomposed state…looks like it…that it…yes it could well…be Peter.’

Covering her face to hide the erupting grief from her company, Hazel instantaneously curled herself up into the foetal position and fell from the armchair onto the hearth rug.

The high-pitched deathly moaning that emanated from her being was almost inhuman.

W.P.C. Coombs leaned across, sank to her knees, and placed her arms around Hazel's quivering form, as both women succumbed to the swelling tide of relentless torture.

They held one another tightly as the eye of the hurricane swept viciously through them. They bobbed and buffeted against the lashing storm of reality.

The merciless din created by such a ravaging loss rose in pitch and fell again without warning or rhythm.

As a mother finally surrendered to her very worst fears.

The fatal sufferance of her only child had been confirmed.

The male police officers respectfully remained stoically silent throughout Hazel's initial reactive maelstrom.

It was some minutes before she felt able to push herself away from the floor and sit up.

Yet her mind would not rest there.

She tucked her knees up to her chin and commenced a rocking motion as her brain assimilated the news she had been dreading for weeks.

The next questions were unwelcoming in principle yet reached out from her conscience, clutching fretfully for answers.

'Oh no Stacey…oh my God…what do I tell his daddy? How can I tell David that his son is dead? How am I supposed to do that, Stacey?'

The female officer attempted to calm Hazel and instructed her as to the next stage of procedure.

'When the forensic team and police medical examiner are finished with their business, the police coroner will be in control of matters. On his say-so the body will be transferred to a nearby mortuary. Hazel…I know this is unbelievably hard…but we are going to need authorised identification of the body from you or your husband.'

'Yes…' Hazel sobbed. '…yes of course.'

'But there's something else, Hazel. You need to know about his injuries.'

A mother's spirit momentarily rose and then descended again, freefalling into her fathomless chasm of despair.

It was all too much to absorb after more than a month of hopeful, hopeless nothingness.

In Peter's absence, all she and David had retained was that with which they were dealt.

An empty, silent void in their lives where a healthy, loving child was born, was reared, and once played.

Where he once shouted and laughed.

But will now never return to his parents.

The distant dream that Peter might just come back to them.

Some day.

One day.

A distant dream that now lay in tatters.

A shattered remnant of woefully misplaced human faith.

The void is now declared permanent.

Her emotions switched again as she now buckled under the expulsion of fury.

'Injuries, you say? What injuries? What have those bastards done to my boy! What have those fucking bastards done to my Peter? Wasn't *killing* him enough? What fucking injuries, Stacey? WHAT HAVE THEY FUCKING DONE TO MY BOY?'

The treatment endured by her only child was depicted in barely appropriate language as the female constable succumbed to her own emotional frailty once more.

Horrendous reality cursed those present.

'We're so sorry…so deeply sorry for you and David.'

Holding Hazel once more to steady her against the surging, grieving anger that now seeped from her every pore, it took several minutes for the female officer to summon her own composure and convey the overall condition of the body.

By their side, the male constable tried to remain staunchly respectful as the detail of Peter's physical condition registered itself.

Prostrate once more under the weight of desolate desperation, Hazel wailed into the cushion of her armchair.

She now felt wanting; wanting to punish herself.

Irretrievably.

Permanently.

In her extreme, regretful sorrow over her son's demise.

And in extreme guilt over her own shortcomings.

The perception that she had unforgivably neglected her son jabbed at her conscience.

Hazel's continual release gradually reduced itself to a pained whimper as she eventually looked forlornly into the eyes of W.P.C. Coombs.

'Why, Stacey? Why did they have to do that to him? Why did they have to disfigure him? My helpless little boy? Oh my God! My handsome…gorgeous, innocent, funny, little baby…OH MY GOD NO! PETER…my poor Peter…'

*****

Three-fifty-five p.m.

Number twelve, Basford Lane.

'Okay. Yes. Fine. Okay love! I know where you are. Yes. Good lad for answering! Do you want me to walk up and meet you? No. Okay, then. See you in ten minutes. Bye-ee!'

Satisfied that Michael was on the last leg of his journey home and was also accompanied by Chantelle, Sharon disconnected the call as she hovered nervously in the lounge.

Setting the handset back into the cradle, she was startled by a loud knock at the door. Peering tentatively through the bay window, she was taken aback by the vision of Hazel Leavesdon with two police officers.

Sharon immediately recognised Stacey Coombs.

Sharon immediately recognised the scent of terror.

Even as she walked into the hall, Sharon could feel her stride becoming laboured and her breath irregular. The upset was already rising and forming in her throat.

Strangely, she knew what was to come.

She knew the reason for the visit.

And there was no hiding place.

This was now the time for the worst news possible.

Pulling open the door, the grief-stricken expressions on the faces of the three visitors under the porch way needed little explanation.

Catching Hazel in her arms as she collapsed over the front step and through the doorway, Sharon pulled her best friend close and looked into the eyes of W.P.C. Coombs.

‘She needed you, Sharon. There was one person she said she needed. We had to bring her here. I’m so sorry.’

Holding Hazel tightly to her, Sharon was forced to crouch down under the weight of her distraught and limp form.

Attempting vainly to console her distress, Sharon squeezed Hazel tightly as the police conveyed the harrowing development.

Once the repetition of the damning disclosure had been administered, Hazel forced herself to gaze up into the lifeless, reddened eyes of her friend.

The best friend she ever had; someone she had loved like a sister for over thirty years.

The sentiment between the two was abundantly clear; the remorse Hazel communicated was mutually agonising.

‘I’m so sorry, Sharon…Peter’s gone…Michael was right…your Michael was right…how can you all forgive me? Poor Michael…he was right all along…’

And as the pair embraced in the open doorway, time stood still as a lifetime of cherished memories flashed before Sharon’s eyes.

She considered their past; their present; their future.

And the one conclusive thought plagued her as she continued to cradle Hazel whilst staring aimlessly at the two police officers.

The unyielding, logic-defying knowledge that their unfolding decades of loyalty, humour and infinite joy could conclude in this horrendous manner.

The unrelenting tormenting realisation that the relationship between two loving mothers should ever have come to this point.

And the conclusion was unavoidable.

That the monsters on the horizons of both mothers were never truly gone.

They were always there in hiding.

Waiting, ever patiently, to strike.

CHAPTER 33

Friday the thirty-first of October.

Ten o'clock p.m; exactly.

The evening news bulletin.

'Our main story this evening centres around yet another tragically innocent young victim of abuse.

The final goodbyes to eleven-year-old schoolboy Peter Leavesdon were conveyed today in a funeral procession through his hometown of Shireheath in Berkshire.

Reporting from the scene, Jenny Booth:

'The streets of Shireheath were today lined with mourning well-wishers who threw lilies and roses onto the cortege as it trailed a resounding backdrop of emotion from local citizens.

Almost eight weeks ago, two eleven-year-olds - Peter Leavesdon and his best friend Michael Tompkins - were abducted outside their own school gates. Police were astounded when just under a week later Michael was discovered alive just yards from where they believe the abduction originally took place.

Despite the absence of any concrete leads, Berkshire police were still conducting a thorough investigation – but as yet, to no avail.

As of just under three weeks ago, Peter's whereabouts remained a complete mystery to all. Until that is, an anonymous tip off relayed the location of a terrible discovery.

A mobile phone call originating from Bootle in Merseyside led police directly to Peter's body, which was discovered on the Yorkshire-Lincolnshire border, near a stream running through twenty square miles of moorland near St. Huntswell.

The boy had sustained terrible impact injuries to his skull, as well as bruising and burns to his upper and lower body.

Most disturbing of all was the wounds administered to the boy's skin. Forensics and medical examiners said that the resulting damage indicated treatment of such ferocity that it defied all known limits of human whim and capability.

Another desperate indictment of our increasingly degraded society, this latest casualty will no doubt eventually be filed with the many other unsolved cases of crime against children.

However, the officer in charge of the hunt for the killer, Detective Inspector Kevin Woodley, was this evening remaining firmly adamant that justice would be done:

'In all my time as a serving police officer, I have never, ever been confronted with such a brick wall in terms of the lack of evidence that this case is currently providing.

All matching forensic data concerning this investigation has so far drawn no match to our files and as such I am currently at a loss for a way forward whilst other lines of enquiry are pursued.

It goes without saying that the thoughts of myself and my fellow officers are entirely with Peter's family at this time, and it is with earnest belief that I claim a significant breakthrough will come.

Violent offences against minors are always traumatic affairs. The circumstances of this case are among the worst in my twenty-five years of experience. Yet the fact remains - somebody out there knows who has committed this awful crime.

It may have been the person that provided the location of Peter's body. It may be some other person. But they are still out there somewhere, at large, and despite their apparent freedom, they are now vulnerable for the taking. Somebody somewhere knows who this person is and where they may be residing at this very moment.

I pledge that this investigation will be ongoing until the murderer...or murderers...have been apprehended and tried in a court of law.

It is my dedicated professional intention to see that the perpetrators of this horrific chain of events are brought to heel by firm justice.

Then...and only then...will I consider my job to be done.'

HARVEST

Five years later…

CHAPTER 34

Tuesday, November the fifth; 2013.

Three-twenty-one p.m.

'Okay you guys…I will need your broadcasting assignments back to me by next week at the latest. As you will have seen from your initial term schedules, this A-level course is very intensive. Time is against you all from now until first formal exams next May. So, no slacking! Did you hear that at the back?'

Michael Tompkins quickly realised attentions in the class were suddenly focused upon him.

Swivelling casually on his chair to face the tutor, he sensibly opted for honesty.

'Erm…no, Miss Simpson. Sorry? What was that again?'

The media arts teacher stood with her arms folded and tried valiantly to hide her emerging smile. Yet, she had quickly discovered with Michael that he was the kind of person that rarely encouraged anything else but amusement.

'I said…outside broadcasting assignments must be in by next week…Friday at the very latest. Okay?'

Now it was Michael's turn to smirk.

'Yep! No problem! All cool! All in hand!'

As the tutor nodded wryly in response, the drone of the bell resonated throughout the college as the signal for the end of another day.

As the throng of students merged in upper floor landing of the building, Michael inadvertently crossed paths with his good friend, Chris Chambers. The pair had been firm associates since their early days at Riverlands Secondary School.

Chris laid a hand on Michael's shoulder to catch his attention.

'You coming to the gym, Mike?'

'Yeah, yeah…I've got my stuff with me now. I sent you a text this morning. Did you not get it?'

Chris promptly retrieved his phone from his pocket and avidly inspected the display as the pair exited through the main doors and down the stone steps of the converted mill-house.

'I don't seem to have it, matey…you sure you sent it?'

Now it was Michael's turn to pull his phone from his inside coat pocket and check its memory.

‘Well, it’s in my sent box. Must be a problem with the network if it hasn’t reached you, yet. Anyway, it doesn’t matter, does it? We’re on our way now!’

The sixteen-year-olds reached the main shopping precinct in Shireheath and followed the bustling main street toward the leisure centre.

Converging with the masses of other youngsters that had recently filed into town from Riverlands and other local schools, the pair forced their way through the screeching throng in something akin to a pincer formation.

‘You done that media assignment then Mike…or what?’

Michael threw Chris a knowing glance.

‘Have I fuck, mate! I haven’t even started it yet! There’s plenty of time! To be honest I’m more interested in breaking the one-fifty mark on the bench press.’

Chris laughed at his friend’s wild boast.

‘What? You’ll never beat one-fifty! If Mark Vickers can’t do it then you haven’t got a prayer!’

On the issue of improving his ever-impressive physique, Michael was always found to be on the defensive.

Especially when it came to discussing his personal capabilities.

‘Yeah? Look…I’m getting there! I’ll have it nailed one day! You see!’

Chris was rather less enthusiastic about his friend’s muscular prowess.

‘Yeah, okay. Whatever! I reckon you’re just out to impress that blonde instructor. Or could it be Miss Simpson that takes your fancy?’

‘Miss Simpson? Not my type. But the gym instructor? Well…who wouldn’t want to impress her? She’s fit as fuck, man!’

Chris Chambers chuckled at his friend’s hormonal fantasising.

‘Way out of your league Michael, my son! Believe me…you’re out of your depth making a play for her! She looks a bit snooty to me, anyway! And she’s got a wart on her chin! Plus, there’s a rumour going round she’s a lesbian.’

‘Fuck me, Chris! You aren’t half picky! Are you really telling me that you wouldn’t do her then if it was on a plate?’

‘Not even with yours, Mate!’

‘You’re full of shit!’

'Well…look who's talking! It's not me going for a double hernia trying to show off in front of her…is it?'

'Fuck off, man! She aint no lesbian!'

'Well…perhaps you're right, Mikey. She can't be, can she? I mean…she's sooooo interested in you, isn't she? Actually…I reckon I might try and put a good word in for you tonight if you're that bothered!'

'Oi! Leave well alone, Chris! Stay well away! You might spoil my chances!'

The two college mates pushed and pulled and shoved one another through the glass doors of the gymnasium as laughter accompanied their entrance through reception.

By magical coincidence, the female fitness instructor at the centre of the debate conveniently emerged from the weights room in front of them and jogged upstairs to the office, completely oblivious to her eager audience.

Chris felt the compulsion to rain on Michael's parade.

'I'll say this though…You've got more chance of bench pressing one-fifty than you have of shagging that!'

'Well, we'll see in a minute…won't we?'

The sound of banter between the two resonated along the corridor as they headed toward the men's locker room. Chris offered a wager to his mildly embarrassed friend.

'Right…ten quid says you haven't got the bottle to ask her out when she walks back into the gym.'

Michael eyed his friend whilst debating the tempting challenge.

'Chris…'

'Yes, Mike?'

'Just get changed…'

*****

Michael was back at home at just after six o'clock.

Opening the front door, he detected from the swirling aromas that cooking had been taking place at some point but sensed he had missed the boat.

Entering the kitchen, he saw his mother loading the dishwasher.

'Hi, Mum.'

Sharon glanced up as Michael dropped his gym bag on the kitchen floor and duly perched himself at the dining table.

'You're too late for lasagne, I'm afraid. Your father and I wolfed it down between us!'

The resulting expression of dejection on her son's face caused Sharon to smirk.

'Ohh…you're joking aren't you, Mum? I love your lasagne as well! What can I have, then?'

Sharon swung open the doors of the fridge freezer and scanned the contents before declaring a choice of dish.

'Pepperoni pizza sound alright?'

'Yeah, fine. Where's Dad?'

'Out with Wallace. He shouldn't be long. Where have you been until this time anyway?'

'Oh…just to the gym with Chris. I think I've overdone it, though. My arms are aching a bit today!'

'I should think so! You pump any more iron those biceps look like they might explode! Was college okay, then?'

'Yeah…good. I'm enjoying it to be honest. It's all cool.'

Switching on the still-warm oven, Sharon unsheathed the frozen pizza as the sound of a rocket exploded and flashed outside, lining the blackening dusk skyline with a hint of gold.

'You planned to go to any firework displays tonight?'

Michael idly flicked through the free local newspaper as he pondered his mother's query.

'Yeah…probably meeting up with the guys in a bit. Just going to the park though, I think. There's a funfair and stuff. Should be a laugh…hopefully.'

Sharon turned to admire her son's athletic frame and chiselled good looks. She also noticed his closely shorn head. A style which had never really appealed to her as his mother.

'What…this park around the corner? Where we take the dog?'

'No, no…the main one…through the other side of town.'

Another opportune chance to tease her son arose.

And Sharon Tompkins, ever the dutiful mother, could not resist.

'Is…erm…Chantelle…going with you…by any chance?'

Michael interrupted his read and glanced over the top of the newspaper, fully aware of his mother's mocking amusement.

'Yes...yes she is...actually! Oh, that reminds me. I've got to phone her when I leave the house, so she knows where to meet me.'

Sharon switched position to check the oven temperature.

'I don't know why you two never made an item. She's such a lovely girl, Michael. You've been friends for years as well!'

'Well, that's just the problem isn't it, Mum. You can't really go out with a long-term mate, can you? Where the sense of fun and surprises going to come from?'

'Well, I reckon you're mad for ignoring her for all this time! She worships the ground you walk on! I saw it the first time I met her. She'd snap you up like a shot, as well!'

Now Michael's attention diverted itself from his read and focused on his mother as she slid the pizza onto the oven shelf.

'What? No way did she say that! You're making it up! How do you know that?'

'Because she told me!' murmured Sharon, desperate not to surrender to her desire to snigger.

Michael reclined in his chair and folded his arms.

'I don't believe you, Mum! You're imagining things! It aint going to happen! So, pack up ribbing me about it!'

Sharon succumbed and began to chuckle as she closed the oven door and set the timer.

'Right, love...your dinner will be fifteen minutes. Plenty of time for you to go and have a shower and shave, young man!'

'No need, Mum! I showered at the gym. Plus, I kind of like the scruffy, unshaven look. In fact, I'm thinking of growing a beard. Anyway, I haven't got time. I've got to get my ass to the park as soon as poss.'

The joyous sound of a mother's laughter echoed throughout the house as a partially embarrassed Michael sat stroking his chin in immediate regret of revealing such a plan.

'You...grow a beard? Fat chance! It took your father thirty years to get his bum fluff to stay on! I'd say you've got more chance of going out with Chantelle!'

Sharon's mirth evolved into a fully-fledged belly laugh as she tore up the empty pizza box.

'Mum...'

'Yes, love?'

'Do some...housework...or something...'

CHAPTER 35

'Yeah…I'm just opposite the post office. I'll be with you in five minutes. Okay, Chaz. Byeee!'

Michael felt the bite of the cold autumn air as he hurried his stride along the high street to meet Chantelle, wishing he'd brought a hat and gloves.

He observed the dark outlines of the scores of adults and children moving steadily in the opposite direction towards the central town parkland, where the annual bonfire festivities were about to commence in approximately fifteen minutes.

As usual, Chantelle was heard before being seen as he veered along the pedestrian precinct. Her tone carried a distinct slant of disgruntlement.

'You're bloody late, Tompkins! You said seven o' clock and its nearly twenty past! I'm bloody freezing!'

Finally joining her shivering silhouette under the amber glow of a streetlamp, Michael half-heartedly issued a vague apology.

'Don't fret…I'm here now, aren't I? I'll buy you a hot dog to warm you up. We'd better get a move on!'

Shaking her head, which adorned a large fleece hat lined with fur, together with fully adjustable earmuffs, Chantelle linked arms with Michael before they quickly merged with the staggered procession making its way toward the park.

'How was the media course today, then?' she enquired through chattering teeth.

'Good…I suppose. Bit boring at times. How about nursing?'

'Oh…thrilling. I learned how to give a bed bath today!'

'Wow! That is one hell of a way to spend your day! Dousing some old codger's privates with a sponge!'

Chantelle laughed out loud and squeezed on Michael's arm a little tighter as they walked with a brisker stride to keep out the cold.

'We don't use *real* people to train with, you fool! We use dummies!'

'Where's the fun in that? I'd volunteer to be a life model if you'd have asked! All those young women in uniform queuing up to wash my tackle! Wow!'

'You're just a pervert, Michael Tompkins! I dread to think what some poor nurse would find when she peeled back your bedclothes!'

'I know I'm a pervert! That's why you hang around with me, isn't it? Don't tell me there's something else you like about me apart from my sick imagination?'

Chantelle giggled into the frosting night air and skipped along with Michael's lengthier stride as they approached the bonfire venue.

The pair soon reached the iron gates of the north entrance to the park and waited impatiently behind the line of patrons.

Excitement seemed to be in the air as the sight of billowing white breath and shining eyes combined with the distinctive aromas of fried food and the sound of a thumping fairground beat.

It was a very happy moment for Michael as he neared the gate.

However, his optimism soon altered as he noticed the chalk-scrawled admissions sign.

'Five quid! Each? It's a bloody scam! You shouldn't have to pay to get in your own bloody park!'

'Oh, shut up moaning and cough up you tight arse!' barked Chantelle, tugging his arm out of his coat pocket.

Once into the bustling arena and having met up with Matt and Clare, two former classmates from Riverlands, Chantelle immediately noticed the absentees.

'Are Kim and Jack not coming?'

Clare presented a knowing smile through the technicolour shadows.

'No…they've erm…got better things to do, apparently.'

'Such as? What on Earth could be more fun that freezing your gonads off in the middle of a field of sludge?' smirked Michael, cheekily.

'What do you think?' Matt intervened. 'They're at it like bloody rabbits at the moment. And to think Kim never even used to like boys!'

'She's found out what she's been missing out on now though, eh?' chuckled Michael.

The group laughed together just as the public address system whined into life, announcing that the bonfire had now been lit and the fireworks display would start in ten minutes.

Convening with the hundreds of other locals, the friends enjoyed the festive atmosphere that fought valiantly to thaw the rapidly freezing air.

The fireworks were loud and very impressive as always, leaving Chantelle to make the obvious comment as the group trudged back toward some warmth.

'So, Michael? Do you think that was worth the five pounds?'

'Erm…ten pounds! I paid for you as well, don't forget!'

'You really are a Mister Miser, aren't you!

He smiled without response as they made their way past the now furious bonfire and into the midst of the throbbing funfair.

*****

For the next hour the group indulged themselves in adrenaline rushes and games of chance and skill, with the rides and attractions offering much scope for competitive amusement between the two boys.

The obligatory hot dogs and burgers were eagerly consumed, with Chantelle declaring that there was one last thing she wanted them all to do.

'Come on! We've got to go on the big wheel! I bet the view of the fair is brilliant from up there!'

Michael cast his gaze up into the deep jet black of the night sky and felt his legs begin to buckle slightly as he studied the height of the wheel's twinkling pinnacle.

'I don't know, Chaz…I'm a bit dodgy with heights, you know!'

'Rubbish! Don't be a chicken! There's nothing to be scared of!'

After a few persuasive shouts of support from the rest of the gang and one or two firm tugs on his arm from Chantelle, Michael reluctantly decided to join his friends in the queue for the Wonder Ferris.

In turn they were shown their seats and Michael reluctantly allowed the attendant to strap him in.

Chantelle gave Michael a nudge as they sat at the bottom of the ride waiting for the cycle to begin once again.

He turned to engage with her child-like stare, which beamed at him with infinite affection.

'No going back, now!' he muttered with feigned annoyance.

'Thank you.' she whispered.

'What for?' asked a bemused Michael, now distinctly wary of the impending adventure he had submitted himself to.

'For coming out to play with me tonight! It's been great fun!'

‘Yeah…yeah it has. Thank you as well!’

‘What for?’ she grinned.

‘For being a brilliant mate all these years. You’ve been a rock for me.’

Slowly, the pair moved their faces closer together as the big wheel’s gear box began to grind into life and the pumping music blasted into the stratosphere.

The kiss was soft and tender.

Just as Chantelle had predicted it would be.

And as the wondrous memory lingered, she felt overwhelmingly compelled to repeat the act.

A move that Michael Tompkins found he had surprisingly little objection to.

As the ride started to gather momentum and took the pair away from ground level, there was an uneasy pause in the conversation as Michael gripped the handrail and braced himself for a bout of all-consuming nausea.

Then another feminine compulsion forced Chantelle into declaring her honest feelings.

‘Michael…’

She observed him as his nervous concentration alternated uneasily between the floor and the sky.

‘Yes. Chaz? Jesus…I’m not sure about this fucking thing now I’m on it! Fuck me its high up here!’

His female companion resisted the will to chuckle as she maintained focus on her imminent revelation and on Michael’s face.

‘Michael…’

‘What’s up, Chaz?’

‘You know that I love you…don’t you?’

Another pause.

Another moment for thought.

Then another declaration.

His response did not carry the sentiment that she had ideally planned to absorb.

‘Well…to be honest, Chantelle…I’m not really surprised! I mean…who *wouldn’t* love me?’

A playful slap on his cheek did little to harm its target when cushioned by large woollen mittens.

‘Well…you can walk me home after this ride…if you want to, that is!’

‘Okay…sounds like a good plan…that is…if I survive this ride! I think I’m going to be sick.’ he concurred.

As the enormous mechanism sent the pair soaring upward and swooped them around and down again, Michael chuckled heartily as he scanned the brightly lit faces staring up at the spectacle from below.

It was a most beautiful, clear evening for November the fifth.

The crowds were buoyant and good natured.

To try and defer attention from his twitching gut, Michael watched the shadowy individuals underneath the axel supports of the mighty wheel as they weaved hither and thither between the various rides and stalls.

All around the congregation at the funfair seemed to have adapted into a universal image of amused contentment.

Then as the Wonder Ferris cast him floor-ward once more, one figure in particular caught his attention as he passed through.

There was a definitive if brief flicker of recognition; yet Michael could not place the vaguely familiar visage.

The man was some distance away from the big wheel; hunched next to a brightly illuminated coffee stand.

His face became only partially visible under the white light bulbs as he held a polystyrene cup to his lips.

Michael continued to study him as the big wheel ground its disorientating cycle.

He observed a cigarette in the man’s hand, which alternated position at regular intervals and was clamped between his thumb and forefinger.

Ensuring to assess the man more clearly on the next downturn, Michael set himself up to fully scrutinise the tall, thin physique and the darting eyes that seemingly bored into the blissfully ignorant passers-by.

On the way skyward once again, Michael’s heart began to thump.

He looked briefly once again at the smiling profile of Chantelle as a sense of discomposure began to claw at his conscience and his chest began to pound with dreadful certainty.

From the very peak of the ride, he squinted down below at the miniature figures in silhouette.

Yet his unnerving focus kept itself centred to the lone body by the coffee stand.

And slowly but very surely, the distant past began to emerge from the shadows and infest the luxurious present.

Long dormant monsters crawled slowly from their lairs and began to darken Michael's peaceful horizon, as finally his curious trepidation gave way to full blown fear.

On the downswing again, Michael scrutinised the man sternly once more, until total conviction overcame the remaining partial doubt.

Surely not.

It couldn't be.

Then once more over the pinnacle of the wheel's arc for the final turn, Michael felt the hydraulic brake begin to gently apply itself and the entire mechanism begin to slow down.

Unlike Michael's heartbeat, which now raged untamed like a war drum.

Keeping a firm eye fixed on the unmoving form doused by the white light of the drinks stand, Michael was alerted by Chantelle's alarmed cry of pain.

'Ouch! Oi! Michael! That bloody hurts, you know! What do you think you're doing?'

Only then did Michael realise he had grabbed hold of her hand and had begun squeezing.

And squeeze he had continued to do.

'Oh…sorry, Chaz…I didn't mean it. The ride…it…scared me…'

Their seat came to a final halt next to the kiosk and the attendant unbuckled them.

Still maintaining his concentration on the refreshment stall, Michael's legs would barely carry him down the few short steps of the ride's plinth and back onto the grass verge.

He retained a fixed view as dozens of flitting silhouettes passed between him and the solitary figure, whose random gaze seemed to be observing no one in particular.

Yet it became very clear to Michael that he was in actual fact observing every single patron of the funfair as they moved around him.

Especially when children came within his space.

As innocent youngsters passed him by, the man's neck would twist slightly, and his eyes would become larger. And then the cigarette would be employed for a second or two.

It was definitely him.

'You coming with us, Michael?'

The sound of Matt's voice distracted him temporarily, yet he continued to behold the taunting vision in the mid-distance as if in some trance.

'Michael? You alright? We're ready for the off!'

Chantelle urged him to move, yet Michael felt himself to be totally rooted to the spot.

His entire body flexed with pulsing anticipation as she took him by the arm and leaned toward his ear to convey an enticing whisper.

'Come on, Tompkins…you promised to walk me home…remember?'

An excuse was needed at that precise second.

He searched frantically for a sound method of extraction to detach him from his circle of friends.

Something convincing.

Something believable.

And it duly arose.

'Listen…Chaz…I feel a bit ill after that ride. Why don't you go home with the others tonight? They'll get you home, alright. I'll make my own way. Is that okay? I just need to find a gents, first.'

Chantelle's evident disappointment was tempered by loving concern as her companion seemingly stared vacantly into the hustle and bustle of the crowd.

'Oh…my baby…have I worn you out? You sure you want to go home alone? Do you want me to stay here with you? I can wait and make sure you are okay?'

A quick and polite reply was required.

A quick and polite reply was duly summoned.

'No, Chaz! I mean…no…honestly…thank you. I'll be alright. Just need to get to bed. I tell you what…I'll text you in a bit. We'll chat later on the phone if you want…okay? I'm sorry!'

Giving Michael a quick peck on the cheek, a somewhat bemused Chantelle bid him a temporary goodbye and joined the others who offered Michael their own inimitable farewells.

Watching his friends finally merge with the ebbing crowd, Michael was thankful to be finally alone.

Yet still he sensed the need for recognition violently piercing at his conscience.

And still he remained unconvinced of his conclusions.

Still wondering; still unsure.

There was only one way of confirming his clawing suspicion.

Michael moved tentatively toward the coffee bar and its inviting veil of bright white light.

As he neared the subject of his intensive curiosity, the previous vague recognition evolved into an overwhelming and completely unwelcome endorsement.

He weaved ever closer; stopping his careful stride to avoid other passers-by and then moving onward again towards his target.

Finally, at the man's shoulder, Michael covertly stared at him whilst he ordered a coffee.

Then, as if mildly disturbed by the uninvited presence, the man turned his head and glared directly at Michael who returned the gesture.

Their eyes interlocked, yet it was evident that he did not see anything remotely interesting about the sixteen-year-old youth standing before him. And despite the difference in their years, both men were now equals.

Yet in that split second period of mutual engagement, for Michael the mystery was solved beyond any need for further speculation.

It was, without a shadow of doubt, his greatest fear.

Returned to haunt him.

The largest monster on Michael's horizon stood inexplicably before him, forcing its former quarry to confront and absorb its loathsome existence once again.

The gaunt, wan face, age-lined like leather.

The snarling downturn of the lips.

The wiry, lean stature that had diminished with time, but still offered a suggestion of strength.

Yes, this was indeed the demon.

The torturer; the abuser.

The killer of Michael's best friend.

Uncle Tim was evidently at large; in the flesh, and apparently free as a bird.

And Michael became instantly consumed by the chance encounter.

Mentally and physically, he sensed himself drain of all rationality to become completely ruled by a sudden pulsating, omnipotent and relentless rage.

Struggling to maintain his composure, Michael handed over his money and quietly pretended to sample his drink. He observed as the man drew once more on his cigarette butt and then discarded it on the floor, before venturing slowly away from the scene.

And this was Michael's opportunity to move with him.

Second by second, as his heart strangely calmed itself and his head began to reclaim supremacy over his emotions once more, Michael found himself beginning to relish the incredulous prospect of reunification with the source of his worst nightmares.

He had made a pledge to himself during his previous encounter with this evil, merciless fiend.

And with the same lack of warning that had preceded the torrid plight of two eleven-year-old schoolboys five years ago, fate had now awarded Michael Tompkins the unexpected opportunity for his ultimate, victorious fulfilment.

CHAPTER 36

The figure sidled into the murk of night. Further and further away from all the fun of the fair.

Away; from the bright lights and the cries of pleasure.

Away; from the beat of the music and the enticing fragrance of food.

Away; back toward the mid-distant treeline and amongst the spiny shadows.

Dropping his own full coffee cup into a waste bin, Michael allowed a few seconds to pass before deciding to trail his nemesis.

With nearly a hundred yards between them, Michael set out to survey the target.

Uncle Tim seemed to be headed back through the centre of the park. There was another entrance gate on the far side which would allow him access to the other side of town. This seemed to be the destination.

Looking studiously around him, Michael could only hear the sound of his own movement as he trod lightly, keeping a firm visual contact with the oblivious subject out in front.

Once Michael had navigated a path through the clawing limbs of the tree line, the vibrancy of the fairground area had now reduced to a distant hum as the pursuit adopted an unearthly silence.

Noticing the absence of any potential onlookers, Michael now felt completely alone in the darkness of the parkland, yet the element of acute danger had barely even occurred to him. It was as if he were following some mystical command.

This was a pre-ordained undertaking. And as such, the compulsion to give chase was something he found irresistible.

Where the impromptu trek would lead him, he knew not.

But nevertheless, he felt that following this person - this thing that had inflicted so much pain and grief into his existence - was the only option at that moment.

The pace picked up a little as the icy cold air seemed to drop a degree or two further.

A twig snapped underfoot.

The breakage of the stem proceeded to echo relentlessly around the vicinity.

Michael stood absolutely still in the blackness as he observed the man stopping his stride. But Michael's immediate concerns regarding discovery were swiftly allayed as the man simply reached into his pocket, lit another cigarette, and continued walking.

Michael breathed a sigh of grateful relief and eventually resumed behind with infinitely more care.

With no other soul in proximity, the parkland felt like another planet, and in truth Michael was pleased to see the orange hue from streetlamps that hung over the south entrance in the far distance.

Uncle Tim's hunched outline began to increase its speed once out into the glow of the residential area beyond the wrought iron gateway.

Once through the exit himself, a thought struck Michael that he ought to turn off his phone. Should Chantelle attempt to contact him, Uncle Tim was bound to detect his pursuer should the ring tone sound.

Michael checked his watch once onto the amber-lit causeway.

Nearly ten minutes past ten.

He deliberated for a moment as the target continued to scurry away along the road towards the main town through route. Then, when content that his presence remained unchartered, Michael recommenced the chase.

As he walked with mindful stealth, another thought cursed Michael's toiling mind.

It seemed utterly inconceivable that this being known as Uncle Tim, who had willingly condemned a boy to his death and caused such misery for others, had remained completely undiscovered throughout the past years.

He had thrived under the very noses of the police.

He had continued to live on the very doorsteps of his victims.

It was an instinctive reaction for Michael to lift his right hand to his throat and feel the rough scarring under his collar. The wizened, churned tissue that served as permanent reminder of what had happened some five short years earlier.

Yet the circle had now turned fully.

Michael was braver; bigger; stronger.

Propelled by sound motive, he continued to follow the calling.

Steadily observing the instigator of such spiritual agony and personal despair, Michael truly believed that it was his divine right to unveil himself and unleash his wrath.

He was not going to pass up the chance of confrontation with his tormentor.

He could not simply walk away under the pretence that he had not witnessed this atrocious specimen in all his despicable glory.

He would refuse to live with himself knowing he might ignore the path laid out before him.

Michael's rules now. Michael's authority.

It was high time to even up the scores.

And with the game afoot, the ball was completely in Michael's court and with every passing minute, the obliging temptation of retribution enticed him ever further.

The march continued through the outskirts of town and into the council estate beyond. A large block of council flats loomed in the distance, notable for its tiny security lights at each of the two stairways.

Uncle Tim did not approach the front of the building, instead choosing to slip down a side service alley, apparently to gain access from the rear.

Michael presumed this to be a customary manoeuvre as opposed to any perceived effort to shake Michael from his tail.

Stepping up the pace to maintain full surveillance at the back of the bleak array of neglected accommodation, Michael quickly re-established a visual as he watched Uncle Tim ascend the stairway to the top tier of flats before striding along the balcony landing.

Michael slowly followed up the same flight of steps and considered his next move whilst squatting in the shadows.

There may be no second chances to establish the monster's actual place of residence.

Some way along the balcony, Uncle Tim ceased his advance outside a door which sported a plastic patio chair positioned opposite on the concrete landing. He reached into his coat pocket and produced what sounded like a set of keys.

Then in the next second, the figure was gone inside.

Inside his own domain; back to the centre of his web.

Blissfully unaware of his grave and uncalculated error.

Unknowingly, penning himself inside his own lair.

Completely cornered by destiny.

Now trapped by a long-forgotten figment of his satanic past.

Taking deep breaths, Michael glanced around to again ensure he was alone before commencing with caution along the landing toward the flat Uncle Tim had entered.

Two white plastic figures comprising the number twenty were screwed unevenly into the door which was roughly coated with blistering red paint. The plastic chair opposite was evidently some kind of lookout post to sit and scrutinise passers-by and fellow residents below.

His heartbeat raced with channelled adrenaline and his chest felt like it would explode in any instant.

The time for a positive decision was now upon Michael, but he could not fully commit himself to the certainty of confrontation just yet.

The moment felt wrong, somehow.

He needed more time to think.

To formulate a more clinical and infallible method of approach.

Suddenly sensing his potential vulnerability, Michael opted to turn away from the door marked number twenty and silently navigated his way back downstairs and along the access alley. He then resumed position to the front of the building and stepped onto the pavement.

Looking up, he saw a black silhouette appear at a top floor window which duly closed the curtains.

And Michael knew at that moment he had made the correct decision to turn away.

But only for the time being.

Away; from the lair of Uncle Tim.

Away; from what would become the venue for long overdue vengeance to be delivered as coldly as possible.

An act that he committed himself to serve over five years ago.

In honour of his late friend and as a simple matter of right and wrong.

And as he walked quickly home, only a trifle disappointed in feeling the necessity to depart the scene, the premise of an imminent return to Uncle Tim from number twenty, positively engulfed him.

CHAPTER 37

Laid in bed later that evening, Michael contemplated his incredulous discovery and the subsequent chain of events.

He sent a text phone message to Chantelle to confirm he had recovered from his mysterious Ferris wheel sickness but did not feel like chatting.

Her response was typically warm, and she wished him a good night.

And she told him that she loved him once again.

His apparent re-adoption of complete normality had fooled all the necessary parties.

He had sat with his parents and watched television for half an hour or so after returning home, absorbing nothing that emanated from the screen and half-heartedly responding to their queries of mild parental interest regarding the park bonfire and fireworks.

He had indulged Wallace in the ritual play-fight until the fatigued canine willingly retired to the comfort and peace of the conservatory.

Indeed, within the walls of number twelve, Basford Lane, all seem perfectly usual.

Yet inside his head, as the time chased midnight and he stared at the bedroom ceiling, Michael's thoughts churned with the prospect ahead. Pure anticipation flowed through his being and fuelled his conscience, already promising to condemn him to a sleepless night.

He needed a plan.

He turned over on the mattress and continued to think.

He needed a plan.

Then, without apparent inspiration or warning, the idea emerged.

Now, he had a plan.

Once assembled in his head, it seemed so simple.

And if the execution were sound, this wondrous scheme would prove as terminal and effective as its blueprint suggested.

The decision had been made.

CHAPTER 38

Thursday, November the seventh.

Twelve forty-eight; a.m.

With his head tilting from the pillow, Michael listened through the dark silence as his parents slept soundly in the adjacent room.

The minutes passed, but he would remain patient.

He had thought of little else for over twenty-four hours.

Fully assured of his mother and father's recumbence, Michael stirred and pulled himself up to the edge of the bed.

Dressing in jeans, pullover and running shoes, he carefully exited the bedroom, closed the door, and descended the stairway. Through the kitchen he passed the conservatory door, glancing at Wallace through the glass. Luckily, the slumbering German Shepherd did not respond to the movements of his human brother.

'Some guard dog *you* are.' Michael mumbled under his breath.

Out beyond the back door, Michael ventured through the darkness to the garden shed to retrieve the weapons and costume he had laid out earlier.

His father's tool-bag was exactly where he had left it.

Michael quickly stepped into the pair of his father's navy-blue work overalls.

Removing the leather gloves from the bag, Michael pulled them on as if preparing to perform some delicate operation. He gently lifted the tool-bag from the floor and double checked its minimal contents. The sensations running through him veered recklessly between utter, shattering dread and a God-like invincibility.

But now was Michael's chance.

No one would take it from him.

Tiptoeing back up the garden and through the house, he stealthily navigated past the dog, into the hallway and listened at the bottom of the stairs for any sign of movement from his parents' bedroom.

Then, with fate remaining his sole ally and protection, he stepped out into the night air and gently closed the front door behind him.

*****

Michael checked his watch as he walked briskly through the local estate.

Nearly twenty-five minutes past one.

Rapidly onward to town, which was thankfully devoid of any living being leaving Michael to follow his route without hindrance.

Along the High Street; through the precinct; to the outskirts of the shopping centre and beyond.

Nobody detected his journey.

He moved with silent determination; never once stopping to occupy his mind with the slightest strain of doubt.

Because there was no doubt.

His concentration would not falter.

His resolve would not waver.

And then at last, the block of flats appeared menacingly before him in the distance.

But Michael Tompkins was now far from fearful.

Inflation of pure will spurred him onward.

The mission had begun; and in turn would soon be completed.

He checked to ensure his continuing solitude before navigating the side alley leading to the rear of the building.

With as light a tread as possible, he ascended the stairway, gently pulling on the tool-bag again to confirm its contents.

Then, deft of foot, along the balcony.

To the blistered red door with an uneven number twenty attached.

As he stood motionless, Michael's gaze rested momentarily on the plastic patio chair.

A most suitable plinth for his imminent trophy.

Once more confirming his gloved hands and the tools in the bag, he took several deep breaths as the murmur of a television set echoed through the wooden door.

Michael lifted his right hand and clenched the fingers loosely in readiness to announce his presence.

It was to be now; or it was to be never.

Destiny had chosen for him.

It was to be now.

CHAPTER 39

The firm knock on the door was repeated three times.

Michael glanced to either side of his position along the shadowy balcony to affirm there would be no unforeseen interruptions.

He waited with growing impatience; eager to embrace the vision of the monster once more.

Continuing to stare at the red painted door, Michael listened carefully to detect any movement from the other side.

The seconds passed.

Seconds which rapidly evolved into a full minute and beyond.

Michael lifted his hand and curled his fingers once again to repeat the rap on the wood.

The sudden clicking sound from the other side of the door caused Michael's heart to leap. Yet even before he had time to evaluate the source, he found himself facing the nefarious visage that had plagued his psyche for so long and for so many nights.

Images from the past flashed through Michael's mind as he continued to engage with the demonic ugliness of his one-time keeper.

Uncle Tim glared dismissively at his unexpected visitor before hissing abject disapproval at the inconvenience.

Then came the all too familiar rasp of that voice.

'What fucking time do you call *this*?'

Michael swallowed his trepidation and referred to his barely rehearsed and hopefully feasible script.

'Yes…I apologise for the early hour, sir. I am from the council maintenance department. We've had an emergency call out which must be attended to. However…in the rush to get here I've forgotten my works I.D. So…you retain the legal right to allow me access.'

'Alright sunshine…cut the shit. What the fuck do you want?'

The harsh intervention only served to anger Michael ever deeper.

Yet still he retained composure and stuck loyally to the plan.

'Some residents on the floor below have reported a possible gas leak. I need to check your appliances…if that's okay?'

In truth, Michael didn't feel anything resembling conviction in the role and his attire would have surely warranted suspicion in any other circumstances.

The gnarled expression on Uncle Tim's face seemed to concur with Michael's pangs of sudden self-doubt.

His words certainly affirmed as much.

'No fucking chance! Come back tomorrow! There's no fucking leak here, son.'

Fully expectant of the obstacle, Michael moved to stage two of the attempted intrusion.

'But sir…I just need to take a quick look at your boiler and cooker. This is…flat number twenty…isn't it?'

'Yeah…*and*?'

'I presume you have a gas cooker?'

'Yeah…*and*?'

'Can you just confirm your name for me…Mister…'

The man's eyes wandered up and down Michael as if becoming increasingly frustrated at the reason for the disturbance.

Yet to Michael's infinite surprise, Uncle Tim suddenly began to operate a policy of reluctant compliance with the fabricated urgency.

The low whine of his voice brought back such vivid memories.

'It's Mister Thatcher. Timothy…Thatcher. Look…can't you do this in the morning? I'm tired out.'

Michael stared with sincere intent at his subject.

'I would…but…with gas…we can't take any risks can we, sir? Very unpredictable stuff is gas. Wouldn't want you to come to any harm now…would we?'

Deliberating for a few seconds, Uncle Tim suddenly moved aside and allowed the door to swing open.

'Okay, son. But I'm warning you…you'd better make it quick.'

With ambition now flushing freely through his system, Michael expressed his appreciation and entered the murky hallway of the flat. The pungent aroma comprised a number of recognisable ingredients, with samples of some appearing to have been smeared on the walls.

'I'll be watching telly if you need me.'

Michael watched Thatcher return to the living room.

'Okay…where's your boiler, sir?'

'Spare room…walk toward me…then turn left.'

The sensation of anticipation was almost unbearable as Michael pushed open the bedroom door and entered. Observing the number of black plastic bags that lay strewn across the threadbare carpet, he made his way to the small hatch in the far wall.

Execution time was indeed nigh.

He placed his father's tool bag on the grime-laden bedclothes before unclipping it. Double-checking his privacy in the room, he adeptly removed a medium-sized claw hammer by the head and laid the handle into his leather clad right palm.

Slowly wrapping his fingers around the wooden shaft, Michael's emergence of power grew by the second.

He then thought of Peter.

He then thought of himself.

He then thought of nothing aside completion of his mission.

Letting his hand fall to his side to partially conceal the weapon, he ventured back into the hallway and toward the living room door which was slightly ajar.

The noises emitting from the television set suggested that Thatcher was indulging himself in a pornographic movie.

'Oh well…' murmured Michael under his breath. 'At least you'll go doing what you do best. Fucking wanker.'

Peering through the gap in the doorway, Michael found himself ideally situated. Thatcher was slumped in an armchair facing away from the door. His attention seemed firmly fixed on the action on the screen and subsequently he did not react to Michael's entrance.

'Nearly done, sir…it won't be long now.'

The figure in the chair issued his disgruntled reply without visually addressing the source.

'Good fucking job…did you find your leak?'

'Not yet, sir. Just need to check your oven connection.'

'Right…well hurry up, son. As you can see…I'm a bit busy.'

Poised behind the armchair, Michael raised his right hand.

Wielding the hammer over his own shoulder to maximise the downward force, he allowed a couple of seconds to pass before uttering his next sentiment to the slouching, gloriously oblivious monster.

'You won't even know I've been, sir.'

Michael mentally counted to three.

Bringing the hammer down swiftly and heavily, it struck Thatcher squarely on top of the skull.

Michael stood above his victim and emptied his lungs, to then finally replenish them with fresh oxygen.

The target's physical reaction to the impact was not pleasant to behold, yet for Michael, it was one he had longed to witness.

Thatcher begun to flail in agonised desperation. His limbs thrashed wildly as his brain quickly haemorrhaged, causing his nervous system to issue random and uncontrolled impulses throughout the body.

He snorted in a low, pulsating groan and violently twisted his wiry form until it fell from the chair to the floor in front of the television. Still reflexing to his brain's random untamed commands, Thatcher suddenly came face to face with the cause of his sudden sufferance.

Michael moved position from behind the armchair and stood menacingly above his victim, whose large white eyes stared back in excruciating confusion.

Crouching down to stare at his worst nightmare, Michael took immense satisfaction from the sight quivering defencelessly before him.

Severely debilitated and rendered to increasing shock, Thatcher tried to speak. His mouth became contorted as his lips dribbled with saliva. His hands and arms twitched whilst his fingers clamoured toward the young man who had just attacked him.

And then, without warning, the vision of the youth with the hammer was slowly eclipsed by an unforeseen darkness that attempted to consume Thatcher as he drifted in and out of consciousness.

His final thought before completely blacking out was a simple prayer that the intense pain in his head would cease.

However, his assailant had other ideas.

*****

Thatcher was stirred sharply back to awareness by a punch in the face. Rousing himself through the veil of incredible pain, his vision partially cleared.

He found he was no longer writhing around on the floor.

Instead, he was positioned seated and bound to a white, plastic patio chair.

Then he heard the voice of his mysterious visitor.

'Lucky you kept those handcuffs, Uncle Tim. Found them under your bed. Thought they might come in useful for the next part of the game.'

Thatcher grimaced at Michael whilst his mouth continued to expel globules of vomit and blood. Summoning all his might, he managed to utter his first question through a stammering, impeded gurgle.

'What…what the…f-fuck…do you think you're d-doing…you fucking maniac?'

Michael smiled as he stood at ease before Thatcher with hands resting behind his back.

He studied the epitome of evil.

This malevolent being, that would soon become the ultimate motif of human maltreatment in reaping what he had sewn.

'I'm getting my revenge…you…fucking…mutant! I've had you in my fucking head for a long time now, Uncle Tim. And now…at long last…I am in yours. I'm finally going to put you out of my misery. And put myself permanently into yours.'

Another stifled yelp of pain screeched from Thatcher as he strived to re-focus on his uninvited companion.

'Why…the fuck…do you keep…calling me…Uncle Tim? I'm not your fucking relative! You don't even fucking know me…you fucking nutcase.'

Michael drew closer, placing his face close to Thatcher's.

The breath still smelled the same.

The booze; the nicotine; the rotting soul.

'Don't you remember me…Uncle Tim?'

The men engaged each other's stares.

'Remember? R-remember…remember fucking *what*?'

'Oh, that's a shame…I'm really hurt that you don't recognise me. Because I can remember you…only too well!'

'What? What the fuck are you talking about?'

Michael grabbed Thatcher by the hair and yanked his face upward.

Closing his own features in on the prisoner once more, Michael began to jog the memory of his twitching prey with a fire-laced whisper.

'Five…count 'em…five…fucking…years ago…you…and that fucking bitch…you used to shag right in front of me. Five fucking years ago…you and that fucking bitch…took me and my best friend for a little ride in the country…'

Thatcher did not respond as Michael continued to relay the torrid chronicle.

'…and if my memory serves correct…you and that fucking whore weren't very nice to us. But as if that wasn't bad enough…worse was to come…because my best friend didn't come home afterwards…because you fucking murdered him. You left him to fucking die. His head all opened up…his face pointing down into a stream. NOW DO YOU FUCKING REMEMBER ME? NOW IS IT A BIT CLEARER FOR YOU…YOU…FUCKING…CUNT!'

Michael unleashed another solid fist which connected soundly with Thatcher's jaw. The loud crack that accompanied the connection incited a massive fracture which began to swell vigorously within seconds.

Michael stood back to admire the effect of his handiwork.

And then he sought to display the evidence of Uncle Tim's.

'You gave me a permanent remainder of my little stay with you and your fucking whore. Remember doing this, do you?'

Pulling the collar of his overalls aside, Michael exposed the ugly scarring across his lower throat.

Thatcher offered no verbal response as his cheek and chin began to bloat around his broken jawbone.

His thin frame hung weakly from the chair as his churning gut once more emitted its acidic contents onto the floor.

'I suppose I should forgive you if your memory isn't so good these days. But rest assured…I'm an honest guy…and what I'm telling you…is the truth…Uncle Tim.'

Thatcher raised his watery gaze to meet with the emotional grimace of his young accoster.

And then, with incredulous arrogance, he summoned the ultimate insult. Thatcher's change of expression twisted itself across his bloated facade as his ailing mind slowly encouraged recognition.

The last words he would ever speak were accompanied by a damning trail of scarlet fluid.

'Oh yeah…the fat one…with blond…hair. Yeah…Porky. With the…with the dress on. Well, considering…how things have turned out tonight…it goes without really saying…son…considering current circumstances…that the only regret I have now…about meeting you both…is that I didn't fucking drown you…as well as your fucking fat mate!'

Now inwardly inflamed by a relentless urge, Michael left the room momentarily and promptly returned with the tool bag. Replacing the hammer, it was exchanged. For a hack saw.

Michael stood before his prisoner for the final time.

'Don't struggle to say anymore…Uncle Tim. I've nearly finished with you. Come the sunrise…come the victory. I've very nearly gotten you out of my system…but not quite. Not just yet. I reckon my darkest days are behind me, Thatcher…yours are only just beginning. I'll even ring the ambulance for you when I'm finished. Not that it will be of much use by the time it finds you. How's that for genuine consideration?'

*****

With his mission accomplished and the weapons secured back in the leather tool bag, Michael stood outside on the balcony and turned to his now limp and almost lifeless enemy, who vacantly stared back without any form of reactive gesture.

The coast was clear.

The task completed.

Fate's ordainment had been obeyed and achieved.

Slinging the armoury over his back, Michael Tompkins switched direction and walked briskly away, leaving the remnants of his visit slumped on the plastic patio chair.

A totem of a life of wrongdoing; on public display for all to see.

*****

Michael watched the tool bag drop instantly beneath the surface.

Containing two hammers, a hack saw and a rolled set of overalls, he observed it being consumed into the still blackness of the canal.

Now it was time for home.

His parents continued to dream their pleasant dreams as he ascended the stairs and returned to the sanctity of his bedroom.

Safely tucked up in his bed by four-forty-five, he switched on his mobile phone and sent Chantelle a brief text message:

I NEED TO C YOU FIRST THING TMRW.

BY THE WAY I LUV U 2 XX

CHAPTER 40

It was some four hours later when Detective Inspector Kevin Woodley received a call in his office urging him to attend the location of a brutal assault.

Arriving at Renton Court Apartment Block at just before nine o' clock, he was due to survey the scene discovered by paramedics at flat number twenty.

A constable guarding the front of the building directed the inspector to the side alley leading to the rear of the residential complex.

Ascending the stairway, the D.I. had received little previous indication of what he could expect to find.

On reaching the balcony, he cast his gaze toward the activity halfway along the landing.

A medical examiner in sky-blue overalls hovered around a figure slumped outside on a plastic patio chair. The D.I. approached with due caution. On reaching the open red door of number twenty, he watched the forensic doctor for a moment or two.

'Morning, sir.'

'Alright, Geoff? What's the story here, then?' asked the D.I., trying to avert his gaze from the unpleasant state of the victim.

The doctor turned to his superior and openly displayed two purple latex gloves lathered with blood.

'A very nasty one! The paramedics found him like this when they arrived at seven-thirty this morning. Seems our attacker liked to take his time. Did a thorough job, as well!'

Kevin Woodley eyed the disorientated, barely conscious victim, whose dismissive scowl remained focused vacantly into space.

'Well…what have you got, Geoff?'

The officer in overalls pointed to the injuries as he described them.

'I don't know how this poor guy has stayed alive. For starters…we have a precise indentation to the top of the skull. Single…sharp…clean impact…perhaps administered with a hammer or similar heavy instrument. There is also a severe fracture and massive bruising to the jawline. Can't be any more exact without an X-ray. Different weapon used there, though.'

The D.I. quickly felt revolted at the mere sight of the physical damage as the man in the chair wheezed feebly in desperation.

'Has he managed to say anything about what happened?'

'No, sir…because it gets far worse for him.'

'What do you mean?'

An element of sympathy leaked into the doctor's tone.

'I don't think he can talk, Kevin. By all standards, this is a pretty sinister assault. Look at this. The back of his neck has been opened up…looks like his spinal cord has been damaged. I've done some basic reflex tests…but it's my estimation he's paralysed from the neck down. He's hardly breathing, either. Luckily, blood loss has been at a relative minimum otherwise we'd be standing at a murder scene.'

The D.I. fingered his grey beard in disgust as he continued to digest the extent of the injuries.

'What about any internal trauma?'

'Once I've okayed him for transportation the medics can get him to hospital. This is a real MOT job…he could be on the ramp for hours, bless him. He'll need wiring up properly to check his vitals. I can't even begin to guess what they'll turn up.'

'Okay, Geoff…thank you…for now.'

The detective inspector shook his head in disgust as he left the medical examiner to his work and gazed at the depressing surroundings.

Stepping tentatively into the dirt-laden hallway of number twenty, he was greeted by the sight of more colleagues from the forensics unit adorned in similar attire.

Inside the spare bedroom, he discovered two officers crouched on the floor emptying the contents of the various bin liners.

'Anything of interest, boys?'

Detective Constable Craig Jones stood to attention with a random handful of items retrieved from the bags.

'Nothing as yet to suggest the attacker's identity, Guv. But we've found one of the victim's old rent books in a kitchen drawer. Timothy Thatcher. Aged forty-one. A resident here for seventeen years. Unemployed…I'd guess.'

Kevin Woodley registered the information before asking the next obvious question.'

'Any form, Craig?'

‘I’ve already checked. Absolutely none, Guv. Mister Thatcher is completely unknown to the police in any capacity. No previous. Though judging by the state of him now…well…he’s obviously been in with the wrong crowd somewhere along the line.’

D. I. Woodley cast his eye over the items D.C. Jones was holding and the subsequent mess on the floor.

‘What’s all this little lot, then?’

‘Well…looks like this is his life’s possessions. Photographs…some old clothes…one or two items of jewellery…just general household junk, basically. We found a few of these as well. Don’t quite know what they’re doing here. Looks like those writing pads that kids use in school.’

D.I. Woodley offered closer examination of the exercise book as he took it from his colleague and quickly flicked through the pages.

‘Looks pretty new…it’s hardly been used, Craig. It does seem a bit odd. You’re right there. Oh well…get this lot scoured…I shouldn’t think it’ll tell us much, though.’

He closed the writing book and glanced lazily at the front cover.

A second later, time stood still for Detective Inspector Kevin Woodley.

His instincts began to thrash wildly as reality crashed its course back through time and history and into the present once more.

‘Oh…my…good…God…’

All officers present in the room turned and faced the D.I., whose customary fearless expression had instantly turned white as a sheet.

D.C. Jones pressed for an explanation.

‘You alright, Guv? You look like you’ve just seen a ghost!’

Again, the detective inspector exclaimed his disbelieving wonderment.

‘Get this lot to the station. And I mean absolutely everything! Everything in the flat. Top to bottom. The job lot. Now. Today! Get forensics to run a DNA test on every single item in this shithole! Every nook and fucking cranny. Gut the place!’

D.C. Jones remained puzzled by the explosive reaction of his superior.

‘But, Guv…the victim…he’s nothing to the police. No history. Just a random…isn’t he?’

D.I. Woodley reinforced his request in a louder, more insistent tone.

‘This isn’t junk, Craig. If I’m correct…you’re currently sifting through Aladdin’s cave, my son! I can’t believe this! JESUS CHRIST AL-FUCKING MIGHTY! I need to get hold of the Chief ...urgently.’

The detective inspector immediately exited the room and ventured outside to commence his phone call.

D.C. Jones looked dismissively at the schoolbook that had just been unceremoniously returned to him.

With curiosity pricked and confusion still residing, he dropped the writing book in the pile with the others.

D.C. Jones was not inclined to read the identity on the front cover.

The child-like inscription was hand printed in blue ink.

Peter Leavesdon

Year Seven Mathematics

Miss Doherty.

CHAPTER 41

Sunday November the tenth.

Ten o'clock p.m. precisely.

The evening news bulletin.

'Our main story this evening: police have now confirmed their belief that the man discovered dying outside his flat in Shireheath in Berkshire on Thursday morning is the same man responsible for the death of schoolboy Peter Leavesdon, over five years ago.

Forty-one-year-old Timothy Warren Thatcher was found by paramedics after they responded to an anonymous phone call in the early hours of the seventh of November. His extensive injuries have left him completely paralysed and he will be spending the rest of his life under twenty-four-hour medical care at a secret location yet to be determined.

Forensic officers discovered the link completely by chance, with Mister Thatcher having retained irrefutable evidence of his connection with the Peter Leavesdon case.

With me now in the studio is the officer who was originally in charge of the investigation into Peter's murder, Detective Inspector Kevin Woodley.

Inspector Woodley, what was your initial reaction to the unplanned discovery?'

'Obviously, it is with immense relief that we have managed to bring this case to a close after such a protracted time. Unfortunately, due to the suspect's condition, a legal trial will be considered totally inapplicable.'

'Are you happy to accept that Timothy Thatcher is the man responsible for the abduction and murder of Peter Leavesdon?'

'It isn't a matter of happiness when something like this occurs. We have all the forensic proof on hand and items from his flat condemn him as guilty beyond doubt.'

'What about Peter's family?'

'They are understandably relieved by what had transpired in the past few days. Though, of course, these developments have come as something of a surprise and shock to us all after such a length of time. It has unfortunately been a long and intensely painful process for everybody.

But I did stake a claim five years ago that justice would be done. This now appears to be the case.'

'And what of the other boy abducted by Timothy Thatcher?'

'We have unavoidably had cause to contact Michael Tompkins and his family. Michael has confirmed the identity of Thatcher as the man responsible. As far as I am concerned...this case is now closed.'

'There was suspicion at the time of the abduction that Thatcher had a female counterpart in events. Can we shed any light on her possible role in things?'

'When we initially gathered statements, there was indeed mention of a female accomplice. And we believe the anonymous caller who made us aware of the location of Peter Leavesdon is directly connected in some way to the murder. However, there has been no single tangible thread of evidence throughout this case to suggest anybody beside Thatcher was responsible for the abduction and killing.'

'So, what of the assault on Timothy Thatcher himself? What do you make of this?'

'Enquiries have so far shed no light on what occurred in the early hours of the seventh of November. No witnesses have come forward and thus far no third-party evidence has been uncovered at the location of the attack. At the moment, I have to admit we are at a complete loss as to who may have committed the assault...or indeed...why...'

'But considering Mister Thatcher's history, somebody out there must be feeling a sense of satisfaction at what has happened?'

'I must concede that for the Tompkins and Leavesdon families, their long wait for closure may seemingly be over. It certainly isn't the brand of justice that I would personally endorse, but there you have it. We shall endeavour to continue with our investigation of this grievous assault along the normal lines.'

'Detective Inspector Woodley...thank you for your time.'

CHAPTER 42

Within the walls of number thirty-nine, Cromford Road, Hazel and David Leavesdon embraced one another tightly as they observed the remainder of the Sunday evening bulletin play itself out.

Across the estate, Sharon and James Tompkins shared a bottle of wine in a low-key celebration of the news.

Michael came downstairs and entered the lounge.

'Have you heard, Michael?' beamed his mother. 'Police have just publicly said it definitely was Thatcher.'

'I know it was, Mum. I identified him. I told them…yesterday.'

A little inebriated, James held up his glass to the television and wiped his tear-strewn eyes.

'Yes, but it's finally been made official. They got the bastard at last! I'd like to find the person that did Thatcher in and give them a knighthood.'

Michael did not respond further.

Instead, he shuffled through the kitchen to the conservatory and opened it. Wallace instinctively made for the hallway and fetched his lead from behind the front door.

'Right…I'll take Wallace for his walk tonight. You two sit and relax. Enjoy the news!'

Michael smirked as both his mother and father looked to their son in astonishment.

'Are you sure, Michael?' asked James.

'Your dad doesn't mind taking him out before bedtime, you know.' concurred Sharon

James stood to his feet with his voice adopting a tone of concern.

'I'll come with you, Michael. Hang on a minute.'

Attaching the lead to Wallace's collar, Michael remained resolute.

'It's no problem, Dad. After all…the bogeyman has finally been sorted...hasn't he? So…there's nothing to be afraid of anymore…is there?'

CHAPTER 43

Monday, November the eleventh.

Nine oh seven a.m.

Detective Superintendent Joseph Barnes observed Detective Inspector Kevin Woodley from across the desk.

The senior officer wanted a response to developments, and he was adamant he would garner it there and then.

'So…what does your experience tell you, Kevin?'

'With regard to which particular issue, sir?'

As was his wont, the Chief Super rose to his feet and stared beyond the window at the dull, damp crawl of rush hour traffic below.

'Attempted murder, Kevin? And you have no suspect despite a flat full to the rafters with evidence? Surely it must link to someone?'

'Yes, it does. It all links to the victim, Tim Thatcher. Initial response from forensics draws a blank on anyone else, sir.'

The senior officer was not content with the D.I.'s mildly flippant reply.

'Someone with a grudge, perhaps? I think you know where my thinking is headed with this?'

Kevin Woodley shook his head.

'If you mean the Tompkins boy, sir, I'm afraid so far there is no DNA match with anything that might connect him to the scene.'

Turning to face his most experienced detective, the Chief Super rested both palms on the desktop. He then stooped to gain better vantage of his D.I.'s reaction.

'Give it time, Kevin. It's him. I'm telling you.'

Kevin Woodley hauled himself from the chair as if to make an exit.

'Your train of thought is perfectly credible, sir. And don't think it hadn't crossed my mind, too.'

The enthusiastic glint in the eye of the superior officer was not a sight D.I. Woodley was accustomed to observing.

'You can nail this one, Kevin. You're so close to cracking the biggest case you've ever had. A result here could change everything for your career.'

The detective was unmoved by the Chief's vague implication of promotion.

'We'll see sir. But aside from an absence of any tangible proof, he has an alibi for that night. He was with his girlfriend. All night.'

The Chief Super was far from convinced.

'Really, Kevin? And I can safely presume you have followed this through with statements from both of them, have you?'

'Oh yes. And his parents. Besides…I trust the Tompkins lad.'

'You *trust* him?'

Kevin Woodley reached for the door handle.

'Oh yes, sir. After all, the last time I doubted his word five years ago, he turned out in the end to be telling us the truth all along...didn't he, sir?'

Chief Superintendent Joseph Barnes turned away from the D.I to focus again on activity beyond the window.

'Keep me updated, Kevin. Close the door on your way out.'

CHAPTER 44

One year later.

Monday; December the twenty-second. 2014.

St. Martyrs Residential Nursing Home; Clerkenwell Close; Thamesbury.

Two o'clock p.m; exactly.

Visiting time.

The receptionist welcomed the first guest of the day.

'Have you attended this centre before, madam?'

'No. First time.'

'Okay…and who is it you want to see?'

'Tim Thatcher.'

The nurse continued to smile as she checked the computer screen and pushed some keys to register the visit.

'Mister Thatcher has just finished his physiotherapy session. Would you care to fill this form in, Madam? Just your basic details. Again, just for security reasons.'

The visitor complied and completed the paperwork in silence.

The nurse eyed the document without suspicion.

'Okay…Miss Grundy. I just need to process a visitor's badge for you to wear today.'

'Please…if you don't mind…I've never liked formality. Call me Sheila. You might as well…I'll being seeing a lot of you in the future, I reckon.'

The nurse's smile broadened as she handed over the lanyard attached to which was the security badge.

'Okay…fine! Sheila it is, then! I'll just ring through and get someone to take you to the rehabilitation ward.'

A minute or two passed before Sheila Grundy was escorted from reception and along a maze of corridors. The accompanying nurse was pleasant and friendly.

'Are you a relative of Mister Thatcher then, Sheila?'

There was a pause before she answered.

'Oh no…just a friend…an old friend.'

The pair entered a brightly lit room with a glazed roof and paned walls which overlooked the frost laden gardens that surrounded the complex.

‘There he is, Sheila. Over there…in that wheelchair…by the window. You are aware that his physical faculties are severely diminished? He won’t be able to speak. He has no dexterity at all from below the neck.’

The visitor silently observed her former accomplice for a moment.

‘Thank you, nurse. You can leave us to it now.’

EPILOGUE

He watched in silence from behind the glass.

Contemplative of the inability to move, his gaze wandered among the lack of activity beyond the window.

Yet that pleasant scene was no place for him.

Not before.

Not now.

Not ever.

His role had been ordained.

He was to be the unseen observer.

Not for him to tread the path of normal men.

For he had been robbed of such luxury long ago.

The female voice resonated in his ear as a necessary irritant.

He could be nothing without her; yet he so resented her constant presence by his side.

His head tilted toward her as his mechanically aided lungs slowly inflated with anticipation.

No further exchange was deemed necessary as she set her mind to the task ahead.

Sating his every whim.

Tending to his every desire.

She would always be there for him…

ACKNOWLEDGEMENTS

I wish to thank the following people for their invaluable expertise and support in helping this book gain wings:
Samantha Thornton; Hannah Bliss; Charlotte Wilson; Robbie Wilson; Carole Thornton, Chris Bliss; Charlotte Bliss; Jeanette Taylor Ford; Sue Hayward; Ford Wood and last but certainly not least, David Slaney for his superb cover design.
I couldn't have done it without any of you.
I am forever indebted.
RJT

Printed in Great Britain
by Amazon

32803840R00200